CLEM READER is a reporter on the celebrity beat who accidentally stumbles on the story of the century. At the same time, he loses himself in a passionate affair with Saroyan Pashogi, one of the world's most famous and beautiful movie stars. As the lovers fall under government surveillance Saroyan finds additional evidence, and the government begins action to permanently silence them along with anyone else who knows the secret. Will the lovers survive? Will the world survive? It's a tale of extraterrestrials, drug running, and political corruption that will keep you going until the final chapter.

THE STORY OF THE CENTURY

a novel by
Karl Eysenbach

iUniverse, Inc.
New York   Bloomington

The Story of the Century
a novel

Copyright © 2009 by Karl Eysenbach
All rights reserved. No part of this book may be used or reproduced by any means, graphic, electronic, or mechanical, including photocopying, recording, taping or by any information storage retrieval system without the written permission of the publisher except in the case of brief quotations embodied in critical articles and reviews.

This is a work of fiction. All of the characters, names, incidents, organizations, and dialogue in this novel are either the products of the author's imagination or are used fictitiously.

iUniverse books may be ordered through booksellers or by contacting:

iUniverse
1663 Liberty Drive
Bloomington, IN 47403
www.iuniverse.com
1-800-Authors (1-800-288-4677)

Because of the dynamic nature of the Internet, any Web addresses or links contained in this book may have changed since publication and may no longer be valid. The views expressed in this work are solely those of the author and do not necessarily reflect the views of the publisher, and the publisher hereby disclaims any responsibility for them.

ISBN: 978-0-595-52757-1 (pbk)
ISBN: 978-0-595-62809-4 (ebk)

Printed in the United States of America

iUniverse rev. date: 7/5/2010

To Karen and Judy, who know what it's really all about
To Netto, wherever he is
To the Alvarados, thank you for everything you've done

PROLOGUE

INSIDE AMMUNITION BUNKER G7
FORT HUACHUCA, ARIZONA

Part of the problem is that no earthling knows how to use it. Imagine that someone gives a caveman a computer, -- a smart caveman. He's curious and patient, using his analytical skills; but he's still a caveman. Generations of boys in white lab coats have given their best shots, and they've all walked away, scratching their heads.

It's not very big, -- only one meter by 1.5 meters by .75 meters. And it's heavy, weighing almost a ton. It's funny looking, -- like a cross between a nuclear power plant and the guts of a desktop computer. The gizmo is welded together a molecule at a time out of metal that turns diamond bits into powder. The computer operates at or below the quantum level. Even the most brilliant minds on the planet, playing around with it for hundreds of years have only the dimmest understanding of what it's really all about. They think they know enough to call it a magnetic interferometer.

It had been taken off of a spaceship that had crashed near Maury Island, Washington in 1947, and Navy divers retrieved the thing from the bottom of Puget Sound. The entire operation was done under the cover of night and the darkest secrecy. Once scientists had a chance to sort through the debris, they found an encyclopedia of mysteries. Some things, like transistors, were fairly easy to figure out. Others, like the spacecraft's propulsion unit were deemed to be so dangerous that nobody wanted to touch it. The magnetic interferometer was in between; tantalizing in what it could offer to humanity, but ultimately too complex and challenging for the puny human brain to understand. Unlike the tiny alien skeletons at Wright-Patterson Air Force Base in Dayton, Ohio, or the more famous curios at Groom Lake, Nevada, this was one piece of alien equipment that never had a single leak about its existence.

So the interferometer sat there for decades, even before World War III. American scientists kept it in safekeeping at a secure spot in the Los Angeles Air Force Base. For some unknown reason, one of the last acts of the dying American civilization was to move the thing to its bunker at Fort Huachuca. World Expeditionary Forces found it in year 12 and made note of the curiosity, but they were not on a mission to discover ancient UFO technology. Eventually, scientists visited, running some rudimentary tests. Months or years later, they would come up with some interesting conclusions that had applications for microelectronics or robots. But even the generations of Platinum Prize winners, the chosen few with access to the device, had only the dimmest idea of the thing's workings.

From time to time, one World President or the other would be curious about the secrets surrounding alien technology. They would take a covert tour of the Army bases and research labs, and they would put their hands on the interferometer. The great leader would receive the standard briefing about what was known about it, and then the secrets would remain a secret. Even the presidents who had seen UFOs violating the laws of earthly physics agreed that knowledge of the space antiques should be dozens of levels above the most secret security clearance.

Going public would mean telling people that the government lied, and that there were there were things that government was powerless to control. It would imply that man is truly a feeble-minded creature. And besides, if the government admitted the existence of the little green men, then the little green men might come. No one knows what would happen then, except that everything would be different. If a protozoon is the starting point of life, and the builders represent superior intelligence, then mankind – Homo sapiens – is about at the level of a rabbit.

Now a rabbit is a wonderful thing. It can be an excellent pet. It is a source of endless amusement and responsibility. There is always the feeding and watering and cleaning up the shit. It is possible to love a rabbit. It can show you some rudimentary emotion. You can hug and play with it, but a rabbit is still a rabbit. It will not perform differential equations or discuss the finer points of atomic physics with you. And if you are hungry…

So there is this feeling, -- that you and I and Jesus, Buddha, Mohammed, Moses, and Zoroaster all rolled into one are but penny ante poker players compared to the beings observing the things we do on this quarantined planet. And the business of this planet, as we all know, is business. The military-industrial complex has funded Big Science projects related to the magnetic interferometer for all eternity. Billions and trillions of dollars were and will be required to get to the bottom of things. An entire military industrial complex has come and gone, disappearing in a radioactive haze with another one taking its place in the quest to understand the mysteries of the magnetic interferometer.

Of course, politicians have always been untrustworthy. If wars were too important to be fought by generals, then the gizmo was deemed too important to be left under the control of any government. There is always the temptation of some political hotdog -- that one guy who's trying to put his name in every history book so that he can say, "Look Mom, I'm famous!" There is the problem of plausible deniability. Sane world leaders and rational intelligence agencies want to deny that the government has anything to do with warehousing machines and bodies of little green men. That is why the magnetic interferometer is the corporate property of Lodestar, in subsidiary control to the Public Private Partnership. When an inquiring UFO-ologist makes an inquiry of government records, the response is:

"All records have been searched. We find no evidence that the government has any evidence at all about UFO artifacts. Have you seen a psychiatrist lately? Let us help you."

That is why the government has its disinformation program, and the secrets still remain secret. UFO believers are all loony tuners, providing a rich source of humor for late night, stand up comedians. Bureaucratic mechanisms are set in place to keep it that way. And now, for some unknown reason, it has been decided that the machine is no longer going to be under the control of human hands. It's going away to simply vanish. Soon, base carpenters will be called in to fit foam and lumber around it. Then a Mexican government truck will pull up in front of the bunker to take it to some other secret undisclosed location. No one knows why, but everyone agrees that the paperwork is all in order. Secretary of Defense Corozon has put his signature to it.

BAJA
CALIFORNIA

Karl Eysenbach

It's been a big week for the smugglers. First they picked up the bag of diamonds at San Felipe. Frog drove down from Tijuana, and had given Jorge a bag of peanuts on the beach. After refueling at Bahia San Antonio, he and Ivan headed south until they reached home base in San Mateo. They picked up their chums in the two other boats there, and within a few hours, here they are stowing their gear in the little suites at Hotel Punta Borego. Abandoning their rooms, they go back to the ocean to fish. After all, they tell other people that this is what they do for a living.

The best way to visit the hotel is by landing on the dirt airstrip nearby; but the hotel never advertises, and it's always empty. Despite this, the Hotel Punta Borego is clean and luxurious beyond belief. It has thirty rooms, a professional staff, an Olympic sized swimming pool, a three-star restaurant, tennis courts, and a nine-hole golf course. You can stay there if you pay $500 a night, but of course no one ever does. If you were foolish enough to try to visit by land, you would have to travel 30 kilometers on roads that are capable of breaking axles, even on four wheel drives. It's a miracle that an empty hotel can be so profitable.

The fishermen go out near Isla Santa Isabel, near the reefs where the waters are literally crawling with fish. The fishermen are lucky, catching some giant sea bass that must weigh a hundred kilos each. They gun the boat motors, and it's back to the hotel in no time. But why should you be surprised? Their boats have outboard motors so large and fast that they can beat a speeding car to Bahia San Antonio 200km away.

Once they get onshore, they stow their gear and turn their attention to gutting and cleaning the fish, cutting them into a manageable size. The kitchen staff stores the fish in the kitchen's giant walk-in coolers. The next morning, the fishermen sit on the terrace finishing up their heuvos rancheros and chorizo, when they see the private plane coming in on its approach pattern. They run to the main desk. The manager gives them some keys, and the six men commandeer Jeeps to meet the

The Story of the Century

plane. As soon as the propeller stops moving, the men load four duffel bags from the plane into the Jeeps. Only after the fishermen are done, does the hotel's ground crew begin the process of refueling the plane for its turnaround.

The fishermen return to the kitchen, hauling the khaki bags, which obviously belong to the Marines. With the help of the kitchen staff, they take packets of white powder out of the duffel bags, placing them carefully inside the cavities of the fish. Then the fish are wrapped in white paper, iced, and carefully placed into Styrofoam coolers. One by one they carry the coolers to the beach, depositing them in their boats. Now it's time to leave.

Jorge and Vladimir walk into the manager's office and pay for their visit with the bag of peanuts that they had eaten on their trip down. The manager dumps the peanut shells onto his desk and smiles. He finds that the diamond count is satisfactory, and he takes out a loupe. Inserting it in one eye, he examines the diamonds one by one. This pleases him too. The blue and white diamonds are of very high quality. Getting out of his seat, he shakes Jorge's hand.

"It was a pleasure doing business with you Jorge. Feel free to visit again any time."

Jorge smiles. "Some day I would like to actually put my name in your hotel register. I would like to stay here with my wife." Both men smile at the joke.

They shove off, and the boats travel north again. This time they land at San Bernardo. It's Sunday, and the fish processing plant is closed. One person is there. Someone called from the hotel, telling the plant manager that a consignment was on the way. He's waiting for the fishermen when the boats dock.

"What do you have here?" the plant manager says, his arms akimbo.

7

Jorge replies, "Five hundred kilos of sea bas wrapped and ready to go."

"Well, unload those coolers. Put them on the back of that flatbed truck, and we'll go to the refrigerator line." The men snap to it, pronto. Jorge gets in the truck cab with the manager, and Puto, Vladimir, and Ivan walk the hundred meters to the large metal building with no windows. Inside the cramped and shabby office, the Filipino plant manager takes one package of fish outside of each cooler; carefully opening the packages as if they were Christmas presents. One by one, he unwraps the fish and opens the plastic bags just enough to place a tiny amount of powder onto white filter paper. Then he carefully reseals each bag. Taking an eyedropper out of his desk drawer, he puts the smallest amount of thick clear liquid on the powder samples. The powder fizzes and turns the same shade of bright yellow. He compares the color to a chart on his desk.

"Very good. Looks like they're all 99% pure or better."

"What do you expect?" Jorge replies. "It's always the same. It's never anything except the best." Jorge doesn't like the fish plant very much. It's always too cold inside, and he hates to wait. But there's nothing he could do until everything is checked. He wishes he was outside, joking with his men in the warm sun.

"Procedures are procedures, you know. I'll find out the exact weight of the fish later." With that, the short, stocky man goes to the wall safe and takes out stacks of $100 bills still in their currency wrappers from the World Bank.

"The gross is $50,000 for the services of you and your men, but we are withholding $20,000 for the usual fees and taxes." This is a polite way of telling Jorge that the fish plant will handle the job of bribing and paying for the cooperation of local officials. The fishermen are going to take home $5,000 each. Jorge stuffs three empty duffel bags and the cash into one bag, and he walks outside with a broad smile. They look around, and all they can see is the empty fish plant, a sleepy Mexican village, and a beach that goes on forever. They are alone. They get into their boats, and they shove off for the short hop to Bahia San Mateo.

As the narrow fiberglass boats skip along the waves, the men smile and shout at each other, happy that they've completed their mission. The boats slow as they go past the headlands, entering the shallows of the bay. The fishermen anchor in their usual spots, some children watching them as they look for clams. The kids are no dummies. They keep their distance. Everyone climbs out of their boats into the shallow water and begins the process of shuttling back and forth, unloading the gear to where their trucks are parked.

Ordinarily, the men would go home and spend a week or more with their wives and family. They would make trips to Cachanilla to deposit their money and to purchase supplies. Some would have patronized the Red Pelican, the local ladies bar, where they could purchase the comfort of a woman. But not today, there's only limited time. As a group, the little convoy of pickup trucks pulls up in front of Carmelita's General Store. The men get out of the trucks, gathering around Jorge -- waiting and listening as he slides a card into the telephone, calling a nearby Marine base.

"Is Sergeant Homero there?"

(pause)

"Sergeant Homero, this is Jorge Estrada. How are you doing? Are your children well? I was wondering if our training session was still on. It is? What time?"

(pause)

"Where should we meet you?"

(pause)

"That's good. We'll all meet you tomorrow morning at 0600. Thank you very much. We'll see you then." As Jorge hangs up, he can hear the collective groan from the men.

"Guys, I know you don't want to do it, but remember. This is what the big money is all about. If we complete the training and we do the job, we can all retire. Be ready to go by five o'clock tomorrow morning. Vladimir and I will pick you up."

The next morning two dusty, bruised looking pickup trucks head south on the two-lane blacktop past the Marine base. They turn right onto the gravel road that goes to the microwave tower. After three kilometers and a few hundred meters of elevation, there's a fork in the road. They turn right again, going onto a narrow dirt path with way too many large rocks, sharp curves, and washouts. Going up and down the mountain for forty more minutes, they come to where the hills turn into a box canyon. An olive drab military lorry is parked at the base of the cliff, where once long ago, families of prehistoric Indians lived.

Sergeant Homero is waiting for them as the beat up trucks stop, raising a cloud of dust. The fishermen get out of the vehicles. There's no need for introduction. They form a straight line in front of the military man, waiting for him to begin this day's lesson. The fishermen are standing at ease.

Sergeant Homero is a tiny, hard little man. He looks Aztec. He looks bitter, and he has good reason to. He's been passed over for Sergeant Major, and that really sucks really bad. Lots of suck-ass politics in the Army. If you don't play the game, you could be dead, Fred. Sgt. Homero is stationed in this desiccated shithole, while his extra creepy brother is sitting in the lap of luxury in Singapore, carrying around some briefcase for some overstuffed general. Hey, thanks a lot Ferdie for all yer support. Now, Singapore was so nice as to cut him some

The Story of the CENTURY

orders that are Cosmic. Oy vay! Train these fishermen on SEAL tactics in top secrecy! Now if that don't take the cake!

Master Sergeant Ignacio Homero is a lifer, and this ragtag bunch in front of him are the strangest things he's seen in his military career. He still has trouble believing that he's doing this, and he would have refused if he hadn't seen the orders addressed to himself from the Commander in Chief of Naval Operations. So he did as he was told. He's already put these men through the equivalent of basic training. He won't admit to himself, but he's glad to see that they are as tough as they are. Week by week, he's taught them and supervised them as they've gone through the training in small arms. They've already been on some tactical games deep in the mountains and out in the middle of the flat Vizcaino desert, and all of this has to be done off base and under deepest cover of secrecy. Not even his lieutenant or the base commander knows where he's done with this crew, or what he's doing today. God only knows what half-baked scheme in Kuala Lumpur this operation is about.

"I know that the World government is screwy, and half of it's corrupt, but what in God's green earth do these people have to do with the price of tea in China?" he thinks to himself.

"Good morning, gentlemen. As you can see today, we are going to learn how to assemble, disassemble, and transport heavy machine guns. We will do this without being detected by the enemy, and we will do this quickly and quietly."

As secret as his training is, Sergeant Homero does not know that the fishermen know a much bigger secret than he does, or that at the end of their training, that the good sergeant will die in a mysterious automobile accident.

Karl Eysenbach

NEW LOS ANGELES, EL PUERTO DISTRICT
FEBRUARY 13th, 6:00 AM

He wakes up with a terrible hangover. Even though the volume is on low, the sportscasters are still standing in front of him, reminding him to get up. He can see through them into his kitchen. It looks like a mess.

"Well Juan, it looks like America is going to go to the World Cup Finals against China."

"That's right, Chao. The New Los Angeles goalie, Rhadavan Khrishna was the superstar in yesterday's shootout with Brazil."

They drone on until Clem tells them to shut up. He shouldn't have stayed up so late milking that source about the Bollywood lawyers sandbagging Tata Studios, but it's part of the job. He orders up strong coffee, raisin bread with apricot jam, and orange juice, and he takes a shower while the kitchen robot is processing it.

What a dump! Once upon a time it had been an 'artistic salon' where he and his wife Salma had put on modern art exhibits every month. Now it's just another slovenly bachelor pad with half the furniture it used to have, and way too much junk from abandoned art projects and fast food wrappers. He told his missus to get the hell out three months ago, and he's going through the worst stage of his loneliness right now. There is too much of her lying around here. The divorce has made him work three times harder than he has before, all in an attempt to forget his life. That means getting to work an hour early after boozing it down until 2AM, but it also means that he's slowly but surely driving himself into a pit.

Breakfast is waiting for him when he gets out of the shower. After eating, he gets on his bicycle to ride down to the docks to catch the ferry for work. The hangover is killing him, and the only good thing is that it's before the major crush of commuters. He locks his bike up on the dock and gets on board. The ferry pulls away, heading south then west past the Palos Verde peninsula, turning north to pass by parts of the forbidden zone and some of the secret installations near El Segundo. The sun is low in the horizon, shining through the fog that is lifting, and the sea is almost calm. The vision of finding Salma in bed with the two young artists flashes through his mind for the ten thousandth time, and he tries to concentrate on what he's going to do this morning at work. This is not going to be a good day. His boss is a well-meaning guy, but they have issues to discuss. Clem thinks maybe he's done less than splendidly well on that his last piece of reporting

By now, the boat is docking at the main terminal. The *Times* Building is across the street. Clem walks with the crowd and through the revolving doors. Up the elevator to the fourth floor, and the gray cubicle farm of the newsroom is waiting. Only one editor is in his glass booth along the wall, and it's Pablo. Pablo Lopez is the Assistant Editor at the *Times*, and he's been at the paper for twenty years. The short, fat, balding man is sitting in his office smoking a cigar when Clem walks in.

"Come in Clem. What's the deal on your Bollywood sex symbol?"

Clem tries to clear his head before he speaks. "Boss, I'm sick of doing investigative pieces about Gary Chindowarry's taste in tuxedos. Can't I get a real piece of news to wrap my hands around?"

"Well, you know, that's what the public wants! We're in the business of selling newspapers. *Comprendas?*"

"Yeah, yeah, yeah. But I'm sick of this Bollywood beat. Is there any possibility of doing something a little more weighty, like the defense industry?"

Lopez's intelligent eyes look at him for a moment, and he's silent. Finally he speaks.

"Look, this last article you wrote was crap, and you look like crap too. You're losing your edge, and you look completely burned out. I need better stuff than this shit, and I'm spiking your story."

This hits Clem like a fist in his stomach. He feels the cold sweat, suppressing his nausea.

"Okay. Okay. You're right and I'm wrong. You know Boss, I've been working for three years, and I need a break. I've build up a little vacation time. Is it okay if I take time off?"

Lopez puts his hands on his stomach, and he thinks for what seems forever. Clouds of cigar smoke form around his head. "Okay. You've got two weeks off starting tomorrow. I want you back on the job and ready to go on the 20th."

Clem thanks him, goes out to the bullpen, and does his job for the rest of the day. That night, he goes home and packs for Mexico.

SOMEWHERE NEAR CACHANILLA, BAJA CALIFORNIA
8:45 PM

Carlos Castellon is hitting his fists on the steering wheel. It's tough enough being a big time road contractor guy, but tonight's the night that he has the *quinceañera*, and then the damn message comes down that he has to do the errand. And on top of this, the *chingadora* pickup truck breaks down!

Although brand new one-ton Honda pickups are very reliable, a tall rock has punctured the ion exchange box in the hydrogen fuel cell. Carlos has done his best with duct tape, but it isn't enough. There's a short circuit somewhere. With luck, he'd be able to make it home. Unfortunately, he didn't. He makes a mental note to have his secretary Conchita write a letter to Mallard Power. He thinks for a bit about the good things Conchita does for him in the afternoon. Then his mind returns to his predicament. Of course, it would have been better if he hadn't tried driving on that boulder-strewn dry riverbed in the first place.

Being stuck in the middle of nowhere is not much fun. It's dark, and it's getting cold. Carlos figures out that the best thing to do is to walk to Ernesto's house, and he's about a kilometer away. After what seems like an eternity, Carlos stumbles to the mechanic's house, lucky to be able to find his way by following the wheel ruts in the so-called road. It's too late already, and Carlos gets to the small, concrete block house with its yard filled with engine parts, small children, and a couple of black dogs with their ribs sticking out. The dogs run around and bark at Carlos as he approaches the front porch with the rusty and bent tin roof. Ernesto's wife Lupe comes out to see what the commotion's about, and the sight of Don Carlos, tired and sweaty, makes her rush to clean off the old metal lawn chair, offer humble apologies, and run inside for a large glass of ice water.

Ernesto comes out, and they talk about the *quinceañera*, Sara Reyna, and the weather. But Carlos is in a hurry. *"Andale! Debemos hier! Regresamos al coche!"* In Spanish, this is a polite way of saying, "Let's stop dorking around and get humping with car repair!!" Ernesto gets into his beaten down pickup truck, and a cloud of white smoke appears, but only temporarily. They speed off, but Carlos is still rattled. When they get to the dead Honda, Carlos' sphincter tightens. He searches in his pockets for his keys to no avail. After about five minutes of frantic searching and wailing, he remembers that he took them out of his pocket when he sat down for water. So they go back to Ernesto's to retrieve the keys.

Ernesto can't work his magic tonight. They drive to a tow truck operator's house in Cachanilla, and the two trucks return to Carlos' fancy paperweight. Carlos pays the tow truck driver extra money so he can take Ernesto home. He gets into Ernesto's truck, guns the engine, and speeds towards the Casa de Piedra. Parking as close as he can, Carlos walks to the main gate to find the party in full swing. He thinks that he slipped in anonymously, but he's mistaken. Even though it's close to the high point of the *quinceañera*, his wife Doña Victoria Reader Castellon spots him, homing in like a heat-seeking missile.

"Where have you been!? You ought to be ashamed of yourself! Of all the stupid days for you to be out playing with your stupid new toy! You have no respect for anyone! Are you late because you were abusing the machinery? That would be exactly like the boneheaded kind of thing that you would do!! I swear I should have taken a gun and shot you myself years ago! No court in the land would convict me!" Her harangue continues like this for several more minutes, and Carlos' cheeks flush with shame. Once again, his wife has intuited what he's been really doing. But Carlos is a proud man, and he lies, dramatically putting his heart to his chest while he declaims.

"*Mi corazone!* Of course I would never do anything like that! The truck was defective. I was just driving along and the thing stops! I had to walk to Ernesto's house for assistance, and we had to go all the way to Cachanilla and back to get the thing towed. I am going to have Conchita write a letter to the automobile company tomorrow. The Japanese should not sell automobiles that have defective engines!"

Carlos doesn't bother to change into his tuxedo, and he's more than glad to see friends to socialize with in order to escape the sermon from his wife. He talks too loud and laughs too much. He tries to calm down, playing the role of gracious host and dealmaker, but there aren't enough social obligations in the world to keep him here one second more than necessary. When he spots the first guest leaving, he walks out, down the dusty road, and back to the beaten up Toyota with 403,543.2 KM on the odometer.

The Story of the Century

He has to go back to Cachanilla, back to the towing yard, and back to retrieve what he's left in his Honda. There's too much booze under his belt, and only one headlight on the truck is functional. But his luck is with him. No Federales tonight. His head nearly hits the roof when he hits the first speed bump, and he sobers up, quickly turning onto the potholed side street up the hill to where the razor wire compound is. The gates are closed, but Somoza's house still has a light on. Carlos bangs on the gate, and Somoza comes out, wearing a grease-stained wifebeater T-shirt. His pit bull barks angrily, jumping at Carlos, strangling itself on its choke chain.

"*Buenas noches, Señor Somoza.* Thank you very much for helping me, especially with Ernesto. Could you do me just one more favor this evening? I am so stupid! First my truck dies. Then I remember that I need to get something important from it. Could you get the keys and give me a flashlight? I can go there myself if I can avoid your dog. I've put you to too much inconvenience this evening."

Somoza shrugs. "No problem, Señor Castellon. Cujo!! Shut up!! I don't want to hear from you any more!" On command, the dog becomes calm and lies down. Somoza goes inside to retrieve the keys. He returns and opens the gate. Carlos goes inside, exchanging money for keys. Somoza hands Carlos a flashlight.

"*Muchissimas Gracias,* Señor Somoza. I don't need to find my way. Thank you very much. I'll only be a few minutes." Carlos smiles a little more than normal, but this is understandable, given what he's looking for. He walks on the uneven ground to the red truck. The dog strains at its leash, and its upper lip curls as it growls. Carlos smiles at the dog as he passes by safely.

"*Pinche Perro, Pinche Perro, Pinche Perro,*" Carlos coos at the dog in an attempt to calm the animal and himself down.

He looks at the dog, and he feels his heart pounding loudly and quickly. It isn't Cujo that makes him so nervous though. "Did the driver or Ernesto find it?" he thinks to himself. "God, I'm in trouble if they did!" He puts the key in the truck door and he climbs in and sits down, closing the truck door. At last, Carlos is alone. He reaches under the seat, and he feels what he was looking for. A smile crosses his face as he pulls out the semi-automatic Colt .45 pistol and slips it into his jacket pocket.

The *quinceañera* just keeps rolling along. Ejido San Mateo has less than 300 souls, and almost everybody is there, with a sizeable component from Cachanilla and San Bernardo too. The people of Cachanilla and San Bernardo have their differences of opinion and their snobberies. The people of one community like to gossip and say bad things about each other, but all of this is forgotten when a fiesta is being given. Most people have put on their Sunday bests to celebrate the Sara Reyna's fifteenth birthday, and everyone is happy.

This is about as good as any *quinceañera* could be. When Carlos and Victoria Castellon put on a party, there's no one who can outdo them, either in their lavish celebration or their hospitality. Hundreds of Japanese lanterns have been hung from the trees. The food and drink are prodigious, and it's all tasty beyond belief. Aunt Victoria gave Clem the task of being an assistant host. He's busy consulting with the band, pouring drinks, bussing tables, and being charming to everyone in the way that good waiters are. He's so busy that he doesn't notice most of the *quinceañera* ceremony, or the fact that Uncle Carlos is nowhere to be found. Only later does he does notice Aunt Victoria fuming when Uncle Carlos comes into the party late and bedraggled.

Bandera music, *cerveza,* and various forms of booze flow freely all night, and there are enough lobsters, turkeys, and paella to leave the families and friends full enough to loosen a notch in their belts. At ten o'clock the mariachi band starts playing, going on until I don't know how many hours after midnight. While the band plays the old

The Story of the Century

standards a few people dance or sing along, but the majority of people sit around talking quietly, drinking, eating, re-establishing relationships and catching up on family gossip. Officer Carcelho is especially happy. He has his own large bottle of champagne. But this is all the party needs for security. The only trouble is the *borracho* mason, Luis, who decides to not only walk, but to try to lie down in one of the fire rings. Only with Roberto's effort does he not burn up. As it is, he's too drunk to feel the pain.

Sara Reyna is standing on the chair with the doll, and the crowd's cheering. Part of the ceremony calls for her to throw a doll (that represents her childhood) to ten or eleven screaming girls, with their hands waving in the air trying to catch it. Aunt Victoria's smiling thinly, and she's thinking to herself, "Where in hell is that *pendejo* Carlos?" The musicians begin to play the special music for the ceremony, and Sara Reyna tosses the doll to Samantha, a ten year old very pleased with her prize. After she steps off of the chair, she leads the rest of the ceremony by starting the dance with her escort, Raul. Clem is dragooned out of being the headwaiter, just long enough to dance with Aunt Victoria, and then Sara Reyna. Soon others join in until the whole party is celebrating Sara Reyna's coming of age celebration.

You can be sure that people notice the fact that Carlos is absent for the ceremonial waltzing. About and hour and a half later, Uncle Carlos tries to quietly appear at the fringes of the party, but of course, Aunt Victoria quickly gives him a loud what for. Perhaps this is the highlight of the party, and it's the first topic of gossip the next day.

Clem doesn't see this, as he's too busy supervising the kitchen detail. As nice as the *quinceañera* is, Clem feels the alienation coming back. It's true that these are his people. His entire adopted family is here. The whole party's one big happy family! And yet Clem continues to feel isolated. Maybe he's been in New LA too long. You can get those city ways, buy he also thinks that maybe it has something to do with his skin color.

Everybody at the party is just like they always are, but the undercurrent's the same. It isn't as if people are deliberately mean or stupid. People like to talk about little things, and they can talk about things that are different. He is some freaky-deaky orphan that Uncle Carlos and Aunt Victoria had taken under their wing. Yes, he's an orphan of Aunt Victoria's cousin, and he grew up in this village, but to this day hundreds of years after the fact, there's still this stigma attached to his skin color, a vestige of prejudice against those who perpetrated the Great Atomic War.

He's heard about it all his life. Well-meaning liberal types try to engage him in weighty, 'meaningful' conversations of, "What does it feel like to be white?" Clem's learned to make flip answers like, "Just like you, except paler." That usually shuts them up. But, but, there's still that aroma, lingering in the conversational air here, -- like something bad you put in the microwave two weeks ago that still hangs around, waiting to be activated when the door is opened.

Officer Carcelho's joke brings Clem back to the present. He's pouring champagne. "Aunt Theresa says that she has always wanted to marry you!" he announces to everyone who is listening. The 80-year-old spinster is totally embarrassed. The whole table laughs, and this puts Caracellho on a roll. "Not only that, but she wants to have your baby!"

"That's true," says Clem with a straight face as he continues to pour the rum into empty glasses. Superficially, he's smiling and playing along with the police officer's somewhat crude joke. At another level, he's busy being a waiter, looking for people to serve the people needing more drinks. At the deepest level, he's embarrassed, just looking for an exit strategy.

People sit around the fire rings talking about new times and old as long as the mariachis play. The stone walls of the courtyard shelter them from the cold desert winds, and friends pull up their chairs to share the heat of the fire pits and each other's stories.

Clem works, helping until he gets tired, and he goes to his room to lie down for a few minutes, maybe a half an hour. When he gets up, it's back to being a kitchen worker again. Put the excess food away, and there are plenty of pots, pans, dishes, glasses, and silverware to wash. This is the most frantic part of the evening for him. The Castellon servants are working smoothly and efficiently, but it's a huge job serving such a huge crew; and kitchen work has its own methamphetamine speed and tension. "God, imagine doing this for a living!" Clem thinks to himself.

One by one, the partygoers drift away. The kitchen is clean, and Clem tells the help to call it a night. Clem is the last man standing. His hands are on his hips as he looks up at the sky underneath the giant bouganvillas twined on the roof of the ramada. Off in the east, there's a gray glow. Dawn's not here yet. As usual, the stars of Baja California are beautiful -- too beautiful for words. Deep black velvet surrounds you. Little pinpoints of diamonds just hang there and twinkle, forming their patterns of clusters and sky threads and constellations. It's good to see all of the old friends that have been waiting for him while he's been away, working for the paper in New Los Angeles: the Pleiades, Orion, the Big and Little Dipper, Mercury, Venus, Mars, Jupiter, and on and on. He has a connection with the sky that he doesn't have with anyone or anything else.

In New Los Angeles, the only stars he ever sees are from the entertainment factories. When Clem gets his rare vacation, he spends every bit he can at the Casa de Piedra. And then there's the drive down. Clem calls it living in the car commercial. He loves to whip along the old road, on the straightaways, around the hairpin curves, up and down the mountains the hard way, not on the superhighways. This is the one road that leads him back to his roots. He goes through the

Karl Eysenbach

Mexican desert, -- nothing but kilometers and kilometers of cactus, mountains, and the rare and welcomed glimpses of the Sea of Cortez.

A window is open, and Clem can hear Aunt Victoria snoring. The patch of gray has grown in the eastern sky, and Clem looks out beyond the stone walls to the little village. Ejido San Mateo is his real home, even if it doesn't look like much to the casual travelers passing through. To them, San Mateo is nothing more than a swelling of nondescript buildings clustered along the highway, stuck in the middle of nowhere, a hamlet that you whiz by in the godforsaken desert.

It's a village of fishermen. Lots of people are dirt poor, and there are still too many cardboard shacks here. But people have made incredible progress since Clem came here for the first time. Brightly painted concrete block houses of different colors are the norm, and the people have neatly ordered gardens next to badly working cars behind wire fences that face out on broad *caliche* streets.

Casa de Piedra is different. Uncle Carlos and Aunt Victoria purchased the huge stone cube with a pyramid roof after it had been abandoned for decades, an artistic pile of ruins. Through hard work, they made their road construction firm into one of the biggest and most prosperous on the Mexican peninsula. As the contracts came in, they plowed money into the hacienda, not only restoring it but also expanding it. You can see it from the highway for kilometers coming down from the north, surrounded by its citrus orchards, facing out on the vast quantities of desert and mountains that Aunt Victoria leases to the *rancheros*.

In the summer time, the heat is oppressive. The only people who visit are demented sports fishermen searching for dorado and blue fin. When the weather cools in October, retirees, vacationers, and others came to Baja looking for adventure. The miraculous thing is, that most of the time they find it without killing or injuring themselves, -- up in the arroyos, through the cactus thickets that grab at you, stinging and cutting your body. There are poisonous snakes, spiders, fish, and plants that will kill you if you aren't careful. There are even the stray drug runners, aligned with some mysterious guerilla operation, but they do not bother ordinary people, unless you stumble into the wrong place at the wrong time.

Closer to civilization there are the crowds and the corrupt cops. There is the pollution. There are the seventy-zillion channels of entertainment and information streams surrounding people in the city every waking second, telling them what deodorant to buy. But out here the air is pure and a deep blue color, and a person stands out distinct, unique from the environment and from other people -- as a person and not as a part of some herd.

Clem's thoughts are interrupted by the sound of a truck approaching. He listens as it pulls up in front of the main entrance and stops. With surprise, he hears the truck's door slam, and the voice of Uncle Carlos as he swears with a vengeance, "Son of a bitch." It sounds like there's some scraping or tearing of paper at the gate, and then a pause. The truck turns around, going back to where it came from. The gate swings open, and Uncle Carlos quietly heads towards the bedroom where he sleeps when he's out of favor with Aunt Victoria. Instinctively, Clem hides himself behind a pillar. Waiting for a few minutes, but it seeming like an eternity, he waits for Uncle Carlos to go to bed. Quietly Clem walks, taking the wrought iron handle to open the gate.

Traces of orange and pink are showing now, and there are some fingers of fog hanging off far in the ocean. He opens the gate to inspect the desert expanse to the north, but he has a rude jolt back to reality as the gate creaks open. Some scraps of paper are on the ground. A poster has been slapped on sometime during the night that quickly reminds Clem of the world news that Baja and some other parts of Mexico have been making for the last year or so. It's still easy to see a half-torn piece of paper where there's a picture of a stylized fist jamming into the air. Rays of green stream out of the fist, and five red stars show themselves prominently. The poster's headlines scream:

VIVA LA REVOLUCION!
POWER TO THE PEOPLE!
ATZLAN LIBERATION FRONT

TWO HOURS EARLIER

Carlos Castellon is driving the old pickup truck south toward San Mateo again. On the way, the one operating headlight shines its cyclops eye at the cars returning from the *quinceañera*. North of the village he slows, searching for the turnoff, as the truck bumps and crawls onto the rocky road. He's headed back to Ernesto's house.

The dogs bark, and the threadbare mechanic's shack is dark; but the red glow of a cigarette shows that Ernesto is waiting. Carlos stops the car, leaving the engine running as he gets out to greet his employee.

"Ernesto, you are a blessing to me in many ways. I would not be able to do what needed to be done without you. Thank you again for rescuing me this evening. We still have to do the errand I told you about. But remember. It must remain a secret forever. Tell no one, or it could mean both of our lives."

Ernesto's eyes widen, and he puts the cigarette out, stubbing it into the dirt with his boot.

"Now let's get into the truck. You drive." With that, Carlos slides himself over to become the passenger while Ernesto walks around to the other side. Off in the distance, two cardboard shacks are lit by the glow of trash fires. They back out, and the truck gets back on the highway to head north again, turning off on the road to the mining district. They go for a few kilometers, and then they go for a few kilometers more.

"Here's the turnoff." Carlos points to the right at what looks like nothing more than a cattle track. The old truck lurches and tosses as if it's on a stormy ocean, as it works its way into the middle of the desert. Even by Baja standards, this is not a good road. Besides the rocks, Ernesto has to skillfully avoid the cactus spines and broken beer bottles. Within a couple hundred meters, the 'road' improves. The silhouettes of the landscape change from scrub to cactus forest, and the road begins to rise. Finally, there is a wide spot where a small pickup can turn around.

Carlos barks, "Stop here. You have your watch on, don't you?" He reaches into a gym bag at his feet and pulls out a pair of very tiny, very expensive night vision binoculars.

"Have you ever seen something like this before?" He hands the binoculars to Ernesto, who examines them with curiosity.

"Put them up to your eyes, and look through there." Ernesto is surprised.

"Everything looks green, but I can see as if it is almost daytime!" he exclaims in surprise.

"Use these to watch me. I'm going to walk up to where the cliff is, but you won't be able to see me when I go around the bend. What time is it now?"

"It's almost 3:30"

"Keep your eyes open towards where I'm going to. If I don't return in half an hour, or you see someone else heading towards the truck, get out of here pronto, and tell the *commandante*."

"Yes, Señor Castellon."

With that Carlos reaches down into the gym bag again and pulls out a large police flashlight. He gets out of the truck. He turns on his light, and he starts walking over the stony ground with cactus surrounding him. He continues walking up, turning on the path leading towards the cliff. The circle of light shows something that does not appear to belong in the vast wasteland. You might find a man in the middle of the desert, but you would not find two nice dining room chairs facing each other five meters from a sheer drop-off.

Out of nowhere, a man steps into the light. He is dressed in black drab military clothing, and he has a black balaclava over his head. You can only see his eyes. Carlos is calm, but he has increased awareness of the pistol near his armpit. The man in black is only known by his *nombre de guerrero,* Subcommandante Insecticida. He is the regional chief of the Atzlan Liberation Front, or ALF. Insecticida speaks.

"Please sit down. It's not very often I get to see an honored and distinguished guest as yourself. This is why I have taken the trouble." First Carlos sits down, then Insectida. Carlos puts out the light, and the two men shake hands.

"How are you, Señor? You are *muy famoso,* and you have much respect among the people. This is an unusual place for a meeting, no? These are very fine chairs. Where did you get them?"

Subcommandante Insecticida smiles a secret smile. "I have my sources. I can't tell you. We both know some things have to remain confidential. Did you have a good *quinceañera?*"

"It was a good thing. I think it's still going on. I got some sand and gravel contracts, and I needed some cement work done."

"Tell me, how is Doña Victoria?"

"I am very lucky to be here on time. My truck died, and she scolded me for being late to the party. Otherwise, she is excellent. You know she always keeps thing under control." Carlos pauses for breath before he continues.

"The *quinceañera* was wonderful, but you know, *quinceañeras* are so much trouble. I'm glad I don't have to go through them every day. I'm sorry you didn't attend. I didn't know where to send the invitation." It's Carlos' turn for a secret smile.

"That's all right. Some of my men attended for me. We better get down to business. Neither of us has much time."

"Yes. You're right."Carlos coughs a little before he begins. "You know, my friend is still very interested in your well being, despite what he publicly says. You know that because he allowed you to get that large shipment of supplies from the Marine Quartermasters warehouse."

"When you see him next time, thank him for me. But we both know that this meeting is not about military rations or weapons. I have another message to deliver to your friends. We cannot afford to wait. We must have the magnetic interferometer immediately!" The subcommandate's eyes almost blaze out at Carlos in the dark. Carlos is clearly intimidated, and he feels a trickle of sweat on his forehead. He wonders whether he will have to use his gun or not. But he speaks.

"Yes. I have been informed that you will find a magnetic interferometer at the Ybarra Loncheria near Santa Ynez at 2300 hours on the evening of February 19th." He pauses, and then he continues.

"Yes. That is right. A magnetic interferometer. I do not know what that means. It will be at the Ybarra Loncheria at 2300 hours on February 19th. It is a curious message, no?"

The hooded figure is silent for a minute, thinking about what he is going to say. He puts his hand to his chin. Finally he speaks. "We are very grateful for this information. Tell Governor Salinas that he is to not worry. Everything is in order."

Uncle Carlos glances at his wristwatch. He does not know what to think about what he has heard. He says, "I will deliver that message. Now with your permission, allow me to get back to my truck. My people are waiting for me. It has been a long day, and I am very tired."

Insecticida stands up. "Of course. I understand. It has been a big day for everyone in the *ejido*, and certainly a big day for your niece. My congratulations to her. I'm sure you need your rest. Thank you for getting involved in delivering this message to me. I will pass it along to my people."

"Believe me, Señor Subcommandante, this is not something I do on a daily basis. I was chosen only as a messenger boy." Carlos reaches down and fumbles for his flashlight. By the time he has turned it on, Subcommandante Insecticida is nowhere to be found. Carlos walks down the path he came, spotting the truck within a few minutes time. Ernesto spots him, and the truck comes to life, its one headlight shining.

"It's a good thing you came down. I was almost ready to abandon you. What did you do in the middle of the desert?"

"I cannot tell you anything, except that I had a meeting with a man. We sat on two very nice chairs. That was unusual." He pauses, and then continues.

"Thank you for your patience, Ernesto. Everything went smoothly as planned. Even more smoothly than I expected. Take me home. You can expect to get some days off, and I will pay you something extra for all the trouble you have taken with me today. I think you will be very happy." A great weight goes off his shoulders, and Carlos begins to get a small adrenaline high of elation.

"I will tell you, that this was not a meeting about business. It was much more important than that. I was asked by someone very powerful, very important, to do what I did tonight. It was an honor for me to serve. I feel like some kind of spy or secret agent."

FEBRUARY 11TH, 1 PM

Clem is digging his hole in the far corner of Uncle Carlos' orchard, and he's trying to dig it deep enough so that a tangerine tree can go in. There's the fast way of digging a hole, and there's Clem's way. He knows that he'll never finish it before he goes back to New LA, but that's not the point. Uncle Carlos and Aunt Victoria humor him. Of all the things he does in Mexico, this is one of the things he loves the most.

He found the little pit waiting for him, partly filled with brush and beer cans from the last time he was in San Mateo. He cleans out the trash. Then he gets down to where he was before. He has everything he needs: gloves, a pick, two shovels, one giant pry bar, and a few gallons of water. Clem likes digging holes because it is hot, sweaty, dirty work fit only for a peon. In other words, it's not like anything he would do in New Los Angeles. He feels that when he returns home, it is important to show his family and the people that he's one of them, and not some gringo prince too good for manual labor. Besides, he needs to lose the weight. Clem is working on his third liter of water for the afternoon. He's in the rhythm now. It's nice outside, and a good breeze is coming in from the north.

When Clem is in his rhythm, he begins to let his mind wander. Right now he is looking at the place during the Ice Age. 12,000 years ago, there was no San Mateo, and the area was 20° cooler. Pine trees grew food for the mastodons. The mastodons were food for the saber-toothed tigers. In this spot, in the scrub and grasslands (not the desert), there was a fast moving stream running with the clearest, coldest, cleanest water imaginable. If you walked to the ocean, about a kilometer further out than it is now, you'd find a beach a meter thick with seashells. You could practically walk on the fish. About four families of cavemen lived here, making tools for dressing hides and crushing the bones of small animals. They sucked the marrow out of bones and threw them in the stream. The rock tools remain. Clem finds one of them as he digs.

Clem thinks about many things while he is digging. Maybe he's an astronaut working the methane deposits on one of Jupiter's moons. He thinks of all the people who have ever dug holes like this; maybe he is an *indio* in a Spanish mission, working for the Franciscan padres. He sweats and sweats and sweats some more. Maybe he is an ancient Assyrian working outside of the City of Ur or a doughboy in a trench in WW I.

Clem is covered with a fine whitish dust the same color as the soil. He wears a cowboy hat, wrap around sunglasses, a bandana, a white dress shirt, jeans, and old work boots. His hair is matted, and his nose is dripping from the sweat. The sun is low in the sky, and it's time to go back to his room. He walks through the orchard, smelling the citrus blossoms as he looks at the sun through the canopy of the trees.

A housekeeper is around, but no one else. He takes off his clothes, and showers in the bathroom with its walls made of rough-cut stone. When he's in his bathrobe, he reaches into the drawer of the old armoire. He takes his stash out of its place. He rolls the joint as he walks onto the patio, checking the wind to see what direction it is going to make sure that no one is downwind. His muscles ache, but not anymore. He thinks many thoughts —too many. He gets tired. He eats what is left of the burned out cigarette, and he lies down on his bed after raiding the icebox, dreaming marijuana dreams.

One hour later, Uncle Carlos returns from work in Cachanilla. Aunt Victoria is reconciling the books for the company, and she will not be back until after 7:30. He doesn't know that Clem just woke up at the sound of the pick up truck. Carlos goes outside to the patio near the trash can. He doesn't see Clem get up, peeking behind his bedroom curtain. Carlos takes his phone out of his pocket and dials Mexico City. He is calling an Assistant Minister of the Interior. Senõr Labastida is the cutout who will tell the Governor about what Uncle Carlos has done.

"*Buenas tardes,* Your Excellency. This is Guillermo. I have a message for our friend. He says he needs the magnetic interferometer on February 19th at 2300 hours local time at Santa Ynez."

(pause)

"I repeat. 2300 hours. February 19th. Ybarra Loncheria."

He pauses while the other man speaks. "Yes, that is correct. Is this line secure? Do you know what a magnetic interferometer is?"

(pause)

"No, I do not know what it means either. Thank you very much. *Adios.*" Carlos takes the cellular phone's battery out, and throws the phone in the trashcan.

Clem does not know what to think of this. He knows that Uncle Carlos has been in plenty of shady dealings in the past. He has never really wanted to know what kinds of side deals his uncle had to do in the course of his business. The road contractor would not be where he is today were it not for doing shady and crooked things. That's none of Clem's business. But what would Uncle Carlos have to do with a magnetic interferometer when he doesn't even know what it is? Who knows what could be accomplished if you had a magnetic gizmo? But there is no one in Baja California, even at the universities, who would know how to use it.

Discretion is the better part of valor. Perhaps he can ask Aunt Victoria some hypothetical questions. Maybe she will give him advice. Then the mystery could be solved.

Karl Eysenbach

KUALA LUMPUR, MALAYSIA
CENTRAL INTELLIGENCE AGENCY

God knows how many black units are devoted to keeping the secrets from before World War III. Take the example of atomic weapons. Research into this area was strictly forbidden, and the military spends billions of dollars monitoring knowledge traffic to insure that A-Bomb information never gets out.

This is the advertised purpose of the underground bunker we are in right now. This branch of the CIA is known as the TCOM Division, the World Government's center for monitoring all internet traffic, looking for emails from terrorists, or searching for key words or phrases that might constitute threats to world security in the vast ozone of human communication. Walls of the bunkers are covered with giant electronic maps of the worldwide web and phone traffic, and other large TV screens monitor world news and military situations.

General Caramehni is idly smoking his pipe, sitting at his gray metal desk, watching the streams of data as they crisscross the Pacific Ocean on the large display screen posted on the far wall through his office window. His aide, Sergeant Singh comes into the office and salutes smartly. "General, Sir! We have just picked up a pattern of transmissions from Mexico, Sir!"

General Caramehni knows that it must be important, as his aide does not usually act this way. "What do you have, Sergeant?"

"Sir! Satellites report transmissions from one Guillermo somewhere in Baja California. He called Assistant Minister of the Interior Labastida in Mexico City."

"Well, that sound interesting, but what does that have to do with us?"

The Story of the Century

"Sir! They mentioned a magnetic interferometer, sir! And they repeated the time February 19th, 2300 hours at the Ybarra Loncheria."

The general smiles. He puffs on his pipe once before speaking. "Well, that is our monopoly, isn't it Sergeant? I want you to start up a file on this matter. It is to be classified as Delta clearance – Foreign Technology Division. This file is to be for our eyes only, is that clear?"

"Yes, general. I will set up the computer protocols immediately." Sergeant Singh walks out the door and down to the hall to his office. He does Job #1, but there is Job #2, -- his own personal job. A long time ago, he installed some extra secret software on his computer. The most extensive hack will not reveal its existence, but when activated by his password, it will interfere with some of the Archives Division's security monitoring systems. The sergeant has a VCR that broadcasts one tape of an empty row of files, and another VCR with a tape of him Xeroxing archive files. The VCRs are connected to timers. Sergeant Singh has been using this computer program more and more lately. He looks at his watch and does some calculations. Then he types 'URANTIA' into the computer. This is the codeword that starts the timers. He shuts his secret program down, and he files its CD disk. He shuts up his office, going up the elevator, and through the security checkpoints. He goes to his jeep in the underground parking lot and he drives four kilometers to the windowless building marked Archives Division. That's where they keep some records on alien artifacts.

SEA OF CORTEZ

Pretty much most of the village is out squid fishing tonight. The Koreans are buying, and although they're paying dirt, they're the only game in town. From the land, it looks like there's a city on the ocean. From the vantage point of the fishermen, there are dozens of pangas, bobbing on the waves, with kerosene and electric lights hanging on poles sticking out over the water to attract the creatures. Often times, entire families are on the boats. Other times, there are three strong men to haul the big bluish gray tentacled monsters up on the jigs.

Jorge is a lone wolf tonight. Everyone can hear him, even though they can't see his boat. That's because he has the only panga that sounds like a B-29. The 300 horsepower inboard outboard motor gives the little craft speed, so much speed that his mungy-looking panga can give a quarter million dollar cigarette boat a run for its money. Anyone with a room temperature IQ assumes that he's carrying product. That's not true, although it certainly is on other nights. Tonight he's on a different journey.

Jorge heads north, giving the squid fleet plenty of room. He passes by the lights of Cachanilla. Periodically, he looks at the little green screen of his GPS system when he isn't admiring the stars. He's headed out to the deep ocean, where no one is and where no one can see him. About 80 kilometers north, he banks towards the east. He's headed towards a destination that only he knows. The water gets deeper and the swells increase to over a meter, but the weather is fair. His GPS system beeps, and he cuts back on the engine. He maneuvers around a little bit, and he kills the big engine, dropping the small auxiliary motor into the water to keep his boat in a steady position. The wiry man with the thin moustache reaches into his pocket and lights a cigarette. Some minutes go by, and his only job is to keep the boat aligned with the waves.

Off in the northwest, low to the horizon, a new star appears near Ursa Major. Jorge watches as it gets brighter and bigger, turning green as it begins to move across the heavens. Its speed increases, and it begins to take the shape of a large, narrow glowing egg. It rushes at him until it is almost overhead. Just as suddenly it stops, hovering for a moment. It's only about ten meters long, but it is low over the ocean. From his vantage, it fills up almost a quarter of the sky. For other people, this would induce panic, but not Jorge. He throws his cigarette in the water, as he watches his boat bob on the waves. Almost nonchalantly he thinks, "It's that time again."

The egg begins to shrink until it becomes an emerald no larger than a plum. The green light throws an intense light on the dark ocean around the panga, and further out, the blackness intesifies.

"Hello Jorge. How are you? I hope that you are well. How is your training going?"

"The men are shaping up well. We worked with heavy machine guns the other day."

"You'll have to use that later on, you know."

"Attu. You know that none of us wants to do that!" Jorge is still indignant that he has to do what he has to do, but he knows that there's no way out. Too much has already passed. Too many deals have been made, and too many people have already been involved. He and his men have been promised big money, and they have been told that they will never have to go through with such a dirty job ever again. He doesn't need to speak this, because he knows that Attu is reading his mind.

"I'm truly sorry that you have to be involved this way, Jorge, but there is no other way. If it could have been different, I would have made it happen. But some things are out of my control."

"I understand." Jorge speaks and then he pauses. He thinks about the decades that he has spent with the green light. One of his first memories as a baby in his crib was playing with Attu while no one was around. He knows Attu, and he trusts him. Attu mentored him, setting him up with RPM. RPM suggested that they start the Atzlan Liberation Front, and Attu approved. The job he will do will be under his other identity, Subcommandante Insecticida. But still, the idea of it turns his stomach. Attu hovers patiently, silently understanding.

"Your training is almost complete. Your men will have to get acquainted with the lifting devices, and there will be a simulation of everything that you will have to do. After that, you'll have some time off."

Jorge looks at Attu with a look of profound disappointment. "Sometimes, I think I'm in league with the Devil."

The glowing emerald waits a half second before speaking. "You know I'm not a devil, Jorge. This is the only way to get the magnetic interferometer. The unit we have is just about at the end of its life. If we don't get it fixed, your planet will die. I can assure you that whatever you do for us will be good for everyone. You are our only hope."

Jorge sighs. "I understand. Sometimes I just wish there weren't such a burden on my shoulders."

Victoria Reader Castellon is a very attractive but stern looking 60-year-old. She's the real force in the Castellon family. Carlos is all charm and bonhomie, but Aunt Victoria is the bookkeeper and lawyer for the firm. The family joke is that her official position in the construction firm is that of bacon saver. How many times has Carlos done something stupid or boneheaded? How many times has Aunt Victoria had to grab Carlos by the ears and lead him to the proper course of action? Don't even ask.

Just before Clem leaves to go back to New LA he catches up with Aunt Victoria where she usually is -- in the library. Clem thinks long and hard about what he has to say as he sits down beside her in a comfortable armchair.

"You know, Aunt Victoria I never interfere in your business, or Uncle Carlos' business."

Doña Victoria puts her book down, and folds her hands. She looks at Clem pensively and she waits.

The Story of the Century

"A few nights ago, I heard Uncle Carlos saying a few strange things on the telephone."

Aunt Victoria keeps her silence and stares at Clem intently.

"He was doing some kind of business deal. He didn't want anybody to know about it. He even threw away his cell phone. I guess he thought I was asleep, but I wasn't."

"He threw away his cell phone?" She leans forward, waiting for more information.

"Yes. He threw it in the trash.'Clem pauses. "Now you know, when Uncle Carlos does his deals, I don't listen, and I don't remember. But this time was different. He mentioned a magnetic interferometer. I think that's what he called it. It sounds pretty technical. I don't think he or anyone else in Mexico has any use for that kind of thing."

Aunt Victoria is silent for a moment. Then she begins to think out loud. "That doesn't make any sense. Why would he use a cell phone and then throw it away? He doesn't trust them. Why would he be talking on a cell phone? And then to be talking to someone about something he doesn't know anything about at all. This is very curious."

Clem hazards a guess. "Maybe somebody gave him the phone to use, and they told him to throw it away after one time." He pauses, thinking about what he saw and heard.

"It sounded like he was speaking to someone important."

"And what did you say he was talking about?"

"A high tech gizmo."

"But what did you call it?"

"A magnetic interferometer. It was going to be available to somebody somewhere, and he called himself Guillermo."

"Guillermo? Why would he call himself Guillermo?"

"Well, this is speculation. If you know anything about cell phones, you know that the government, various companies and individuals

37

can trace the location of a cell phone when someone is talking. Uncle Carlos did have a brief conversation. That might have allowed anyone tracing the call to narrow the calling area down to a particular cellular tower, and it's a big calling area out here in the desert. I think it would take a longer time to pinpoint Uncle Carlos' exact location than he was on the phone."

Clem continues. "So, this sounds like some kind of espionage thing. Someone gives Carlos a telephone. Tells him to call himself Guillermo, and only call when there is something important. Then they tell him to throw the telephone away so his identity can't be traced. That's expensive and sophisticated. That must have been some important phone call."

Aunt Victoria snaps her fingers. "Maria. Would you come here a minute please?' Maria enters the library. As usual her uniform is starched stiffly, and she looks impeccable.

"Maria, would you ask Jose if he found a cell phone in the trash when he emptied the trash?"

"Right away, Doña Victoria." Maria turns and exits. A few minutes later, she's back in the library. "Jose says there was a cell phone with no battery. It is in the dump now."

Aunt Victoria continues to think. She puts her hand to her chin. Looking up, she quietly dismisses the maid, and says, "Thank you Clem. I appreciate your telling me this. I hope you have a good journey back to America and that you continue to be a success on your job." She reaches out to hold Clem's hands between hers.

"You know I hate to see you go. We see you so seldom. You know, we love you, and we only want the best for you."

"I love you too, Auntie. I know you do."

"Thanks for spilling the beans to me about your uncle. When Carlos does something like this, it's always important to have a plan. I'm thinking that I'm going to try something new."

The Story of the Century

They say goodbye and give each other a heartfelt *embrazo*, and Clem heads out to his car. Everything is ready to go. Aunt Victoria has already made certain that there's a supply of cookies, oranges, tamales, water and coffee for the trip. It's a long way to New LA, and Clem will have to pull an all-nighter to get to El Puerto. At around 2 AM, he passes through the Ejido San Ynez, and his mind is wandering. A semi passes, and Clem concentrates more on the road. He worries about Uncle Carlos. What was he getting into? Why would he talk about a magnetic interferometer, whatever that was? Why would he call himself Guillermo? And who or what had told him to do all those crazy things? There are way too many questions going on here. As much as he hates to admit it, there are lots of warning lights flashing about this phone call. His reporter's instincts are going off, and he resolves to do some serious digging when he gets back to Nueva LA.

Victoria Reader Castellon is in the rose garden, inspecting the grounds with her husband. There are examining the yellow roses for aphids and caterpillars, and there's nothing wrong with them. Flowers are everywhere, and the leaves are healthy. But the David Austen rose is more temperamental. In patches there are aphids, and there's black spot too. Aunt and Uncle Carlos have been talking about the roses for about five minutes now, but Aunt Victoria is in the process of setting the trap -- now.

"Carlos, by the way, what is a magnetic interferometer?"

Carlos stops in his tracks and looks up from the ground. *"Mande?!"* This is Baja Spanish for, "Say What?!"

"I said, what is a magnetic interferometer? I've heard that you're planning a project with this machine, and I need to find out how much it will cost, so we can revise the budget." She tilts her head a little, curiously.

Carlos would really like to get his eyes to the size of pie plates, but he resists the temptation. Instead, he narrows them a little until they become slits. "Where does this witch get her information from? She has better spies than the the CIA!" Instead, he calmly says in his most innocent voice:

"What are you talking about, Cara Mia?"

"A magnetic interferometer."

"A magnetic what?"

"A magnetic interferometer."

"Yes, that's what I thought I heard you say. Where did you get such foolishness?"

"Rumor has it that you're very interested in the magnetic thing. If you're doing a project with it, I need to know how much it will cost."

Carlos smiles smugly, and he blinks. "Frankly, I've never heard of such a thing in my entire life." He pauses for a moment and points down.

"Now look at the poor little Green rose. Nobody ever pays too much attention to it. It looks like it needs water." He bends down to gently touch its petals.

Doña Victoria has seen this trick for over thirty years. "Why did you throw away your cell phone?"

Carlos feels another arrow enter his chest. "The keys were not working right lately. I've already got a newer model ordered. "His jaws clench, and he shuffles his feet a little. He knows that she is turning into a courtroom attorney.

"But why didn't you use the cell phone that you left in the desk? It's perfectly good." She pauses. "While we're asking questions, why were you riding around in the arroyo the other day with Ernesto? Is that why you had to leave in the middle of the party?"

The Story of the Century

This is too much for Carlos to control. He rolls his eyes "I wanted to go out for a little ride. I was very frustrated about the truck breaking down."

"What were you doing out there?"

"I went out to check the fence. I thought that part of it might have been broken down."

"In the middle of the *quinceañera*, with hundreds of people at your house, you go out to see the fence?"

"I told you. I wanted to go out for a little ride. I was frustrated."

"So you're in the habit of riding in the dark with Ernesto? How long has this little affair been going on?"

"*Cara Mia!* It was nothing! I wanted to get out under the stars, away from it all!" His eyes are bulging now.

"So you headed out into *bandito* country! That's pretty stupid! Were you meeting any *banditos?*"

Carlos shrugs his shoulders. He grins slyly. "You know, we all do stupid things some time. No harm came of it."

"So, why were you talking about magnetic interferometers?"

This is the straw that breaks the camel's back. "Look, you stupid woman! I'm the man of the house. I can do whatever I want to! Do you understand?"

"Yes, Carlos. I understand." Doña Victoria only pretends to back off. Like a skillful angler, she lets a little tension out to play the line, just long enough to tire the fish some more. She speaks softly.

"You know, Carlos. If you're doing something illegal, you should tell me."

Carlos stamps his foot. "*Basta* woman! I will hear no more of this shit! How dare you accuse me of illegality!! The next thing you know, you're going to start accusing me of dealing with the Atzlan Liberation Front!" The moment he says this, he knows that he has gone too far.

Doña Victoria looks at him calmly under the moonlight in the garden. She looks at him, and lifts an elegant eyebrow. "So, is that who you were talking to near the arroyo? Well?"

Screaming inside himself, but trying to keep a normal tone of voice, Carlos replies. "I'm the man of this house! I want no more discussion on this issue!"

"Fine. There will be no more discussion." With that, Doña Victoria Reader Castellon turns on her heels and walks into the house, to the room she sleeps in when she is mad at Carlos. Carlos feels his blood pressure going up and up. He paces back and forth in the garden for what seems to be forever. He opens the main gate, and spends more time tearing at the ALF poster remnants still stuck there. Then he spends the longest time throwing stones into the desert.

Carlos wakes up the next morning at seven o'clock. He has business to attend to at the office. He gets out of bed, takes a shower, shaves, and gets into his bathrobe. Usually by the time he's made this much noise, a servant will have placed his business suit and a clean shirt and tie out on the dressing stand for him. Today, there's only the collection of clothes that he left on the floor from the night before.

"Maria! Come here! I need my clothes." Carlos yells. There is no response, only silence. The lord of the house opens his bedroom door to the hallway, and shouts one more time, "Mah Reee Ahh!" There's a faint little singsong echo in the stone hallway, but nothing more. "Where is that woman?!" Carlos half-thinks, half mumbles to himself, "This is not like her."

The thought occurs to him that she must be occupied in something important. "Oh well," he says to no one in particular. He returns to his room, closing the carved oak door behind him. Fumbling around, he

The Story of the Century

slowly gets dressed in his rumpled shirt and slacks, being careful to add extra deodorant and cologne.

Señor Castellon walks down the grand staircase, through the living room, to the breakfast area. Ordinarily, the kitchen computer monitor is on, showing its links to the Mexico City newspapers and construction journals. Today there is only a blank screen.

"*Chinga su madre!*" is one thought that crosses his mind as he boots up the computer, tediously waiting to activate the links one by one. "What is wrong with the people I pay to run this place?" This is a shout that Carlos is not happy about the monkey business going on around here. For good measure, he yells, "I am not happy with the monkey business going on around here!"

Usually, the kitchen staff has been up for an hour preparing Don Carlos' ritual breakfast. For the last fifteen years, he's had the same breakfast, a strong cup of black instant coffee, a large glass of freshly squeezed orange juice, and a delicious plate of *huevos rancheros*. There are two eggs, slightly runny set beside some *machaca* and refried beans. The whole plate is lightly drizzled with mild green sauce and white cheese. Ah, delicious! A feast fit for the gods.

Today the breakfast area and the kitchen area behind it are spotless. In fact, it's even more clean and sanitary than usual. All the pots and pans are sparkling and in their place. The floor has been mopped to the point where not even a mote of dust can hide. He does not observe any of the household ghosts, although they are watching him with some amusement. The kitchen staff has spent extra time and attention in securing the place so that they could go somewhere else.

After Carlos has fiddled around with the computer, he notices how clean the kitchen is. The kitchen is far too clean to accommodate the fixings of his meal. He goes to the large stainless steel refrigerator, and he opens the door. Like everything else, its insides have been scrupulously cleaned, and old food has been thrown out. Unfortunately, the staff failed to stock up on new supplies. Carlos sees a head of lettuce, half a pitcher of iced tea, and a can of chocolate sauce.

The big construction boss stands in the kitchen tapping his forefinger to his forehead, and thinking about what he should do next. He thinks back to his last visit to the doctor's office. Dr. Velasquez lectured him both about his weight and his cholesterol count. "Perhaps," he thinks to himself. "Perhaps I should change my life a little bit. If I go on a diet, I can drop a few kilos and look more sexy." That is a good thought, as a small flash of self-awareness passes over his face. He feels in his pockets to make sure he has his car keys and wallet. He doesn't. So he returns to his bedroom and hunts around until he finds them. He walks downstairs again, goes outside, and climbs into his pickup truck. Ernesto has seen to it that it's been fixed.

Things were as he's left them at the office. Piles of paper are lying around everywhere on his desk from the Hermosillo repaving project. The engineering specification book is still opened to the middle where Carlos made notations yesterday. He's usually the first person into work, but today, he wishes that Victoria were here to help him with some of the fine points of legalese he has to contend with.

At 9:30, Conchita comes in. Cara Mia (as he calls her) walks in through the front door five minutes later, passing by Carlos' office as if he were invisible. We will not repeat what Carlos thinks to himself at this point. Conchita is one of Carlos' favorite things. She's in her late twenties, and she has the most amazing bullet shaped breasts. And those hips, Mama Mia, Cara Mia! Conchita, like many Latin women, is not averse to displaying her assets. Her office attire is a cross between dress for success and come fuck me. As Senór Castellon's personal secretary, she is probably the most important person next to Señora Victoria. Today is going to be a busy day, as the deadline for bid submission is at midnight.

The Story of the Century

Conchita comes into Castellon's office with his morning cup of coffee, and Carlos accepts it gratefully, giving her a little squeeze on her butt in the process of complementing her. At least someone is paying attention. Doña Victoria is incommunicado, so it's all right for Conchita to give Carlos a little French kiss. He thinks to himself," One of the nice things about her is that besides fooling around, she also does productive work around the office." Carlos assumes that, besides the perks, that she will help him put the company's bid proposal into the hands of Planet Express by the end of the afternoon.

"If we work together now, I can get my afternoon pick me up." This thought distracts him from his bid specifications. What Carlos is really looking forward to is that 3:00 hour. That is when Conchita comes into the office with another cup of coffee that she places on his desk. She makes sure that the door is securely closed. Then she will climb under the desk, unzip his fly, and suck his dick.

Unfortunately today, Mrs. Castellon has had a few discreet words with Conchita before work by phone. In a totally non-threatening manner, Doña Victoria coos in Conchita's ear sweetly with just a touch of frostiness, "I know how hard you work, and how important you are to Carlos. Señor Castellon and I think you need to take some time off, -- especially before three o'clock."

As the day passes, Carlos notices that Conchita seems somehow distracted. She is not quite up to snuff today, but he's patient. At 2:58 Conchita comes into Carlos' office with a cup of coffee, but she does not close the door. She's holding the back of her hand to her forehead, and she has a kind of hangdog expression on her face. She asks Señor Castellon if it is all right if she can go home early today. She is having a horrible migraine headache. She flutters her eyelids ever so slightly. The mighty Carlos is as macho as a warm puppy. "Of course, my dear. Don't even think about it. Go right now."

45

Conchita thanks him profusely, gives him a big hug, and exits. After she leaves, Carlos realizes that he's now solely responsible for bringing the bid proposal to completion. This means cutting and pasting, dictating to the computer, proofreading, revising, rechecking the numbers, printing the first draft, rereading the whole document to make any last minute changes, printing out 75 pages in triplicate, collating, binding, faxing the original to Mexico City, and making sure that Planet Express picks it up on Blue Ribbon Extrafast service.

Carlos does the only sensible thing a man can do in this situation. As he sees Conchita drive away through the window, he roars like a wounded bull and pounds both of his fists as hard as he can on his desk. After four very satisfying poundings, a couple of things happen. First, he feels a twinge in his heart, and he breaks out in a cold sweat. Second, Doña Victoria comes into his office for the first time today and asks quietly, "Is everything all right, Dear?"

Carlos tries to regain his composure. "I'm afraid we're both going to have to work a little late tonight." He feels a drop of sweat trickling down his forehead.

"I have a hair dresser's appointment at 3:30. I should get going."

"I would be really grateful for any assistance you could give me." He speaks calmly, but he is pleading with a crazed look in his eyes.

Doña Victoria stands in the office doorway with her arms crossed. She looks at him calmly and patiently, pausing for what seems like a minute. Then she speaks.

"I will help you. But first, do you want to tell the truth?"

SANTA YNEZ, YBARRA LONCHERIA
FEBRUARY 19TH, 11:00 PM

The Ybarra Loncheria is one of those places you can only find in Mexico. Both the truckers and the military know that it's the only place to eat between Sanispac and El Chicon. It isn't much to look at; just an open faced little concrete block building with sliding glass doors and big windows facing the roadside. It has a thatched roof and a detached bathroom ten meters away from the kitchen area. The Ybarra family has been operating the place for forty years as a 24-hour tortillaria.

This is not as big a hardship on the Ybarras as you might think. The restaurant looks out on the two-lane blacktop where a truck or car might drive by once every fifteen minutes if it's busy. If it's not busy, you can wait for hours or even days before you see a vehicle coming down the road.

Tonight is not busy. The wind is cold and clouds cover the sky. The Ybarra family is huddled in their beds, sleeping with all of their clothes on. Not that they've been sleeping very well. The dogs have been barking all night, and they won't shut up. Papa Ybarra keeps getting up to make sure the cow is all right. He doesn't want to have to mess with the coyotes out in the dark that are obviously up to no good.

He crawled back to bed and was nearly asleep when he hears the two trucks pull up on the gravel driveway. The family can see the lights of the headlights streaming through the curtains, and they hear the honking of the horn on the jeep. This is the sign that the regular customers are here and hungry. Mom, Pop, and the three children pile out of the single bedroom. They light the kerosene lamps and fire up the griddle.

"*Buenas noches,*" says Lieutenant Alvarez. "My men have been driving for five hours, and we would like something to eat. Is this possible?"

Karl Eysenbach

"*No problemo*. Welcome. Please, have your men sit down. Here is the menu. It will be a few minutes before the water is hot enough for coffee."

The small detachment of Marines is grateful to be out of the big rig and the jeep. They sit down at the plastic tables, and they rub their hands to get warm. Nobody wants to sit out on the patio tonight. It's just too nasty outside. Because there is no moon out, it's the kind of night that makes people glad to be near anything that resembles civilization. The desert is big, but it gets infinitely bigger on a night like this. And you can feel yourself getting smaller -- too small for the desert on a night like this.

The Ybarra children are busy in the restaurant. Obviously, the Marines want to talk to the girls. It makes no difference that they're only 10 and 12 years old. Girls are still girls. The six privates are all talking at once, both with each other, and with Alejandra and Sandra. Alejandra and Sandra are talking to the soldiers, but they're also putting tinder and wood in the pot-bellied stove, handing out menus, and making sure that the kerosene lamps on the tables are okay. Manuel, the only Ybarra son is starting the electric generator and turning on the boom box. The ranchera music is a little loud, but it has to compete with the wind rattling the little timbers that support the roof. Mom and Pop are back in the kitchen getting ready to take the orders.

The children stand by while the people at the tables scan the menus and order. Table one has six coffees and five waters to start. They order one hot cake, one scrambled egg, two hamburgers, and two orders of beef tacos in multiples of three and four. Table two has coffees and waters, and they order pisole and menudo. The sergeant and the lieutenant order the most expensive things on the menu.

One thing the Ybarra Loncheria is famous for is not its fast service. When a group like this comes in, you can be sure that everybody's going to stick around for at least an hour and a half. It's probably going to be two hours before anybody even thinks about getting down the road. This gives the Marines more than enough time to inspect the outhouses, the cow, and the interior of the restaurant as well as the trucks.

Despite the cold wind and the blowing dust, the loncheria is a clean and cozy place. Still, the glass doors rattle in the gusty wind. Getting up from the table, the men huddle by the stove looking at the Tecate posters, or they examine the display cases. The counter area with the cash register sells a variety of things including chewing gum, candy bars, sexy comic strip novellas, and CDs of ranchera and banda music.

But the thing that makes the loncheria special is not just the good food, which is in fact superb. It's the pictures and memorabilia. The Ybarra are the descendants of the famous General Cesar Ybarra. General Ybarra distinguished himself as one of the leading explorers who worked with Akili Alvarado in the Great Explorations of North America after World War III. The whole *loncheria* is filled with historic photographs and souvenirs.

Here's a picture of General Ybarra standing with his men in the atomic wastelands of old Los Angeles. Everybody looks slightly silly in their facemasks and yellow bunny suits that protected them from the radiation. But you can tell that the men had been forced more than once to use their weapons. Then there are the pictures and framed newspaper articles of General Ybarra receiving his medals personally from the President of Mexico; President Nunez-Brooks, the last President of Mexico before the President became Governor, and Mexico became the 54th state in the new World Government.

For an hour and a half, there's more than enough time for the troops to inspect the pictures and the ceremonial sword in the glass case. Everyone has finished eating dinner, and the Ybarra girls have just gone to the kitchen to start washing the dishes. At zero hours, seventeen minutes, and thirty-three seconds on February 20th, the Ybarra Loncheria becomes world news. Lt. Alvarez is going to speak to his sergeant, and the conversation would have gone like this if they had had time to speak before it happened.

"You know, Sergeant, this whole operation has been screwy. The brass does some weird thing sometimes. I mean, do you believe the instructions on this detail?"

The old sergeant looks at him. "Oh, lieutenant, I've seen worse."

"But the routing on this thingamabob is really strange, don't you think? The orders come from Singapore; go through someplace I've never heard of in the Ministry of Defense, and then it's diverted somehow through the Office of the Secretary of the Interior in Mexico City, before it goes back to our Marine base. And all the time it's in segregation before we get our hands on it. Why did they do it that way?"

"The routing is all scuttlebutt and politics. That's what it is sometimes when you have a hot cargo. Maybe not. You never know, and don't ask. We're all here just to follow orders."

"Well then, tell me why there wasn't more security on this detail if it's such a hot cargo? If the thing is that valuable, why wasn't there a convoy and more coverage?"

"Begging the lieutenant's permission, sir, that's pretty obvious." The sergeant lights a cigarette. "This is a low profile operation. Nobody pays any attention to us, and we all go back to base tomorrow. Nobody raises any eyebrows, if you know what I mean."

"What about the travel itinerary? Do they usually specify, 'Drive five hours. Stop for dinner at Santa Ynez at 2300, and proceed to Ensenada, refueling at San Quintin?"

"You know the brass as well as I do, lieutenant. It sounds like some control freak to me. Me? I don't care. I just work here. Me and the three hash marks on my sleeve."

The Story of the Century

This conversation never took place. Something happens that will make the Ybarras talk about it for generations. Next week is the week of the sirens and the helicopters. It will be the week that the white vans with satellite dishes come. News reporters from Africa will ask them questions through interpreters speaking broken Spanish. The Governor of Mexico will arrive in a black limousine and give them a check for more money than they've ever seen in their life. A convoy of trucks from the Marines will unload enough food to feed everyone in the desert for a week. Anonymous men in dark glasses and tan chinos will fiddle with strange boxes attached to the underbellies of helicopters. Jet planes will fly overhead that they have never seen before. They'll cry, burying their dead.

At 00:01:33 February 20th, all hell explodes. The south windows shatter into a million pieces, and splinters of wood and glass lodge themselves into tables and bodies. Everyone in the restaurant dives for cover, and there are screams of fear and mortal pain. The flash of a machine gun from the hill across the road is raking through the restaurant. The lieutenant is killed instantly, while the sergeant falls into a creeping pool of his own blood. He will die within the hour.

Some of the enlisted men at the big table are temporarily lucky. They race out the side door towards the outhouses and the trucks down on the gravel driveway. The first thing they see is the Holstein cow, black and white. But the cow's eyes are wide and unseeing. Pieces of fresh hamburger are flying out of it towards them, hitting them in the face and stomach. Out of the six Marines at table one, two lie dead inside the restaurant; three are wounded, and one is still unharmed, but not for long. Crossfire from an automatic rifle to the east kills or mortally wounds everyone in its path, including the Ybarra boy, who made the mistake of looking out the window. Not a single Marine was armed. They all left their weapons in the trucks.

Two men dressed in black camo gear come from out of the east. One has a Colt .45 automatic pistol, the other an M-16. They systematically shoot each Marine in the head one time. Then they search through the oozing bodies, retrieving wallets and car keys. They nervously get in the trucks, back down the driveway, and roll 20 meters in the direction of San Quintin before they stop. Two more shadowy figures walk down the hill, lugging a tripod mounted machine gun.

Gunfire erupts from the jeep and big rig, but it's not gunfire with conviction. The Ybarra family is screaming and crying, and the banditos know that the Marines are dead. Tires squeal, and the trucks disappear into the night.

60 KM SOUTH OF CATAVINA
2:00 AM, FEBRUARY 20TH

Subcommandante Insecticida is different from the others. He hears the voices talking to him, and he sees things sometimes that the other men never see. Even if the green light is near him, others might see nothing and think he's crazy. But Insecticida is a leader and a genius. In this respect, he's like an ancient Aztec priest, a man who can communicate with the gods.

There are only ten men in the Baja who are active members of the Atzlan Liberation Front. While they handle large quantities of valuables, most of the money goes elsewhere to people and places that they never even know about. They support and are supported by their families. They're truckers and fishermen, making a few dollars here and a few dollars there when they can. But in a land where work is only a sometimes proposition, it's easy to say that you're going to be gone for a few days or a week and say nothing more. And nobody wants to ask too many questions.

The Story of the Century

When called upon, the band of guerillas meet at one spot or the other in the mountains, sometimes following the old abandoned missionary trails. At other times along the highway, trucks park in the middle of the desert, idling their engines waiting to deliver the illegal cargo that passes through the military checkpoints. With a different message, they're on the ocean with their hotrods of boats eluding honest Navy patrols and hooking up with the corrupt ones to deliver the cargo.

But tonight is different. This is a first and last time. The four men in the trucks have been training for this operation for months, and until now things were smooth. It's fun playing war games, but when you see real human blood, it's a different thing

Puto is driving, and he stuck his head out the window five minutes ago to throw up. Vladimir and Fidel are covering their faces, bending over, crying as quietly as they can. No one has ever killed a human being in cold blood before. Insecticida is totally silent and stoic. He's got a lot on his mind right now. The trucks roll down the highway quietly and at the speed limit. Only the wind and the sound of the tires on the road can be heard. The headlights throw their puny little rays out into the big darkness.

Insecticida has begged, pleaded, and cajoled, using every ounce of his persuasive powers to convince the men of the necessity of the mission. Half of the ALF had simply refused to have anything to do with it, with too many meetings and too many arguments. It was finally decided that $100,000 would be given to each person in the Baja cell, and that the actual evildoers would receive something above and beyond as a reward. Only now they've found out that money doesn't mean much in these circumstances, and everyone in the truck knows that if caught, they will either immediately die in a hail of bullets, or failing that, they'll be sent to prison and denied water, dying the slow death of thirst.

The two trucks continue to roll silently through the desert. The landscape begins to be less hilly, flattening out, and the curves in the road get less dangerous. After traveling for about sixty kilometers, the trucks come to the paved road going left; and the little convoy turns at the sign marked '*Bahia Gonzaga.*' A series of paved roads were laid out, stretching from the main highway to the Pacific Ocean and the Sea of Cortez. Supposedly the yacht owners would sail to the marinas to pull their boats out of the water to be transported to the other side. There were only two problems. One was that the marinas were never built. The other was that the big boats never came. In the end, the only person who ever made money from the project was Carlos Castellon. Two Marine trucks go down this two-lane blacktop towards the ocean and the middle of nowhere.

Insecticida gets out his GPS system, monitoring the changes in elevation, longitude, and latitude as the trucks slows down to 30 KPH. The jeep and the big rig slows even more as they get closer to the nowhere destination. Finally, Insecticida stops the jeep, and the big rig halts behind it. Both trucks turn off the road, starting to travel at walking speeds true north into the barren salt flats. All the while Insecticide focuses intently on the little screen, marking out meters and microlatitudes. When Insecticida yells out, the convoy halts. The landscape is no different from any other place, totally undistinguished and black as pitch. They're 200 meters off the blacktop, and 7.382 kilometers from the Pacific Ocean.

The men get out and open the back of the lorry. Inside are hydraulic lifting equipment and the machine gun with its ammo. But there's something else too, -- a large wooden box with metal strapping. The whole thing weighs a ton if it weighs an ounce. It's way *pesada, hombre!* The men begin attacking the project with adrenaline. The object is to put the crate on the sand, lying just so. Lifting heavy objects is

The Story of the Century

something they know about. After all, the late Sergeant Homero taught them everything. More importantly, the physical exertion is a release from the nightmares that they've just created for themselves.

For an hour, they grunt and sweat like pigs. They have to slide the box to the back of the truck, and then there is the slow ballet of lowering the crate to the ground. Even with the hydraulic lifters, it's hot and dangerous work, and the men divert themselves from their waking nightmares for just a moment as they stand around and wipe their brows. The work is done. The men put the lifters back in the lorry. They get back in and start the trucks, heading onto the asphalt road towards the ocean. Both the jeep and the big rig travel to the ocean at almost top speed. Time is running out. They have to be far, far away before dawn.

Just before the surf, the convoy stops, and the men get out. On either side of the asphalt there's a rocky beach. Insecticida gets out of the command car, and he picks up a small boulder. The door of the jeep is open, and the engine is running. He puts the rock on top of the accelerator, and the jeep's tires scream, leaving a smoking path as the jeep lurches towards the water. When it hits the waves, it actually skips like a stone a little bit before it gracefully sinks under the swells.

The driver in the other truck moves the lorry closer to the waves before he stops. Puto curses and prays as he jumps off the running board of the big rig, and he tries to do the rock trick as well as Insecticida did. Not only does he have to jump farther than Insecticida, but he nearly sprains his ankle by landing on the rocks. The big rig begins to lurch forward too, with not as much velocity but much more mass. When it hits the surf it collides with a huge splash before it slowly tilts over like a dying elephant. Its wheels spin furiously in the surf before the engine short-circuits with one big blue spark.

Karl Eysenbach

The moon is rising in the sky now, and the clouds have begun to break. It's going to be a good day tomorrow. The lunar crescent lights their paths as they pick their way down the beach. Eventually, after a long walk it becomes more sandy and sheltered. This is where their boats have been stashed since the day before. There's no one around for kilometers, and the boats are loaded with nets and fishing gear, untouched by human hands. The men struggle as they walk down the beach, carrying duffel bags as they sidestep and climb over the rocks. At the pangas the men strip down to their underwear as they get out of their black balaclavas and assassin's gear and into their fishermen's yellow slickers. When that's done, they start pushing the boats into the water and start up their motors, the engines making a loud and whining sounds in the silence of the desert.

The boats pull out into deep water, and they head for a time due south towards Punta Catharina. There are no more than five meters between the boats, but they're not going fast. Off in the distance, they can see a pod of dolphins pacing them. Insecticida yells out over the waves, "It's getting to be time;" and on cue the two pangas cut their engines and begin the process of letting their nets out.

Off at the edge of the horizon, they see a light suddenly pop up. No matter how many times they've seen it before, it never fails to fill them with a mixture of awe and dread. The light, at first small and almost starlike, soon morphs into a glowing green ovoid shape as it whizzes silently over them at incredible speed. Just as suddenly as it accelerates, it stops, hanging over the desert. They stare at it, and they see something they've never seen before. A brilliant blue beam appears between the green egg and the ground. Even bobbing in the waves, with unsteady hands on binoculars, the men can see a tiny speck rise from the salt flats into the belly of the craft. The thick, almost translucent light goes out, and the glowing emerald egg streaks back to where it came from, hanging over the horizon as a star before it winks out.

Insecticida and his men are lucky. The robots on the ground and in the spy satellites have not yet been alerted to the fact that a group of Marines has been massacred in the desert. The cameras were not been programmed to follow the convoy. But the cameras have always been programmed to target green ovoid shapes. Langley, New Columbia, and Singapore receive real time images in 3-D detail of the comings and goings of the saucer. The spy camera also captures the gomer fishermen bobbing in the water staring at the thing as it lifts the magnetic interferometer.

DAWN

Subcommandante Insecticida and his men have been moving their pangas a full throttle for hours towards the empty beaches south of Punta Borego. Both the wind and the sea are fair, and they slice through the waves as the two boats move towards the long finger of desert land extending out into the sea. At first nothing but a barely visible line at the horizon, it grows slowly until the rocky outcropping can be seen with the sandy beach off to the south. Giving the resort hotel a respectful distance, the guerillas move past the white stucco buildings with their terra cotta roof tiles.

They go on until they see the fish camp, a collection of shacks made out of nothing more than driftwood and cardboard and rusted metal sheeting. The men beach their boats in the gentle surf and wade ashore, pulling the boats behind them. When the boats are secured, they start unloading gear with hardly any conversation. At last, they flop down in the little shacks with no floors with all the fatigue in the world, trying to shut out the atrocities they performed the night before. Two of the men don't even bother taking their clothing off. They just make a pillow out of their gear and immediately fall asleep. Puto strips down to his underwear, gets a sleeping bag out and climbs in before he passes out.

Insecticida is exhausted too, but he's got work to do. As traumatized and tired as he is, he has a very important appointment to keep. He reaches into his duffel bag for a small brown glass vial and a metal tube. Retrieving an old beer can on the beach, he taps some of the white powder onto its bottom. He performs the ceremony and snorts the meth into each nostril. He feels the rush, and starts the engine.

He retraces his journey past the resort and San Bernardo until he goes back to his home anchorage at San Mateo. As soon as he gets into the bay, he gets a ride into the village to stock up on supplies. It's going to be another long journey north. One of his cousins helps him as they put food, fuel, water, and camping supplies into the old pickup truck. Then his boat is restocked, and within an hour he is headed out of the bay towards Cabo Insurrgente.

The boat's motor drones on, and Insecticida keeps himself amused by listening to music on his headphones. He drinks his water, eats his food, and sips on cups of strong coffee from his metal thermos. All the while he concentrates on reading the ocean and sky. Even as he's doing this, he keeps doing instant replay on his butchering. He's diverted from his thoughts by a pod of dolphins that appear, racing with the boat off of the starboard bow. They play their game of 'shadow the *panga*' before they lose their attention, turning away and moving out into deeper water. The wind picks up a little bit, and Jorge has to pay careful attention to the passage of the boat as it jumps through the waves.

At last, he reaches the little cove with the agate beach. Cutting the motor, he drops anchor before wading towards the shore. The area where Insecticida has landed is truly one of the most remote and isolated in all of Baja. Between Cabo Insurrgente and Bahia San Antonio there's nothing -- not a house or even a cow, nothing for at least a hundred kilometers. Because of this, the ocean is pristine. Insecticida spots a small school of tetras swimming, their brilliant yellow bodies flashing like neon gold in the water.

Insecticida walks up the beach towards a narrow arroyo. The sun is getting high in the sky, and Insecticida feels the sweat sticking to his shirt. He's not just sweating from the heat. He thinks about the bullets he fired last night again, the faces of the dying Marines in agony, the way he had to pull the trigger at the men's heads in order to dispatch them. He tries to get these thoughts out of his mind, concentrating on what's ahead.

As he walks through the arroyo, the walls began to close in, sheltering him from the sun. He picks his way between the narrow cliff walls, dodging spiky mesquite bushes and stepping over the fossils of giant chambered nautiluses. The fossils are museum pieces, but here they're just nuisances to stumble over. Once upon a time, a fast stream of pure, fresh water surged through here full of trout and salmon. The air was filled with the aroma of Douglas fir and cedar. Now the arroyo has the faintest aroma of desert flowers. He begins to feel less like Subcommandante Insecticida the mythical revolutionary terrorist, and more like Jorge.

About a kilometer inland, he's gained about a hundred meters of altitude, and the cliffs get closer and closer, and the ocean disappears from view. At some points he has to squeeze sideways to make progress through the cliffs. Then the dry stream bed broadens out, and the cliffs get lower. At last Jorge stands in front of a large shaded area in the side of the cliff. It was here that a Neolithic family dug out the hollow to make their home along side the fast running brook. They had made the floor flat, and individual sleeping quarters had been dug out in the walls. It must have taken thousands of hours to do, and it was all excavated by hand with shells and rocks.

The thing about this place is that it almost looks as if the cavemen had abandoned it yesterday. The only clue that this isn't the case is the dust that covers everything. Ashes are still in the blackened fire pit. The three bed spaces in the wall still have a generous layer of dried grasses lying on top of twigs, and there is a pedestal standing in the middle of the living space. When the cavemen were digging here, they carved everything out of the *caliche* slowly and patiently with hands and stone tools and reed baskets. Here they skinned and dressed rabbits, snakes, and other animals. The pedestal still holds the polished stone dressing tools where the family left them.

The pedestal is different from the rest of the area. It's the only spot not covered by dust. Jorge picks up the tools, and he sits down on the pedestal. He plays with the polished stones for a while, but he doesn't have to wait long. By now, the entire arroyo is in shade. It's late in the afternoon. Everything is quiet. Not even the birds sing. Coming down the arroyo from further up, there's a presence, moving towards him. He tenses a little, waiting. There is no sound of movement at all, just some quiet white noise from the wind. The walls of the cliff begin to turn an emerald green. Then the diamond-shaped object floats into the family cave, hanging there about a meter away from Jorge and three meters above the dry creek bed.

"Hello there, Jorge."

"Why did you tell me to kill the Marines? It was the worst thing I have ever done! I will never be able to forgive myself! And my men will never forgive themselves! Did you know we murdered an innocent child?!"

"I understand your feelings. If I could have made it any other way, I would have done things differently. There is a committee in Singapore that makes all the decisions. They say how things will be delivered

The Story of the Century

to me. To them, the World Government is like a giant windup toy. The admiral that could have done things differently had the flu that day, and it went to General Caramehni instead. Once he got hold of it, there was nothing anyone could do. It was his recommendation to sacrifice the Marines."

"Why couldn't the Marines have left it for you?

"The general is stupid, but there are other reasons. They have to do with Mexican politics and the world government…" There is a pause, "Many things. If you want to know more, I can tell you."

"No thanks. I'm sick of politics, and my men are sick of politics. This Atzlan Liberation Front stuff is getting old. And besides, there is the money."

"Yes, I know. Arrangements have already been made. Money from an armored car will be made available to you at Rancho Ayala. The time and coordinates have already been placed in your GPS system. You need to send a message to New Los Angeles. The internet address and message are on a piece of paper underneath your life preserver in the boat. I've put enough money there too for the men who were with you. This will allow your people to survive for a while."

"I'm afraid."

"You should be. This whole incident has been very unfortunate. The world press has descended on the **loncheria.** Because of this, you and your men are in great danger. The safest thing to do is to take a bus to New Los Angeles with some of the money."

"What will I do there? How will I contact you?"

"Don't worry. I will make arrangements. I'll stay in touch with you."

"What about my men and their families?"

"Everyone will have enough money for the time being. The families should continue doing what they have always done. They should not change their routines at all now. Just have them continue to go on with their business as usual in the village. Spies are everywhere. But the men should think about moving to cities, Mexico City, Ensenada, New Los Angeles, the Texas District. There is safe work there, and opportunity. The government will not be able to find anyone there."

"I am very tired and very hungry."

"Go back to the boat. Your sleeping bag is on the beach ready. A fire is going, and there is hot food waiting for you."

"One last thing. Do you know what is going to happen now?"

"I cannot say. I think it is possible that many more people will die. I hope that this will not be the case. This general made a big mistake."

TWELVE HOURS LATER

Jorge is sleeping on the beach, When he left the green light, he found a fire going, a pot of *pozole*, and his sleeping bag open and warm. Mom couldn't have done better. He's slept the sleep of the dead, except he has this damned tape loop of a dream where he's looking at his hands, and they're covered with blood.

He is lying in a sheltered cove in a sandy spot, and the sun is shining in his face. Rise and shine! Greet the new day with a smile. He remembers how he used to jump on his brothers' beds, singing at the top of his lungs in the world's worst singing voice, "WAKE UUUUUUP----WAKE UUUUUUUUUUUP----IIT'S TIIIIIIIME TO GET UUUUUUP."

He thinks about how strange it is -- that he can organize cold-blooded mayhem for some purpose that he's only the most dimly aware of -- a hit ordered by a green light from outer space. And here he is, in the middle of the wilderness, by himself -- camping in comparative luxury as if nothing out of the ordinary had ever happened.

The Story of the Century

Part of the problem of living a secret life and compartmentalizing is that your alter egos have a tendency to go running off on their own. For example, is it Jorge or Subcommandante Insecticida? Subcommandante Insecticida or Jorge? Jorge is getting extremely tired of the Insecticida dude. Once upon a time Insecticida and the Atzlan Liberation Front were exciting. The intrigue, the secret messages and dead drops, the training for the mission, but gradually the politics of holding it together got to be a bummer. Then he killed those people. Now the village and the world have nothing else to talk about except that asshole and that hellish organization. And don't talk to me about internal politics! Surely whoever did the massacre must be cokeheads, world terrorists, criminals against humanity, illegal drug runners, and schizophrenics with paranoid tendencies for some of their better qualities. And they don't even know that he's a deadbeat dad too!

For a moment, Jorge is a baby in his crib. He is two years old, and he keeps trying to touch the little green light as it bounces around in front of him playfully. He remembers Attu talking to him the first time.

"Your name is Jorge, isn't it? My name is Attu, and I want to be your friend. But I'm your secret friend, so don't tell anyone." And that's the way it's always been. As a boy, Jorge got away from his family by roaming in the desert. Sometimes he'd meet Attu in an arroyo, and Attu would tell him lots of stories. Jorge found out about the 23 kinds of life forms that Attu has encountered in his lifetime, -- Grays, Vikings, shapeshifters, *chupacabras*, Michelin men, red plastic giant devils, little green gnomes, and winged cats for just a start.

Now things have changed, and there is this horrible uncertainty. Why, if Attu and the other lights were so all seeing and all-powerful, why did they set up a bloody scheme that had made seven people die? Why did the lights go along with a mistake that some fucking general had made? Was this evidence of a lack of power on their part? Or was it part of some deeper, more sinister plan? Was it fate or free will that made the lights commission a massacre? And what's going to happen to himself?

How much more can I take?

He thinks about the Marines again, laying on the linoleum floor in that restaurant, lying in thickening and spreading pools of deep red molasses, some of them blinded by their own wounds and blood, and some not. The broken tape loop keeps playing the same old song over and over again. He remembers the ones who aren't blind, looking at him in their last moments on earth as he pulls the trigger and makes their heads explode.

He wonders whether the lights actually govern everything he's ever done. Are they steering him all the time to do the things he does? Is he some kind of pet to them, something who has a tendency for free will, but who's still under their control?

There are no answers.

Once upon a time, he had been happy. He had a wife and children. Jennifer had been a beautiful Asian wife that he found washed up on the beach. She had escaped from Hong Kong with a big time heroin habit. She had tried detox 99 times. She was broke and starving, and she had terror in her eyes. Jorge rescued her. Together they had worked to free her from her drug habit. As Jennifer grew healthier, she became even more beautiful, and she began to make contact with her parents in Kowloon. They were overjoyed, as they had given her up for dead.

Jennifer was more than just an ex-junkie. She was the daughter of a *chaebolista*. Her father owned a thousand robots. He had a large candy factory, as well as a company that made 3% of all the dinnerware in the world. Her parents chartered a jumbo jet filled with relatives for the wedding in Cachanilla. San Mateo had a fiesta for three days. Everyone was drunk and happy.

The Story of the Century

Despite her parent's wealth, Jennifer and Jorge lived modestly in the village. A little two-bedroom house was built with a low stone wall around the property. They planted oranges, limes, lemons, peaches, apricots, and pomegranate trees on the hectare of land. Jorge was still a fisherman, but he had the best equipment and the best wardrobe of anyone in the village except for Carlos Castellon. The Estrada-Tse family eventually included a girl and a boy. This made Jennifer's parents even happier, as these were their first grandchildren.

Good things never last. Jennifer's parents got tired of flying between Hong Kong and Hermosillo. They didn't like the commute. These things were for common people, and the Tses were not common. They did not like Mexico. They did not like that Jorge was still a fisherman. They offered him a job as bodyguard, but he turned it down. He did not want to learn Chinese. He did not want to go to university. He did not want a job in the chaebol at any level. He wanted to be free.

Jorge didn't know it, but Jennifer's parents began to conspire against him. They began to give Jennifer more tickets to Hong Kong. For a while, Jorge went too, but not always. Jorge and Jennifer began to fight. Once he even slapped her in the face. The children screamed. A few days later, Jennifer got into the car with the children, saying that she was going to go to the grocery store. Three months later, the police called at Jorge's house. They wanted to know what he was going to do about the car that had been abandoned at the Tijuana airport.

Now the house is more or less empty, not quite a trash pit. It's always filled with comrades in arms, rather than a wife and children. The smuggling and the ALF has become more important, and he devotes less time to actual fishing. RPM made its demands, and Jorge/Insecticida delivers.

He thinks about the faces of the dead and dying Marines again. He thinks about the surprised expression on that sergeant's face when he puts a bullet in his forehead. He's sure that he'll see it staring out at him from the front cover of *WEEK* Magazine in one or more of the stores when he goes to downtown Cachanilla. Slow the boat for the harbor.

By now, Jorge/Insecticida is at the Cachanailla dock. Puto is there waiting for him. Somehow, someone had told him what time he would be arriving. Jorge gives Puto an *abrazo,* and says, "I've got a down payment for you in the boat."

Puto smiles, "Well, I can always use money, but how about later?"

Jorge gives Puto a smile, even though he doesn't feel like it. "I'll meet you at the fried chicken shack near the waterfront in an hour or so." They get into the pickup truck, and drive to the internet café. Lisbeth is in the little office, and she greets him warmly. Jorge has been a regular customer, and she hasn't seen him for a long time. She asks him how things are, and he lies. "Everything is fine." He sits down in front of the computer and does what's needed to get into his email. He finds 173 messages, the majority of which are spam. 54 of them are pornographic come ons. Jorge is a lonely guy. Twenty seven messages detail fishing conditions in the Sea of Cortez, but they're old news. Three emails come from Hong Kong, discussing the goings on in the candy factory and the dinnerware concern. This is boilerplate from the Tses. Jorge scans in vain for any sign of Jennifer and the children. There is none. He deletes in disgust. Two of the emails are from Victor. One is a routine spam note on RPM, wishing everyone a Happy Chinese New Year. The other is personal and encrypted. He prints the coded message, deleting it.

The rest are bulletins on the news in Baja California. Evidently, there had been a massacre of Marines in the desert near Santa Ynez. Jorge follows the developments with great intensity as the story unwinds. It takes total will power to keep from screaming at the computer. At the same time, he has the sick thrill of finding himself the subject of world news. Although

The Story of the Century

neither he nor the ALF are ever mentioned as suspects, Jorge sweats, and his face is contorted as he looks at the computer screen.

He feels a hand on his shoulder. "Are you all right, Jorge?" It's Lisbeth. She's seen him looking very anxious and sad, mumbling to himself as the different screens pop into view.

Jorge jumps. "I'm sorry. I've been out fishing. I didn't know that all those people had been killed at Santa Ynez. I loved that family! And they served such good tamales!"

He turns to the computer. At hand, he pulls out the paper that Attu has given him, and he copies the email message.

TO: AXOLOTL@LODESTAR.COM

FROM: JORGE22@MX.RPM.NET

SUBJECT: MOTHER'S TREATMENT

MOTHER IS HOME. SHE NEEDS HER MONEY TO PAY DR. AYALA. PLEASE TELL MR. JONES. 63712

The electrons go to Lodestar in Hermosillo, and are forwarded to some national security establishments. In Singapore at the Department of the Treasury, this message starts a funds transfer from the Central Bank to an armored car company in Tijuana, specifying $2.3 million in unmarked bills for eventual delivery. At another, even more secure routing, Admiral Hideo Sakamoto receives the message at a remote outpost on Reunion Island. As he watches the message flash on his computer screen the admiral turns to his aide, and says, "That is a 63712 message Colonel, isn't it?" The colonel looks over his shoulder and says, "That it is, Sir, confirmed, -- a 63712 message."

The admiral turns in his swivel chair and looks at his aide.

"Forward this message to the grays, please, Colonel."

Karl Eysenbach

IN A MOTORCADE OUTSIDE OF MEXICO CITY

Esteban Salinas has one or two things going for him. One is that he's one of the most drop-dead gorgeous men on the planet. He's a ladies man. The second thing going for him is that he's the bachelor Governor of Mexico. It's widely anticipated that he'll be elected as Mexico's next senator as soon as his term is through, and he's bandied about in the press as a future presidential candidate for the Founding Fathers' party -- the one in charge of the planet now. The whisperings in Mexico City are echoed in Singapore as well. It's easy to see him as a World President. He's only in his early forties, and he's making all the right moves and news.

All that is in the future, though. Governor Salinas has no time for reflection. Like any head of state, he's horribly busy. Right now, he's in his limousine, having just personally delivered condolences to Sra. Amelia Castro, grieving mother of one of the Marines tragically and mysteriously martyred in the desert of Baja California. Although the house in Toluca is less than 100 KM from Los Pinos, the Governor's Palace, it seems like an eternity as the motorcade speeds through the traffic lights.

The police have cordoned off all of the intersections. Right now, Governor Salinas is in the third limousine, surrounded by his chief of staff Miguel Castenedas, his secretary, Elanor de la Torre, various junior aides, and the head of the Mexican Film Board, Ramon Navarro-Montes. While he would have preferred to be there for the local delegations of Toluca or hobnobbing with the press, the Governor is very busy today. This is a working journey.

Castenedas and the aides congratulate the Governor about his appearance with the dead Marine's mother. Not only has he snagged all the national media and print people in Toluca, but he's managed to snag

The Story of the Century

a sizable press contingent from South America and Africa in addition to the Singapore boys. Two world networks will show him offering condolences to the grieving family tonight. This leads to discussions about the Governor's trip tomorrow to Santa Ynez. Limousines and bus motorcades have been assembled in Tijuana. They'll meet the Governor's helicopter just outside El Rosario and travel for an hour through the desert to the massacre site. Castenedas and the aides all agree that 100% of the major networks will be covering his visit to the Ybarra family. He'll spend the night camping with the Marines before hiking through Catavina the next morning. His helicopter will pick him up at Hotel La Pinta at noon.

Gov. Salinas isn't horribly interested in the logistics. His aides will point, and he'll go in that direction. He's far more interested in the kind of progress that's been made regarding the capturing of the killers. Military intelligence indicates that the rebels have a stronghold around the Cachanilla area. Gov. Salinas requests more intensive police and military personnel to the area without publicity. There's a discussion as to whether there's enough reward money for the time being. Salinas says that more publicity should be given in the Cachanilla area for the $1,000,000 bounty.

One of the aides from the Ministry of Health talks about the upcoming campaign for school vaccinations. It seems that there are spot shortages of measles and chicken pox vaccine. Salinas puts his index finger to his temple and stares intently. He's pretending to be deeply interested, but his mind has wandered off. He's reviewing what he did with that chesty airline stewardess and her friend the night before.

At that moment, the telephone rings in the limousine. Sra. De la Torre picks up the phone and replied "Hello. This is 12-21-19-34." She listens for a while, and then she turns to the Governor and speaks.

"Governor, Victor is on the line. Do you have time for him?"

The Governor's face beams, as he reaches for the phone.

"I always have time for Victor." They make small talk for a few minutes, and Esteban agrees to meet with him when he's in the city. He hangs up the phone, and turns to the small crowd in the black car.

"Where are we now?"

"Discussing the vaccine shortages, Governor." Sra. De la Torre speaks.

"Okay. Can we put a request into the World Department of Health to help us out a little on this? I understand that the Chinese vaccine factories don't have any problem pumping this stuff out."

"Right away, Governor." Castenedas replies.

The mundane business of state resumes again. The Under Assistant Minister of Agriculture gives a briefing on the *campesinos* conference. Farmers are still unhappy about the level of crop subsidies that the Governor has promised. While the Governor's sympathetic, he has to think of the upcoming budget. There's a brief review of the amount and level of subsidies for various agricultural products, and Gov. Salinas says that the Ministry should try to be as generous as possible for rice and corn. But he wants the highest level of subsidies reserved for fruits and vegetables. He's firm on that.

He knows, and everyone else knows that 99% of the issue will be decided in a tangle of committees between the Ministry and the Legislature. Salinas is putting his two cents in right now, knowing that the final answer is months away. Esteban Salinas likes to eat fruits and vegetables, and that's his policy input.

By this time, the motorcade is getting closer to the center of Mexico City. Sirens grow louder as more police motorcycles join the convoy, and there is more than one horn honking from disgruntled motorists who have to wait through two or three green lights until the motorcade speeds through the cleared intersections. The last items for

The Story of the Century

discussion are the pubic works budgets for Sonora and Chihuahua. A short speech on Mexico's counterinsurgency policy has already been prepared and faxed to the limousine. The Governor studies it for a minute. He will deliver the statement to the press when he disembarks at Los Pinos. Then he'll go inside to meet with the delegates from Central America on regional immigration policy.

Esteban Salinas' mind is elsewhere as the discussions take place in the car for the rest of the trip. He asks his secretary for a notepad, and he begins writing in his lap. He thinks and composes a brief note to Ms. Saroyan Pashogi, and he hands it back to Sra. De la Torre with instructions to put it on his best stationary for his signature.

Sra. De la Torre is a thin and proper woman in her early 60s, and she's always a straight arrow. She looks at Governor Salinas with wide eyes as she puts her hand to her mouth before touching her hair. She blushes slightly.

ON LINE

PRESIDENT HOK AUTHORIZES $10M BOUNTY FOR MARINE KILLERS

A GRIEVING WIDOW'S STORY: ROSA ALVAREZ SPEAKS.

OFF LINE

EJIDO SAN MATEO

They're huddled around in the bare little room with a naked light bulb. Once upon a time it had been a gay little place, the master bedroom of Señor y Señora Jorge Estrada. Now it's just one room of a flophouse for the collection of smugglers, political misfits, drug abusers, and recent mass murderers. All the perps have posttraumatic stress syndrome to one degree or another, and this ragtag collection of deviants -- these ten unshaven Mexican fishermen -- constitutes the entire terrorist cell of the Atzlan Liberation Front. They're scared shitless.

This group of mass murderers and conspirators are sitting in the plastic beear chairs looking at their leader, and they have issues. Insecticida sits with them in this little room that's actually his bedroom. As leader, he's said that people should speak what they're feeling, but there's the need for an agenda too. He writes what people want to talk about on in an old black and white composition book.

First there is the Marine massacre. The people who pulled the triggers want to talk about it almost as much as the people who didn't. But there are the different reasons for wanting to talk. The people who killed yell at the people who hadn't actually pulled the triggers. And the people who hadn't killed anyone are yelling at the assassins, telling them that this whole project is no good to begin with. It was the work of the Devil, and only the Devil would have people do what's been done.

Throughout, Insecticida wants to scream, but he remains silent. He has to bide his time, waiting for some of the anger to subside. He has to channel that anger and direct it towards the details of what will be done in the future. He deflects the conversation five degrees. They begin to talk about what they've seen on television.

The Governor of Mexico has sent his entire police force after them. The Secret police are after them. The President of the World wants them dead. There is a reward of $1,000,000 for anyone who can provide information leading to their deaths or capture. Satellite trucks and all varieties of military and law enforcement are infesting the area like malarial mosquitoes. Everyone in the room can smell the fear.

The Story of the Century

This is a good thing. It removes the reality of the situation. Puto has been coached beforehand. He talks about how dangerous the situation is for everyone. No wife or girl friend could ever know about what has happened. Everything will have to remain a secret. No one outside this room can know **anything**. This is Puto's talking point.

"Everyone in this room will die a horrible death if you talk. Your family and friends will die a horrible death if they know. If they are lucky, they will only die of shame. They will be branded for life as the people who helped the assassins. I know when and where the money is going to be delivered to us. It is important that we should not spend any dollars here. What we all need to do is to relocate to a big city. Mexico, Los Angeles, Guanajato. It doesn't matter where, as long as you can get a job or start a business. There will be more than enough money to provide for all of your family. I have the confirmation on that from the government."

They talk about money. A week from today, an armored car will be headed south from Tijuana. Insecticida has talked to Old Man Ayala about having a fiesta for the boys, and they've already made the arrangements. The party will be at the new farmhouse. "Does everyone know Old Man Ayala?" Everybody knows him.

Subcommandante Insecticida is a little stoned. He's been dragging on his cigarette way too long. "Gentlemen, you have already seen what I can deliver. Hasn't the fishing business been good from RPM lately? I deliver, and I'm going to continue delivering. I said that the money was from the lights, and no one believed me. I told you that the box was for space aliens, and no one believed me. And then you saw the lights. The lights have told me that each of us gets $100,000 per family, and the people who took part will get extra money. I deliver, and the lights deliver."

There is silence in the room. Insecticida is smart enough to look at his notebook to figure out what to do next. They discuss the logistics of the money. It will be in small bills (big and bulky), and people will have to figure out how to deal with it to avoid the law. An armored car will arrive at Old Man Ayala's new house on March 22nd, and Leader says that everyone will be pretty much on their own from then on.

This is a major bone of contention, and now it's Vladimir's turn. Vladimir is the devout Communist (everybody knows that Stalinists are such jerks), and Vladimir DOES NOT THINK THAT BREAKING UP THE ALF IS A GOOD IDEA! He launches into his canned sermonette -- workers oppression, the bosses, the contradictions of capitalism, yadda yadda yadda. The worst part about Vladimir's speeches is that he's got good Marxist analysis, but it still doesn't negate the fact that he's an asshole. He goes on and on and on.

Now it's Insecticida's turn to be macho. *Quien es mas macho?* All the John Wayne movies you've ever seen have prepared you for this moment. He gets up out of his chair.

"Gentlemen, pardon me for a minute, I'm going to get the GPS system." He walks out of the room and comes back and he throws the GPS system at Vladimir. Vladimir fumbles, but he catches it.

"Here Pilgrim, you got control of the whole ship. Dude! You're in charge now! You can issue a communiqué under Subcommandante Insecticida and claim full responsibility for anything if you want some street cred. Me? I don't give a rat's ass. I'm a retiree. You can count me out from now on. Is there anything else to this meeting? If I don't hear some big objection, it's adjourned. Those that want to be retirees, stay here for reefer and *cerveza*. Anyone who wants to stay with the ALF, get the hell out! And folks, the money deal still stands. You got your invites to the clambake"

Like a startled and confused herd of cattle, the group gives a sharp little jump, and there's confusion in the room as people shift their chairs, while others begin the process of leaving. Four guys leave the room. Six guys stay put. It's like watching an amoeba splitting in half. Outside in the dark, the new Subcommandante Insecticida gathers his little flock. "Gentlemen, now here's what we're going to do.'

KM 161, VALLE DE LAS ROBLES
MARCH 22ND, 8:00 PM

After the cardboard and corrugated tin favelas, after the military checkpoint, the two lane blacktop begins to twist and turn. It climbs up and around the mountains covered with green vegetation. For a while, just a little bit, the road straightens out for a few hundred meters. Off to the north, beyond the stand of oak trees lining the road, there is a lush truck garden. Two houses huddle off in the distance about a kilometer away, one old ramshackle place with aged gray wood and broken windows, the other small and neat and painted bright red. A half gravel, half dirt road leads to the farm houses, and a hand painted sign along the highway proclaims, *'RANCHO SE VENDE.'* Welcome to Rancho Ayala. On the porch of the red two-room farmhouse is an ancient, withered man sitting on a rocking chair. This is Leonardo Ayala, but no one calls him that. Everybody calls him Old Man Ayala, even though he is hardly 60. Old Man Ayala is pissed, and I mean really pissed! He built the new house for his son, expecting him to get married. He has or HAD a son who was going to amount to something, but he turned out to be gay! Old Man Ayala found his son, Raul in bed with Chuy, the local fairy with tight purple jeans and dyed blond hair. Boy, did the shit hit the fan when he walked into the bedroom!!

Old Man Ayala has figured out that Raul (AKA Vladimir) is a lieutenant in the Atzlan Liberation Front, and he hears that there is $10,000,000 reward for information leading to the killers of the Marines! Damn! He's just won the lottery! Old Man Ayala doesn't know whether the ALF killed the Marines or not. He knows they've been doing plenty of funny stuff in the last few months. Truth be told, he doesn't really care whether the ALF did anything to the soldiers or not.

What Old Man Ayala did, he went to this Marine sergeant, who went to his lieutenant, etc, etc, and so it goes until Kuala Lumpur, Singapore, God, the Devil, and the entire pantheon of Confucian Mandarin codebreakers are all interested in these little goings on. Indeed, it looks as if the most powerful boob toob watchers in the world are going to watch this little TV game of '*Survivor,*' only none of the ALF players know that they're going to be videostreamed by some Marine lieutenant and his crew.

The old man on the porch and the Marines in the bushes watch as an armored car comes down the dirt road and stops. Three guards get out and start unloading sacks of moolah, tastefully arranging the blood money for the cameras. A Marine officer gets out of the bushes and signs for the paperwork, and the armored car guys get in the truck and drive away.

About half and hour later, Raul drives down the short road to the old homestead. He's nervous about confronting Dad, but the party is here, and he has the backup of his affinity group. The men jostle against each other as the truck bumps downhill toward the two buildings. Going through the trees, they get into the clearing where the 20 hectares of cabbage, broccoli, and winter squash are growing. Up ahead is Dad, puffing on his pipe, motionless like some kind of smoking statue. Old Man Ayala is sitting in his rocking chair with the confidence of a Florida elections clerk. The truck pulls up in front of the house near the beer cooler, and the men get out. It seems like ages, but the old goat finally gets out of his chair and stands up from his rocking chair.

Somewhat hesitantly, but knowing that he must, Raul screws up his courage and approaches his father. Off to the side, he sees the case

The Story of the Century

of Pacifico iced up and the bags and bags of cash. There is the most tentative of *embrazos*. Old Man Ayala is as stiff as a board, unyielding to the hug of his son. The other men are standing near the truck.

"Dad, thank you very much for hosting this party. It will be a great celebration, and you will be rewarded."

"Yes, I know. Some day God will forgive you for being such a pervert." He pulls away from Vladimir, making the excuse that he has to go to the bathroom. Curiously, he closes the front door and locks it. Just then, Fidel points to the line of trees.

"Look, over there!" A bank of floodlights glares at the little cabins, and a booming voice barks from a loudspeaker.

"FREEZE. -- GET DOWN ON THE GROUND WITH YOUR HANDS OVER YOUR HEAD."

Unfortunately, everybody who is an ALF member takes this opportunity to panic like scared rabbits. Hector tries to run behind the house towards the woods. Vladimir and Fidel attempt to make a stand behind the pick up truck. Vladimir and Fidel spend the last second of their lives watching each other produce bullet exit wounds from various parts of their bodies. Hector is fatally shot in the back by a military bullet.

At this moment, Jorge and Puto are late to the party. They had some car trouble, and it took a while to figure out where the electrical short was. As the battered crewcab cruises up the road north, Insecticida and Puto sense that a situation is developing. There's been way too much heat on the road, and it's been getting thicker as they go along. There's a *tienda* off to the side of the road, and they park the car. Suddenly they hear gunfire off in the distance. Jorge turns to Puto. "Is that coming from where the Ayala place is?" Puto nods his head yes. He tells Puto to follow him.

Later the shop owner is wondering what that beater in front of his store is doing, and he makes a phone call. Some basic police work leads the authorities to believe that some ALFs may have taken for the hills. Jorge and Puto have a head start, but the Marines have the manpower and technology. A detachment of Marines is sent out from Jorge's abandoned pickup in pursuit.

ON LINE

In a stunning piece of police work near Ensenada, Mexico a unit of the 17th Marines, Special Battalion hunted down and captured members of the Atzlan Liberation Front, a guerilla organization that has terrorized the west cost of Mexico for more than three years. Three of the guerillas were killed, and four were later captured. Although not formally charged, the World Prosecutor's office in Mexico City today issued a statement charging that these members of the ALF may have been responsible for the bloody massacre of Marines in the desert of Baja California.

SOMEWHERE IN THE MOUNTAINS SOUTH OF ENSENADA, 1:45 AM

Things are not going so well in this part of the world. 320 kilometers south-southeast of New Los Angeles, Jorge and Puto are in a race for their lives. Their heads are filled with nothing but fear. They're totally aware of every sight, every sound, and every movement or smell. Right now they're statues, trying to overcome muscle cramps from crouching for so long. They stifle their breathlessness. They know the Marines are close. Too damn close. When the time is right, they scramble from brush to behind giant oaks. Then they wait to go behind the large rock outcropping in another brief mad dash.

Sometimes they can hear the voices in the forest. There are units talking to each other over radios, crossing off sectors where the manhunt has been unsuccessful. Sometimes they hear airplane and helicopter sounds, but they're invisible as long as they're under the canopy of the trees. The good news is that they're only 18 KM from the fringes of the greater Estero Beach area. The bad news is that Insecticida has left his maps and compass in the pick up truck. He's crossing through rugged unknown country, and he has only the vaguest idea of how he's going to contact a friendly living in Colonia Hildago near Ensenada.

This is not going to happen right now. Jorge and Puto are in a poison oak thicket near a clearing. The Marines have an idea there might be someone east 200 meters, and they're right. The lieutenant decides to send a squad out through the woods. He radios headquarters and gets the go ahead. Puto turns towards Insecticida and says, "Pull my finger." Insecticida does with predictable results. *"Frijoles,"* Puto says, and he laughs quietly. Both men sense movement 200 meters to the west.

Simultaneously, the two fugitives get out of their crouching positions, ignoring their urge to scratch themselves silly. This is make or break, and they're not sure if the Marines aren't going to catch them. They head towards a clearing for no good reason. It's a final whim perhaps. Suddenly, the dark night lights up from the sky. It shines down on the men in the clearing with a fierce intensity, and both are frozen in its blue-white glare.

They find themselves floating up out of the oak forest. They can see the hills of the valley drop below them as they feel the weightlessness of floating through the air. They can hear the whiz of a hundred bullets, but not one comes close to hitting them. The lights of Estero Beach begin to be visible as they rise above the hill They're trapped in a blue column of light that's drawing them towards the silver disk that is growing bigger and bigger each second.

Neither Puto nor Jorge remembers any of this, but the flying saucer hovers over the clearing and draws the two men inside its belly. It fires yellow rays at the Marines in the forest below. They drop their guns, and fall to the ground screaming. In two days all of the men will have died from the worst cases of radiation poisoning that the military has seen in over two hundred years.

It's classified as a secret, and it's a scandal. Every action is taken by the World Government to insure that no mention of this incident will ever be reported to the press.

NEW LOS ANGELES
NEW LOS ANGELES TIMES NEWSROOM
8:30AM, FEBRUARY 20TH

Clem is on the net, looking for sites about 'magnetic interferometer,' but this is just a brief diversion from work. He's happy to be here. Like the first day back on any job, he's busy. He's already placed preliminary phone calls into Pepe Lopez's office about setting up an interview with Saroyan Pashogi. And he's wading through the small mountain of press releases that have piled up on his desk while he's looking at a description of a magnetic monopole.

"I wish I knew what this means," Clem thinks as he continues to play catch up. He's scheduled to go in to see the boss about the Bollywood superstar. Since Ms. Pashogi has a chick flick opening soon, Clem hopes he can get an exclusive. And he remembers that he and the sex goddess hit it off quite well when he interviewed her a couple of months ago. She isn't as dumb or simple as her movies make her out to be, and there was chemistry to the interview that went beyond the trite pablum that the publicity mills demand.

On the way to the boss' office, Clem and everyone else on the fourth floor pause. There's a late breaking news flash on the tube. ALF guerillas have massacred a contingent of Marines in a remote section of Baja California. "Wow!" Clem shouts, "I know that place. I drove by there the day before it happened. I practically know those people!" There's a silence in the newsroom, but Mbake Methune looks over his glasses at Clem and says,

"Whatever."

It might mean something to Clem, but to most news guys it's just another item in the news hole, another piece of paper in the in box, another thing to scratch off the 'to do' list before the next edition. Feelings have nothing to do with it if you're a hardboiled journalist. Clem walks into the boss' office. He sits down in front of Pablo Lopez's desk and says, "Did you just see the news? I drove right by there 48 hours ago."

"That's great. I want you to do a background piece for the next edition, but Emilio is going to take the lead on this. He's our guy in Baja. Maybe you can call him up and fill him in on what he's going to be looking for."

"Great. I'll get right on it. Changing the subject a little, I feel like a million. If this were another world I'd want to do the story down there as a lead. But I've got too much movie stuff on my plate right now for my first day back at work."

"For instance, what?"

"Well, for one thing, Ravi Guptara has the reputation for being the biggest asshole in Bollywood right now. He's a real screamer, and there's been a lot of palace intrigue."

"Is there a story there?"

"Not now, but things will develop when the lawyers get moving"

"Just be sure to let Chollie Knickerbocker in on some of the gossip. He loves those hanging rumors with a twist of innuendo. Just to change the subject, how are your aunt and uncle?"

"They're great. As soon as I got down there, I had a *quinceañera* to butler for. It was for my niece Sarah."

"You look more brown than you did two weeks ago. You even look like you lost a little weight. Are you ready to work?" Lopez has his hands folded across his big belly, looking at Clem.

"You bet I am! I've already made new inquiries with Saroyan Pashogi's agent, and it looks like we can get a new angle on the case."

"Good. That's what I like to hear. I expect a Pulitzer Prize from you on this piece." Lopez smiles with wicked little corners of his mouth.

Clem groans audibly. Pablo Lopez is famous for mixing bad jokes with obscure historical allusions. Clem counters quickly, "Strive for excellence at all times." That had been one of the dorkier slogans President Hok used to win in the last election.

"All right, the first thing I want you to do is to do the background for the next edition. You know, a travelogue kind of thing. And then do a recap on the guerilla activities down there. I expect to see lots of news in the hole by the end of the day. I'm glad you're back."

The first, second, and third times that Clem tries to call Emilio Robles, the line is busy. On the fourth time, he can see Robles' taut face focusing out on the traffic he's passing as he looks out the windshield of his car. Emilio is going down the toll road at about 200 kph. It's a bad time to call. Half an hour later, Emilio returns the call. This time, he's a little more relaxed. He's sitting in the jump seat of a helicopter as it speeds south out of the Tijuana airport.

"How's it going pal? It looks like you've got a hot one."

Robles' image breaks up a little. "It's not every day you get a wienie roast like this. I'm going to be busy for the next ten days or so."

"I understand. That's why I called. I think I have some background for you." As Clem speaks, he keeps one eye on the breaking news from the hologram.

"As near as I can tell, the massacre took place outside Santa Ynez. Now as far as I know, there's nothing on the ground anywhere near there except for a taco stand and a military checkpoint."

"You're broadcasting." Clem hears his words repeated back to him in an electronic echo. Emilio is entering the last 30 seconds of their conversation onto his portable computer. Emilio is also downloading the computer pictures that Clem has pulled up from the morgue on Santa Ynez and the ALF. Emilio's voice crackles a little. "Anything else you can tell me?"

"I don't do marines when I'm down there, so I can't tell you anything about the dead guys. But I know a Marine detachment is stationed at Ejido Santa Clara. A Major Cervantez is the big dog there. I can tell you more about the *taqueria*."

"Roger and copy."

"I think the place is called the Ybarra Loncheria. It's as old as the hills. They've got great food and pictures on the wall of some old Mexican general. He must have been in the family. That's an angle. I remember they had their Holstein cow tied out between the outhouse and the restaurant. Real nice place."

"OK, sounds like some human interest. Anything else you can tell me?

"Nothing I remember." "Okay. Thanks Clem. I'll get back to you. Signing out." Clem scratches that off his list, and for the next six hours he works hard to put out two news pieces. It hasn't been made any easier by the fact that incoming details are changing the story as he writes, and the scheduled item in the news hole still need filling. It's about the rediscovery of an ancient 20th Century technology known as breast implants, and their impact on Bollywood.

The computer beeps. It shows the both stories on the Marine massacre have finally passed muster along with the tit story. They're already out on the net, and at the printing presses. Clem is pleasantly surprised and happy. He stays at work late that night, tidying his desk and deleting unwanted computer files. With some free time, he rifles through the internet some more, looking for citations on 'magnetic interferometer.' But somewhere near Kuala Lumpur, a military computer is trying to track Clem's electronic inquiries. With prejudice.

GENERAL COMMUNICATIONS HEADQUARTERS, TELECOMMUNICATIONS DIVISION

It hasn't been a picnic today. There was the FLASH notice that a group of Marines had been killed in Baja California, Mexico just a few hours ago. There's conversation in the bunker about the bastards who did it, and both the robots and the manual surveillance personnel have been busy combing through recordings of internet traffic for the last month to see if there's been any extraneous references to Company B, of the 16th Marine Detachment, Transport Group. Unfortunately, the search has revealed hundreds of messages from faraway lovers to their soldier boys. Since the news got out, these internet messages have gotten more pleading and more desperate. It's depressing watching wives and lovers asking for the whereabouts of their menfolk, without getting any response.

This is not the only thing that occupies TCOM's attention. The bunker is examining internet traffic going out of the 16th Marines or other areas to see if there's been any compromise of security. So far there's nothing. It isn't like looking for a needle in a haystack. It's like looking for a needle in a field of haystacks, and as fast as the robots review everything, there's still that frustration of knowing that some clue must exist somewhere on the net that's just waiting for discovery. This is occupying much of TCOM's time, but there are layers of secrecy, like onions, above and beyond the ordinary that need looking into that are not entrusted to the rank and file workers in the bunker.

General Caramehni is the only person in the Army General Staff who knows the real purpose for the massacre. After all, he's the guy who planned it and made it happen; what with his meetings and conversations with the Secretary of Defense and the Public Private Partnership. Such interservice rivalry!

The blinds are drawn in front of his office, and an MP stands guard, signaling that the General is doing a special, classified search for key words and email addresses. Some of these deal with physics. Phrases like 'magnetic interferometer' and 'magnetic monopole' are high on his list. There are other phrases as well dealing with astronomy. 'Alpha Centauri' and 'Callisto Base' are some of ten or twelve phrase searches he's examining. Last but not least, he's screening these phrases to see if any of these have traveled through the Mexican government or Lodestar, especially its Hermosillo operations.

While he's doing a manual search, he's put his own robots on the case. Occasionally, his computer will beep at him, and he'll pull up an amateur astronomy club in South Africa, or a graduate physics class in China. He'll call up the screens to spy on them, and he takes notes. But it all looks very routine. When he digs further, Caramehni finds that there are good reasons for these people to look at these websites.

He's just gotten up from his desk to check on how the people outside are doing, when he's called back by the beeping noise coming from his desk. With a few clicks, he brings up the internet file. This time his attention is riveted. Someone in the *New Los Angeles Times* has made an Octopus search on the phrase 'magnetic interferometer.' Caramehni watches with interest as someone in the news organization scrolls back and forth between the search directory and through the websites on the phrase, including an extensive search on the information that Lodestar has posted related to such things.

This is of great interest as the newspaper is the only media source in the entire world that's doing this search now, and it's occurring after the bodies in Baja aren't even cold. A review of the *Times*' web traffic over a three-year period has revealed no searches for the phrase 'magnetic interferometer' until now. That means that either there's an extremely unlikely coincidence that the newspaper is planning a science feature on a very sensitive subject, or that there is one extremely good investigative reporter (with a hotline to the mojo wire) at the tabloid. Caramehni wants to know more, but he's frustrated.

"Sergeant Singh, will you come in here a minute please?" He barks into the intercom. In a few moments, the sergeant comes in. Singh has been doing most of the monitoring in the astronomy area in his office next door.

"Yes, General. We've been looking at a variety of astronomy magazines and websites showing star maps of the Southern Hemisphere, but not much else. Do you have anything going on?

"Yes, as a matter of fact I do. Look at this." He points to his computer screen, and the sergeant bends over his shoulder to look.

"An Octopus search on the phrase 'magnetic interferometer.' That IS interesting, General. Who's initiating the request?"

"It's coming from the *New Los Angeles Times*, but I can't see who is doing the search. It's obviously from their news division, and their firewall is very, very good. Is there any way we can penetrate it to find out who specifically is doing this?

"I'm afraid not, General. That's one of the weak spots in our systems. I wish our interfaces into the press were better, but you know those damn constitutional requirements---"

The Story of the Century

"Yes I do, Singh. What do you think we should do about this? I'll continue to monitor it. We can set the whole thing on automatic function from now on, but where do we go from here?

"Well -- General, have you considered the Mighty Wurlitzer?"

"Ah yes! Excellent idea, Sergeant. Notify Gordo at once, and see what he can do with it."

"I'll put in the request immediately." With that, the sergeant turns on his heels and exits, returning to his office.

Everyone in TCOM is busy for weeks, and they receive a Presidential Citation for the good work they've done. But Sergeant Major Singh has other, related things on his mind. At the first opportunity, he gets a 24- hour pass. Taking the utmost care on the subway to evade anyone who might be following, he gets off at the KL Sentral station and pushes his way through the crowds of downtown Kuala Lumpur until he sets down at the computer of the first internet café that he finds. Few people notice the athletic man from Bengal, and no one pays any attention as he sends an email to a certain real estate consulting firm in New Los Angeles.

TO: KHYL@CASTLE&BISHOP.COM
FROM: OTROMONDO@XYZ.COM

There is material that you need to look at. I need to talk to you personally on how we can do it. I really believe that the time has come. Yours in everlasting bliss. May the Archangel Michael guard and protect us all.

DOWNTOWN NEW LOS ANGELES

Clem is walking through the Castellemare district of downtown after dark. He strolls down the boardwalk on the beach, passing by the trolley station, water taxi dock, and private marina. He has no desire to walk to the forbidden zone tonight, as he'd done more than once when he was going through his divorce to Salma.

When Clem was breaking up with Salma, he had left the fifty-story building of polished granite and glass, walking south along the coast as the buildings got progressively older, shorter, and dirtier. Neon signs multiplied, advertising the pachinko parlors, resale stores and karaoke bars. As he mourned the breakup of his marriage, he had passed through the restricted zone of South Santa Monica filled with its grubby concrete block buildings housing *maquilladoras*, taco vendors, and flophouses. And then there were the homeless people. In Venice, he had seen the Third World slum stretching out into the distance; cardboard and sheet metal shacks jammed with four and five children families. He saw the babies without diapers playing on the trash heaps near the railroad yard. Clem didn't bother to walk through the yard to touch the rusting chain metal fence going out into the ocean that marked the boundary of the forbidden zone. Instead, he had turned around, going off in search of a hotel room to grab some short, troubled sleep before he went back to work.

The hurt of the divorce has healed, and Clem isn't doing the distance tonight. He's only walking a few blocks from the *Times* office to the restaurant district. Clem's mind is occupied with work. He thinks about the press releases and phone calls inviting him to cover the public appearance of Saroyan Pashogi at the Tour de 'Argent. For some reason, the thought of the movie star is sticking in his mind longer than it should have, and he begins to fantasize about her. At this moment, 37,415 other men on the planet have something of the same idea, but most of them do not have an interview set up with the sex bomb on Tuesday.

He thinks about the publicity machine, how everything is built on an exchange. I'll give you an exclusive interview, if you buy so much advertising. 95% of all the 'hot' Bollywood gossip in the world is highly refined and processed fish food, and reporters like him are the fish, eating it up without questioning. What they shit out is then passed on to the general public as the Real McCoy, something worth remembering and fantasizing about for thirty seconds before they get the urge to go shopping for the knockoff of that handbag that they've seen the star carry to the awards ceremony.

Clem thinks about Mexico again. What's happening at the Ybarra Loncheria now? What a zoo that place must be! He feels sorry for the Ybarra family. The updated reports from the hologram have talked about one of the children dying. This doesn't elicit Clem's pity because children die in Mexico every day. No, the pity is for the innocent family being put under the ordeal of the twenty white satellite vans descending on the little rest stop like some kind of land-based sperm whales. He envisions the news hens powdering their noses before they step into the glare of the video cams.

By now he's standing in front of Sochi's, a little sushi joint that the newsmen frequent. Clem's hungry, and he hasn't had any Japanese food in a long time. He steps inside and smells the mixture of fresh fish and tobacco smoke. Mbake Methune is at the bar eating some sashimi and downing sake. He spots Clem coming through the door. "How are you, my little brother?" Mbake says a little loudly as he waves Clem to sit down beside him.

Mbake is the military affairs correspondent for the *Times*, and he has about ten years seniority on Brother Reader. When Clem thinks of adjectives to describe Mbake to himself, the words 'cold,' 'haughty' and 'condescending' usually come to mind. Methune has looked down on Clem somewhat in the past, thinking that Little Brother Reader is not a 'true' reporter because of his Bollywood beat.

Times (and the *Times*) change though. Mbake has seen some of Clem's bylines on the Marine massacre. This pleases Mbake no end, as his workload has been increasing. He hopes that Clem will be interested in what he has to say, maybe even volunteering to help Mbake with his workload. The military affairs reporter has uncovered some exciting news, and by his third jar of sake, he actually gets warm and emotional.

They have a good-natured argument about the nature of journalism. This is an old standard that's been repeated for more than a few hundred years. Half of the argument is a lying contest. "I'm more cynical than you are!" The other half is the ritualized doggy sniffing of rear ends. After dishing the dirt on the *Times*, they eventually get down to the real business of dishing the dirt about military affairs.

"Little Brother, -- the secrets I know."

"Tell me more," Clem says as he puts a piece of California roll into his mouth.

"For example, there are a tremendous number of old secrets from before the war that are being pulled out from the ice fields and the forbidden zones, both here and elsewhere."

"I would imagine so," says Clem. It's the younger reporter's turn to be calm and laconic while the old hand waxes enthusiastic.

"The easy secrets are the ones they let me investigate." Mbake uses his fingers in quotation marks. "No doubt, you've read about the things like the spy satellites and the devices that monitor the internet?"

"Like Net Owl III? I really liked your story on that the other day."

"Thank you," Methune replies. "But as wonderful as these things are, they are nothing compared to some of the things from the Nevada, Arizona, and Ohio districts -- all forbidden zones, as well as here."

Now the elder reporter stops for a minute to see if anyone is listening. The place is empty except for the sushi chef, sitting in the corner of the kitchen reading his Japanese comic book. Nevertheless, the goateed Kenyan reporter with the salt and pepper hair lowers his voice to a whisper as he bends close to Clem's ears. Out of his mouth comes a barely audible "alien technology."

Clem looks at him with a confused expression. Mbake repeats the words, "alien technology." Clem's eyes give him the go ahead to tell him more.

"Starting in the old pre-war year of 1947. They have metal as thin as toilet paper that cannot be broken or cut. They have a collection of strange devices that no one knows how to use, and they even have a collection of bones that come from no animal that ever lived on this planet." Methune looks around again to see that he's not monitored.

"Now these are only some of the things I have heard about from my most secret sources, but there are some problems with everything. For one thing, there are never any documents. This person says this. I can never get two people to talk about the existence of the same thing, and even if I can, what does it mean? Even if twenty people were willing to go public on such a thing, they would be immediately branded as lunatics or even silenced forever. So you see, there is the need for documentation, but I have never seen any documents. If I could lay my hands on those papers, not only would I win a Platinum Prize, but I could retire as a famous and wealthy man. Such a story would be the story of the millennium!"

"But there are other problems besides getting people to agree to the existence of such things and the proof that they exist." Methune bends closer and whispers in Clem's ear.

"I believe that the government would make a serious effort to ruin or kill me if I found out. But if such a danger could be avoided, it would be the story of a lifetime. That would be a prize!"

Clem picks up the tab for both men, and they walk down the street to wait under a light at the trolley stop. They are along on the platform waiting for the Pink Line to take them back towards the *Times* Building. The sake has loosened Methune's tongue, and he raises his voice to the night.

"Call me a madman if you want, but I believe that our government actually has a way to communicate with the space aliens. I don't know how, and I am guessing by reading between the lines. But I have heard a rumor that the government has even returned some piece of alien equipment back to the creatures from outer space. Who knows why?"

ON LINE

Hu Jin Tao resigned today as Vice President of Tata Studios, Brahmaputra Productions citing irreconcilable differences with studio head, Ravi Guptara. At a press conference Mr. Hu stated that Guptara's interference in Brahmaputra Productions was responsible for the string of box office disasters the film and media unit has been suffering lately….

Three of the most recent features released by Brahmaputra have bombed out, including remakes of *Heaven's Gate, Gigli,* and *Battlefield Earth. Heaven's Gate* was particularly painful, costing $200 million to produce and grossing only $10 million to date….

The law firm of Wang, Jhangvi, and Olivares was a key player in forcing Mr. Hu's resignation. Despite his string of failures, Mr. Hu had what many in Bollywood considered to be an unbreakable contract with Tata.

OFF LINE

It's a busy day in the newsroom. Clem is focusing on the press releases, trying to work on his rewrites while trying to connect with

Saroyan Pashogi's agent. Other newsmen are working hard fleshing out the details of the Mexican massacre, while the senior correspondents are seeking reactions to President Hok's speech before the Congress.

Sometimes being a reporter is like being a one-man band. Beat the drum. Play the accordion, and breathe through the harmonica, all while you're trying to keep in time with yourself. Clem's in his 110% production mode, scanning the press release screen while monopolizing two ancient data processors with articles at various stages of completion. At noon, one of the robots passes by his desk, putting close enough for what looks like lunch on his desk, while busing out the tray from the so-called coffee break. It's a miracle that Clem has time to go to the bathroom. The 2PM deadline for the afternoon edition comes and goes, and Clem arranges his electrons just in time, getting editorial okay with less than a minute to spare. The afternoon is more laid back, -- time for making phone connections.

The video console lights up, and Saroyan Pashogi's manager appears on the screen. Clem and Pepe have been playing phone tag, and they finally review time and place requirements for the Star and Newsman. Some time is taken in backgrounding how the interview questions should be phrased, and there's *Zorro*. With Bollywood being Bollywood, where appearances are always more important than reality, it doesn't matter that *Zorro* hasn't even been greenlighted yet. Pepe tells Clem that a suite at the Bellagio in Malibu has been arranged for the interview tomorrow at 10AM, followed by a small press lunch at Pashogi's home off of Alvarado Drive at noon.

Clem is just finishing up dealing with one Lopez, when the other one shows up at his desk. Boss Pablo stands in front of Clem and motions for Clem to follow him into his office. Clem thanks Pepe, gets off the phone, and goes across the newsroom to plop into a chair facing the editor's desk.

"Boffo box office biz lately, eh?" said Lopez.

"You bet. When it rains, it pours, boss." Clem waits expectantly.

"I know that you're busy, but here's a chance to do some of that heavyweight reporting that you've been hounding me for. Is there any possibility that you could do a little detective work for Emilio Flores? He's been stuck in Santa Ynez filing stories a little bit longer than anyone anticipated. This story about the loncheria has a set of legs."

"Well, given the fact that I'm living the life of a Buddhist monk, I might as well put in some overtime." This is as much a joke as Clem can muster in the afternoon, but he wonders what the punch line is.

"OK. Good. Call up Emilio and talk to him. You know his number. And thanks for doing a little extra work. I know you've been busy." Clem heads for his cubicle. He dials Emilio's satellite telephone, and Emilio's face pops up on the screen later rather than sooner. Clem has a feeling that this conversation is already being watched by God knows who.

"How's it going, Emilio?"

"Hello, Clem. I'm pretty busy. How are you?"

"The juke joint's jumping up here too. Of course you're partly to blame. What's going on down there?"

"An awful lot, let me tell you. We've got the usual crews from the media, and the military is as thick as fleas. I just found out that Governor of Mexico is going to make a personal appearance tomorrow. Rumor has it that he's going to donate money to the Ybarra family. He's making the rounds right now of the families of the dead Marines. As usual, we've got a lot of reporters interviewing other reporters. Santa Ynez is not exactly one of the world's flesh pots."

"How well I know. Since I've volunteered to be your part-time slave in New LA, can you clue me in on what's going on down there? I mean really going on down there?"

The Story of the Century

"Well, there are some strange things in Santa Ynez, -- things that don't add up. For example, you'd expect to see one or two CIA dudes down here in a situation like this, but the place is lousy with spooks. Not only that, they've got two strange Air Force units down here. Nobody from these units has any identifying insignias, and they're all stationed the hell away from everybody with unfriendly barbed wire and MPs around them. The only way I found out who they were was from asking some of the Marines, and they. "At this point, the video breaks up, turning Emilio's face into a collection of squares before returning to normal.

"Do you want me to research these guys?"

"No. Don't worry about them, Clem. I've got a bunch of guys in Singapore and military affairs covering that. There's more stuff that doesn't add up. I want you to look at some military hardware that has its origin in Alta California."

"OK. Go ahead and shoot."

"Well, there's been a lot of aerial activity in the desert. You'd expect that if they were looking for guerrillas. There are more than enough helicopter gunships and spyplanes doing overflights. But some of the helos landing here have white metal boxes jury-rigged on them from the Lodestar group, and that's in ...." At this point, Clem's video screen becomes a jumble of static. Clem tries redialing two or three times without success. After five minutes, he reestablishes a successful video connection.

"Howdy, Cowboy. We seem to have been kicked the hell off."

"Yes, indeedy," says Emilio. Clem can see him wink one eye as he continues. "I think I was talking about somewhere in New LA. Where was I when we left off?"

"You were talking about white boxes and Lodestar." The screen jumps and freezes before it returns to normal.

"Yes, I think little pitchers have big ears. I'll tell you what, Clem. There's other stuff I need you to research for me right now, but let's just concentrate on what we've talked about now for the time being. I'll try to give you some additional information through additional channels, but it won't be as fast as this one. I'll just tell you. Something down here smells big, -- really big, -- and spooky."

"One question before I sign off Emilio. How are you surviving down there? There aren't any hotel bars down there, much let alone any hotels"

"The Marines and the Mexican government have been really good to us. We've got our own captive cerveza truck, and they hauled star wagons all the way down here from Ensenada for us to sleep in. I have to share it with two other guys, but at least it's in the shade. As for food, we eat with the Marines." Emilio pauses.

"One more thing before I sign off. Can you get some nice cocktail glasses, lots of good tequila, five decks of cards, and some fresh limes down on the shuttle? I'd be grateful, and I might be able to talk to a few people over a poker game."

"Hey, Emilio, I'll arrange for everything ASAP. I'll just check on how we can requisition it all to you."

"Man, that would be great. I'm signing off."

It's getting closer to closing time for some people, and Clem goes over to Mbake Methune's desk to ask him a few questions.

"Oh Big Brother, what do you know about the Lodestar Group?"

Methune takes his eyeglasses down a notch so that he can look over them before he speaks. "How many volumes do you want? I could spend a few years telling you about the ins and outs of one of the finest companies in the military-industrial complex."

Celebrate Recovery®   LESSON 16

AMENDS

Principle 6:
Evaluate all my relationships. Offer forgiveness to those who have hurt me and make amends for harm I've done to others, except when doing so would harm them or others.

> *Happy are the merciful. Happy are the peacemakers.*
> Matthew 5:7a and 5:9

Step 8:
We made a list of all persons we had harmed and become willing to make amends to them all.

> *Do to others as you would have them do to you.*
> Luke 6:31 (NIV)

A _____ the hurt and the harm

"Do not judge others, and God will not judge you; do not condemn others, and God will not condemn you; forgive others, and God will forgive you."
(Luke 6:37 GNB)

M _____ a list

Treat others as you want them to treat you.
(Luke 6:31 LB)

E _____ one another

And let us consider how we may spur one another on toward love and good deeds.
(Hebrews 10:24 NIV)

N _____ for them

"Love your enemies and do good to them; lend and expect nothing back."
(Luke 6:35a GNB)

D _____ it at the right time

Each of you should look not only to your own interests, but also to the interests of others.
(Philippians 2:4 NIV)

S _____ living the promises of recovery

If it is possible, as far as it depends on you, live at peace with everyone.
(Romans 12:18 NIV)

Celebrate Recovery® — LESSON 16

Amends List

I OWE AMENDS TO	I NEED TO FORGIVE

LEADER'S FOCUS

How can you begin to live the promises of recovery? What promises of recovery have come true in your life?

© 2006 Celebrate Recovery

The Story of the Century

"OK," Clem pauses for a little sarcasm. "Let's say there's some new piece of military technology that's not quite ready for prime time, but they rush it into the field for use on helicopters in Mexico?"

Mbake immediately knows what Clem is talking about. "Oh, you mean the ZX-47 equipment? Yes that is experimental, but Lodestar is quite proud of what they've been working on." With that, the military affairs reporter turns his back to Clem and spends a minute or two pecking at his computer. Consulting the *Times* operations manual, he spends another half minute doing more typing in silence while Clem waits.

"There. I've just downloaded all the files and press release on ZX-47 to your station. I'm sure that you'll have hours of endless fun playing with your new information." Methune smiles smugly.

"Thanks for the help. That's good for a start, but can you give me the name and number of a real human being that I can contact?"

"Ah, yes, Little Brother. You want to talk to Charlie Fong. He's a research engineer, and he's been with the company since they started playing with transistors." Methune turns his back to Clem. This time a picture and short biography of Fong comes up on the screen, and the older reporter prints it out, handing it to Clem.

"Fong is the project director for the ZX-47, but you can't call him now. It's 4:30, and all the engineers have already left for home."

"Nice work if you can get it. Don't you think we're in the wrong line of work?"

"Ah yes. Government and government funded employees. I know them well. Obviously you've talked with the boss." Methune pauses expectantly.

"Of course, I'd be crazy coming over here to harass you if I didn't have permission, especially after our conversation the other day."

"I don't know what you're talking about. Ask me if you have any more questions. Happy hunting. As for me, I think I will say hello to my wife and children."

With that, Methune reaches for his fedora on the hat rack, and walks out of the newsroom.

Clem goes back to his cubicle to spend a few hours calling up files on the ZX-47. He does not know that his research is getting the broadest distribution. The ZX-47 is sensitive information to the World government. While technically a civilian project, its development has been based on what Lodestar scientists found in working on the magnetic interferometer. Because of this, all internet queries on the machine are closely monitored, and the robots make every effort to backtrack the source of any internet search. The *Times'* computer firewalls mask Clem's identity as he does his research, but this query sets off alarms in the military-industrial complex.

What the world defense establishment doesn't know is that Clem's transmissions are going to an even larger audience. Clem's rambles are also being broadcast to a tiny robot that digests his information, waiting to display the highlights of what it finds as a narrated slide show for a conference that's going to take place on the 45th floor of an ordinary looking skyscraper somewhere on the third planet from what Earthlings call Alpha Centauri.

WORLD TELEMETRY PROCESSING CENTER

Colonel Gordon "Gordo" Nkrumah is the Jedi master of the Mighty Wurlitzer. To the slightly larger number of people outside of the intelligence community who know about it, it's known as the Lodestar Deepbase III, a computer program designed to allow its operator to collate and sift through a wide variety of very different sources. The

The Story of the Century

insiders in the intel business call it the Mighty Wurlitzer because if you pull out the stops right on Deepbase, you can make some beautiful, powerful music.

Gordo is simply the best in the business. He's a hereditary computer geek. His father used to be a programmer for WNN. The first memory Gordo ever had as a baby is sitting on his father's lap while the old man worked a super graphic for the World Cup finals. His mother is still a professor of computer science at the University of Singapore. When Gordo junior was three years old, his birthday present was a laptop. Gordo is a shy and retiring person, more comfortable with machines than people. After he was appointed to the World Army Academy, he majored in computer science, minoring in mathematics with a specialty in logic. Graduating with high honors, he was immediately assigned to the World Security Agency where he's been ever since.

Gordo is only one of three people in the entire world who have full knowledge of the Deepbase III. To say that the Mighty Wurlitzer is user unfriendly is an understatement, but Nkrumah is blessed with a photographic memory. With his training and talents, Gordo can do the equivalent of Bach organ cantatas when he sits down at the keyboard, only what he does is to ferret out the most obscure and hidden information in an ocean of data, putting it together into a short, sweet coherent package for targeting intelligence.

The Office of the President emailed him an hour ago requesting a computer investigation of the events behind the massacre at Santa Ynez. Click click click click click. The first thing he pulls up on the screen is the order and routing slips for the delivery for the magnetic interferometer. A click pulls up WNN footage of the most recent coverage of the massacre. Seven more clicks, and he retrieves a map of North America, showing the route the magnetic interferometer took before it disappeared.

He sits and thinks for a moment. Given that the interferometer has disappeared in the deserts of Baja, where could it have gone? He types in today's secret code asking all networks for information on significant events recorded during February 19th and February 20th between San Quintin and San Ignacio. He sets some parameters on what he's looking for. Then he goes out for coffee and a gnosh while the computer does its search routine.

When he gets back, he has a list of 2984 collections of data encompassing 12,308,384 discreet items. With robots and key word searches, Nkrumah has worked through the emails for February 18th and 19th in just under two hours with nothing to show. He's grateful that there are so few to sift through. The middle of the desert is not a high traffic area. Just like any random sample of ordinary chitchat, mostly boring. Homesick Marines talking to their wives, girlfriends, and family back home. About a quarter of the messages are come ons for internet sex. Gordo always enjoys spying on other people's sex lives. In between glancing at selected emails, he spends some time doodling on paper. He's designing an algorithm to filter out irrelevant traffic from critical messages based on key words and phrases. He exits from Deepbase for a moment, testing his algorithm on the internet traffic file that he's created, and he finds it works.

February 20th and February 21st are different. Everything has changed in Baja. The colonel spends more time than he should have on the routine emails. There is the concern, the anxiety, the sense of desperation. Families and friends from all over the world are trying to contact Marines, trying to find if their sons or boyfriends are all right. And there are the Marines writing home to reassure parents and sweethearts. The colonel spends hours on this traffic, and then he finds one very strange report from a Coast Guard vessel. He reads it twice, and this begins to change his thinking on how to deal with the massacre.

The Story of the Century

About 0349 I saw something really weird. I was on watch and I saw what looked like a bright green star appear fifteen degrees above the horizon in the southeast. Through binoculars it looked like an egg. It moved rapidly towards the mainland and stopped for approximately ninety seconds. It then accelerated rapidly again, moving from the southeast to the south before blinking out and disappearing. I never saw anything like this before. I wish I had been drinking!

He thinks a bit, sipping on his fifth can of World Cola. The Marine convoy appears to have disappeared off of the face of the earth. There are several alternatives. The convoy and its cargo could be hidden in the desert, waiting for the heat to die down. Or there could have been an attempt to move the cargo by some other way than by land.

His intuition tells him that it would be unlikely for anyone to try to smuggle the dead Marines' cargo anywhere now. That would mean that perhaps the interferometer was airlifted out. He returns to the main menu of the Mighty Wurlitzer, and he finds the back door of the World Reconnaissance Agency (the WRO). Click click click click… Gordo decides to call for an automated review of air radar traffic for the area in a twenty-four hour period before and after the massacre.

Nkrumah enters his password and the daily code, specifying general latitude and longitude for central Baja, and high gain image retrieval as his parameters. He waits until the menu appears on screen, and he clicks on Eager Beaver. On the submenu, he clicks on Archive. Eager Beaver is the spy satellite designed to capture unusual aerial activity.

With a few more data entries, he specifies the time periods and dates he wants searched, as well as a few other parameters. The WRO will do all the work for him, but it'll take a while. He leaves the computer to do the work for him overnight, and he calls it a day.

The next morning at 0800, Col. Nkrumah is back at work. Working his way through twelve layers of access codes, ID verification, and security clearance confirmations he finds that the WRO Image Intelligence Acquisitions Division has completed his work for him. He makes his menu choices, and he clicks on a few icons, finding a satellite map with color-coded air traffic. Light blue lines show the flight paths of airplanes headed to and from Loreto or Cabo. One red line is curious, starting nowhere and seemingly ending nowhere. The screen goes black for 10 seconds, and a small photograph appears. With one click, he enlarges it, and with another click he activates the movie. After thirty seconds of loading, an image fills the screen.

There's a lot of real estate to look at 500 kilometers up in space, but the satellite has captured the image of what looks like a green star hanging just south of San Pedro de Martir. With no warning the emerald dot goes from zero to 9000 kilometers per hour, stopping just as suddenly near the shore 30 kilometers NNE of Cachanilla. It's time to freeze the movie. Do the point and click. Magnification click. Magnification click click freeze. With a little computer magic and fuzzy logic, he calls up the image enhancement subroutines. Not only can he see everything as if he was only ten meters away, but he can follow the saucer's every move automatically. At a power of a thousand times, he sees the bay and the road, even if the whole picture looks as if it's made of tiny squares. There's an emerald green ovoid shape hanging above the landscape, giving the land a greenish tint. Carefully, he freezes the image and moves the cursor. He moves over to the surf. He sees what looks like a submerged jeep and lorry. He moves the cursor back to the glowing green light. The saucer's image is frozen on the screen.

Unfreezing the image, Colonel Nkrumah puts the movie into its slow motion mode. The saucer moves slightly and hovers over what appears to be a large wooden crate. The brilliant flash of blue light beams down on the box. Parts of the screen turns white. The green shape lifts the box, and the blue shaft of light turns off. For a moment,

The Story of the Century

the image breaks into random pixels until the computer catches up with the green egg's acceleration. Nkrumah backs out and reruns the whole thing three or four times, wondering what he's just seen. Then he saves the file and exits.

Looking at a manual for a moment, the colonel clicks for the appropriate security codes and enters what's needed for ACID. ACID stands for Alien Craft Identification Designs, a computer intelligence program classifying flying saucers by their shape, history, and origin. Where information is available, a saucer can be identified by the star and alien type associated with the ship. Nkrumah opens the UFO video file, pulls up a close up image of the saucer, and imports it into the ACID program. The computer screen goes black for only a second, and a blue screen appears with white lettering:

ORIGIN:ALPHA CENTAURI
TYPE:NEAR EARTH TRANSPORTER, CALLISTO BASE
   TYPE
PROPULSION: GRAVITY WARP DRIVE
OCCUPANTS: GREEN LIGHTS, POSSIBLY GRAYS,
DIMENSIONS: 10m X 5m X 5m

Nkrumah saves this with the UFO video file. By now it's almost lunchtime, and he realizes how hungry he is. He goes to what passes for the cafeteria near his secure area, and he puts his coins in the vending machine for his sandwich. While he's eating, the thought comes to him that General Caramehni has made a request for information to him in the hall about a magnetic interferometer. He isn't sure whether the files have been downloaded into his computer or not by GCHQ. The request is about a week old. Is there some tie in between the flying saucer and the magnetic interferometer?

There's that jeep and lorry in the surf. That's certainly circumstantial evidence. He feels a little stupid that he hasn't thought of that before, and he's worried about not responding to Caramehni as quickly as he should have. But if his hunches are right, he might be able to kill two birds with one stone.

At 1302, it's time to be a good little bureaucrat covering his bases. Nkrumah takes some breathing exercises for relaxation before making the call to Caramehni's office.

"How are you, General?"

"Just fine. Just fine. Do you have anything?"

"Yes, General. I've been working on your request this morning. I have some questions. Do you know what kind of escort and security vehicles were carrying the interferometer?

"Isn't that in the information I sent you?"

"No sir. Not that I've seen."

"Let me see a minute." There was a pause on the line. Nkrumah can hear the general in the background question his sergeant about the particulars.

"It says on my screen that Company B of the 16th Transport had one jeep as a command car and a five-ton lorry."

"That's very interesting, General. You'll be happy to know that you're the first person I'm telling this to. I've just found in my research what looks like an abandoned Marine command jeep and a five-ton lorry in the surf at this area --." He pauses to call up his Oilsource IV program onto his computer screen to see the exact location of the military vehicles.

"They're at a place called Bajia Gonzoga, General."

"Excellent work, Colonel."

"Sir, could you review for me one more time what you've found at your end General?"

There's a long silence at the other end of the line from Nkrumah. Finally, the general clears his throat and said, "Okay, Colonel, one more time. First, we had some telephone traffic in Mexico February 11th between the Cachanilla area and Mexico City referring to a magnetic interferometer. This was a Level 4 occurrence -- very unusual. We tried to get a fix on the call from Baja, but we only managed to isolate it down to a cell area. Someone called Guillermo phoned Juan Labastida, an undersecretary at the Mexican Ministry of the Interior. Labastida made contact with Gov. Esteban Salinas, who was responsible for transporting the interferometer from Arizona to Hermosillo. But this call stood out because it didn't appear to be consistent with the paper trail on the machine."

"Was there any fix on Guillermo?"

"No, we tried, but all we got was a phony name and address in the town of Cachanilla."

"What did you do then?"

"Over the next two weeks, we monitored all Level 4 traffic on the magnetic interferometer, but there wasn't anything too unusual about this stuff. There was some internet chat from a graduate physics class at Lagos University and a scientific trade show in Shanghai. All of this was in addition to the Level 4, Level 5 & 6 traffic going from Fort Huachuca to the Mexicans, Lodestar, and the Marines. All of this took place before the massacre at Santa Ynez, but we determined that all of this traffic was routine.

"Right after the massacre, only about nine hours later, we got a funny hit from the *New Los Angeles Times*. Someone in we think the news division did a query on the magnetic interferometer, and it happened just after Company B of the 16th bit the biscuit. We tried to ID the leak at the *Times*, but the paper's firewall is just too good."

Fortunately, while Caramehni's been talking Col. Nkrumah has been able to call up all the pertinent information on the screen. "Let me do the final wrap up, and I'll be back to you by the end of the day, General. Let's keep the Nautica Escallera just to ourselves for a few hours."

Oilsource is on the screen. The map displays the area around the Nautica Escallera. Nkrumah pulls away until he can see all of Baja California with one blue dot showing where the UFO hovered near the Nautica Escallera. Downloading the video file of the UFO, he does a conversion routine to the longitudes and latitudes of the green egg's flight path. A blue line now appears, extending from the Nautica Escallera, ending somewhere in the mountains in the interior 147 kilometers northwest of Loreto. Calling up the information on Guillermo's conversation is easy enough, and now there's a shaded area of the cell tower's calling area. It appears to cover the Ejidos San Mateo and San Bernardo. The saucer's flight path almost bisects the calling area. Last but not least, Colonel Nkrumah calls for a blue dot for Cachanilla. It's in the next calling cell area less than 16 KM away from Ejido San Mateo. Gordo can see that things are very tight in Old Mexico.

He thinks about the inquiries concerning the magnetic interferometer from Lagos and Shanghai, but they're not priorities. Science students and technical trade show dudes might be expected to make an internet inquiry. The big deal is the *New LA Times*. Nkrumah knows that their firewall is one of the best in the world. You can't crack them head-on. While the government can know with certainty that an internet hit came from the *Times*, who on the inside was responsible for the query?

Before he calls up the home page on the *Times*' site, he stops for a moment, taking some deep breaths. He needs all the concentration he can get. "Here's where we get the money." Nkrumah says out loud as he breaks into the newspaper's mainframe with one of with one of his special home-brewed computer worms. He knows enough not to try to track the mystery internet request for the magnetic interferometer.

That's too obvious, and the systems administrator will figure out that someone's hacking them. Nkrumah goes for the *Times'* personnel files instead. His queries will use less space, and will be far less obvious.

The message on the screen announces that the worm has done its job. Typing in a search for 'military affairs,' the colonel gets three names: Editor Pablo Lopez, Senior Correspondent Mbeke Methune, and Junior Correspondent Clem Reader. A search for 'science and technology' shows that Nam Phoc Tran is the editor, Joaquin Saloberto is the senior correspondent, and Fidel Ochoa is the junior correspondent. 'Mexico' shows Emilio Robles covering Baja, and Fernando Flores as the Mexico City correspondent. Gordo harvests these names along with all the individuals' personnel file information.

Then he shuts his computer down. Leaving his office, he heads for the CIA's main library. The computers there appear to the *Times* mainframe as if they're just another cyber café in Kuala Lumpur, and there will be no danger of contaminating his own machines. Getting on the *Times'* home page, Nkrumah indicates that he's a premium subscriber. He asks for a series of queries from the newspaper archive, and he finds lots of stuff on recombinant DNA, cloning, and gene splicing. An archive search on UFOs and extraterrestrial life reveals nothing. "Good" Nkrumah thinks to himself. Eventually, he pulls up 153 articles. Using a standard subroutine, the colonel arranges them into the following categories:

#1. magnetic interferometer / ZX-47

#2. Santa Ynez massacre

#3. Atzlan Liberation Front / Mexican rural poverty / Baja

#4. Gov. Esteban Salinas / Mexican domestic politics

Downloading this onto a CD for future reference, Nkrumah knows that he'll have to have a long talk with the Mexican desk later. Taking the information back to his office, he performs an author search. For the three articles related to the magnetic interferometer, he finds two old citations with Mbake Methune. These are basically rewrites of Lodestar press releases. Clem Reader has written an article only a few days old on the ZX-47. Nkrumah makes a note of Reader's name. For Mexico, he finds that Emilio Robles had written 79.3% of the articles on the Baja massacre, with Fernando Flores penning 18.8% of the articles. 1.9% of the articles have the double byline of both Robles and Clem Reader.

Nkrumah's eyes get big. Looking more closely at one of the articles under dual byline, it appears that one of the reporters is talking about his personal experience with the Ybarra Loncheria before the massacre. Talking to himself again in excitement, he says, "Verrry interesting!" Clem Reader is moving up in the charts with a bullet. There doesn't appear to be significant information from the other author searches on either #3 or #4, except to indicate that Flores and Robles are still suspects.

It's time to go back to what he's stolen from the *Times* personnel files and the number one suspect. Clem Reader's basic personnel information came up on the screen. Bingo! Gordo finds these words:

"In case of emergency notify:
Victoria Reader Castellon, Castellon Construction Company
PO Box 1142
Ejido San Mateo, BCS, Mexico
Phone: 001 52 615 161 11547

It's not anything that would hold up in a court of law. It's still only preliminary intelligence, and yet Col. Nkrumah needs less than a second to think. He strokes his chin. It's time to pick up the telephone.

"General Caramehni, -- Gordo here. I'm going to call the President."

Clem is calling from New LA to Aunt Victoria. He's been worried about what's been going on down in San Mateo.

The Story of the Century

"Hello, Auntie, how are you doing?"

"Oh Clem, how nice of you to call. I wasn't expecting this. Was your trip up north good?"

"Things are going okay. Work as been very good lately. I got a raise today."

"That's wonderful. You must be doing well. I hope the rest of your life is as good."

"No problems Auntie." Clem pauses. "Say, I wanted to ask you a question. Did Uncle Carlos ever tell you about that gizmo we talked about?" He can practically feel a cold blast of air coming through the telephone. Aunt Victoria replies.

"Yes, he told me everything he knows about it. But it wasn't much. I will tell you that this is one of the most stupid stunts that he has ever played in his life. He's lucky he's still alive, and it wouldn't be just me killing him. I'd have to start giving out numbers. If I catch him so much as doing anything like that ever again, I'll divorce him and make a big scandal and take everything he's got."

"Well, that's a little bit more than I wanted to know. I hope Uncle Carlos learned a lesson. I'll tell you what, if you want me to give you moral support, I'll call Uncle Carlos and grill him."

"That's probably not a good idea. I've done a good job of humiliating him. Besides that, I don't think he should be going around explaining what he's done. It was pretty shady."

While Clem is talking on the phone, he looks at his computer and notices that his story has gotten approval and prominent placement on the front page. "Well, okay, Auntie, you're the boss, you know. I just got my first front page story in a long time. You've got to be just about ready to eat dinner. So I'll let you go. Say hello to Uncle Carlos for me. I love you very much."

"I love you too, Clem. When do you think you're coming back home?"

"Not for a long time. I'm too busy in Bollywood. I did a little story on the Santa Ynez massacre, but I don't see being sent on assignment anytime soon."

At this point, something unexpected happens. The iciness of Aunt Victoria's first reaction is nothing compared to the cold that he feels now. There is silence. It seems to go on forever. Finally Clem decides to speak.

"Auntie, are you all right?"

There's a cough on the other end of the line. At last, Victoria speaks with a dead voice. "There's no reason why innocent children needed to die because of drugs or money." At this point she hangs up the phone. Clem listens to the disconnect. There isn't one click. There are three of them -- click click click.

Uncle Carlos doesn't come home until an hour later. He's gotten the road contract for the mainland, and there had been work to do at the office. The kitchen staff has prepared some tortilla soup and salad, and the servants have gone home. Aunt Victoria and Uncle Carlos are now home alone. Dinner is uneventful. They talk small talk -- talk about Clem's phone call, about village gossip and what needs to be done around the house.

It's dark outside, and the wind has picked up from the north. It's blowing quite strongly. They retire to the living room to watch the hologram, when they're interrupted by a knock at the patio door. This is unusual, as people usually announce themselves by ringing the bell at the gate outside.

"I wonder who that is?" Carlos gets up from his chair, and Victoria follows him. She's curious too. A man and a woman stand at the patio door. The Castellons' spines stiffen immediately, sensing both threat and danger. Carlos stands at the French door with one hand on the knob. Victoria hovers close behind.

"*Buenos noches,* what can I do for you?" Carlos asks sternly, masking his fear. It's well past sunset now, but both strangers are wearing the darkest wraparound sunglasses. It's a miracle that they can even see. He's wearing a black fedora and a somewhat antique dull black suit with a stiffly starched white shirt and narrow black tie. She's wearing a severely tailored black suit made out of the same material as the man, and her blouse has a stiffly starched white ruff. Her hair is pure white, done up in a very hard permanent wave. Carlos can't help but notice her giant lapel pin. It looks as if someone had turned a real crysthanthemum into solid gold. Both have withered, albino faces with almost no noses, and they're scowling with tight, thin lips. The man reaches into his pocket and takes out a wallet, holding it in front of Carlos' face for inspection. There is a solid six-pointed badge.

"We're **special** agents with the World Security Agency."

Carlos doesn't know what to think. "Do you want to sit down? We can sit at the table over there." He motions to the furniture on the patio. No way does he want these creeps inside of his house. He continues. "I didn't catch your names. My name is Carlos Castellon, and this is my wife Victoria." As courageous a woman as Victoria is, she's actually trying to hide behind Carlos. There is a silence that seems to last forever. The two strangers are impassive and silent, not moving. The woman in black speaks now. She has almost the same voice as the man.

"Yes, we know who you are. Our names are not important."

Here the man in black takes over as if he had the same brain as the woman. "We have a warning for you. If you value your lives --," Here is another horrible pause. "You'll never mention the words 'magnetic interferometer' -- **ever** again." He pauses, and then he continues without taking a breath. "And it's not nice to throw away mobile telephones."

Carlos and Victoria are dumbstruck. There is weirdness, and there is high weirdness, but this is off the charts. They turn to look at each other with fear and amazement, and then they turn again to face these horrible strangers. They're in for another surprise. Although it's only been a second or so, Carlos runs to turn on all the yard lights. They feel their hearts fluttering in their chests. There's no one on the patio, and there's no one on the property.

ON LINE

So, Esteban darling, do you have time to see me in New LA? I'd really like to see what kind of sweetener could be added for the pictures. Ravi Guptara treats me like a jerk, and he refuses to sign the contract until the Mexican government can throw in a million dollars more. I need to see you so much. XOX Saroyan

OFF LINE

Saroyan Pashogi is holding court at the Tour de l'Argent just outside of Malibu. It's the typical Bollywood restaurant scene -- 150 ivory tapers burning, acres of fine white linen, horribly tasteful interior decorating with teak paneling, a red velvet cord holding back the peasants, five pieces of sterling silver and vermeil tableware for each setting and six muscular, well dressed menacing men, each one wearing inky black glasses and earpieces. In the center of it all is the most beautiful man in the world sitting with the most beautiful woman in the world.

Behind this fluff is ambition. She's become a star in part by sleeping with countless men and not a few women. World news organizations have made hundreds of millions of dollars on her romance with her most recent boyfriend, Rhadavan Khrishna. What the press doesn't know is that Saroyan has already become deeply disenchanted with the soccer goalie. She appreciates his strong, muscular body, but she's realized that soccer players are still just soccer players.

SP, as the press called her, has already started exchanging email messages with Esteban Salinas, the Governor of Mexico. More than anything for Saroyan this is just a business proposition, as she's gotten the Governor to commit money to her project that she badly wants to get the studio to greenlight. It doesn't hurt that Saroyan has never gone to bed with a world leader before, and besides that, the guy is handsome.

It's been a long 36-year journey for the Iranian superstar. Beneath the glamour, behind the façade of the most beautiful female body in the world is a lonely little orphan girl from New Tehran. She showed some talent in school plays, and she won a beauty contest in high school. Out of more than 3,000 young women who auditioned for a Double Happiness soy milk commercial, she walked away with the starring role. This got her a bit part in a Bollywood musical, and Saroyan distinguished herself by capturing everyone's attention even when she was in a crowd scene. The rest, as they say, is history.

These thoughts are far from her head as she greets other celebrities and drinks champagne while the camera lights bathe the whole scene with their intensive white glare, taking in the star of *The Maid of Givenchy* and her most handsome boy friend. Saroyan has allowed the paparazzi into the restaurant, and they look lovey-dovey for the media-fish as they pose in Booth #1. The news hounds shout questions and take almost as many pictures of Krishna as of SP, but the young soccer goalie has a petulant, quiet and sullen air that contrasts sharply with the breathless, razzle-dazzle of the sex goddess. It's a small miracle that either Saroyan or Rhadavan manages to take a bite of their $500 per plate meals.

SP's meal includes a fine assortment of sushi, baby greens salad dribbled with vinaigrette dressing, and a caramelized pear in brandy sauce. Rhadavan's meal consists mostly of a one-kilo tenderloin steak well done with a few potatoes. Khrishna calls the waiter over and requests a jar of mango chutney that he promptly slathers all over the steak. Saroyan is secretly horrified.

"Mmmmmm!" he says, "just like Mummy used to make!"

Saroyan pays for the meal, and a crowd follows the 'happy couple' outside. On their way out, Saroyan turns to the maitre'd and says, "Tell Victor thanks for everything." At the valet parking they wait for Rhadavan's latest toy. Treasure hunters were wandering in the ruins of Las Vegas when they discovered an underground bunker, and inside the intrepid explorers found the world's largest collection of antique cars from the 20th and 21st Centuries. Rhadavan spared no expense in bidding for one of them at auction. Then he spent an additional $500,000 or so to restore it, customize it, and convert it to hydrogen fuel. The press churned out megawatts of coverage on this artistic project.

The black 1932 Dusenberg coupe pulls up to the front door of the restaurant, and the doors open for Star and Star. Rhadavan tips the attendant, and they speed down the Pacific Coast Highway in the direction of downtown NLA. Rhadavan turns briefly to Saroyan as the moon shines on the water. With that killer smile he says, "Your place or mine?"

"Mine." Saroyan says somewhat absentmindedly. Rhadavan loves his car. Saroyan absolutely despises it. The car is like everything else about Khrishna. The guy might have a pretty face and a great body, but everything else about him simply screams, "I'm a baboon!" The car drives through the quiet residential neighborhood towards Alvarado Drive. Finally, it glides silently through the gate and up the short driveway to the garage. Saroyan lets herself out of the passenger side and walks to the front door. She says hello to Jeeves, the hologram butler standing at the front door, and he opens it. Both soccer player

The Story of the Century

and movie star move through the living room. She gets to use the bathroom first, and he follows.

Saroyan takes off her robe and climbs into bed, and a minute later Rhadavan enters the bedroom. He makes sure that Saroyan sees his purple silk boxer shorts with the soccer ball embroidered with solid gold threads, taking them off in front of her before he climbs into bed. Mr. Sticky Sweet Meaty Breath climbs up on top of her without so much as a "How do you do?" and starts humping away. Saroyan has spent months giving an Academy Award winning performance as someone who is somehow, actually passionate about this romance, but she's getting tired of this playacting.

Johnny Fuckerfast is done in a minute, but to Saroyan it seems like an eternity. She thinks about an incredible number of things while his hard, fleshy, sweaty body moves up and down on her almost motionless form. The first thing to cross her mind is the statement that Albert Einstein once said about the theory of relativity.

"A minute sitting on a hot stove can seem like an hour, while an hour talking to a beautiful woman can seem like a minute."

This is one of those hot stove moments. She spends some time thinking about her character, Doña Maria, in the remake of *Zorro* that she's trying to shoot in Mexico. She thinks about the mannerisms that she's going to have to act and the inflections of her voice. Rhadavan switches positions slightly as he speeds up, approaching climax. This distracts her.

The thing about Rhadavan is that he's very proud of his lovemaking ability. Saroyan always thinks about how tiny he feels inside of her. As he progresses in his up and down and up and down, his penis feels tinier and tinier until Saroyan can't feel anything downstairs at all. She thinks of Junior, her big fat gray cat. The first time that Junior started humping Missy M, her semi-wild tabby, Junior's penis was on top of

Missy's back instead of her vagina. Junior thought that this was just fine until Missy turned around and gave him a good smack. Rhadavan is just like Junior.

Just then, Junior decides to jump on top of the bed. He's been attracted here by several things. First, the bed is squeaking. The sounds of the bed indicate that sex is going on, and Junior likes sex, even though he's been neutered. Secondly, he smells beef sweat. Junior likes tenderloin steak. This is an irresistible combination.

Saroyan notices Junior beside her on the pink silk sheets. She reaches out with her right hand to stroke Junior's fur. Junior rubs appreciatively against her hand. Rhadavan suddenly notices the cat. He yells, "Oh Shit!" as the back of his hand sends Junior flying across the room. The cat yowls as it goes airborne. On his way out of the bedroom, Saroyan notices that Junior squats and sprays on Rhadavan's purple shorts.

Saroyan smiles and whispers, "Oooooooh" as Junior leave the room. This is as much to encourage Rhadavan to finish his work as it is in appreciative pleasure for what Junior has done. Her thoughts continue.

Why couldn't Rhadavan be more, well -- white? The sexual prowess of white men is legendary. White men all have supersized kabobs, and they make love for hours at a time. White men can do it five times a night, no problem. Saroyan has slept with a lot of men before, but she's never slept with a white man. The image of that *Times* reporter pops into her mind. He's a white guy, and he's kind of cute. She noticed the cute bulge in his white pants. What was his name?

At this point, Rhadavan comes, and he immediately slides off Saroyan in his usual ungracious manner. "Was it as good for you as it was for me? He smiles.

Saroyan gives a little V-shaped smile and says, "Of course, Dear." Then she lights into him.

"Why did you do that to my cat?" she cries.

"The stinking cat was on the bed while we were making out!" Rhadavan's sunny smile darkens just slightly.

"Junior didn't mean any harm! He's the only thing in the world that cares for me! You don't care for me!" She says this icily, clenching her perfect teeth.

"That's not true, Honey. Of course, I care about you." Khrishna says this half apologetically and half defensively.

"Care about me?!" Saroyan pauses for emphasis. "Care about me? That's a big joke, you -- you -- big baboon!" She throws a pillow at him.

Now Rhadavan knows that Saroyan is mad at him. "Now listen, Sweetie. I don't know what's gotten into you lately. You don't seem the same any more. Hey, you know I love you a lot." He thinks that this will be enough of a statement to answer any questions or doubts.

"If you really cared about me, you'd know how important Junior is to me!" she snarls.

"Oh, Baby. He's just a cat. Why do you have your tit in a wringer? Khrishna replies lamely.

"Just a cat!" Saroyan is now on the verge of tears.

"Gee, sometimes I think that fat furball is more important than I am."

"Now that you've figured that one out, you can just pack your stuff and leave!" A good deal of hysteria has now entered her voice.

"Oh, Baby --." Khrishna starts to talk, but he's immediately interrupted as a perfume bottle flies by his ear and smashes on the bedroom wall.

"Get out! Get out! Get out!" At this point Saroyan is a banshee. Anything and everything she can get a hand on is being used as a missile.

Although Rhadavan does not have a particularly high IQ, even he begins to realize that discretion is the better part of valor. Crouching and ducking as rapidly as possible, he gathers his clothing as he beats a retreat for the door. His last words to her before he slammed the bedroom door were, "Next time, go fuck your cat!"

Saroyan continuous sobbing, her faced buried in her pillows. She hears the Dusenberg go down the driveway, burning rubber. Missy M is rubbing up against her perfect, naked thigh.

BELLAGIO HOTEL

Having a 10AM interview with the most beautiful woman in the world at one of the most expensive hotels in the world is not as romantic as you would imagine. A 10AM interview usually means getting to the hotel by 9AM to inspect the press packet while waiting on chairs in the hallway outside of the Imperial Suite. Clem is number 6, which means that he gets to observe media things numbered 3,4,5,7, and 8 and their entourages.

Two news hens powder their noses. One cameraman sits around with his head hanging down, his arms hanging between his legs, obviously working off a major hangover. Another cameraman looks surprisingly like a shaggy bear with his short, dirty hair and scruffy beard. The bear is reading a comic book. YTV's representatives are clearly a group to themselves, resplendent in their greasy purple hair, tastefully ripped and sown back together pieces of clothing, and dark wraparound sunglasses. The purple hair group is chattering like a family of magpies among themselves. The whole scene reminds Clem of some surreal waiting room at a Beverly Hills dentist's office.

Ms. Pashogi's personal assistants disrupt the waiting room periodically, hovering over the news crews to make sure that everyone has enough water, juice, coffee, tea, and pastries. Every fifteen minutes or so an incredibly slender, callow black clad minion will whisper in a news dog's ear that it's time to get ready. Mr. Hangover gathers his gear together, while a news hen looks at herself in a mirror before a personal assistant opens a door for them. Pepe escorts one TV crew out before motioning the next crew in.

When Clem is ushered into the suite, Pepe escorts Clem over to Saroyan, talking to him while he shoos the hired help away. SP is resplendent in her form fitting black gown complementing her smoldering dark eyes and lustrous hair that falls to her shoulders. The hotel suite is resplendent, too. It's like a large living room in an English country manor. The recessed and molded walls and ceilings are tan and taupe, and the overstuffed furniture in crème and ivory brocade clusters around a late 18th Century mahogany coffee table. The sex goddess is seated in a cream-colored silk club chair at one end of the room. Kleig lights have just been turned off, and she is being attended to by a maid serving her water and a smock-clad make-up man attending to her nose and forehead.

He can hear her say, "Thank you Guy, I don't need much powder right now. Maybe later when the lights are on," as he walks towards her.

The movie star dismisses her helpers and gets up out of her chair to shake hands with Clem. Pepe is there saying, "Saroyan, you've met Clem Reader from the *Times* before. He's doing a major piece on you." Then Lopez seems to disappear. Star and Reporter make eye contact with each other, and shake hands. Eye contact and hand touching lasts just a bit longer than usual before they sit down. Clem is surprised.

He's at the edge of a giant sofa, putting his recorder down on the end table as he takes out his pad and pen. This ritual is about as freewheeling as a multinational's presentation of its annual report. Everything about star interviews is structured. The first fifteen minutes are to be spent discussing Ms. Pashogi's latest movie *The Maid of Givenchy*, a typical Saroyan Pashogi movie in theaters scattered from here to the wild reaches of Angola. Then time is to be spent on what she's bought lately (like some $500 shoes and a big fat sapphire necklace).

Two minutes can be spent on her appearance at the Tour de l'Argent with the love of her life, Rhadavan Khrishna. The last six minutes is set aside for her upcoming new movie, *Zorro*. *Zorro* is seen as a daring breakthrough for the star. SP is branching out, trying her hand at production in addition to starring in the movie. The negotiations with the studio are not complete, and Pepe hopes that SP's conversation about striving for more depth, complexity, and maturity will be a publicity push that can apply pressure on Ravi Guptara. Clem is also supposed to ask about the rumor as to whether Antonio Matamoros is going to costar. That's the way it's supposed to go.

Banter between Star and Reporter seems loose and unstructured, but in actuality, the actress is repeating her lines for the sixth take of the day, with more to go before the celebrity lunch at noon. Both Reporter and Star have multiple thought balloons running through their heads as they recite their lines in the script.

REPORTER: "Tell me about Maid of Givenchy."

STAR: "I loved making it. It's the kind of story that's a fantasy set in the court of the French king. I'm an innocent young woman who finds herself suddenly caught in the spider web of a plot. I love doing love stories that are sweet and romantic, but with just a whiff of danger and intrigue. It was intense working with Hu Yabang. Every time I work with an actor like Hu, I learn so much."

One thought balloon that both share is, "What time is it now?"

The two internal voices also say, "How's my face? Am I looking sincere enough? Do I have the right degree of animation and emotion? Am I being appropriate and attentive enough in my body language?"

The Story of the Century

REPORTER:"Is it strange doing a role that's set so far away from where we are today? After all, Louis XIV is ancient history. Why should people see this picture?"

While Clem is asking this question, both he and Saroyan think, "How is Pepe doing over there in the corner?" SP's manager is sitting in a club chairin the corner. The small, fat man with the eagle beak is the official attitude inspector, in addition to some of his other functions. Although he's famous for his charm and deference, it's obvious that nothing escapes his oversight. Everything has to be just right. He earns his 10%.

STAR: "*Maid of Givenchy* is a picture that has universal appeal. You could put the story into a contemporary setting, but it wouldn't have the atmosphere, the costumes, or the spectacle. It's the kind of picture that everyone can see and relate to. If you liked *My Last Love Affair*, you'll love *Maid of Givenchy*."

As they run through the litany of questions, several things happen that are unusual. Saroyan Pashogi stares more intently and longingly than usual. Once or twice, she glances down at Clem's crotch before returning her gaze to his eyes, smiling slightly more than usual. Clem's just doing his job, but he's oblivious. He thinks to himself, "Is there anything wrong with my shoes?" After a while, Clem begins to sense that Star might have more interest in him as more than as just a publicity transmitter. This makes him a little nervous, but he keeps to the script.

REPORTER: "How was Tata Studios in its support for you doing this picture?"

STAR: "As usual, they were fabulous. I can't thank Ravi Guptara enough for giving me the chance to play in a starring role in a picture as great as this. They gave me absolutely everything I needed, and Jackie Chan is just an incredible director."

At this point, Star's thought balloon goes like this. "If I get stuck in another oat burner like this one more time, I'm going to slice my wrists. But I was tied into the contract, so like what choice did I have? And as for Ravi, what a schmuck! I hope he chokes, but not before he gives final sign off on *Zorro*."

Reporter's thoughts are different. In addition to playing his part, Clem's mind is filled with fear, apprehension, anticipation, and lust. At some basic level, he identifies with her. Unconsciously, his body shifts closer to her, signaling to her, "I'm deeply interested in you." But at the same time, he's cool and professional.

Saroyan emotes on, talking about her role as Therese, the good wife of an evil duke, who is slowly drawn to love a humble but handsome dance instructor. The Duke of Givenchy discovers their passionate romance, and he has her true love thrown into prison for plotting against the King. Therese discovers that the Duke is the one plotting against the King, and courageously tells him the truth during a court ceremony. All of this is sandwiched between six songs and three dance scenes.

Saroyan is thinking that Clem is not only sexy, but a real human being -- not like that creep, Rhadavan. This reporter seems intelligent, sensitive, and interesting. Saroyan unconsciously moves closer towards Clem, coming so close that she touches the sleeve of his jacket with her hand. By now, Pepe has discovered that the interview is going off track. His eyes begin to bug out, and he puts his hands to his forehead in an expression of exasperation. The interview should have sounded like this:

REPORTER: Tell me about your relationship with Rhadavan Khrishna.

STAR: Fabulously. Maybe you were at the Tour de l'Argent the other night. We had a fabulous time. He's in training now for the World Cup. We talk on the phone every night now that he's in Rio getting ready for the big game." Instead, it goes like this:

"You know, I couldn't make it to Tour de l'Argent the other night.

The Story of the Century

"That's okay. You know how some publicity events are."

"So, how's your boyfriend?"

"Do you want to know? Do you really want to know?" Saroyan's eyes begin to get red and moist. There is a pause. "I'm not seeing him anymore. I can't take it from him any more. He's too possessive and crude. We have nothing in common." She grasps his arm, and realizing what she's done, she suddenly pulls back to formal interview position. Clem instinctively puts his notepad down and holds the movie star's hands between his own. This gives Saroyan a case of the secret shivers inside.

"Gosh, that's all right. You can feel like that if you want to." Suddenly both Star and Reporter feel a presence hovering over them.

"Why didn't you tell me that you had broken up with Rhadavan?" From the angle where Saroyan and Clem are, Pepe looks quite a bit like an eagle, a bald eagle.

"I'm sorry, Pepe. It just happened, and I didn't want to upset you."

"Well, dear, we could have handled it. As a matter of fact, we can rearrange things before lunch." Pepe snaps his fingers. Three personal assistants appear from out of the woodwork.

"Juan, did you know that Saroyan has broken up with Rhadavan? Did you, Jesus? Norma, put a little make-up on Saroyan. "Appropriately chastened, both Star and reporter eventually get down to business.

REPORTER: Now what about your next movie? I hear that *Zorro* is going to be something of a breakthrough picture for you."

After the Q and A is over, things begin to degenerate again. Saroyan holds Reporter's hand between hers. She gets up out of her seat and continues to hold Clem's hands for two or three beats before she says, "Thank you, Clem." By now, Pepe's in the Saroyan zone, effusively thanking Clem before ushering in the camera crew from YTV. The only clue in the hall that something's amiss is that the unflappable

Pepe seems flustered and Reporter seems mildly befuddled. Clem is actually blushing. Saroyan notices this, and thinks he looks even cuter. As an aside to Clem, Pepe rolls his eyes before he lets him go.

"Thank you very much, Mr. Reader. You provided a badly needed breath of fresh air. We'll make all the necessary adjustments before the lunch at noon."

Instead of hanging around the waiting room, Clem wanders down to the hotel lobby in search of a secure location. In a small courtyard, he opens his phone and dials the *Times* main number.

"Chollie Knickerbocker, please. This is Clem Reader. Chollie? How are you doing? I've got a hot one for you. Yeah, it's big. You can put it on the web right now. This is a world wide exclusive, a scoop. Saroyan Pashogi announced today to this reporter that she is no longer involved in any way, shape, or form with soccer star Rhadavan Khrishna. That's right. Not even Pepe Lopez knew about it. I got it straight from the horse's mouth. That's right. She told me personally, and she had to know it was for publication. Pepe Lopez is going to break the news after lunch, but we've got at least a one-hour jump on everyone else. Yeah, I imagine it might be front-page news. See if you can call up Khrisna for confirmation. It was definitely unexpected. I'll see you later."

At 11:20 a smaller complement of journalists gets on the bus for the drive to the press lunch. Clem is feeling pretty smug as the bus drove south on the Pacific Coast Highway. It isn't every day that any kind of reporter gets a scoop of this proportion. In a day or two, there will be headlines all over the world, and he, Clem Reader will have been the guy responsible for breaking the story. Pablo Lopez will be in his hip pocket for at least a few weeks, and Chollie Knickerbocker will be his most obedient servant for life. But other thoughts run through is head as the bus passes by what had once been called Dan Blocker

Beach. Clem is surprised at his wonderful luck in being able to break such a big story, but he wonders why he got the story first and not some worldwide hologram reporter.

Now, the press bus pulls up to SP's white modern mini-mansion overlooking the San Fernando Valley. The five palm trees in the front are all more than a hundred years old, and they cast tall, narrow shadows on Alvarado Drive. Jeeves is standing by the door giving directions for the meal and camera placements. Inside, the reporters find a large, sparely furnished living room and dining room, with the glass wall looking out onto the baby blue kidney shaped swimming pool. The weather has turned uncooperative, so a few black leather chairs are clustered around a glass coffee table where the star will eat and give more interviews. Everything has been arranged to make a good background shot for the photographers.

Pepe claps his hands for attention after most of the newshounds have nearly finished their box lunches. "Ladies and gentlemen, we have news for you. We have just learned that Saroyan has just broken off her relationship to Rhadavan Khrishna." Almost in unison, people begin to shout questions at the elegantly dressed, short, beak-nosed man and the star sitting, almost hiding, behind him.

"Why did you break up with him?"

"How did you decide to give him the boot?

"How did you feel when you told him it was over?"

Clem stays in the background. He takes in the scene. The reporters are a bunch of hyenas, looking for some fresh meat to tear apart. Pepe holds his hands up to quiet the mob, and he begins reading a statement that deflects some of the harsher questioning. It talks about the cost of being famous in different fields, how two people sometimes have to go off in search of different areas of interest, how Saroyan only gradually realized that she was drifting apart from him, and how as painful as the parting is, she only wishes the best for him,etc,etc. Assistants pass out copies, and Lopez indicates that after reading, reporters are entitled to ask questions one at a time if they're respectful and dignified. Clem opts for the food. He feels slightly unclean about what he sees happening. He doodles on his notepad, letting the recorder do all the work. He only drifts in and out of attention, catching snippets of SP's responses.

Star does her best, but she's an animal caught in the spotlights of hunters. Her answers are well thought out, but there's something missing. Sometimes she talks in a low monotone. Then the reporters yell at her to repeat her answers. Occasionally, she'll touch her cheek to catch a tear.

"Sex wasn't an issue in my decision."

"I love Rhadavan passionately. It's just that we can never be a couple again."

"I just want to say, that it's personal differences, and it's all my fault. We're two different people, and I wish him every success in the world."

The news jackals have their way with her, and the press conference begins to wind down. Saroyan is posing for photographs as if nothing has ever happened. As usual, there's that indescribable chemistry that exists between Saroyan and a camera. From whatever angle, it's impossible to take a bad picture of her. Even when she was admitted to hospital for an appendicitis attack, and the press had nearly smothered her, she still delivered that irresistible radiance to the electronic beasts that captured her image. Today's no exception, and yet Clem is surprised. Saroyan is moving her hands and legs ever so slightly from pose to pose, but she's looking at him all the time. It's as if he is the only person in the room, and Saroyan looks at him as the only person who ever mattered in her entire life.

Pepe thanks everyone for coming and the crowd makes moves towards getting back to the bus. While the camera crews pack up, Saroyan goes to Clem alone, getting close.

The Story of the Century

"You're not like the others are you?" she says.

"What do you mean by that?"

"You didn't fall for the publicity tricks at the Tour de l'Argent, and you weren't shouting rude questions about my sex life for an hour and a half."

"I'm not that kind of boy. I really am here to do a story about you and *Zorro*." By now this statement is more than a white lie.

"Can I whisper a little secret to you?" At this point, Star gets closer to Reporter, putting her hand to his ear. "I think you're absolutely right. We need to talk more -- privately. Can I borrow your pen and paper for a minute?"

Clem immediately obeys, flipping his notebook to an empty page. He hands his pen and paper over to Star. Saroyan writes for ten or fifteen seconds before handing pen and paper back.

"This is my private number, and that is my personal email. You can call me any time to set up an appointment." She gives him a brief peck on the cheek and walks towards the glass door leading to the Japanese garden. She coyly turns and waves before she disappears. Clem is stunned and immobile until Pepe, Jeeves, and a personal assistant surround him.

"Are you ready to get on the bus, sir?"

Clem has taken the trolley back the *Times* Building after the press bus dropped him off. For the most part, he's been unconsciously focusing on the bulge in his pants, which has grown quite a bit; and it's refused to lie down. His conscious thoughts are fixated on the movie star. Clem calms down by the time the elevator door opens on the fourth floor, and he sees Pablo Lopez waiting at the door.

"Come on in, Clem. Have a cigar on me." It isn't every day that Pablo Lopez shares one of his Cubans with ordinary press wretches.

"That was some scoop you got, son."

"It wasn't anything, boss. I just happened to be in the right place at the right time."

"So, you were just sitting there, in front of her, when she spilled the beans?"

"Yup."

Lopez comes right to the point. "Look, I talked to the big boss, and she was impressed. How does an instant bonus sound to you?"

"Gee, I don't know what to say."

"Well, you've been doing plenty good work lately, and I want you to do a story on Lodestar. You said you wanted to do something military."

Clem's in a daze, and he shakes Lopez's hand. He walks back to his cubicle. There's been a lot of action at his desk while he's been away. One note is from Alejandro Wong, a project Engineer at the Lodestar Group. Mr. Wong wants to set up another appointment about the ZX-47. Yet another note is a generic looking thing from Pepe Lopez, thanking Clem for taking his time today at the interview. The most important note is an animated tape loop. Clem opens it up and turns the volume on his computer up just a bit. It's Saroyan Pashogi.

"I just wanted to thank you for the way the times handled the story about me. Can we get together a little later today?" She's breathless and demure. Clem's brilliant intuition tells him it's more than just a publicity thank you. He thinks a moment, and he replies by email.

"I'm sorry I missed you, but I was busy. But I usually get off work before six o'clock. Maybe we can go out for sushi later on. Get back to me so we can make arrangements."

In the middle of typing up Saroyan, Alejandro Wong appears on the screen from Lodestar. "Just a minute, Mr. Wong. I'm finishing up an email." Clem is happy that he doesn't have to play phone tag any more. It's a good sign that Wong has called him. Perhaps the Lodestar executive has run out of real things to do, and actually wants to talk to the press one more time about some white box with secret electronics, welded underneath some helicopter cruising the Mexican desert. This is the ZX-47 story.

I hate to interrupt the story, but this is an excellent time to look at some of the most current thinking as to what constitutes the nature of time and space. One theory being bandied about by physicists and cosmologists concerns the concept of the multiverse.

In technical terms, multiverses are X-dimensional entities simultaneously existing in the same space and time. This is a helluva lot more interesting than it sounds like, kids. In English, this means that one action can go X-different ways at any time, creating way different consequences. Do I dare to eat a peach? Depending on your answer, you could be creating different realities. You never know. Let's look at some of the consequences arising from this seemingly simple phone call.

Take Example A. Clem talks to this engineering bozo, who spins one-eighth of the truth. But while he's lying, Marines storm an alien base in Baja where the magnetic interferometer is located. The professional killers are very good at greasing little green guys, but before they die, Attu radios for back up. The alien command decides they've had it with the killer rabbits, and they send a full-scale invasion force towards Earth. We can't fight against superior technology, and there's a global bloodbath that eventually results in the sterilizing of our planet so that the universe is safe from such murderous morons. In the process, they leave the Earth for a more worthy race, -- beings who were forced from their home by their sun turning into a red giant. This is one particular multiverse.

Or take Example B. Alejandro Wong actually decides to tell the truth.

"Yes, Clem, it's true. Lodestar put these white boxes on military choppers to look for a thing called a magnetic interferometer. This interferometer is a piece of alien, extraterrestrial technology that the government has had in its possession for some time. The Marines who were massacred were moving it to another base when they were ambushed."

Clem gets some news pals on the phone to hear this, and they decide that the guy isn't crazy, as he faxes them all sorts of documentation. On a whim, they decide to follow the evidence, and they get some military guys to admit that, "Yeah, that's what we're doing." Eventually, the World Congress raises questions, and the President is forced to acknowledge that, "The World Government is in control of some pieces of extraterrestrial hardware, and we don't know what many pieces are for, as they come from civilizations far in advance of our own." The government throws open the door on what it's got stashed up in the attic, and this leads to a profound philosophical evaluation of who and what we are. The aliens decide that we are at least capable of toilet training. They make peaceful contact with the Earth, and everybody lives happily ever after. Clem is famous for breaking the story. He becomes a media millionaire-star in his own right, and he marries Saroyan so they can settle down and have kids, just in time to appear on the cover of *Persons* magazine. Universe #2.

Now let's look at what really happens.

"Thank you Mr. Wong for getting back to me. I appreciate the time that you're taking out of your schedule for my questions. I'm interested in the ZX-47 program."

"Well, that is one project in my area of responsibility. What do you want to know about it? Usually, I talk with Mbake Methune at the *Times* about program questions. But I talked with people in your shop who told me that you're working on this for Mexico. Is this right?"

The Story of the Century

"That's correct. Our correspondent down there indicated that some ZX-47s are attached to military planes in Baja."

"Well, I'm not the person that you would want to talk to because I don't have any military authority."

"I understand that, but I'm interested in some of the technical information surrounding the ZX-47. Would you be more interested in being a background source, rather than being quoted. It sounds like you're not interested in publicity."

"Mr. Reader, you're a very clever man. I'm not for attribution"

"What can you tell me about the ZX-47 in twenty five words or less?"

There's a pause. He's the very stereotype of the California aerospace engineer, but the pictures on the wall of the corner office in the background show that he's not just a drone bee in the corporate hive.

"We're very proud of what we've managed to accomplish with the ZX-47 project. Although it's not ready for production yet, it shows a great deal of promise for the commercial market. This is proprietary technology, and we will closely control the ZX-47's licensing and distribution."

"We can see uses for it in the pure and theoretical sciences, in mining, geology, and perhaps military areas. In a nutshell, it is capable of producing extremely detailed maps of magnetic and gravitational patterns. It also has a nose for gamma rays, x-rays, and the decay products of radioactive isotopes. Scientists could use it to get better predictions of earthquakes. Miners could use it to find gold, silver, radium, and uranium deposits."

"How does the ZX-47 relate to the Marine massacre?"

The phlegmatic but amiable face grows dark and worried. "This is confidential and strictly off the record. I cannot be used as a source. He pauses. "They could be using the machines to search for old mine shafts in the area."

"How can I get confirmation on this?"

"I didn't say so, but Lt. Commander Juan Columbo is the Public Information Officer for the 4th Marine Division. He might be able to give you some kind of official statement."

Clem's mental shit detector is flashing a yellow light. From what he's read, the ZX-47 is a poor piece of equipment to be looking for abandoned mine shafts. If the Marines could corroborate it, Wong's story is good enough for now. And it's getting late. Reporters are some of the laziest people in the world, and Clem is in his fish mode where he's willing to digest any kind of crap without questioning it. It's time to wrap the story up.

"How successful has the deployment of the ZX-47 been?"

"We haven't heard any complaints yet."

"Can I get back to you tomorrow to ask some more technical questions?"

"Sure, I'm here any time. Lodestar likes to pride itself on having good press."

Okay, I'll try calling you about 4:00. Is that a good time?

"No problem. See you then."

Clem calls Lt. Commander Columbo, and he confirms that yes, the Marines are using the Lodestar technology. He's not at liberty to say what the equipment is being used for, or how successful it's been. The good Marine faxes Clem a press release that allows the reporter to send in a story for tomorrow's edition. There are delays in getting off the phone system and clicksall over the place; Kuala Lumpur, Singapore, and the conference room on the other star system are all ears. And the extraterrestrials have passed this call along to higher ups who have the power to destroy the solar system.

ON LINE

Although not highly publicized, military authorities have enlisted the aid of modern technology to hunt for the killers of Company B, of the 16th Marine Transportation Group Detachment, at Santa Ynez last week. With equipment and men on loan from the Lodestar Group, military helicopters have been plying the Baja in the hunt for the assassins. The ZX-47s as they are called, have been installed on helicopters to search broad areas of the desert for the suspects, using the most advanced secret technology. "While we have not yet located the killers, the ZX-47 has been incredibly helpful to us in narrowing the area we have to cover," says Lt. Commander Juan Colombo.

OFF-LINE

It's almost home time. Clem is goofing off for a few minutes shooting a toy basketball into a net that someone had placed a long time ago on the newsroom wall, just below the hologram of WNN. The anchor's giving a wrap-up on the nightly business beat. Hang Seng averages are up. Singapore Ordinaries are down. Sao Paolo is up fractionally.

Clem goes down the elevator with a herd of reporters, but he splits off on the street. The sun went down fifteen minutes ago, and it's gotten cold from a north wind. It's drizzling now. Clem pulls up his collar, and holds it around his neck. Seemingly out of nowhere, a black limousine pulls up along side him and stops. The window rolls down, and Saroyan pops her head out. "Are you cold? Do you want to eat?"

Clem looks around. There are surprisingly few people on the street. This is good, considering to whom he's talking. "Sure, can I get in?" Saroyan opens the door and slides over. "It certainly is good seeing you again." He thinks about holding her hand or giving her a kiss on the cheek, but he thinks again. It would be inappropriate.

"Where do you want to eat? We could go to l'Hermitage or the Palm. I'll pay, for the interview, you know."

Clem frowns. "Hmmn. That would be a bad idea. With the publicity you've been getting lately, you'd draw a stadium. I suggest someplace more discreet, somewhere were you could actually try to be anonymous."

"Ooooh! You are so clever. I can take care of being anonymous." She reaches into a large handbag on the floor and pulls out a plain silk scarf, a pair of horn-rimmed glasses, and a semi-transparent plastic raincoat. "Now where do you want to eat?"

"Do you want to go to this little newspaper bar near here? They serve some okay sushi."

"Do you like sushi too? I love it. It's my favorite food." Saroyan looks deep into Clem's eyes as she begins to fiddle with her disguise.

Clem is almost beginning to feel like a cool guy. "Driver, do you know where Sochi's is? It's about six blocks away from the *Times* Building. I can give you directions."

In no time, the limousine is there. Clem gets out of the limo alone and goes into the restaurant. He passes by the sushi bar where some reporters are clustered, whom he tries to avoid. He finds Sochi in the kitchen and whispers in his ear. The chef suddenly grins and gives an OK sign. Clem goes out through the back, around the alley, and gets into the car.

"Sochi says that it's okay to use the banquet room. It's not being used right now, and we can access it through the kitchen entrance, and Sochi has promised me that he will keep the back area private for us."

The limo goes up the alley, and stops by three trashcans and a dumpster. A door is open, and Sochi's waiting there expectantly. Clem

The Story of the Century

turns to Saroyan and says one of the most significant things in his entire life. "Do you think it's okay if you let your driver go back for the night?"

Saroyan looks at him for what seems a minute or longer (although it wasn't). She puts her hand to her chin, thinking. She smiles, "Sure. That's a good idea. Harold, you can go home now. I'll call you if I need you." Now Clem takes her hand, and with that they get out of the car to shake hands with the restaurant proprietor.

Sochi is absolutely flabbergasted that THE Saroyan Pashogi is actually in his restaurant. The short man with the paper hat and white apron bows low, and he has a grin on his face a kilometer wide. He wipes his hands, shakes hands with the movie star, and Saroyan promises him an autographed picture to hang in his restaurant. Sochi thinks to himself that now maybe he can send his three daughters to college.

It's not like any interview Clem has ever had before, and he'll remember almost every word for the rest of his life. They talk about many things. They quickly discover that they're both orphans, and they talk a long time about what that means to them. She tells Clem some of the things that she's not proud of. Saroyan realizes that she's self-disclosed more than she's ever told anybody, and she begs him for his confidence. The thought balloon in her head says, "I can't believe that I said that. I don't know what's happening to me. Am I getting crushed out?"

Clem listens sympathetically, and he promises total confidentiality. He puts his notepad down, never to pick it up again until it's time to go. He asks her to tell him more. She talks about the orphanage and how she finally broke into TV commercials. The rest, as they say, is history. He finds out that Saroyan is really a quiet, complex, and private person. Ultimately she says that she really feels alone. Clem says that he feels that way too. Saroyan says that at one point she had to face the possibility of living on the streets, and this concentrated her resolve. And she has to admit, that lucky first audition was the turning point in her life. She's very deliberate and cunning in marketing herself, but what she's created is alien and foreign. Clem's thought balloon reads, "I can't believe that I'm so calm and collected. With any other beautiful woman, I'd be slobbering like a dog and acting like a fool. I don't know what's happening to her or me. Is this going to lead to a relationship?"

Saroyan speaks. "When I see one of my films, I think that that woman must lead a very glamorous life."

There is another Saroyan Pashogi who will always follow her around. She's made of paper. She's made of film stock. She's made of electrons. She will never die. She will never have a period. She never has to brush her teeth or take a piss. She's never unhappy except for brief cinematic moments, and she never cries, except for as long as it takes to resolve the plot.

"Who is this woman who looks like me? She always looks perfect."

Now she's in her mid-thirties. She's begun to think about having children, but she's afraid. What could it do to her career? Does she really want children? And whom out of that ocean of men would she want to have a child with? She thinks long and hard about this question each time. Finally, she always said, "No."

"I'm afraid to have children too." This was an issue that helped to destroy his marriage to the beautiful Salma. Clem wants to tell Saroyan about Salma and his divorce. He wants to tell her about how much he's suffered, but he stops. He changes the subject.

"Where do you want to go in life? What do you want to accomplish now?"

This is a standard interview question that Saroyan has answered a thousand times. The rote phrases pop into her head, but she stops them from coming out. Now things are different. She talks about looking

The Story of the Century

at the prospects of growing older. Some day she knows that she'll be an ugly old hag. Not even the best doctors in Tokyo or anywhere else can prevent people from eventually getting old and dying. They can only slow it down. Saroyan wonders about how much more plastic surgery will be necessary to prolong her career. She's already had that butt surgery.

"Would you like to feel the *nalgas*?" This is a thought on both people's minds.

At this point Clem realizes that they've been talking for hours. Reporter and Star look at each other. Clem says, "It's getting late. Would you like a drink?"

Saroyan says, "Sure, but where can we go?"

"Get on your disguise. I'll show you where I do my drinking." Clem talks to Sochi and pays the bill. Saroyan leaves an extravagant tip on the table.

The couple walk down the alley towards the main drag. It's still drizzling. They get to the water taxi terminal, and it's getting close to the last run of the evening. There are less than a dozen passengers sitting on the terminal benches. Clem and Saroyan sit close together, and it's not just to keep warm. They talk about everything and nothing in one of those conversations that cover cabbages and kings. The more they talk, the more they find they have common bonds. It's one of those rare times in life when you find out that the stranger sitting next to you is in fact your soul mate.

The boat docks, and only five passengers get on board. No one's on deck. Clem and Saroyan go outside to watch the lights of the city through the mist and spray as the ship chops through the water. They try standing without holding on to something, but this doesn't work. The boat is moving too much. There's a bulkhead with a bench for two at the rear. They sit down. They look at each other, and Clem finally kisses her hard on the lips. For the next half hour they make out like amorous teenagers in nirvana. Finally the boat slows, docking at El Puerto.

By the time the yellow lights of the cargo cranes announce the end of the line, Saroyan has adjusted her hair, her makeup, and her disguise. Clem stays close by, feeling her body heat through his clothing. They walk arm in arm to Shanghai Red's. Shanghai Red's is famous as the bar where once upon a time, they rolled suckers to take one-way trips to Quito and Jakarta. The Chinese waitresses still have on these tight red Mandarin dresses, and they wear entirely too much makeup. The occasional drink of the house is still the 'Mickey Finn.'

Saroyan and Clem walk in, and the whole place lights up. Even with her disguise, Saroyan has the looks to launch any ship with her brick shithouse figure. Clem still wants to continue the conversation, but Saroyan wants champagne. Clem proposed boilermakers, and Saroyan compromises. A round of beer and a shot of good whiskey are given to everyone in the house while the bartender scrounges up some bubbly for the couple. Someone in the corner starts singing a naughty sea chantey, and everyone joins in. Forty-five minutes passes by like a second.

Clem bids farewell with Saroyan, his arm draping around a beautiful *nalga*. Saroyan will find out that night that it's true what they say about white men. The man in the corner who started the naughty sea chantey takes out a cheap paper notebook. Boson Ernesto Gomez, Naval Intelligence is making his report.

"Reader and Saroyan Pashogi seen exiting for home 2350."

NEW LOS ANGELES POLICE DEPARTMENT CONFIDENTIAL MEMO

TO: ALL WATCH COMMANDERS
FROM: C.Z. VAZQUEZ, CHIEF OF POLICE
DATE: 15/04/57
SUBJECT: SECURITY PROVISIONS FOR ONGOING WORLD INTELLIGENCE OPERATIONS USING THE 1421 CODE

World Special Intelligence operations now being directed at local citizens, some of whom are either very influential or famous. In order to assist the FBI and CIA in this area, there has been the request that the NLAPD take steps to limit the street presence of paparazzi or other free lance reporters and photographers on an 'instant notice' basis.

Upon World Security authorities request to this office, code 1421 will be broadcast by police radio. This will notify you of the need to immediately implement contingency plans developed that will divert attention away from a World investigation site.

For example, a radio report of a 1421 at Central HQ would mean that all units in the vicinity have five-minute warnings to divert paparazzi from a three-block radius around Central HQ. Arrests of reporters should be only used as a last resort.

The following techniques are more acceptable alternatives to a 1421 broadcast:

• Broadcasting of false incidents at prominent night clubs, restaurants, hotels, and galleries (see attached list)

• Employing homeless people and transients as obnoxious attention getters away from said locations near paparazzi.

- Using celebrity security personnel to create a situation that paparazzi will be drawn to, such as assaulting private citizens or drawing weapons.

Please take steps to implement contingency plans for the 1421 code within ten days. Please call my office if you have any questions.

ON LINE – CHOLLIE KNICKERBOCKER REPORTS -- FLASH --

It was a hot night just before dark when Gary Chindowary and his entourage arrived at the Macambo. The rugged, good looking star of *The Spy Who Loves Me* series got more than he bargained for when he was suddenly accosted by Jojo Zimbabwe, a deluded street person who insisted that he would play the villain against Chindowary in his next spy thriller. Things got even hotter when Chindowary's security personnel showed the hapless Zimbabwe their high voltage tazers. An elegant evening quickly dissolved into a three ring circus complete with the mandatory fire truck and ambulance, as well as the appearance of more than 50 paparazzi, all of whom immediately converged at the mayhem at the Macambo. This is one time when Chindowary wished that he had stayed in bed…

TRANSCRIPT OF TELEPHONE CONVERSATION,

30/4/57 - 5:03 PM

    S: Oh Clem. I've been waiting for you to call.
    C: Hello Saroyan. The paper is just about put to bed.
    S: I've missed you so much.
    C: I've missed you, too. I really want to see you.
    S: Is there anything the matter?

The Story of the Century

C: No – yes – I mean – It's very complicated. I've got all sorts of conflicting emotions in my head right now. You mean everything to me, but I don't want to get hurt, and I am hurt.

S: What do you mean?

C: Well, I was thinking the other night. We're really involved with each other, and I think that you feel the same way about me the way I feel about you. Now, we've been trying to be discreet, but I think that the word is beginning to get around that we're an item. The guys in the newsroom are beginning to look at me funny. You know, making jokes about me, and the paper has rules about fraternizing with people you're interviewing so that's one thing.

S: So, Clem, you were telling me that you wanted more than to do the Bollywood beat. Why don't you go into Pablo Lopez's office and ask to do more work on defense or Mexico or something?

C: Gee, that's a really good idea. I feel better already. But -- but -- there's another thing that's been bothering me.

S: What is it love?

C: Well, this shit, -- you know -- about the President, I mean the Governor of Mexico and that charity ball. It's just that you know, I'm a loyal and I uh, -- don't sleep around, and this publicity sucks. I mean, I'm not jealous, but this Salinas stuff is ripping me up inside.

S: Darling, darling. I can't tell you how much I love you too, but you know that, -- well it's my job not to be faithful (laughs). I told you that Governor Salinas can bankroll my project, and that can get me the greenlight. You are a special person to me. I can say things to you I can't say to anyone else, and you are the only one who can make me laugh. I need you for that, and besides, you are a great lay. Honey, you can be my friend any time you want.

C:That means a lot to me.

S:Do you want to come over right now?

C:I'd love to do that. You are so everything to me. God, I could make love to you a million times.

S:(giggles) Well, that would be a good start.

(breathing)

C:But you know I'm still really having problems with this whole thing. I mean I'm not a millionaire playboy.

S:Honey, you are so hot. Millionaire playboys are a dime a dozen. You are not a millionaire playboy. That's why I love you so much.

C:But there's more to it than that. My job is bothering me. I'm still covering the show biz beat while I'm doing some of the military stuff, and things are getting hot and heavy around here.

S:So, is that why you haven't seen me lately?

C:That has a lot to do with it. But Saroyan, you're so gigantic in the news lately, I'm afraid that one of the news vultures from *Show Biz Tonight* is going to take my picture, and then I'll be on the front page of the *Times*. A newspaper reporter is not supposed to become part of the story.

S:(pause) So, I'm just a source to you? Is that all I am?

C:No no no. Things could get really dangerous for me. You're a movie star. I'm a reporter. I've already had this feeling that I've been under surveillance by somebody outside of work.

S:So you're saying we need to be discrete.

C:Exactly. I think that that's best for both of us. I don't want to be a kept man with no job. But I'm crazy in love with you, and there's a lot of dangerous stuff going around lately, and it's not just my fear of flashbulbs, or getting on the cover of some trashy magazine. It's a lot more than that. Can I see you tonight?

S: Oh, Clem, I want that more than anything. What do you want me to do?

C: How about a walk on the beach? How does Zuma Beach sound in an hour and a half?

S: Oh, Clemmy, you are so smart. I'll drive down in my beater, and I'll meet you in the parking lot.

C: That would be great. Do you want to eat first?

S: I sinned tonight, and I ate burger already. When we get to the beach, why don't we go skinny-dipping?

C: I'd love to do that, kitten. Oh Saroyan, I've wanted to see you so much. You are my be all and end all. You are my own private goddess. I worship you.

S: Clem, you turn me on when you say that.

C: You turn me on every minute of the day. I really need to see you right now. My head has got so many different feelings inside. I'm confused and jealous and a little afraid.

S: Oh, Clem, darling. You sound like you need to put your head on my shoulder. We really do need to spend some time together.

C: Do you think we can wait until six?

S: I don't know. It's going to be tough.

C: Well, I better get going. I will sin with a burger or a hot dog too. It will only take me a few minutes to wrap up at work.

S: Okay, darling. Oh, Clem, I can hardly wait. You naughty boy. You need to see me more often.

C:I love you Saroyan.
S:I love you Clem
C:Byebye.
S:Byebye.

PRELIMINARY SURVEILLANCE REPORT ON SEXUAL ENCOUNTER BETWEEN CLEM READER AND SAROYAN PASHOGI AT ZUMA BEACH, CALIFORNIA, APRIL 30, 257 6:24 PM

Van was prepositioned on Pacific Coast Highway by 6:00PM. Agents with night vision and listening equipment were stationed on hills across highway and in parking lot. An additional agent was positioned on the beach with a boom mike. It is noted that surveillance conditions were extremely difficult due to wind and atmospheric conditions. Parts of the conversation were blotted out by surf and other noises. All tapes will be subject to analysis at FBI and other labs for enhancement.

Camera recorded suspect Pashogi driving into beach parking lot at 6:24 PM in a green '47 Mitsubishi Allegro two-door. At that time two other cars were parked in the lot. Background checks revealed that these belonged to XXXXXXXX and XXXXXXXX of Sylmar and Paso Robles. Request for further identification revealed no known connection to either Reader or Pashogi. Pashogi waited in car. She was wearing horn-rimmed glasses and a short red wig as a disguise Her car radio could be heard. It appeared that she was reading a book, later determined to be *The Death of Socrates*.

At 6:31, suspect Reader drove up and parked his car directly next to Pashogi's. Reader got out of car and talked to Pashogi at her car door. Pashogi remained inside. At 6:32, car belonging to XXXXXXXX drove away. Spot surveillance of all vehicles by special surveillance instruments observed no unusual electromagnetic transmissions, bugging devices,

The Story of the Century

or radioactivity. Reader got into Mitsubishi front passenger seat after XXXXXXXX left at 6:32. Pashogi and Reader spent twelve minutes kissing and fondling. At 6:44. XXXXXXXX of Paso Robles left.

Sound equipment did not appear to pick up any conversations from inside or around the car. Improper settings and a loose jack were determined as causes for audio surveillance failure. All visual surveillance was working, showing Reader and Pashogi in an extended kissing and fondling session. Reader appeared to have his hands underneath Pashogi's blouse. Pashogi appeared to unbutton Reader's shirt and pants. Suspects rebuttoned clothing before exiting car at 6:45. At that time, couple and surveillance crew were the only people in the area.

Pashogi and Reader started to run out of parking lot in NNW direction along the shoreline, continuing to a point 0.8 kilometers before stopping at 6:55. Sound technicians attempted to fix equipment, successfully tracking part of the conversation.

CONVERSATION RECORD, PART I, PARKING LOT AND BEACH

> S: Oh, Clem, darling, darling.
> (heavy breathing, surf, wind 45 seconds)
> C: If I told you you had a beautiful body, would you hold it
>   against me?
> (breathing, surf, wind, 38 seconds)
> S: Darling, I've been so lonesome without you.
> C: It hasn't been like I didn't want to see you. You've been in my
>   thoughts 24 hours a day.
> (kissing, moans, breathing sounds with surf, 2 minutes, 9
>   seconds)

S: I want to hear about how you feel, Clem. I felt so sad on the telephone listening to you

C: God, you mean so much to me. I've never experienced anyone like you before. But you've probably heard guys tell you that all your life. (pause) It's really weird reading about your romances with soccer stars and politicos when I go to the drugstore. I'm not sure I know how to handle all of that.

S: You wouldn't be jealous would you?

C: Jealous? Well -- no --yes -- I mean -- It's very complicated. I've got all sorts of conflicting emotions in my head. Right now you mean everything to me, but I don't want to get hurt, and I am hurt.

S: What do you mean?

C: Well this shit – you know – the date you have for the charity ball. On the one hand, I know that you have to do a lot of Bollywood things. It's part of the culture. But at the same time, I'm stupid. I'm faithful. I just need some reassurance.

S: Darling, darling. I can't tell you how much I love you too. But you know that.

(3 second pause)

S: Oh, Esteban is like Rhadavan. It's almost the same thing. He's been pursuing me because of the fame thing. His fame and my fame, but he's a phony. This fame thing in two different worlds is getting kind of old. I think he gets some thrill out of being seen with Saroyan Pashogi, whoever she is. He's not my type. He's kind of oily. He's not a sports star. He's a politician. My problem is that even though I don't like him as a person, I need him so he can contribute enough money to make *Zorro* happen. Ravi Guptara is a real slimeball, and he's a tightwad too. He's withholding signing off on the picture for sure until every last dime has been squeezed out of Mexico, so I'm kind of trapped with Gov. Salinas for a while. I hope that we can start shooting down in Loreto in October.

C: So, business is business?

S: A gal's got to do what a gal's got to do. I don't know, is the term for it called business fucking? You know the corporate culture.

C: But you know, I'm still having problems inside Is there any way you can help me?

S: Oh babyface, I can tell you something that only I (UNINTELLIGIBLE, -- 2 minutes, 1second) secret just between you and me.

C: You mean that?

S: Absolutely

C: Well, that makes me feel a little better. Why don't you get a little closer? I need a little body heat.

C: You know this is a very good place to meet. There's absolutely no one around. Did you have any trouble in getting free?

S: No. Not really. Pepe wanted me to have a business discussion on my production company, but I told him it could wait until tomorrow. Everybody pretty much understands.

(UNINTELLIGIBLE, 25 seconds)

C: That's another thing.

S: bad, but it sounds important.

C: It is important. It's the biggest story I ever handled, and it was given to me on a silver platter. (UNINTELLIGIBLE, 41 seconds).

S: That sounds like something out of a Gary Chindowary movie. What do you think it all means? How exciting!

C: Yeah, but I have to admit I'm scared, too. This is really big stuff.

S: I guess it means we have to be careful about where we meet and things. (pause)

S: This wind is cold, but you're so warm. (pause) I have an idea (pause) Last one down to the point is a rotten egg.

C: Tag, you're it.

(UNINTELLIGIBLE, surf, wind sounds, some laughing 10 minutes, 22 seconds)

S: You mean like this? (pause) Say, tiger, let me help you with that.

C: I can help you too. Lie still.

(surf sounds, wind, 3 minutes, 49 seconds)

S: Oh God. That's fabulous. Gee, the ocean looks good tonight.

C: You can't do that to me. Wait until I get my hands on you.

S: Catch me if you can.

WRITTEN SUMMARY, VISUAL INTELLIGENCE

Couple started running down beach for almost eleven minutes. Wind gusts prevented full recording of conversations. Couple took off all clothing and waded into surf at 7:11. Water fight occurred at 7:15. At 7:17 couple waded out of water, running NNW along shore until 7:20 when they returned to Pashogi's handbag. Pashogi took out large beach towel, and couple lay down, commencing to have sex until 8:03 Reader was on top of Pashogi. Then Pashogi was on top of Reader. No significant conversations occurred during sex.

From 8:03 until 8:08 subjects were involved with getting dressed and gathering personal items. From 8:09 to 8:37 couple walked back to their cars. Wind died down, making recording of activities easier.

CONVERSATION RECORD, PART I I, BEACH

S: You know, we need to do that more often.

C: Well, yeah. I'd have to agree with you there. Practice makes perfect.

S: Purrrfect. You are my tiger (pause).

C: I wish I could have you all to myself.

S: Well, maybe some day you will. Can't you imagine us all old and gray sitting on some rocking chairs somewhere. I'd be a washed up old movie star, and you were some retired big time editor or publisher.

C: That's a nice thought. You are special to me, and I -- I'm just afraid of getting hurt.

S: Remember our little secret?

C: Yeah.

S: Well, business is business, and you're just not business. You (pause) are in a category all by yourself to me, and I want to keep it that way.

C: Well, remember in my world, I'm supposed to be invisible. I can't afford to have my picture in the *Times*.

S: So you're saying we need to be discreet.

C: Exactly.

S: Darling, darling. You don't need to be jealous of anybody at all. Maybe once upon a time I was in love with Rhadavan, but maybe it was because we were both famous, but from different worlds. He was in sports, and I was in the movies.

But did you know that he really was unrefined and crude? Not only that, he had no brains.

But you. You're different. It was almost like magic the way we met and got together. Pepe almost had a cow when he found out when you and I started going together. I consider you my secret. That's one of the things that's exciting about you, Clem.

C: You're my secret too, Saroyan. But what about this Mexico guy?

(UNINTELLGIBLE 2minutes, 34 seconds)

C: Not my idea of fun. But (pause) well, if business is business, I need to take care of business on my end too. Can you do me a favor?

S: Oh Clem, you know that I'd walk on hot coals for you. Is this what you have in mind?

(54 seconds, surf, wind, kissing sounds)

C: That was nice, but that's not what I had in mind. I've been doing work on that Marine massacre in Mexico. Do you remember that?

S: I think I remember some of the pictures on the hologram.

C: Well, the next time you do pillow talk with Governor Salinas or whatever his name is, can you talk to His Excellency about what happened in Santa Ynez?

S: Santa Ynez?

C: Yes, Santa Ynez. That's where the marines were killed.

S: I'll try to remember that. (2 minutes, 34 seconds surf/wind sounds)

S: Here we are.

C: Way too soon. I may have to say good night to you here.

S: You don't have to. Why don't you come home with me?

C: I have to be up early for work.

S: Jeeves can wake us up in time, and I can get the driver to let you off at a Pink Line station.

C: Well okay. Let's get in our cars. I'll follow you home.

At 8:45 both cars left the parking lot for Pashogi's Alvarado Drive residence. Charlie team surveillance team recorded activities there as a separate report.

Once again, audio reprocessing is necessary and being worked on. Final draft of report should be available in one week.

2323 ALVARADO DRIVE, 11:35 PM

An unknown amount of time has passed. It seems to last forever. Her soft yet hard body is pressing on top of him, and they move together -- sometimes faster and sometimes slower. There are times when they stop altogether, when they look deep into each other's eyes before they start moving rhythmically again. It seems as if they've been making love forever. Clem remembers that he woke up to find Saroyan kissing him and petting him on the shoulders. The present comes back. He feels her inside of him as she surrounds him with her body. He imagines what it feels like to be Saroyan, just as she is imagining herself as Clem.

He fixes on her pendulous breasts, and he puts his hand to feel her flesh and nipple as the back of his hand brushes over his chest. Everything is concentrated on the moment that always changes from microsecond to microsecond. He looks at her hip with part of her leg visible above the bedcovers. The centers of their bodies are the dictators, commanding all of their senses and body parts. He gently grasps her narrow waist, and he feels her stomach laying on him warmly and softly.

His breathing intensifies. He's panting now. He feels himself go into another dimension. He feels his sweat on the sheets underneath him, and he hears that funny squishing sound. Everything clears from his mind except for that driving motion, and the urge to complete himself.

TIMES NEWSROOM

Clem reads the wire service reports on the upcoming presidential election, but it doesn't register. He does remember waking up with this heavenly nude creature lying beside him. He remembers writing a love note to Saroyan, leaving it on his pillow. One more time, he sees himself kissing her awake as he's ready to go out the door. He remembers almost having to pry himself away, resisting the overwhelming temptation to take off his clothes and linger in bed for another two hours.

Clem doesn't remember the water taxi ride to work because he was thinking of Saroyan all the time. He's had less than three hours sleep, but he's full of energy. He replays the events of the night before over and over again in one pleasurable loop, and he wants the memories to repeat themselves until he dies.

He more or less floated off the boat and through the terminal. He doesn't remember having to walk across the street to the elevator or into the newsroom. At his desk, he hardly pays any attention to the 72 press releases, 14 phone messages, or the half written article on the ongoing debate going on in Lion Studios as to whether the *Fidelio* project is appropriate in a Bollywood format. He doesn't remember doing the fact checking on whether the venture costs $56 million or $66 million to date.

To the other people in the newsroom, it's obvious that something's going on with Clem. He has this glazed beatific stare, and anyone who gets close to him notices that he smells funny. Clem has sleepwalked through work all day. He comes alive four or five times when he takes calls from a famous movie star using assumed names.

"I have never had anyone like you."

"Oh, darling, when can we get together? I want to see you so bad."

"My love, I've set aside a hotel suite at the Ritz. Do you want me to meet you after work?

"It's suite 2266. I wish I could pick you up. How soon can you be here?"

That was four hours ago. Right now they're in the middle of experimenting with each other's bodies, seeing what is most intense and most comfortable.

At that moment, nobody knows it, but there's a slight perturbation in the universe. At this point, Clem changes his train of thought that he's been on for twenty hours or more. He begins to visualize what his life is going to be like after his great romance with Saroyan Pashogi is like, out in public. He'll have to get a $100,000 wardrobe. People with cameras will crowd around him. Others, total strangers, will try to go up to him to try to kiss him. He doesn't know whether he's ready for that.

"Gee, I wish I could get out of this shit."

Clem does not know whether he is ready for such a major turnover in his life. His job is okay. He would have to leave his job. He kind of likes the guys and gals at work. He doesn't know what he would do for a living except to be a kept man. What would he do if and when the romance ended?

"This is extreme. This is very radical."

Karl Eysenbach

PABLO LOPEZ'S OFFICE

The small talk about sports has already been completed, and Pablo's sitting there, waiting for the punch line. He can see that Clem is nervous. After a second that's way too long, Clem finally clears his throat.

"Um, boss, -- is it all right if I close the door? I've got something personal to say before anything else."

Pablo looks at him quizzically, but he waves his hand in a go ahead gesture. Clem gets up, closes the door, and sits back down. Pablo is waiting.

"Ummm, boss, -- I've got a new girl friend and it's been giving me personal problems."

"How so?" Father confessor speaks.

"Well, nothing has ever happened like this to me before, I mean, she's a swell gal, but there are issues, -- issues dealing with work."

"Love is a wonderful thing, so?"

"Well, I know that I'm never supposed to be part of a story, but I might be coming part of a story. I've been seeing this girl, and for the life of me, it's a miracle that we haven't been picked up by the paparazzi."

"So you're dating a news story?"

"And how" Clem begins to stammer as he says this, "Boss, I'm a little embarrassed to say this, but I'm having a love affair with Saroyan Pashogi. There, -- I've said it."

At this point Pablo does a classic comic double take. If he were Danny Thomas, he would have sprayed coffee all over everything. He breaks down into hysterical laughter, and he can't stop. Tears come to his eyes. He almost calms down, until he looks at Clem again. Then he starts laughing all over one more time. After a few minutes, he almost has his composure. He slaps Clem on the back and says, "Clem

Reader, you old dog you! Getting any lately?" He starts to laugh again. Then he gets at least mildly serious.

"You old dog you. Well, you're right, sleeping with the biggest movie star in history when you're on the Bollywood beat is a conflict of interest.' Then he slaps him on the back one more time and laughs some more.

"Well my old news daddy told me, 'I don't care if you're sleeping with elephants. You just can't cover the circus.' From now on, you're off the Bollywood beat, and I'm putting you on defense and military affairs 100%. Things are heating up with all that Baja stuff. That ought to make Mbake happy."

"I know. You told me to get on the horn to Emilio, and there are problems with the leads in Los Angeles."

Pablo cocks one eyebrow, "Like what?"

"Well, you remember the Marine massacre at Santa Ynez?"

"So?"

"Well, why were they killed?"

"It was the guerillas."

"No, there's more to it than that. What were the Marines doing down there?"

"That's simple. They were returning to base."

"But there's more to it than that."

"So what were the Marines doing?"

"Emilio has some good indications that there's something being covered up. You know, the spook boys had this ZX-47 down there."

"You broke the story on that. So?"

"Well the problem is, is that their cover story has more holes than a 50 kilo wheel of Swiss cheese. The ZX-47 is a device that is best suited to detecting anomalies in gravity waves. Lodestar and the military say that the thing was looking for mineshafts where the guerillas might be hiding. They've also said that the military was doing Lodestar a favor by doing R & D, but I haven't gotten any answers as to why they'd want to do a testing thing on such an incredibly high profile news item. On top of that I've checked on historical records with the UABC Department of Geology, and all the abandoned mines are on line. There was no need for anybody to use a gizmo to look for mineshafts where the guerillas were hiding because everybody knows where they are already."

"So, that sounds like a good follow-up story."

Now it's Clem's turn to smile. "I've got you on that one, Boss. I've already typed that one up and it's waiting in the box for your approval, but there are more unexplained questions. When the 17th Marines flushed out those ALF guys, they were hiding in an oak forest near Ensenada. I checked around, and there are no abandoned mines near where they were captured for over a hundred kilometers. Not only that, but Emilio tells me, they're still using the ZX-47s on choppers, and they're still using the cover story about abandoned mines. That's out of the horse's mouth of the Marines' public information officer. I talked with Alejandro Wong at Lodestar, and I get the impression that the real purpose of a ZX-47 is to detect gravity waves and disturbances in gravitational patterns. Why would the military continue to search for 'mine shafts' after they've gotten the guys who greased the Marines?"

"Maybe they're still doing R & D for Lodestar."

"But wouldn't their story change?"

"That's a good question."

"Here's another one for you. Emilio and I have been trying to communicate about this, but we both get the feeling that we're being closely monitored. Is there any way the two of us could get together for a confidential conversation?"

Pablo thinks for a minute. Finally he gets an answer. "Okay, it says here that the Tijuana bus station has been remodeled, and they're having a grand opening tomorrow. I've assigned Emilio the job of covering it, but he needs a photographer. You've got a vacation with pay tomorrow."

STATION CENTRAL, TIJUANA

The Delegado of Baja Frontera and the Mayor of Tijuana are wearing their red, white, and green sashes over their dark business suits. They take the giant gold scissors and cut the ribbon as the crowd applauds. Clem is on one knee as he is furiously taking pictures of the festivities. After the applause dies down a few reporters buttonhole the elected officials and transportation planners about what it all means. Clem follows at a respectful distance. As the crowd moves inside the new building, Clem gets Emilio's attention.

"Hey! They didn't tell me I was going to have photo back-up on this gig. How did you get here?"

"I just happened to be in the neighborhood. When do we get a serious conversation?"

"I'll tell you what," Emilio says looking around. "Why don't we take separate taxis and do lunch at El Muelle? They've got some killer ceviche."

Clem loiters around the bus station taking more pictures while Emilio hails a cab. Five minutes later, Clem does the same thing. Within twenty minutes they're sitting in the yellow restaurant with hockey sticks and movie posters on the wall. They have their pitcher of beer and plates of food. But this is a working lunch, and the booth is littered with papers. Emilio's talking about the ordeal in the desert.

"You know those margarita glasses and drinking supplies were life savers. There wasn't a whole hell of a lot of things to do down there for a week. You can only get so many photo opps in the middle of nowhere. I mean, how many shots of the empty desert can you saturate the world media with? If you want desert pictures, buy a coffee table book. The military was bored out of their minds, too. They all complained about the wild goose chases they were on out there. The Marines really didn't like the CIA guys or the boys in the white lab coats. I guess it's that, 'Oh, you think you're better than me?' kind of thing."

"But soldiers always like to gripe, don't they?" Clem signals the waiter for another round of cerveza.

"I eventually cleaned the Marines out of most of their chips, and I took my winnings so I could play with the spooks and scientists. Very wisely, I just about lost everything to the CIA guys, but it was worth it."

"All on the expense account of the *New Los Angeles Times*." Clem smiles drolly as he takes another sip.

"Well, at first, the company boys were not what you call talkative about anything, but we developed rapport over time, and the margarita mix didn't hurt. I mean, after a while, they almost became human. They were complaining as much as the Marines, but for partly different reasons. After a while, they admitted that their cover story was pretty cheesy."

"How so?"

"There was one moment about two hours into a poker game when I referred to the gravity of the situation -- the massacre, you know? And one of the spooks blurts out, 'And magnetism, too.' The other spooks at the table give the poor guy looks that would kill. A few more hands to fold, a few more bottles of tequila, and they loosened up enough to joke about little green men."

"Did you ask about the ZX-47?"

"Of course I did. They said it cost a gazillion dollars an hour to operate, and that it wasn't going to find the Marines killers or a single damn thing, for that matter. I guess they thought of it as some giant waste of taxpayers' money."

The Story of the Century

"What did they have to say about their cover story?"

Emilio looks around before he speaks. "When they were drunk enough, they admitted that their cover story sucked, and they wouldn't go any further than that. All I could get out of them was that the dead Marines had something in the back of their truck, and that this thing was stolen. The ZX-47 was trying to find the thing that was stolen.

Clem asks, "Did you follow up on what the Marines were carrying?"

"Sure. The public information officer said that the dead guys were carrying electrical generator parts. He even showed me some of the documentation. I mean, there doesn't appear to be any story there."

Clem's on the case. "I'm not so sure. Let's play Sherlock Holmes. The ZX-47 is looking for some magnetic or gravitational disturbance, and generator parts wouldn't give off gravity or large magnetic waves. Is there any chance you could hit up the public information officer one more time and do some questions?"

Sgt. Singh has been anticipating this train of thought. He's been monitoring military and press communications between Baja California and the *Times* main office in addition to the news. Very thoughtfully, he puts a new piece of information into play that just happens to be targeted at the public information officer at Camp Magellan. Later, the authorities will have a great deal of trouble determining how Lt. Commander Columbo got this piece of information, and Columbo will be forced to retire from the Marines early. The brass will look for leaks in the system, but they'll come up empty handed.

Clem has an idea. "Why don't you call Lt. Commander Columbo right now and ask him some questions. I mean, it's after lunch, isn't it?"

"Emilio has Camp Magellan on his speed dial. The Marine officer's face appears on his cell phone screen. Emilio is as charming as ever.

"Juan, how are you this afternoon? I just wanted to touch base with you again. I have some follow up questions about Santa Ynez."

"It's funny that you called, a new piece of information on that just fell into my lap. Fire away."

"I'm not going to take up too much of your time. I pretty much have just one question. Now I understand that Company B was carrying parts for an electrical generator when it was hit, is this correct?"

"Wow! You must be psychic. That's the piece of information that I just got. The Marines were not, I repeat not carrying electrical generator parts. The new information that I have is that they were carrying classified material that I'm not at liberty to talk about."

"Classified material?" Clem looks at Emilio and starts writing notes to him.

"Yes, that's right."

"Could you hold on for just a second, Juan? Are you still with me? Good. Were the Marines at Santa Ynez carrying anything called a magnetic interferometer?"

There's a significant pause on Camp Magellan's side. Juan clears his throat and says, "No comment. I'm not at liberty to say anything about the cargo."

"Was there any extraterrestrial technology involved?"

"Again, I really can't say. What the Marines were carrying is classified as top secret. There's nothing more to say."

"Okay, one last question, Juan. I can take it from you that there was a secret cargo. Do you have anybody I can contact as a confirmation on that?"

"I'm sure the main Office of Public Information in Kuala Lumpur can confirm that. Their number is 001-345-59-68-888, extension 17."

"Thanks a lot Juan. You're always a great guy to talk to."

He clicks off the phone, and the two reporters give each other high fives. They order another round of beer in celebration. The story runs the next day, and Lt. Commander Columbo calls up Emilio as one extremely angry dude. It appears as if Lt. Commander Columbo is being blamed for everything, but by then it's too late.

TIME: UNKNOWN
PLACE: UNKNOWN

They wake up in a large cold room. It's very white. Puto and Jorge blink and look at each other. They've been miraculously cured of poison oak. They're wearing their own clothes, but their shirts and jeans look as if they've never been worn before. There isn't a hint that they've ever spent more than a day playing fox to the Marines' hounds. Both of them are sitting on red foamy couches, which are the only pieces of furniture in the room. There's no door but there is a picture window with rounded edges. There's a view of nothing but black outside. Both men have a sense of missing time. This is their first memory in a long time. They're comfortable. They don't need anything. -- Funny.

"I just thought I'd say goodbye to you before you got back to Earth," says Puto. "I'm going to be assimilated by the blue light, and you're not going to remember any of this information that I'm giving you. We're still friends, and we always will be; but you won't be seeing me for a while." A small smile appears on his face.

Jorge blinks, and he dreams this, but he must be dreaming with a vengeance while he's sleepwalking. Here he is standing in front of Concepcion Ayala's door in the suburbs of Ensenada. It's 7AM, and the sun is rising fast. He looks around at the narrow dirt road with pastel-colored concrete blockhouses running up the hill. The door opens, and Concepcion stands in her dark hallway looking at him with some suspicion.

"You look respectable. Come on inside."

The little concrete house doesn't look any better than anything else in the colonia, but it's neat and clean and newly painted. Inside there are some beaten up chairs and a table. In the other corner of the room is a gray couch with a busted spring, and a big picture of Jesus hangs on the wall in its fake gold frame.

"Sit on the couch, and wait a minute."

She leaves for the kitchen. Jorge sits down and looks at the television, watching the infotainment. Five minutes later two greasy dudes weighing a collective 300 kilos wearing wifebeater T-shirts enter through the back door. They look like they could bite the head off of a Buick. They hold on to their lug wrenches as they talk quietly with Concepcion in the kitchen. Occasionally, one or the other brute will glance into the living room where Jorge is sitting. After a geological era, the three of them come into the living room. Concepcion sits at the table, while the giants get closer to Jorge. Jorge gets up from the sofa.

"Insecticida, don't you remember me? I'm Frog."

Reflexively, Jorge gives the monster an *embrazo*, even though he has trouble remembering.

"This is Canejo. You finally got here. We've been working on our truck, and we've got a job for you arranged in New Los Angeles. Word came down from Victor."

BONAVENTURE HOTEL

The five-star hotel has always been a magnet for the elite. So you can imagine the scene at the 14th Annual Child Abuse Charity Ball. There's a traffic jam of limousines, and police barricades have been set up to contain the thousands of gawkers as well as the herd of media vans with their satellite dishes. Everyone else who's everybody is there. There are bleachers for the proletariat and a hectare of red carpet for the glitterati, with ten meters of security in between. Searchlights pierce the sky with their sweeping patterns, and the front of the hotel is saturated with glaring white light. The hologram reporters go on and on about SP's new movie, *The Maid of Givenchy*, and how marvelously it dovetails with the evening's event.

Saroyan Pashogi causes a stir when her limo drives up, and the masses find out that Governor Esteban Salinas of Mexico has SP on his arm. The crowd roars, and 3,259 flashbulbs go off in a matter of a few seconds as they go inside. The main ballroom looks like a replica of what was once known as the Hall of Mirrors in the long-lost Palace of Versailles. Hundreds of event staff are in 18th Century style costumes. Everyone else, being a paying customer with $5000 or more to burn for a ticket, is in a tuxedo or formal wear.

The real reason why people are here, is -- money -- making money. Connections are to be made. For example, right now the publisher of the *New Los Angeles Times* is being buttonholed by a major property developer named Ken Ho Yunghai Lee. Mr. Lee has promised to substantially increase the amount of his advertising, and in return the publisher will do a Sunday feature on Mr. Lee in the paper's magazine. Since it turns out that Clem Reader is an old classmate of Mr. Lee, the publisher decides that Clem will be the reporter. But this is the way Mr. Lee structured it.

"Look, Saroyan Pashogi is just entering the room!"

As if on cue, the crowd of thousands turns its eyes on the couple entering the hall. The music suddenly changes to that of a processional. An announcer excitedly broadcasts what everyone already knows; the main event is about to happen. Saroyan Pashogi and Governor Salinas are the guests of honor.

Imagine standing behind the beautiful couple as they bask in the lights of five global networks and the standing ovation of over 2,000 of the best-dressed people in the world. Then there is a back stage meeting of Saroyan, Governor Salinas, and Victor. Victor and Governor Salinas do a little business about tax free investments, and Victor says that he's interested in bankrolling an eight-picture deal for his syndicate with Tata Studios. He's going to see Ravi Guptara. Saroyan pretends not to notice because she's too busy getting ready for her finale. She ends the show by hoofing a song and dance number in a diaphanous blue gown with a million sequins in front of a huge chorus line. Afterwards, there's a party after the post show party at the mayor's house. Two stretch limousines filled with Star, World Leader and entourage pull up at the brick mansion. There is yet more applause as the couple makes their way inside through a small crowd of well wishers.

"Do you see how much they love us?" Saroyan whispers in Esteban's ear. The mayor greets them as servants take their drink orders. Saroyan gets a white wine, and Esteban receives his jalapeno martini. Esteban continues to whisper sweet romantic nothings in her ear, as party guests intrude. But when he sees some men gathered tightly together, his mood changes. Esteban puts on the mask of the great Governor of Mexico, and he takes off his Latin lover skin.

"Excuse me, darling. I have business to attend to." The governor immediately goes to a corner where some gentlemen are smoking cigars. Saroyan recognizes C.Z. Vasquez, the police chief, but she does not know the other gentlemen. They are the biggest heroin pusher in town, the local CIA station chief, and a well-dressed, good-looking man by the name of Ken Ho Yunghai Lee.

Clem has just woken up. He's had trouble sleeping, and it doesn't make any difference that he has to get up early tomorrow. He lies in bed for a while, just thinking. Then he gets up and goes to the kitchen for a

The Story of the Century

beer. For lack of anything else to do before getting sleepy, he turns on the hologram to WNN. There's some problem down in Guatemala about some general who got blown up. Central America is getting hotter, and a military expert says a lot depends on what Mexico does. Then there's the Bollywood news. Saroyan Pashogi is basking in a thousand flashbulbs with her escort of the evening, the Governor of Mexico.

At this moment, the Saroyan-Esteban tryst is not being recorded for the benefit of publicity. Saroyan and Esteban finally have a chance to be alone together in the Presidential Suite of the New Bonaventure Hotel. The lights of the city shine below. Saroyan is already in bed but in her nightgown, and Esteban is taking off his clothes. Saroyan is thinking about rolling a bomber.

"Would you like some marijuana?" The Governor nods yes as he caressingly holds Saroyan's hand to his mouth to kiss it. Saroyan weasels away as she reaches into her purse by her bed to take out the baggie, rolling papers, and rolling machine. "Panama Red," she says. "From Michuocan."

Esteban smells it deeply, savoring every THC molecule. "Yes," he says. "I know it well. It's one of my favorites." He watches as she takes the looks-like oregano and produces a flawless doobie. As much as Esteban would like to have sex, Saroyan keeps him at bay. She talks about how badly she wants to make *Zorro*. She talks about how much it will mean to her. It will be her transition. She says that unless the governor can help her, she won't be able to fulfill her life's dream. She talks about how much it will mean to the studio to have the financial support of the Mexican government in the making of this motion picture. She says that the studio has been burdened by giant turkeys recently, and that Ravi Guptara is standing in the way of her being a good movie producer. If only Esteban can see in his heart to release a few million dollars, they'll be able to make history together.

"And it's the money thing you know? Pictures are sooo expensive. I mean caring for and feeding an army of movie workers for months on end. Do you have any idea how much that costs?" She hands the joint to Esteban.

The Governor of Mexico takes the blunt and sucks in for five seconds. Finally he exhales and smiles. "Yes, I know. They are called my relatives." The dope has acted like a mental laxative. He speaks freely and in confidence, -- a potentially fatal disease for any politician. "Yes, money is a concern of mine too. I have money problems all the time."

"You do?"

"Certainly, not only with the government. I have to deal with billions of dollars every month, but I mean for me, personally as well."

"Why is that?" Saroyan is relieved that she's sidetracked him.

"Well, for one thing, there's always the government appointments. Everyone wants to be the *patrone* or *delgado* of his or her village. That's easy as long as I can put them into some office position. The problem is that they all need more to live on than what they get from their salaries."

"I don't understand."

"Look at me. You see before you one of the most important men in the world. Viva Mexico! But for all this power and glory, what do I get? Only a $100,000 a year salary! Why, that's hardly enough to maintain myself, much let alone my family."

"That sounds serious! Do you have a big family? That really is a problem."

"So you see how much money is a problem? Yes I do have a big family." Esteban takes another long toke.

"Verry good. Now where was I? Oh yes. So I have to get other sources of income. It's very necessary. I do what I can with campaign contributions. The businessmen are very helpful there, but there's still not enough. Most of those contributions have to go for the campaign apparatuses, signs, banners, TV commercials. On top of this, political campaigns come only once every two years or so. People have to eat in other months too, you know."

"So what do you do?"

Esteban smiles. He passes the joint to Saroyan who takes a ladylike inhalation, and she passes it back to him. He grasps the joint close, as it is near its end. He inhales, holds his breath, and exhales a thick cloud of blue smoke.

"Smooooth! I will tell you a little secret." His eyes are red. "I have other businesses. Businesses that take advantage of supply and demand functions." An ironic smile crosses his face.

"What does that mean?" Saroyan is truly puzzled. What kind of dope rant is this?

"Supply and demand. It's very simple. You know about the extremely heavy world taxes on cocaine and some of the hard drugs?"

"I think I've heard about them. I don't know."

"Okay. The world government pretty much outlaws these drugs, so they tax them. They tax them a lot. A cocaine license costs $5000 a year, and you have to go to all these stupid drug education classes to maintain you right to use coke."

"Yes, some of my friends complain about that."

"The truth is people don't want to do that, so they break the world law. But I have friends who can buy cocaine for 1/100th of the official world price. They can sell below the world price and allow poor people to use cocaine too."

"I see, so they give you money?"

"Yes and no. Everything has its price. They will give me money, and they will give me drugs for what I need, but it's more complicated than that."

"How so?" Saroyan's eyes are red, but she gives Esteban one of her patented wide-eyed innocent looks.

"They want something in return. Did I tell you that I have some cocaine for us to share later, heart of my heart? I got it at the Mayor's party." Esteban looks slightly manic, and he's leering at Saroyan. She reads him like a pamphlet, and she gets out of bed, running outside to stand on the balcony.

"I need some air. Does it feel warm to you?" She looks back at Esteban and flutters her eyelashes.

"Carumba! Close the damn door." Esteban yells, but he has been distracted. Saroyan has succeeded.

"I'm sorry Esteban." She closes the door. She walks back to the bed and sits on it. "Now tell me about what drug dealers want and your money problem."

"Where was I?"

"You were saying that people give you drugs and money, but they want something in return."

"Oh yes. That's the other side of the supply-demand equation. You know that no one in Mexico is allowed to own guns?"

"I didn't know that. Tell me more." Saroyan looks at him seductively.

"I am going to make up a quote. 'To live outside the law you must be honest.' The people who help me live under their own rules. Contracts and lawyers don't do them much good. They have to maintain their business standards by other means, and that's where I can help."

"How so?"

"The government has a monopoly on firearms. Only the police and the military can own handguns and automatic weapons. The people who give me money from drugs are willing to give me tens or even hundreds of times more money if I can supply them with the necessary firepower."

"And that is how you feed your family?"

"Precisely. I wouldn't be in the position of being where I am today if it weren't for my business arrangements. So you see, it's good for me, my family, my business associates; everyone benefits!" Esteban smiles proudly.

Saroyan looks at Esteban, and she gets closer to him. "Oh, Mr. Governor. I had no idea that your job was so hard. Would you promise me a big, big favor?" She puts her arms around him, looking deeply into his eyes.

"Would you promise me that you'll give $2 million to Tata Pictures as a good faith effort to help me make my movie?"

The governor looks at her as he puts a hand around her waist. One hand begins to feel her precious breast. "Why for you, my love, I would do anything. I promise. I promise that I will get it done, starting tomorrow." He kisses her passionately. Saroyan is listening to some noises outside in the hall.

Just then, there's a knock at the door. Saroyan gets out of bed and opens the door. She covers herself. A man in a dark suit and an earpiece is there with a cell phone.

"Ms. Pashogi, there's a telephone call for the Governor. It's Singapore. The President wants to talk to him."

"Oh my! That's important. Esteban!" she yells, "The President of the World is on the telephone. He wants to talk to you!"

"Oh shit!" Saroyan has never heard him use that language before. "Tell him I'll be there in a minute. He adjusts his clothing to be more presentable. Saroyan looks at the security man.

"Can I take it to him?" She walks back to the bed quickly. The security man silently goes inside a few steps.

"He's on this phone. You can take it where you are." Saroyan hands it to him.

The President is sitting at his desk in Singapore. It is just after an early lunch, and he's worried and concerned. He's calling Governor Salinas because he has secret information indicating that General Rios-Arbenz had some affiliation with the Atzlan Liberation Front. CIA reports indicate that there is increased ALF activity in the districts of Chihuahua, Nuevo Leon, and Mexico City. President Hok's intelligence indicates that the general shorted some guerillas on a drug deal, and they were just paying him back for his impoliteness. President Hok is going to ask Gov. Salinas to step up his anticrime operations against the ALF. He is also going to ask for the Governor's assistance in solving the succession problem that is now plaguing the generals due to Rios-Arbenz's death.

"Mr. President. How are you tonight? I will do anything I can to help you."

Governor Salinas at first appears tall and proud, but his expression begins to change. His eyes start to get bigger and he begins to curl his upper lip.

"I did not know that that was the case. This is very serious."

"It begins to get obvious to Saroyan and the security man that Governor Salinas is now more influenced by the cocaine that they snorted in the car than the marijuana they've just finished smoking. Esteban puts the palm of his hand to his forehead and he tilts his head back. An expression of anguish comes over his face. Suddenly his body jolts as if he had been given a quick electric shock.

"YOU WANT ME TO DO WHAT?!" (pause)

"I heard you the first time!! You listen to me! I carried your water on that magnetic interferometer thing. You heard me, the thing from Arizona! Now you're asking for my blood!! I can only fight so much crime and corruption. Why are you really calling ME? There must be some ulterior motive!" He is shouting into the telephone. Saroyan is beginning to be afraid.

"One general. Some Marines in Santa Ynez. It looks like something is seriously wrong in your shop, Mr. President. Don't tell me how to run my state!"

Saroyan can see the veins standing out on his forehead. Governor Salinas yells, "*Chingada!!*" and he throws the cell phone down on the floor. He grabs an overcoat and storms out of the hotel suite. The slamming door can be heard all over the hotel floor.

MAY 21st
NEW LOS ANGELES & SINGAPORE

Around noon Saroyan and her entourage visit Tata Studios to see Ravi Guptara about *Zorro*. It's not going to be a nice meeting, no way. Ravi Guptara is the biggest sleazeball in the industry. It's not that he makes bad product. No, Ravi's problem is that he is the collection of all the bad personality traits that can infect a big cheese in the entertainment industry. His usual good mood is that of an enraged water buffalo on a crystal meth jag. You don't want to see him on one of his bad days, like today for example.

Saroyan has been jerked around for months while Mr. Guptara held up the Mexican government for extra cash, and yesterday Esteban took care of it. But Ravi is such an asshole that he still doesn't want to finalize the contract. You might say there was a personality conflict between the two. Saroyan has a personal grudge against Ravi taking advantage of her sexually when she was a rising starlet, and Ravi gets his cheap thrills by being the tiny dick in the power seat. It isn't about the money so much. It isn't all about who controls production. It's about revenge, too. Theological questions arise to no end:

"What is your definition of the net gross?"

"What is your definition of residual distribution rights?"

"How many Bollywood lawyers can dance on the head of a pin?"

All of this has kept Saroyan, Pepe, and her legal and accounting help working into the graveyard shift; but with thirty seconds to go in the game she's still ahead by two. Saroyan and her attorney Olive Montgomery have been in a meeting with Mr. Guptara for just under two hours. Most of the meeting revolves around discussions of things like Appendix B, subparagraph j, and line 17, and they've actually succeeded in getting a mutually agreed upon format for the final contract. Even a grade 'A' prick like Ravi Guptara knows that there's nothing worse than being pecked to death by a Bollywood lawyer. Saroyan manages to hold her own by mostly keeping her mouth shut and batting her eyelashes. Things look like they are 99% nailed down in favor of Star, but there's that 1-% uncertainty. Ravi refuses to sign the contract, even though Saroyan has put her John Hancock to to the paper.

Saroyan survives the meeting, but her blood pressure goes off the scale too. As for Ravi, his blood pressure is 300/200. Modern medicine has made him not dead yet, but he pays super premium prices for his health insurance. The odor of his antiperspirant mixes with the heavy scent of his *Paco Rabane* cologne. Ravi says that everything depends on what happens in the next meeting, and until that's settled, he's sitting on things. Saroyan's meeting is over.

On the way out, she runs into Victor in the hall. She squeals, and she gives him a big wet French kiss. Their conversation goes like this:

"Ooooh Victor, I had no idea that you were going to see Mr. Guptara today."

"Saroyan, you look wonderful. I had no idea you were going to see him either. I'm on my way in to see about bankrolling some of his future films."

She looks up at the big man with her doelike eyes, and she keeps her arms around him. "Victor, dahhling, would you do me a big, big favor?"

"Anything I can."

"Victor, -- would you tie your financing to making sure that Mr. Guptara abides by the contract with me on my production of *Zorro*? Make sure he signs my contract right now, today."

He pauses for a moment and then says, "Sure Saroyan, anything you say."

The meeting with Guptara goes well for Victor. He manages to send some financial product into the Brazilian-Asian money mojo, and he gets a 12% rate of return guaranteed for the next ten years. It's a win-win situation. Half an hour into the meeting with Victor, Ravi signs Saroyan's contract. He also signs onto an $80 million participation note with some of Victor's Cayman Islands shell companies. No one knows if Victor gave some blow to Ravi, but it's a fact that the studio CEO dies of a humongous stroke in the wee hours of the morning. And the Coroner's Office finds that Ravi had significant traces of cocaine in his system. But the documents for Victor and Saroyan have been signed and vetted by the accountants and attorneys

----

It's later, and, Clem is sitting in a little taco bar somewhere in Venice. It's a spur of the moment date between SP and the reporter, and the restaurant is really off the beaten path. Theoretically the place is closed, but that's because he's eating machaca with Saroyan. She puts down her fish taco and begins to tell tales from out of school.

"This is really delicious. Did I tell you about what Governor Salinas was talking about at the charity ball the other day? It was really crazy."

Clem looks up. "What do you mean by that?"

"He talked a long time. He started out talking about how many people he had to support. I guess in Mexico, politics is a family operation, and he has a big family."

"I guess that's to be expected. I think it's like that everywhere."

"But he went on to say that he couldn't make it financially on the salary he gets as Governor of Mexico, so he depends on campaign contributions, but that isn't enough."

"Sounds like he's got money problems, that's for sure."

"But wait, it goes further than that. Esteban says that he doesn't like the way the world deals with cocaine."

"Hmmmn. That sounds odd."

"Yes, so he's in business with people who are in the cocaine business, but he kept talking, and eventually, he said something like he has to pay the cocaine people with guns that the government has."

"Whoa! That sounds like a story."

"But wait, it gets even weirder. I was smoking dope with him, and later I even did some coke -- only one line. But we're in this hotel room, and he gets a phone call from the President of the World."

"Wow! If I was a hot babe reporter, I would have had more than one front-page story. So tell me what you heard on one end of the phone."

"Well, Esteban was a little crazy from the coke. I think he must have had some before I saw him. Anyway, he was really angry and rude to President Hok. The President told him something he didn't want to hear, and he began to yell and scream at him. I just covered myself hoping the security man wouldn't see me."

Clem grimaces when he hears this, but he says gamely. "Go on. What was he talking about?"

"I remember what he said. He said, 'I carried water for you on that magnetic interferometer thing. Now you're asking for all of my blood.' That's what he said."

Clem's jaw drops, and his mouth forms a big 'O.' His face freezes for a moment until he regains his composure. It's Clem's blood pressure moment. He clears his throat and asks Saroyan, "What thing did Governor Salinas carry water for?"

The Story of the Century

Saroyan says, "It was something called a magnetic interferometer. I think that's what it was. Yes-- ."

At this point, Clem jumps up out of his chair and starts to do a dance around the empty restaurant. He keeps yelling, "I can't believe it! I can't believe it!" When he finally calms down, he goes over to where Saroyan is, and gets her up out of her chair. He pulls Saroyan to him and gives her an extended full mouth kiss. "Darling, darling! I don't usually get so emotional with my reliable sources, but you've just made my day! If I get one more independent confirmation, I've got a Platinum Prize story. You don't know how happy you've made me!"

He thinks for a moment, and his expression changes. He gets more serious. "Is there any possibility, -- if you see him again, that you could ask him more about what he meant about guns and coke?" What Clem doesn't know is that he's just started to commit the ancient curse of getting what he asks for.

At the same time and moment, in a really bad part of the San Fernando Valley, near the end of the Pink Line, Jorge Estrada, formerly known as Subcommandante Insecticida, is asleep in a decaying stucco bungalow. He's employed as a dishwasher at the Tour de l'Argent, and he's in the arms of Lupe, a set up chef that he met at work. Nothing happened to him today except that he worked like a beast of burden.

Meanwhile in Singapore, President Hok is looking at himself in the bathroom mirror. He's on the fifth floor of the Otani Hotel overlooking the waterfront. Everything in the suite is in a tasteful modern gray with brushed stainless steel bathroom fixtures. The President is looking in the mirror frowning; standing with a towel wrapped around his waist. He doesn't like what he sees; a short, slightly overweight middle-aged man who used to be young and better looking. In the background he sees Yvette lying on the gray silk sheets. Yvette used to be a bikini model. She was born in Tahiti. She's a lobbyist now. She works for Lodestar. After their little sexual encounter, she delivered a message to the President, and the President doesn't like what he's been told. "Call Rigoberto about the AHITF," she says. He'd rather eat a bar of soap, but he has no choice. He's boxed in. He's got to make the goddamned call to the goddamned Secretary of Defense, whom he knows has him by the short and curlies.

Secretary of Defense Rigoberto Corozon is the rat-bastard of the Cabinet. He looks very much like Donald Rumsfeld. Corozon is from Brazil. The Brazilian Mafia -- they are as thick as fleas with Lodestar, and they're all up to their armpits in military contracts. If it were up to Hok, every last one of those assholes would be picking their way through the Brasilia municipal dump, scrounging for their weapons contract money. Unfortunately, deals with the devil had to be made in order to get the President elected. The boys from Brazil had to sign on the bottom line before he could become Leader of Us All. So, Walter Casopedro had to be picked as Vice President, and Rigoberto was part of the package.

And what makes Hok even madder is the fact he likes to fool around a little bit with Yvette in his spare time. The boys from Brazil put their heads together, and voila! They have no problems from El Presidente as long as she's around. Sometimes, just sometimes, Chun Hee Hok wonders why he's so stupid. This is one of those times. So Yvette is here, and President Hok has to deliver a message to the Secretary of Defense. He looks away from the mirror, and turns to his poisonous flame, his bikini model. "Give me the cell phone, Yvette."

President Hok looks at the cell phone, and he speaks. "Get me the Secretary of Defense, it's personal and encrypted." Within ten seconds, the picture of the Corozon is on the screen. Corozon is sitting at his desk, and he's ready.

The Story of the Century

"Yes, Mister President?," he says. The Secretary of Defense's hands are folded, and there's just a trace of a smirk on his face.

"Call the committee, Mr. Secretary."

"The committee, Mr. President, -- which one?" Now Corozon has a bigger smirk on his face. As if he didn't know. He's been expecting this call from Hok.

"AHITF. The Ad Hoc Interagency Task Force. Yvette is here with me."

"Very good Mister President. I'll do that immediately." The cell phone screen goes black. It's just the start of another convoluted, bureaucratic government procedure. Except that this procedure will eliminate Clem and Saroyan, and some other people will die.

EL PUERTO, NEW LOS ANGELES
245 HARBOR DRIVE

Clem knows the situation is strange, but he feels lucky at the same time. On the one hand, he's not used to interviewing old school chums at the personal request of his publisher. On the other hand, it isn't like this story has to be put to bed before midnight. The way he figures it, this interview is a good excuse to go home early and clean out the excess fast food wrappers. Here he is sitting in the waiting room of Castle Property Management & Bishop Real Estate Consultants LLP. Of course no one ever calls it that; everyone just says Castle & Bishop. To say that the waiting room is palatial is an understatement. It looks as if it's bigger than Saroyan's house. Carrara marble columns go up seven meters, and the parquet floor has the Castle & Bishop logo inlaid in precious woods.

Right on time, Ken Lee appears from behind the giant carved oak doors. The moment he sees Clem, he comes up to him and gives him a bear hug of an *embrazo*.

"Old chum. It's so good to see you. I can't believe that it's been so long. You look like life is agreeing with you."

"You don't look so bad yourself, Ken. I'd say that life has agreed with you pretty well too." They share a small laugh. Clem continues.

"The big boss called me herself, and told me to do a special assignment on you. I jumped at the chance to get a reunion with you."

"Well, I'm glad you did. That's interesting that Madame Cheung decided to send you to cover me. I'm not **that** newsworthy." He pauses. "Come on inside, you should get to see what a real office looks like."

Clem has to admit that he's impressed. Not even the moguls in Bollywood have more spectacular or luxurious digs. Ken holds his own, and the studios can't match this view through the bulletproof glass wall overlooking the harbor.

"I'm here to do a human interest story for the Sunday magazine. You'll probably be on the cover."

"Human interest, human interest, human interest. I want to talk with you about **your** old times. I want to find out what you've been doing. Would you like some brandy or a cigar?"

"I don't do that while I'm working Ken. I've got an idea. Why don't I do my job now, and then we can go off together somewhere, and you can interview me."

"Sounds fair to me." The interview begins with all of the standard life questions.

"Tell me about your early life."

"How did you get started in the business?"

"Why do you get up in the morning?"

"Talk to me about the way you see the business climate today."

"What would you like to accomplish in the next five years?"

Lee is in the middle of responding to question # 3. "Well, I was really lucky. I was just flopping around after college with nothing to do

The Story of the Century

in either Shanghai or Hong Kong, and my Uncle Chou said I should go back to New Los Angeles to work for this friend of his at Acme Property Management. I walk into the place. It was in the New Bradbury Building downtown, and I walk into Feng Go Dentu's office. He was the old boss man. I told him that my uncle told me to see him. He looks up from his work, lowers his glasses, and he gets up out of his desk. 'Follow me,' he says. I wound up working in the mailroom."

Clem is taking notes, but his shit detector's flashing yellow. He senses that that he's on TV, but who is his audience? Ken's sitting there, going on and self-disclosing about his life, and Clem has the old paranoia bug biting him.

Of course, Ken didn't stay in the mailroom long. He had a rapid rise through the ranks, getting to know every part of the business in quick rotation. "Why, I even cleaned up some apartments for a couple of weeks, just to get the feel of how things go." Lee continues. It turns out that Lee didn't stay in Los Angeles all the time. His father called him home for a few years, and Lee was managing property in Hong Kong and Manila for his dad's firm.

"I didn't mind it for the first year or two, but there was so much hassle dealing with the government as a landlord, that I finally had to break away from my dad, and declare my independence. I came back to Castle & Bishop." That was only seven years ago. By that time, it seems that the other real estate sharks had been eating C & B's lunch and dinner. When he returned, he found the company near the edge of bankruptcy.

"I had to take no prisoners. I worked on a 100 hour a week crisis mode for more than a year before I turned it around." And turn it around he did. Much to the chagrin of his local competitors, Castle & Bishop had managed to increase its business by 35% a year for seven years running. Within the last six months, Lee has acquired Wangpo

Realty, a company that was once upon a time much bigger than C & B. It's obvious that he relishes his role as bad boy of the real estate market. He talks about his somewhat unconventional style of doing business, but he's interrupted when chimes begin to softly ring in the office. A friendly female voice comes out of the wall. "Mr. Lee, your three o'clock is here."

"Thank you Mrs. Beasely. Well, old chum, it's time to go. Let me see you out to the lobby before we say goodbye."

Clem gives Lee a knowing, somewhat secretive look as they walk out together. Lee has his arm around Clem's shoulders as they pass by the security cameras. Lee whispers in Clem's ear. "You know that my office is bugged six ways from Sunday?" Clem's eyes widen a little, and he nods his head yes.

In a voice for more public consumption, Lee continues. "Old chum, when do you want to get together again?"

"Well, when do you get off work?"

"For you, I'll get off work at five. Where would you like to meet?"

"How about at Shanghai Reds?"

"That's good for a start. Why don't you meet me out in front at five, and we can walk there?"

Clem walks the three blocks back to his studio. He phones into the paper to tell them that he isn't going to return to work, and he takes some time to sort through the litter that was the old art gallery. After he changes his clothing, he returns to the Castle & Bishop Building. He only has to wait a minute before Lee appears in the lobby.

"Was that enough for a story?"

"I think so. Interviews like this are not exactly rocket science. Most of our questions have been predigested a thousand times. Any reporter guy could have probably have done the thing in his sleep."

"Well, that's good." Lee looks around on the street. There are some people walking around, going home. It's a good sign. He surprises Clem again.

"With the traffic here, it will be harder for anyone to bug us, but it will be easier for them to follow us. We have to assume that wherever we go, there will be someone tailing us and trying to record us. I suggest that we start out at Shanghai Red's for a drink, but we should go to the Inferno Disco if we want to talk. That will drive the audio guys crazy."

Clem looks at him. "My, my school boy, you sure do get around."

Ken gets close and whispers in his ear. "If we're going to see each other on a regular basis, we're going to have to practice some spy craft of our own. Don't say anything but 'Sure' when you hear this. How is your hunt for the magnetic interferometer going?"

Clem's eyes get very big. Reflexively, he yells out, "What?!" Ken Lee just smiles, and he puts his finger to his lips. "Silence is golden," he says motioning behind himself. "I think that car over there has a directional microphone. You see, we have a lot to talk about, but this conversation is going to have to wait until later. We've got to change the subject." Clem stays silent, trying not to look at the slouching men that he notices for the first time in the very clean and basic bones four-door sedan across the street.

Ken brightens somewhat artificially as he chirps loudly, "Well old chum, you've got to tell me about your life. Remember, it's my turn to interview you." Clem talks about high school and journalism school. He talks about his marriage to Salma when they were both out of college. He talks about his work on the alternative weekly and his big break by being picked up by the *Times*. He talks about the break-up of his marriage, and his reaction to that horrible experience. And he talks about his budding romance with Saroyan Pashogi. Ken takes great delight in this piece of news.

"You lucky dog! I should trade places with you! Millions of men go to be bed each night dreaming about what you do on a regular basis. How did you manage to keep it secret for so long? No one in my circle knows about this."

"Well, don't tell anybody. I'm lucky I still have my job. I basically walked into my boss' office just in time to avoid getting fired. You know, stuff like this is not only against company policy, but I don't know if I'm in the mood to be broadcast all over the world as the Sex Goddess' newest boy toy."

"Well, that still doesn't explain how you've managed to avoid the photo-vultures."

Clem smiles. He says, "Spy craft."

By now, they're at the bar. Clem orders a beer, and Ken orders a Singapore sling. "Everything is on my tab," he tells his reporter friend.

While they're sharing a drink, Lee steers the conversation strictly away from anything even remotely resembling business. In typical guy fashion, they're talking sports trash. The World Basketball League is starting its season, and most people in NLA rooted for Shanghai, Delhi, or Mexico City. Clem says, "Hey! I've got to be a Mexico City kind of guy!" In the middle of sports chat, Lee whispers in Clem's ear one more time.

"You see that guy over there in the pea coat? He's a regular here. He works in Naval Intelligence, and he monitors the talk from the sailors and anyone else he can listen to. The guy's a regular vacuum cleaner."

Clem knows that it's time to go to the Inferno. He remembers that guy from the time he took Saroyan here, and he wonders how much of their visit (and everything) else is now a matter of government record. By now the streets are deserted, but Lee helpfully points out the stray surveillance vans and cameras. Finally, they go inside the disco. Hanging out in the hallway near the dance floor, the noise is low

The Story of the Century

enough to allow each other to talk without shouting at each other. In a loud voice Lee says, "I love discos. If someone is bugging you and the conditions are right, you can just about destroy their equipment."

"So it's safe to talk here."

"More or less. I'll bet you're wondering how I knew about the magnetic interferometer, but everything I tell you has to be completely off the record. I can be a source, but I can't be close to being identified."

"Okay. I mean that's obvious"

"People say that I'm not your average real estate developer guy, and they're right. By the way, that's the last quote you're going to get from me this evening. From now on, you'll have to swear in public that you've never talked to me after the magazine interview."

"So how did you know about me and the magnetic interferometer?"

Lee smiles a wry smile. "Little pitchers have big ears. Let's just say that I have really, really good sources. Okay, twenty questions. Have you ever heard of B Company, 16th Marines, Transportation division?

"Uh, I think so. Weren't they the guys who were murdered at Santa Ynez?"

"Bingo! What do you think they were carrying? I've got another question for you. Who is a Platinum Prize winning physicist who's a big cheese at Cal Tech?"

"That's a little tougher. Bertrand Russell?"

"Incorrect. His name is Wong Fat, and he is the guy who has lots of answers about magnetic interferometers. You should try to do a Sunday feature on him, since you're getting so good at doing this."

"You know all this stuff?"

"Sure do, chum. I have really -- good -- sources. You're just going to have to trust me. We're going to have to practice some really serious spy craft. From now on, if you want to contact me, write a very small note, and attach it with chewing gum to the underside of ticket counter #2 at the main ferry building across the street from your office. I'll contact you by leaving a small note on the back of the drinking fountain in your newsroom. One more thing, you need to buy a book called *The History of Art in New Los Angeles*."

Clem doesn't know that he's being used as a pawn. He doesn't know that Ken Lee is in the same nutso religious cult at Sergeant Singh, or that they have carefully planned to play him like a fish on a line.

ON-LINE

THE MYSTERY OF COMPANY B

By Clem Reader and Emilio Flores

A new mystery has developed around the massacre of the Marines of Santa Ynez. Military officials at first gave contradictory messages about what Company B, of the 16th Marines, Transport Division was up to on the nights of February 19th and 20th. Now military officials have gone on record as saying that the Marines were on a mission 'vital to world security,' and the Department of Defense has classified all documents related to the mission as top secret. There have been a variety of speculative theories as to why the Marines were in the Ybarra Loncheria on that night, and there are a variety of speculative ideas as to what they were carrying.

MORE OFF LINE THAN ON

Clem is in his cubicle. He's been on the phone playing phone tag for three days with the secretary of the world-famous Wong Fat, Lodestar Chair Professor of Physics, California Institute of Technology.

Clem has sent over a raft of material to Professor Fat for inspection. He's haggled over four or five issues for the interview, and Fat has been generally noncooperative. And yet teeth are pulled. Somehow, Prof. Fat has actually agreed that 1:30 would be an acceptable time for a short chat. Wong Fat's haughty Mandarin face is on the screen facing Clem.

"So, is 1:30 an acceptable time for a one hour interview, Mr. Reader?"

"It sure is, Professor. I assume that you got a list of the questions."

"Yes I did."

"Then I'll talk to you after lunch. Thank you very much for taking the time for this interview. I really appreciate it, and so does the *Times*."

Some people can be a royal pain in the ass, and Professor Fat is shaping up as a cheese wheel in that category. Clem has use of a company car to drive to Cal Tech. While he's stuck on the freeway, you should have a little background information about the New California Institute of Technology. This is not the same Cal Tech as the Cal Tech of the 20th Century. After World War III, when there was a manhunt for war criminals responsible for starting the holocaust, Cal Tech people were very high on the list. The fledgling world government decided that Cal Tech should be torn into a million pieces before it was scattered by the wind. After about fifteen years the government changed its mind, and considerable effort was made to rebuild the campus in Redondo Beach. The new, improved Cal Tech has words in its mission statement that say, 'the peaceful research and development of science and technology.' Yet it still has 12 chairs by Lodestar, 14 endowed chairs by 3Way, and 3 chairs by Mitsubishi. Go figure.

By now, Clem is standing in front of the physics building. It's a giant white oval building with large black plate glass windows. There are several reasons why Clem is interviewing Prof. Fat. One is that the alumni association wanted an article for fundraising purposes. He's one of the preeminent scholars at the school, an expert on theories about magnetism. Clem is feeling a little insecure right now. Everyone around here is a genius. Clem is afraid that he'll be like the *Chicago Daily News* reporter who had an appointment with the Italian physicist, Enrico Fermi. Professor Fermi had just finished a little venture that fried Hiroshima and Nagasaki. The reporter visited the famous scholar, and he had a simple request:

"Doc, can we get a picture of you placing the atom in the machine, -- a picture of the atom smashing, and then a picture of you sweeping up the pieces?"

Clem knows that he'll sound stupid and boneheaded no matter how hard he tries. He got a "D" in differential equations in college, and he nearly dropped out because of that and his bad grade in physics. But here he is.

Now he is at the professor's gray metal door with a number on it. Like many an academic Prof. Fat has plastered his door and surrounding walls with physics jokes. One joke is the word 'HANDLE,' with an arrow pointing at the door handle. Another is a red bumper sticker that reads, "IF THIS LOOKS BLUE TO YOU, SLOW DOWN." Those science guys are a million laughs. Clem knocks on the door, and sees the gray haired, middle-aged man with thick glasses and an unlined face who answers the door.

"Come in, Mr. Reader, I assume."

What he sees is a large office completely lined with bookshelves. There is wall-to-wall carpeting, but you'd never know it because it is covered with piles of papers. There are piles of PhD theses Fat has read or not read, piles of papers that he is, has, or will coauthor, and piles of papers he will not respond to. There are stacks of books. There are stacks of magazines and scientific periodicals. There are a scattered selection of newspapers, government documents, and documents from various global corporations. On Professor Fat's desk there is a high mound of paperwork and books concerning his most urgent and important business. Other than for a narrow, winding path from door to chairs, the only other paper free space is the area directly around his computer.

The professor smiles weakly, "Excuse my mess, Mr. Reader, you're going to have to put up with my filing system just like everybody else. When you've got as many irons in the fire as I have, a rational filing order just won't do. All my secretaries and interns have tried to reform me, but I'm just a reprobate. I eventually reform them." Like others before him, this self-deprecating humor relaxes Clem, but everything is downhill from here.

"Pleased to meet you, Professor. Thanks for taking time out of your schedule to meet with me. I'm really glad we got through." He follows the professor as they zigzag through the piles. Clem sits down on the hard metal chair with the leather seat, while the professor sits in his black leather executive chair. For forty-five minutes they run through the standard questions regarding Prof. Fat's background, growing up, how he performed in school, and his rise to the top of his field. Clem glances at his watch. There's still time to do some digging about the magnetic interferometer

"Okay. I think you know that our readers aren't very sophisticated in physics. I'm not very sophisticated either, but I've been studying, and I've been talking to other people. So I hope I don't sound like a total ignoramus. But I'd like it if we could use the most non-technical language possible."

"Okay, well if we have to speak to kindergarten kids, we have to speak to kindergarten kids." Now Clem is feeling humble.

"I've read *Science World* on a regular basis, and I've seen some good educational TV. A lot of people don't even absorb that much."

"Well, that puts us at first grade level. I must say that some of those shows are informative (especially the ones I've produced). There may be hope yet. First let's start with dimensions. You know one dimension, two dimensions, three dimensions, four? Time and space. Where we are now? You can see the second hand on my wall clock moving."

"Yes sir."

"But you know that our most recent theories of the universe say that it actually works best in ten dimensions. Some people say, "Eleven." No one really knows, but math being math, ten is more elegant, you know."

"Yes go on. How do those dimensions fit into the picture?"

"That's actually a good question. Now we're stuck in 4-D. The other dimensions are wound up in smaller and smaller spaces inside each other. Extra dimensions are wound up inside of quarks. They're too small to measure. "The professor lectures on and on. Clem doesn't understand any of it. It's time to change the subject.

"What could mankind do if it could separate and isolate the magnetic poles?"

"Remember, if we were able to do that now, which we're not, it would take an enormous amount of power interacting on only one atom. It might take more than septillions of volts or even more to make one magnetic monopole. If we could create that much power on a regular and controlled basis, we would never have an energy shortage. But if we could do it, we'd be well on the way towards creating an antigravity device. We might even be able to transcend the current limitations of time, space, and the laws of physics as they operate here."

"So if you could really control magnetism by splitting the poles, you might even make something like interstellar travel possible?"

"We'd certainly be a lot closer to that than we are today."

The professor begins to talk about magnetic monopoles in an extended non-answer. The professor is obviously in love with his own

The Story of the Century

brilliance, and Clem tunes him out. "It's time to strike," Clem thinks to himself.

"Id like you to comment about the recent news concerning the Marines who were massacred at Santa Ynez."

Professor Fat immediately straightens up and enters his official mode. "I really don't know much about it. What do you want me to talk about?"

"It just came out today. I called around about what the Marines were shipping the night they died. The first source I talked to said that it was some spare parts for a generator. Another DOD source said that the Marines were transporting a device called a magnetic interferometer." Clem's not totally lying, but he is playing poker.

The professor puts his fingers together like a bridge. He frowns a little.

"All of that sounds a little bit interesting. If they were taking a magnetic interferometer, they were taking something that doesn't exist. Really, there's no such thing. I really don't know what to say about that massacre, except that it's too bad all those soldiers died. I really hope they've found the people who did that job." He doesn't tell Clem that he was in the meeting with Secretary of Defense Corozon when they planned the massacre.

"Well, some people think that the Marines were transporting some kind of alien technology." Clem is cut off short. The professor scowls, and it's clear that the learned man is mocking the ignorant reporter.

"So, little green men, I suppose. Why don't we talk about the Easter Bunny or Santa Claus? Mr. Reader! I thought you had a first grade education. You need to go back to kindergarten! Why not talk about the international banking conspiracy? How about those automobile tires that last a million miles, but the auto companies suppress? You have really punched my buttons! I don't know why I wasted my time with you!"

"I apologize Professor Fat." It looks like, from Clem's perspective that Fat had punched a buttom himself somewhere. As if by magic, a voice sounds out of the wall. "Your appointment is here, Professor Fat."

"Thank you. We're just winding up, aren't we?" Fat cocks one eyebrow at Clem with a slightly menacing expression. They exchange limp pleasantries as they meander to the door.

"Send my secretary a copy of your article. I'd like to see it before publication."

"No problem, Professor." Clem suddenly finds himself out in the hall as Fat closes the door a little too strongly. There's only one person in the hall -- a mousy young woman in a plaid skirt, white bobby socks, and a ratty gray sweater. She's clutching some books, and she looks like a graduate student.

"Pardon me," Clem says. "Do you happen to know where a snack bar is?"

"I'm going there now. Follow me. We have to take the elevator." On the way down, the girl surprises Clem. She turns to him. "Were you just interviewing Professor Fat?"

"Yes, as a matter of fact. I'm a reporter with the *New Los Angeles Times*. My name is Clem Reader."

"Pleased to meet you. My name is Pham Nguyen. I'm one of Professor Fat's graduate assistants. Did he treat you harshly?"

"No, not really. The interview went really well, and then he had another appointment."

"Were you talking about magnetic things when he got angry at you?"

Clem is a little surprised to hear this. His thought balloon says, "How does she know that Fat got pissed off at me? Is she some kind of mind reader?"

He says, "I started asking him questions about what those Marines were carrying when they were killed in Mexico a couple of months ago."

"You know about the Marines?" she asks.

"I've written a few stories about them."

Nguyen's curiosity is piqued. "In 25 words or less, what did you say about the Marines in Mexico?"

Clem puts his hand to his chin. "I said that there was some mystery as to what they were carrying the night they were killed."

Nguyen is turning into a reporter, and Clem is now the interviewee. "How so?" It's beginning to look like butter would not melt in the mouth of Miss Nguyen.

"Well, I'd rather not say. There was an issue with the Department of Defense, and then everybody does a 180. I haven't seen such a clam up about information in a long time."

Miss Nguyen smiles. If she were a cat, there would be a feather in her mouth. "The professor knows a lot about the Marines. He was lying to you."

"How do you know the professor was lying to me?"

"Because I've seen the minutes of the meeting that he was in last year when they discussed what was going to happen to the magnetic interferometer."

"What did you say?"

"The professor had a meeting last year when they planned what would happen to the magnetic interferometer."

"This is a bolt from the blue," Clem thinks to himself. By now they're at the empty snack bar in front of the vending machines. They're sitting a a table, eating their one dollar treats.

"I'm sorry for being so rude about the professor. Everything that Professor Fat told you about the magnetic interferometer is bullshit. He's worked on that piece of equipment for years. He had me do field-testing with it in the Arizona district. I apologize. I've said too much already." She covers her hand over her mouth.

"No, that's all right. Please tell me more." Clem is trying hard to keep his hands from shaking, and he's beginning to sweat.

"Much of the theoretical work the professor has done on magnetism has come from working on the machine. The professor is withholding much evidence from the public."

"That's a pretty serious set of charges. Can you back any of this up?"

"Yes I can. I've seen the documents, and I've done some of the filing on them."

"Why are you telling me, a total stranger about this? What you're saying is very serious. Your position could be jeopardized."

Nguyen looks at him and her eyes begin to get red. "I don't care. He has used my work and me for his own purposes. I was supposed to have gotten my PhD a long time ago. I made a big mistake, and I put him on my graduate committee. He has held me like a prisoner. He has refused to sign off on my PhD thesis. I have done his empirical dirty work, and he has gotten rich off of the papers I wrote under his name. All I got was the need to pay more tuition."

"But if you tell me about the magnetic interferometer, wouldn't you be jeopardizing your own position?"

"No, not any more. I am almost ready to tell the professor that I am going to abandon my schooling at Cal Tech. I'm engaged to be married to a wonderful man, and I won't have to worry about physics any more."

"So, you said you could get documents that say that the professor has some knowledge about a magnetic interferometer?"

"I certainly can. There are file cabinets full of documents that I can show you."

"Well, let's start with the professor planning what would happen to the magnetic interferometer, along with some description of what it does and what it looks like?"

"I can do that."

Clem thinks for a moment in the empty snack bar. Then he opens up his notebook. "Give me your name and telephone number. Here is my business card. I'd appreciate it if you could copy this information down instead of taking the card. I think it would be advisable if we practiced some spy craft. Would it be possible for you to get your hands on the book, *The History of Art in New Los Angeles*?"

NEWS ROOM DRINKING FOUNTAIN

While bending down to take a drink, Clem feels the water cooler's backside. There's a small plastic bag taped there that he detaches and puts in his pocket. When he gets to the men's room, he goes inside a stall and sits down. Only then does he open the bag. Inside are some squares of toilet paper with neat printing that Clem decodes:

"Meet me at Location A. You'll need about an hour to lose your tail. One way of doing this is to pretend to get on the ferry going home, but jump ship at the last minute like you forgot something. Run out of the terminal into the *Times* Building, and go out through the loading dock. Get a taxi, and ride around town. Congratulations on breaking the story. There are bigger stories and more to come."

Clem thinks to himself, "Is this really worth it?" as he flushes the message down the toilet. He buries the baggie in the waste paper receptacle, and he washes his hands before he goes back to work. At five o'clock he follows the crowd out the door. It's been a slow news day, and the leads that he had on the big story have all gotten very cold and inhospitable.

Outside, things look normal enough. Pedestrians and vehicles are in their going home mode. A zoned-out Rastafarian is playing his clarinet for money ten feet away from the entrance to the *Times* Building. About 15 meters away, there's a man in a pea coat. He looks vaguely familiar, as if he were a neighbor in El Puerto. Clem doesn't dare look at him. Mr. Shadow. What's his name? Boson Something of Naval Intelligence. His own personal spy. Clem is thinking these things as he crosses the street and goes into the terminal, echoing loud with crowd sounds, announcements, and hologram news. He walks up to ticket counter #1 and pays for a monthly pass. Final boarding for the 5:15 is in two minutes. The announcement comes for the final boarding of the ferry for the Harbor area, and Clem walks across the metal gangplank to board the vaporetto. Instead of sitting down, he stays near the railing and the gangplank, looking down at the water and the pier.

The crew is getting ready to shove off. This is the moment for Clem to hit his forehead and curse. "Oh my God! The Veeblefetzer story!" Surprising the deck hands as well as the passengers around him, Clem dashes down the gangplank just as it starts retracting into the boat. He has to jump a half-meter gap between boat and pier, but he lands on dry land in a crouching position. A security guard and a deck hand help him to his feet. Clem is slightly out of breath. It isn't every day that he pulls a stunt like this.

"Thanks guys. I'm really sorry. I mean really sorry. I'm a reporter from across the street, and I forgot about the deadline on this story. If I don't get it done tonight, my boss is going to kill me." The two men relax their grips. Glancing towards the water, Clem can see the ferry getting up to speed. One man at the fantail appears to be livid with rage. He keeps banging his hand on the boat railing. Is he talking into his pea coat? The security guard opens up the terminal gate for Clem.

"You're lucky, Bozo. Don't make a habit out of it. The next time you do something like this, I'm going to call the cops."

"Thanks Officer." Clem quickly and steadily exits the waiting room and crosses the street. He presents himself at the main entrance.

"Al, how are you doing?"

The Story of the Century

The guard recognizes him and opens the giant bronze doors. After he signs in, he returns to his desk and opens up his computer to do some internet browsing. He sees how things are developing in Central America and the Congo. He leaves his machine on. Instead of taking the elevator, he takes the stairs in the back hallway that wind up on the loading dock. Security is a little surprised, but he shows them his work pass. Outside, Clem looks around. The streets are empty. Turning the corner, he comes upon the taxi stand that serves the Grand Hotel. Going to the head of the line, Clem gets in and says, "Drive me around town, but get me to 7th and Broadway by six."

Burger World is not his idea of fun. If it were up to him, the damn fast food chain would have gone bankrupt decades ago. Meat flavored, spicy, high fat, genetically engineered tofu burger is still fast food, and candy cane striped plastic seats at Formica tabletops are not his ideas of fine interior decorating. But here he is. Ken Lee is in the corner dressed in jeans, a leather jacket, and a baseball cap. Clem goes to the counter and orders a McSushi and a giant green tea. Then he comes to the booth and sits down.

"How are you doing, sport?"

"I didn't have any trouble getting here, did you?"

"Well, there was a little excitement at the ferry building. There was a very unhappy camper on the ferry going to El Puerto."

Lee thinks for a moment, "The fact that we're meeting together, and the fact that you broke your tail means that things are going to get hotter from now on. You really annoy the boys when you do something like you did today, and they don't like that."

"Is that why you got in touch with me?"

"That's one reason. Look, I'm going to do everything I can to protect you, but you should know that things might get dangerous from here on. Are you up to it?"

"Hey, if it means the big story, I'm game. But I have a lot of questions. Are you up to it?"

Ken Ho shrugs, "We're here. I've got the time. Fire away."

"My first question is, I've been pursuing this magnetic interferometer thing, whatever it is. It looks like the whole world has been interested in the thing. I talked to the military, and they almost said it was a magnetic interferometer on the back of that truck in Santa Ynez before they shut the whole thing down. The way it looks now, the mystery of Santa Ynez will never be solved because everyone in the government just refuses to talk about it. So I don't know where to go from here. Do you have any suggestions?"

"I do. The first thing you have to know is that this magnetic interferometer is just the tip of the iceberg. Do you remember those movies where everybody is running after something? It could be gold, or diamonds, or a suitcase full of cash; it doesn't matter. They're all after it. The magnetic interferometer is the same thing. You need to look at **why** everybody is either running around like a chicken with their head cut off, or in deep ass-covering mode."

"So, why is everybody running after this thingamajig?"

"I'm glad you asked me that question. The reason why is because the thingamajig is a piece of alien technology. That's the simple answer."

There is some silence.

Clem looks at Ken Lee almost mockingly. "Oh, you mean little green men? Flying saucers?"

"See, you've been conditioned just like everybody else. A lot of time and money has been spent on disinformation. You know as well as I do about how many woo woos and granola heads get all cosmic about President Hok's space alien baby. Well, did you know that for every nut case who saw a big wienie in the sky, there's another woo woo who's actually on the government payroll? Yup, their job is to be weird, just so that people won't believe in UFOs? And there are others, who are professional debunkers who are up to their armpits in dealing with aliens on an almost daily basis."

"Now it's my turn for another big question, old chum. Just how DO you know all this good stuff?"

It's Lee's turn to smile. "To the world, I'm just a humble millionaire real estate developer, but I have a day job, too. Let's say that the CIA, for example, has to carry lots of stuff all over the world. Now, it can't go on a military ship because it's under deep cover. So, let's say they need civilian front companies to do their work for them. There are trucking companies. There are offices. There are warehouses. How do you think the Company does its job?"

"Let me guess. Castle & Bishop?"

"Bingo. You know what I always say as a manager. You can learn a lot by walking around. The CIA has been very, very good to me, and I have seen some pretty funny stuff in my warehouses going out on ships."

"So, you're telling me, that you've looked at pieces of alien hardware pass through the port?"

"Not only that, but maybe a few little green guys too. The government is involved in all sorts of weird shit."

"There's no doubt that what you're telling me is an absolutely gripping story, but there is that perennial problem. Where's the beef?"

Lee puts his hand on Clem's arm lightly. "Believe me old chum, you're closer than you realize. You already have established the mystery of Santa Ynez, and I saw your Sunday supplement on the great Professor Fat. By the way, how did that go?"

"He's pretty full of himself, but I guess he has a right to. Not everyone can win a Platinum Prize in physics."

"How do you think he got the Platinum Prize?"

"I don't know. The space aliens gave it to him?"

"Close but no cigar. Have you ever thought that maybe Professor Fat did some reverse engineering at some undisclosed location, and then somehow miraculously came up with his amazing breakthroughs in science?"

"That sounds plausible. He sure clammed up when I started mentioning the 'magnetic interferometer' words. It was like listening to a prerecorded announcement, and after the interview I had to hold the crying towel for one unhappy grad student who said that Professor Fat has been working on alien equipment to get his reknown, and that the good professor was in on the meeting where they set up the Marines to bite the biscuit in the delivery of a magnetic interferometer. I took it that in addition to some dissertation problems, she might have had some sexual problems with the great professor. And, just to cover my bases, I told her about the book that you recommended to me. On top of that, the grad student says that she can get me documents to prove all of her assertions."

At this point, Ken Ho Yunghai Lee almost calls attention to himself by getting so excited. He waves his hands as he talks. "Baby, you're so close to the money, you can touch it! I know that you need documentation to break all this stuff that I've been talking to you about, but that grad student wants to give you the keys to the Mint! Ask her about Agenda Item #9 of the Public Private Partnership meeting of May 14th of last year. That's one of my golden oldies! Or how about, what Professor Fat has been doing in the Foreign Technology Division in the Department of Defense? I mean, I can give you more good questions to ask, but that will do for now."

As good a set of news as all this is, Clem is still a reporter; and his job is to be a cynical skeptic. It's time to ask Ken the big question. "Can you get me some supporting documentation on what your experience is? What you've been seeing?'

"Sure. No problem."

Suddenly Lee clams up. The old school pals are sitting in a back booth in Burgerville, and Lee is in a corner, his back to the wall. Clem can see his jaw clench up, and his old school pal is looking behind Clem as he starts to scribble something on a napkin. Suddenly Ken Lee is a stranger. Lee gets out of the booth with his food tray, and he goes out of the restaurant. Clem turns around, and he sees a tall, muscular man with short hair follow him onto the street.

Looking down at the table, Clem sees what Lee's written:

"A bad guy from Lodestar is in here. See you later and burn this."

DEPARTMENT OF DEFENSE BUILDING, KUALA LUMPUR ROOM 2948A, RING C

The Ad Hoc Interagency Task Force (AHITF) is buried so deeply in the bureaucracy that no one ever pays any attention to it at all. Its office is literally a broom closet. A computer box without a screen or keyboard is on a shelf. Next to the floor polish there is an answering machine. Somewhere there is a post office box that never gets any mail. This is the equipment for the executive offices and the support staff. An Army general has gotten a greenhorn lieutenant in Botswana to write papers about things like the importance of standardizing shoelaces between the Army and the Navy. Fresh out of officer's training, the lieutenant has been informed that this is a good way to get a promotion. He has been misinformed. No one ever reads them. Fifty copies of his report have been made as cheaply as possible with the AHITF logo on them. They are in various dust covered file cabinets in giant warehouses. Other than for the lieutenant's output, there are no traces of the AHITF's existence. The front guy is some alcoholic lifer colonel who has been put in charge of day-to-day operations as a punishment detail.

Surprisingly enough, such an obscure agency has stellar talent for its secret executive board, which oversees the real work on a need to know basis. It includes a senior member of the World Security Council, a Blue House Deputy Chief of Staff, an Undersecretary of Defense, and various members of the Joint Chiefs of Staff. The three people who do the heavy lifting are a general, an admiral, and the Director of Special Operations for the Central Intelligence Agency.

You are very lucky. There is a meeting of the AHITF going on right now. Three conservatively dressed gentlemen are sitting in a spartan government conference room. Papers, folders, and bound documents (many bearing the Lodestar logo) are scattered around the gray metal table in front of the men. The data has been highlighted and color-coded with stick-on tabs. These documents have been reviewed and rehashed again and again by the committee.

Photographs and news articles are pinned to the wall. One of the photos is of Clem and Saroyan on the beach. There is an article from the *Singapore Post* on Governor Esteban Salinas. There is a *New Los Angeles Times* article by Clem featuring Ken Ho Yunghai Lee. There are some ID shots of currently enlisted Marine sergeants and officers, and a group portrait of the students and staff of the Cal Tech physics department.

Ivan Golytsin is the general. He is one of the few Russians in the world, and he has an IQ of about 200. He is a short, clean-shaven balding man. As a 60-year-old guy, he can bench press a fuel cell. His most impressive facial features are his extremely intense, blue squinty eyes. He's the tactical genius of the group.

Admiral Hideo Sakimota has been in the Special Branches of Naval Intelligence for the last twenty years. He gets around. Last week he was on a hi-lo drop mission in Kazakhstan. For those who don't know, that's when you jump out of an airplane at 10,000 meters or more, and you pull the ripcord at 100 meters. It's quite thrilling. Sakimota has been kicking himself ever since he had the flu one day, and the Joint Chiefs designated Gen. Caramehni in his place for a meeting. Admiral Sakimota thinks that General Caramehni is an incompetent twit, and he's right. If the Admiral were at that Public Private Partnership meeting of May 14th last year, none of this would have ever happened.

The chair of this meeting is a desiccated old prune. He looks like an extremely well tailored but decadent librarian, either that or a president from the Dong Wa Greater Amazon Bank. It's hard to tell. He's one of those Brazilians I've been telling you about. Alberto Comaraso, Central Intelligence.

They are meeting in this dreary little anonymous conference room in the Fascist-modern skyscraper known as the Department of Defense in downtown Kuala Lumpur. There are two stainless steel government issue urns on a gray enameled steel stand. One is for coffee. The other is for water. Cheap drinking glasses and plain white coffee cups complete the décor.

Comaraso speaks. "I believe we all know why we are here. There has been a determination that there has been a clear case of breach of world security that calls for immediate action." Heads nod in agreement. He continues. "As you can see, there are a variety of options facing us here. Some or all of these people may be selected."

Admiral Sakimota speaks next. "That is true. However, I will go on the record and say that there should be definite priorities in the selection process. Some people are more worthy of consideration than others. Let's review the evidence."

General Golytsin interjects. "Gentlemen, we don't have the time to review any more. This needs no further review. This needs immediate attention."

Comaraso nods his head. "Point well taken, General. We all have to agree that significant intelligence gaps continue to exist in this matter. The question remains as to whether Mr. Reader knowingly eluded surveillance that one time. And we haven't been able to isolate the sources of all of our leaks."

General Golytsin smiles a weak tea smile. "That is correct, Mr. Chairman. However, there is nothing to prevent us from making additional determinations in the future. In the meantime, I believe we must be as conservative as we possibly can be in making our decisions."

Everyone agrees that this is a good idea, but Admiral Sakimota rolls his eyes when the others are speaking. "I would still urge caution. Why is it that our best intelligence equipment is subject to what I can only call mysterious failures? How many leaks are there, and where are they definitively located? And there are indications that our most secure channels are being monitored from somewhere, we don't know."

Comaraso gets a little grumpy. "Admiral, these are all excellent points, but we need to stay to the subject that is at hand. The reporter is a protected class in the Constitution, but someone is feeding him extremely dangerous information, and this information must be retrieved."

General Golytsin raises an index finger. "I believe that the resources are at our disposal to take care of all the problems surrounding Mr. Reader, wouldn't you agree?"

Now it is Admiral Sakimota's turn for a weak tea smile. "There are serious repercussions for everyone on our suspect list. Wouldn't you agree?"

General Golytsin is an excellent tennis player. He lobs a backhand smash at the admiral. "We can certainly look at the situation of Governor Salinas, Mr. Lee, and Ms. Nguyen, and of course Sergeant Singh, wouldn't you agree?" The admiral knows he is outvoted, so he will make it a unanimous vote.

Alberto Comaraso looks over his reading glasses. "Gentlemen, there is still the issue of Saroyan Pashogi."

Now it is the admiral's turn. "I believe the situation with Ms. Pashogi is identical to that of Mr. Reader. (pause) Wouldn't you agree?"

General Golytsin gives another weak tea smile. "Point well taken, Admiral, but with a different set of circumstances, wouldn't you agree?"

Alberto senses closure. Alberto likes quick meetings. Alberto knows how to read body language better than anyone. "Gentlemen, I sense a vote."

Admiral Sakimota speaks. "I would vote for Plan Epsilon."

"Plan Epsilon. Is there any discussion?"

General Golytsin speaks. "I advocate Epsilon. We delete Delta."

Admiral Sakimota thinks for a bit. "I think that is very wise of you. Go Epsilon and delete Delta."

Alberto says, "Well, I believe we have closure. We can begin implementing immediately."

SOCHI'S

Clem and Mbake are having a few drinks after work, and they've gone through shop talk. The older reporter has decided that it's time to do a little chain pulling. "So let's talk about what's really important, Clem. How are you doing with SP, and how come we haven't seen your bright and shining face on 'The Waldo Show' or 'Hot Romance of the Week?'

Clem blushes just a little, "I don't know. Maybe I'm lucky, but we try to be really careful about not showing up in public places where there are lots of Nosey Parker reporters like you around. But I don't complain. We see each other about twice a week. It's our separate schedules, you know. Speaking of which, would you mind if I borrow your phone for a minute? I'd like to talk to her."

"Okay, I'll lend you my phone, but it'll cost you 10% of the net gross."

Clem raises a fist in a mock threatening mode. "Why, I oughta! Just give me the phone. Would you settle for 7% of the gross and three blocks of commercial property in the Castlemarre?"

Clem gets the phone, and he steps outside. Saroyan's face pops up on the screen. She is obviously glad to see him. "Oh, honeybunny! I was just thinking of calling you. This commercial they've got me on is a low-grade nightmare. We're on our 37th take. The food handler is not happy with the way the dessert tray looks on screen. When am I going to see you?"

"How about tonight? Isn't the shooting just about done?"

"Hmmmn. I think I'll take matters into my own hands. What if I lay down an ultimatum that shooting is going to stop at seven? Maybe you can stop by and pick me up."

That sounds like a good idea. The studio's on Burbank, right?"

"Right."

"Okay, I'll be there at 7:15. Is that good?

"As good as you are, tiger."

"Okay. I love you, Sweetie."

"I love you, Honeybunny."

"Bye bye."

"Bye bye."

Clem is also phoning another woman. He has been thinking about what Ken Lee had told him. It's time to place a call to Phan Nguyen. He reaches into his wallet and pulls out her number. Her face appears on the screen. She is mildly surprised to see him.

"Is that you, Mr. Reader? I thought that you might have forgotten me. I want to apologize to you for my behavior last week. I certainly didn't want to appear forward to you, and tell you my problems. Again, I am sorry."

"Think nothing of it, Ms. Nguyen. I've been thinking about what you told me that day, and I believe that you have very important things to say. Where would be a good place to get together?"

"I don't know. I am a little afraid lately. I feel as if I'm being watched. I don't know who is watching me. Am I wrong to assume this, or am I just a silly woman?"

"No, I don't think so. I do have a favor I'd like to ask of you. Your conversation with me sounded like there was a lot you wanted to talk to me about, but could you provide any documentation about what you've been talking about?"

Clem can see that she is thinking. "Yes, there are many papers I can share. Where should we meet?"

"I hope you remember your reading. How about Sunday at 2PM at Mrs. Jeremiah Barnes' house?"

SATURDAY AFTERNOON, EL PUERTO

Clem is at loose ends. Saroyan is in Mexico. The plate glass window at the front of the storefront still shows the site installation about New LA. The sign on the door says, 'Closed. By appointment only. Call 5134-0247." That's a joke -- as if anyone ever came down this street in search of a modern art purchase Behind the gallery space is the living space of tall ceilings and bachelor furniture with mail scattered on the floor with old bills and ads for robot upgrades. Clem idly watches the present that Saroyan has given him. It's a hologram of her cat, Junior, and it helps him from getting lonely. Clem really likes Junior. The tailless gray Persian jumps from box to furniture to box. Clem goes into the kitchen and pours himself a generous portion of scotch. Some things are still done best the old-fashioned way.

He goes back to the main area and says, "B.B. King. No pictures." The computer hears him while he's rummaging for the book. The old Chess records disk has somehow survived the centuries, and *The Thrill Is Gone* begins to fill the room. He pulls the coffee table book out from underneath a pile of newspapers and turns to page 110, looking at the picture of Mrs. Jeremiah Barnes. Junior is at his feet, rubbing up against him. He looks at the image in the book again. Then he goes about mentally rehearsing how he'll do what he has to tomorrow.

He's spent Saturday relaxing, gathering strength and supplies for the week ahead. He hasn't been under visible surveillance, and that's good. Before he goes to bed, he calls Saroyan. The lovers have that kind of conversation that two people have when distances separate them. Saroyan is excited and upbeat. This is the first shooting for *Zorro*. Clem is supportive, but he knows in his mind that the Governor of Mexico has to be lurking somewhere in the background. They talk in code a little, as they know they're really broadcasting. Clem reminds her to milk Salinas for information on his domestic activities. Eventually they hang up, and the silence returns to the gallery.

Sunday morning is gloomy, threatening, and cold. The clouds bump into each other in their own traffic jam. There are layers of clouds resting on top of other layers. It's the kind of cloudy that wants to last forever. He goes down to the docks early enough and boards the water taxi. Only two other people are going downtown on the trip with him, a bum and a cleaning woman. Clem guesses that the bum is his tail, but he's wrong. It's the cleaning woman. The ocean is in a sullen mood. Wisps of cloud are torn apart on the Palos Verde peninsula, and there's a short and nasty chop to the thick gray water.

For hours, Clem traverses the Los Angeles Basin, with his phony work at the office, numerous cab rides to nowhere, and various forms of public transporation. All of this takes place in a world barely

The Story of the Century

inhabited by people, and it gives Clem entirely too much time to think about the situation he's in. Sure, he's excited about the prospect of actually being able to crack open one of the stories of the century, but he can feel the tails breathing down his neck. He knows he has way too many unwanted vistors on his electronic traffic, and he wonders how much danger he's getting himself and other people into. Would the government take steps to actually kill him or other people if it thought that one of its most closely guarded secrets was compromised? Clem shuts that thought out of his mind quickly. "I'm only doing my job," he thinks to himself as he watches the landscape pass by under the threatening skies; but at the same time, he can't help but wonder which supposedly innocent looking person on the Gold Line is actually an employee of the world security apparatus.

It's Cepeda Avenue, and the shuttle is waiting to take Clem and the tourists to the Huntington Gardens. Pasadena and San Marino are islands of civilization in the radioactive wilderness. Despite the fact that Pasadena had been as hard hit as anywhere, the world government and the real estate developers have taken the trouble (and the clean-up money) to make the area into something resembling its old self, only with a tenth of the people.

The Samuel Huntington Library is a world heritage site by any stretch of the imagination. After all, there aren't many places left where you can see how 19th and 20th American plutocrats lived. Clem follows the tourists off the shuttle that deposits them in front of the ticket booths. The Gainsboroughs have been restored a few years ago, and they're housed in a new pavilion. Attendance is sparse, and the few people visiting are not going to the old mansion. When it's sunny, the two-story sandstone mansion looks sumptuous and elegant, sitting in the middle of hectares of manicured landscape and lawns. Today it appears to be haunted, looking like the home of some sinister legislature.

Walking up the circular drive, he has a good idea of what's waiting for him, but he wonders about what will follow from this visit. The giant bronze and glass doors open silently onto the polished marble foyer. On either side of the main entrance, alabaster stairs curve and disappear on their way to the second floor. On the right is the bronze statue of Diana, the huntress. On the foyer wall, there's a portrait of an 18th Century English woman, looking out seductively in her flowing white diaphanous gown. Standing underneath the portrait of Mrs. Jeremiah Barnes is Pham Nguyen. She's dressed just as Clem had seen her before in her Japanese schoolgirl uniform. They shake hands.

"How do you do again, Mr. Reader."

"Ms. Nguyen, I really appreciate the trouble you took to come here. I know it hasn't been easy for you, and I've given a great deal of thought to our conversation at Cal Tech. I know that what you have to say is important. I appreciate your determination."

They sit down on a carved marble bench underneath Diana. Clem continues. "Maybe you need to begin by telling me why you want to talk to me."

He can tell just by looking at her that she's paranoid and distraught. She's afraid, but at the same time, she has determination because she's been hurt. Clem thinks that she wants to spill the beans on Professor Fat as a way of breaking away from the university. He listens.

"Ever since I was a little girl, I was always interested in physics. I used to plot the trajectories of toy cars that I pushed off of tables. I was always a good student. In every grade, I got nothing but 'A's. In high school I won the Tesla Prize for my state. There was never any question that I was going to be a good physicist some day, and I was going to teach and do research at a good university. Now all that has been destroyed. I can't take it any longer, and I've decided to break free. Up until now, I have been in prison. Cal Tech was where I've been shooting for ever since high school, but I'm very close to leaving the university. I have fallen in love with a nice Vietnamese boy."

Here she takes a picture out of her wallet and shows it to Clem.

"He is a high school science teacher. He was attending night school at Cal Tech where I was graduate teaching. He's changed my entire life. It was very hard for me to come to grips with what my life's ambitions were, and the trap that I have found myself in. But I would rather be a lowly high school teacher than the bird in the golden cage."

"How are you a bird in a golden cage?"

"It all began as an undergraduate. As a senior, I got to take an honors course with the great Professor Fat. It was as if I were close to realizing my dreams. Here I am, sitting in the presence of one of the greatest physicists of all time. You can imagine how honored I was. And the man is brilliant and charming. He still is. We went through the theories of gravity and electromagnetism, and his discourse is brilliant. I felt that I learned more in one class session than I had in a year of undergraduate studies. And he paid attention to me. After all, there aren't many people in the world who are even at a level of understanding of the professor's theories. He encouraged me to pursue graduate studies at Cal Tech. He said I was a brilliant student, and he pulled levers to get me a full scholarship. This is how my graduate career began, but that is a long time ago."

Clem listens sympathetically, but he wonders. "So how did that lead you to searching out me?"

"I began my graduate studies, and I went through my masters in a year. The professor was very encouraging, and he shared with me some of his concerns about the theories of magnetism. There are holes and mysteries, and he suggested the topic and course of investigation for my PhD thesis. Of course this pleased me a great deal. Being in this position almost guarantees fame and importance in the science world.

I was so excited. I had him as the head of my graduate committee. He was my mentor. He was a father figure, and we became intimate. That is where the trouble began."

"Wong has always been a ladies' man. He has more than his share of groupies. While he was interested in me for a while, he found new sport. Slowly, I changed from being his lover to being just a research animal. I thought I could handle him sleeping with other women, but the shock came when I had written over half of my paper and I read the latest copy of *Physics*. The cover article was by Professor Fat, and it was my dissertation chapter word for word. I confronted him on it, but he didn't have much to say. He knew that I was good. That was why I was doing field testing on the magnetic interferometer."

Clem perks up "You said the magnetic interferometer. What did you do with it?" From here, Clem gets Ms. Nguyen to walk him through her responsibilities as test supervisor in the Arizona desrt, and he gets her to promise to supply the documentation on the alien technology at their next meeting. But he needs more How real is she?

"I have another question for you. I know how terribly wronged you've been by Professor Fat, but are there any other reasons for telling me about all of this."

"Well, yes. I think that the world should know that Professor Fat has accumulated his reputation on false pretenses. All this time, he's had access to machines that laid a whole roadmap out for the breakthroughs in physics that he's claimed. As a graduate student, I did all of his work for him, and I just as easily could have claimed credit for those so-called breakthroughs. He's used me, and he's used other people in the past just like me. I think the world needs to know that."

"For me being a reporter, I have a couple more questions. Can you provide me with any documents that can back up what you're talking about?"

"Sure, although some documents really are under tight lock and key. But others are just lying around on his office floor. Not only did I do the work on a lot of them, but I was responsible for filing them. How many documents do you want? I can get things to you in a week or so."

"That's great. I'd appreciate it if you could start compiling things for me. Now, the last question. Is there anyone else you know who might be able to corroborate what you've been telling me?"

Ms Nguyen bites her lip, and looks down. She raises her head and says, "Maybe my boyfriend. Maybe another graduate student. I don't know."

"Okay, please get back to me on that. That's very important. Now, for our next meeting, can you bring all of your documents?" Nguyen nods her head yes, and Clem continues:

"Okay, how does June 12th at 11:00 AM at the main bus terminal restaurant sound? Can you have everything ready by then?."

There is anger and determination in Ms. Nguyen's eyes. She looks straight at Clem and says, "I can do it. I will be there."

Now it's time to go, and the two walk along the paths to the parking lot. A weight seems to be off of Ms. Nguyen's shoulders, and she seems almost cheerful. "Believe it or not, I drove here. Would you like a ride somewhere?"

"No, I better not. This is a business expense, so I can afford a cab. Thanks anyway." They shake hands, and Clem watches the grad student get into a beater of a Honda Mini. He watches as the car goes down the drive onto the public streets, and he busies himself with calling a cab. He doesn't see the olive drab sedan with three Navy SEALS in dirty jeans and T-shirts as they take up their position three car lengths behind, following Ms. Nguyen all the way home.

Clem is halfway decent at the craft of espionage, but Nguyen is a newby. Various channels relay information on her to Kuala Lumpur and Singapore. General Golytsin and Alberto Comaroso monitor the radio traffic, and they agree that Plan Epsilon needs to be implemented immediately. By conference call, the Executive Board of AHITF also elevates their threat evaluation of Clem Reader.

IN LA CAÑADA MANY YEARS AGO

Little Clem is sitting in his sixth grade class at the Latin School near New Los Angeles. Uncle Carlos and Aunt Victoria have sent him to America in hopes that he will be a lawyer working for the family firm. Right now little Clem is thinking about what he want to be when he grows up -- maybe an astronaut, maybe a policeman. Last month, he wanted to be a media conglomerate owner. This made him start working on the school newspaper.

Clem is something of a loner and for a good reason. He's still trying to adjust to the fact that his guardians shipped him out over 1200KM to this strange place called Southern California. He thinks it stinks that they can't visit him every weekend. Heck, sometimes they don't even videophone every weekend. Being an 11-year-old boy isn't as easy as it's made out to be. For one thing, there are the yahoos who make fun of him because he's white. There are the stray bullies, but Clem can hold his own. Growing up on a ranch has taught him to hold his own. Clem is often homesick, but then he gets angry because his aunt and uncle abandoned him. Clem is also bummed out by the other students at the school. He thinks that most of them are just stuck up rich kids.

Because of this, Clem concentrates on making his teachers and other adults happy with him. His roommate, Ken Lee is okay for a Little Richie Rich, but he's weird. Ken's family is into this weird outer space religion. He talks about Space Brothers and Sisters all the time, and that bores Clem to tears. Ken's a good friend though. They

The Story of the Century

both work hard in school, and sometimes Ken helps Clem with his homework in chemistry. Clem helps Ken in Spanish and art. Studying hard is a good excuse for minimizing his dealings with other students.

Right now the teacher is starting a history lesson, his back to the class while he's writing on the blackboard. Clem is looking at Leticia, whom he thinks is very pretty. Andres is in the corner making faces at everyone and no one in particular. Normal people think that Andres is such a total king jerk. Mr. Arce-Gomez turns around to see Andres wipe his stupid expression off of his face, giving him a silent stare of cold steel. Andres shrivels. This gives Clem, Ken, and Leticia a great deal of pleasure. Mr. Arce-Gomez starts to talk about World War III.

"Last week, we studied the 20th Century. This week, we're going to study World War III and its aftermath. Right now I want you to open your books, and do silent reading on Chapter 17, page 203." Almost in unison, the twelve children in class open their books and begin:

WORLD WAR III: THE GREAT HOLOCAUST

Almost 300 years ago, the Earth had achieved a high degree of economic, artistic, and scientific development. White people ruled the earth. The most powerful and prosperous country was called the United States of America. However, other countries like Russia, and countries in Europe were important too. The world had a population of over seven billion (7,000,000,000) people. Out of those seven billion people, perhaps 10,000 were extremely wealthy and powerful, controlling nearly everything. Another five hundred million (500,000,000) people led comfortable lives, and the rest lived in some form of poverty. The majority of people who lived comfortably were white, although there were many rich and powerful Asians, Africans, and South Americans.

Karl Eysenbach

One of the reasons for white people's power, as well as their destruction, was the discovery and invention of nuclear weapons. Nuclear weapons were very expensive to make, and they are now outlawed. Before World War III, they were looked at as peacekeeping weapons. It was thought that no one would want to use them because of their destructive power. However, once other countries knew how to make atomic weapons, they began to make fission and fusion devices. Other countries like Israel, Pakistan, North Korea, China, India, Iran, and Saudi Arabia also produced nuclear bombs. White countries like the United States, Russia, Great Britain, and France did not approve, even though they had far more nuclear weapons.

The people of Israel believed in a religion called Judaism, and they did not get along with their neighbors, who were Arab. Most Arabs practiced a religion known as Islam, and they said that they were the sworn enemies of Israel. They said that they wanted the State of Israel destroyed and pushed into the sea. In the decades before Year Zero, the Arab states and Israel fought several wars. One of the reasons for war was the Palestinians, Arabs who lived under the control of the Israelis. The Palestinians lived in horrible conditions.

In the old year 2012, a revolutionary government took control of Saudi Arabia, led by an army colonel named Hafiz Ibn-Saud. Saudi Arabia controlled a large quantity of oil. Oil is a rare, black, gooey substance found in the ground. At the time, oil was used to operate most of the world's machinery, and the troubles in the Arabian Peninsula caused major problems for the world economy. While the white countries wanted to overthrow the new Saudi government, they were prevented by the fact that Saudi Arabia had recently obtained nuclear weapons from its ally, Pakistan.

Saudi Arabia and other Arab states imposed an oil blockade against Israel and the United States. Arab religious leaders called for a holy war against Israel, called a jihad. The United Nations tried to solve the problem, but it was unable to. On the old calendar day of December 25th, a nuclear weapon destroyed the Arabian city of Mecca, the center of Islam. It was suspected that the atomic bomb had come from Israel, but nobody knew where it came from. The countries of Pakistan, Iran, and Saudi Arabia declared war on Israel and the United States. On December 31st, 2012, the cities of Tel Aviv and Jerusalem were destroyed in Israel. New York City in the United States also had an atomic bomb explode that day. The United States of America launched nuclear strikes against areas of Pakistan, Iran, and Saudi Arabia, where it was suspected the bombs came from. Russia sided with the Arab countries, and it sent some of its nuclear weapons against the United States and its allies in Europe. The United States destroyed Russia.

This brief period was known as World War III. In six months' time, over 500 nuclear explosions occurred throughout the world destroying almost 99% of the world's population, creating an Ice Age that has existed to this day. The nuclear explosions created numerous earthquakes and volcanic eruptions that caused more damage to the environment. While hundreds of millions of people died from nuclear explosions, many more died of starvation and disease. Plagues of flies and cockroaches overran everything. The nuclear explosions destroyed the ozone layer, and this allowed radiation from the sun to kill most of the plants on land and life in the ocean. For many years, no one knew whether mankind would be able to survive.

REVIEW QUESTIONS

1) What were the major factors that led up to the start of World War III? Go to your library to research your answer.
2) Who was most responsible for starting World War III --- Arab countries, Israel, Russia, or the United States?

a) Write a paper giving reasons to defend your choice.

b) Organize into teams to present your information to the class

Set up a debate between teams to argue your position.

MONARCH HOTEL
JUNE 12TH, 6:30 AM

ON-LINE BULLETIN

Graduate student Pham Nguyen, 27 was found dead in her dormitory room at the California Institute of Technology today in an apparent suicide. Police found an empty bottle of sleeping pills and a note expressing her despondency at not obtaining her graduate degree. In other local crime news, police arrested today three members of the…

OFF-LINE

Clem wakes up with a start. Even unconscious, the news has filled him with a sense of anger and confusion. This is not a good way to start the day. He yells, "Shut up!" and the announcer disappears at the foot of his bed. To make sure he hasn't been dreaming, he tells the news robot to rerun what it said before, only to shut if off halfway through its spiel. Ms. Nguyen is neurotic, but she isn't that neurotic. He calls up the police report as he rapidly eats breakfast, but it doesn't tell him anything he doesn't already know. That old tightening in the pit of his stomach makes his oatmeal feel as if it were buckshot. What if Ms. Nguyen's suicide wasn't really a suicide? What if it's really a murder? Did the government do it?

He looks at the pile of clothes from the night before. He doesn't know it, but he's been very lucky to work as late as he did last night, checking into the downtown hotel after running down some late night angles on the magnetic interferometer. There was supposed to be a meeting with Lee near the Forbidden Zone, and for some reason he never showed. So Clem checked into his favorite cheapo hotel to get a head start on work.

Clem ponders the possibilities as he showers and dresses, and none of them are very appetizing. He feels the need for revenge against who ever did this. Maybe Professor Fat killed her himself. Clem ponders telephoning the police as soon as he gets to work. That might be worth investigating. But what if the police killed her? Clem wonders about her fiancée, and how she related to him. He begins to feel as if he was five years old and has just discovered that his parents are gone, and they aren't coming back. He's frightened and confused. He goes downstairs to the coffee shop for a light breakfast before he crosses the street to go to work. Instinctively, he reaches for his cell phone. He calls Saroyan and a curious message comes on from the phone company instead.

"We're sorry, but this number has been temporarily disabled. Message 212. If you feel you need assistance, please stay on the line, and an operator will assist you." Then there's silence. Clem hangs up. He calls Saroyan's number again. This time there's a fast beeping followed by silence. He tries calling Pepe Lopez. There was nothing but silence on the line. What a time for his phone to be on the fritz! He feels like tossing the damn thing in the ocean.

He's walking the three blocks towards the *Times* Building. The city looks all bright and sunny, but to Clem the city has the soul of an internet hooker. Clem and the crowd surge through the street. When he gets to the lobby of the *Times*, he finds another nasty surprise. Ordinarily, security's invisible during working hours except for the deskman. Today Oscar the security chief is standing there with two robots waiting for Clem.

"Mr. Reader, I'm sorry but you need to see Mr. Lopez immediately. We'll go up with you?"

"What's wrong?" he asks incredulously. Now what's going on?

"I'm sorry. I can't say. That's for Mr. Lopez to talk to you about." With that, Clem and the detail go into an empty elevator to go to the fourth floor.

"God, what the hell is this all about?" Clem says this out loud, but there's only silence from the other parties in the elevator. Clem's thoughts could fill an encyclopedia, though. His anxiety level is continuing to climb. If he were a caveman, he'd be ready to kill a mastodon. The elevator opens. It's still early, and not many people are there. The business editor is at the coffeepot, and it's as if Clem was invisible. Mbake is at his desk hard at work. He looks up at Clem, but it's the longest second before he makes even a motion at saying hello. Even then it's the most tentative 'How do you do?' that Clem has received in months. Clem feels as if he's a criminal. He remembers when he was a cub reporter with the really shitty police beat, and how he had to interview some poor woman whose son had died in some bizarre traffic accident. He knows how she felt watching him come to her door.

By now they've walked the ten meters or so to Lopez's office. Security waits by the door while Clem goes inside. Lopez looks up at him with a deep scowl. His face is ashen, and he looks like he's six hours away from having a heart attack. A cigar is clenched in his jaw, and he's spewing smoke, which is easily winning the war against the ventilation system.

"Sit down and close the door." This is all he can say for a minute. As Clem sits down, he notices that a computer, piles of documents, and some of his personal effects are sitting on the floor. If Clem's anxiety level was high before, his fear factor just went up another quantum level. Clem begins to feel faint, but the pain in his stomach keeps his attention. Lopez places his cigar down on the ashtray before he speaks.

"What the hell have you gotten into, you stupid fuck?!"

His expression changes. He doesn't look outraged any more. Now he looks like he's just about on the verge of tears.

"Do you realize what I'm going to have to do because of your threat to world security? I woke up at 4:30 this morning with a call from Madame Cheung. She sounded like she was scared out of her mind. The FBI sends two agents over to her house last night and told her all about what's going on with you. She calls me up, and now I've got to do what I've got to do."

"Boss –"

"Shut up, you stupid piece of shit!" He pauses. "Clem, in the years I've known you, you've been a mighty fine reporter. I've almost come to look at you as my own son. But this Mexican story that you and Emilio were working on! You should have known better! Threat to world security – possession of classified documents --, you do know what I've got to do, don't you?"

"Uhm, no uh –" Clem stammers, but he's beginning to be able to take a pretty good guess.

"This is your last day on the job. Actually, this is your last five minutes. That's how much time you have to pick up your personal things from your desk. You should be lucky you have that much time. I've given you a head start. I lied to the FBI and said that you had been on assignment in Mexico, and that you were on your way up. That might buy you a few hours. Here's cash and a receipt for what your pay was up until today. We keep all your notebooks and source material. If I ever see you near this newsroom again, you're going to be arrested."

Lopez passes an envelope across the desk to Clem. Clem takes the envelope, feeling the bills and small change through the paper, and extends his hand to Lopez for a final farewell. The only thing that Lopez can mumble is, "I'm sorry." As Clem leaves the office, he can see Pablo rubbing his face.

Security surrounds him while he inspects his desk. There's a dirty coffee cup and a couple of photos. He puts the photos in his pocket, and leaves the cup. While Clem appears to be functioning physically as viewed from the outside, on the inside he's spiraling into some black, unknown pit. He's dazed, confused, shocked, and afraid. The thought occurs to him. He needs a drink really bad. Billy Goat's Tavern is open, and it's only two blocks away. It might as well be two light years. As he walks Clem tries to make some order out of the chaos in his brain. Rational thoughts are pieces of wheat flying in an airstream of irrational chaff. Now he's sitting at the barstool inside Billy Goat's.

Billy Goat's is located in the basement of the city. It sits underneath the freeway overpass on streets reserved only for the big semi-trucks. By some arrangement with the police, it's open 24 hours a day, seven days a week. Although reporters and pressmen sometimes come here, it's more regularly frequented by the sweatshop crews, pick up laborers, sex workers, penny ante hustlers, and miscellaneous low life scum. Other than for the red neon bar sign and beer ads, it could be almost invisible to traffic. It has a picture window, but everything on the outside is covered with a thick coating of grease and road dust. Inside the bar, the view of the trucks makes it look like they're passing through a film of gritty tan jello.

Clem looks at Billy Goat. The fat Mexican has a short greasy ponytail sticking up on the top of his head and a black goatee. That's how he got his name. Clem is a semi-regular, and the bartender knows his face even though he doesn't know his name.

The Story of the Century

"Hiya doing, Pal?" The bartender is wiping a glass with a tattered gray rag. Things are slow. Two customers are truckers. A cop and a hooker are sitting in a booth by the window. Billy Goat takes a few steps to serve his only customer at the bar.

"The usual, kid? I'll tell you. You looked bummed out. I'll tell you what. This one's on me."

Clem slumps at the bar. He glances down at the thousand-year-old linoleum before he raises his head again.

"I lost my job."

"That's a piece of shit."

"Gimme a double scotch on the rocks. I'll pay."

"Don't worry about it, Pal." The bartender begins to pour.

"God. Jesus. Why me? Why me? I didn't do anything wrong." Clem watches as the bartender puts the glass in front of him. He winces as he downs it in one gulp.

"Gimme another one, Billy Goat. I pay for the rest."

"Okay, Pal."

After the second double, Clem can begin to see that he's been partly responsible for what he's done. Some of the stuff he's been doing was dangerous and a problem to the *Times*. Clem talks about this in a general way with the bartender as he glances at the cop in the booth. Pablo Lopez's words come back to him, and Clem realizes people are looking for him right now. At this point, Clem's going to be as rational as he's going to be for the rest of the day. The bartender listens to Clem complain about his ex-coworkers.

"What are you going to do next, Pal?"

"Get drunk. That's the first thing. I'll make my plans later."

"Coming right up. Here's another double."

Clem's in his cups now. He begins his standard discourse on the Clem Reader Theory of the Universe. There's his view that sub-subatomic particles are powered by the same things that make up the biggest structures in the universe. There's the multiverse, and the millions or billions of Clems and Billy Goats who are right now in heaven, hell, and somewhere in between having this same conversation.

Clem's getting pretty spacy now, and he's beginning to get into those rare thoughts that he has when he's really stoned. "For some undetermined time, it was all a giant hallucination. I didn't go looking for any of this. They came looking for me. I was just the messenger. There are conspiracies, and there are conspiracies wrapped up inside of the conspiracies. It's all a giant figure-8. Saroyan is a green light. Pepe Lopez is a robot. The Atzlan Liberation Front is in outer space. The President and Lodestar know all about it, but they don't really know. Even the masters controlling the beings who control the space aliens know that they will have to answer to God. There is no god. It's all just a collection of strings and membranes. A subatomic particle is a universe and vice versa. Beelzebub is wrapped inside of Beelzebub. Where's Allistarr Crowley when you need him? Life is eternal until it ends. The CIA knows all about me. Why am I being singled out? I'm the messenger, not the message."

When Clem becomes conscious, he feels his shoulder and neck hurting more than the other joints in his body. He's also incredibly thirsty. His head is in a cramped position, and it's lying in some hard corner. There's that queasy hangover feeling of being sick and cold. He opens his eyes, and he sees a street scene that he doesn't recognize for a few seconds. Then it dawns on him that he's a few blocks from his home. He puts his feet on the pavement and looks at the bus station shelter with its smoked glass and movie poster. He remembers Billy Goat's Tavern, but he's confused. How did he manage to wind up here? He can see the rising sun reflect off the dome on the Castle & Bishop Building. What time is it? What day is it?

The Story of the Century

He looks up and down the street. There's no traffic. El Puerto is a rough neighborhood. Cops don't pay much attention to winos sleeping it off on a bus bench here. He rubs his eyes and feels the stubble on his chin. He looks down, and what he sees isn't very pretty. His fly's unzipped, and he notices a puddle of urine near his feet. He wonders if it's his. Slowly the outlying regions of his consciousness begin to function. He feels in his pocket, and his wallet is still there. He has about $200 and change. He debates a moment whether to quench his thirst at a local gin mill, or go for an alternative. Since he isn't far from Sacred Grounds, he decides that the espresso joint's the better option.

Dave is in there, just setting up for the new day, and Clem is a regular. But when Dave sees him walk in the door, he gives Clem that look. And Clem feels both embarrassed and ashamed. Wisely, Clem decides to take the offense.

"Yeah, I look like shit because I was on an overnight drunk. It's not anything I'm proud of, but I got fired yesterday."

Dave just looks at him; "Do you want the regular?"

"Yeah, gimme a café americano. Make that a double. That would be good, but could you also give me a two-liter of water? And I think I need to clean up in the bathroom." Clem lays a couple of bills on the counter.

Coming out of the john, Clem looks slightly more respectable, but there isn't a spot on his clothing that isn't wrinkled. He walks outside to get a copy of the *Times*. He's jolted from haze to hyperreality when he sees the bottom of page one. "**Police Manhunt on for Ex-Times Reporter**." Clem doesn't bother to read any further. He hides the front section of the news under the sports section, and goes back to retrieve his drinks.

"Have you seen the paper yet, Dave?"

"Nah, I've been too busy."

"Who do you think is going to top the league in soccer this year?"

Dave's a sports fan, and they get into a good discussion for ten minutes, and finally Dave lets Clem alone. Some of the regulars begin to fill in for their java fix. Clem feels for his cell phone, but it isn't there. He saunters to the back door to where the pay phone is. He wants to call Saroyan, but there's no answer. Even worse, when he dials the number, there's that dead air again. On his second attempt, there's just silence. He doesn't know, but he suspects that her phone and area are blocked. Only later will he find that Saroyan has been involuntarily committed from her movie set in Loreto. As the phone's ringing, Saroyan is enjoying her 'vacation' at the Happy Valley Clinic for Psychiatric Disorders. Her room is a padded cell, and she's ripping her hospital gown to shreds.

Yesterday Sergeant Jawaharlal Singh was in his office when he was interrupted by General Caramehni and four MPs. "Singh, you've been cut a new set of orders. You are to accompany these gentlemen and report immediately to Reunion Island for medical experiments." The soldier-cops grab Singh by the arms and legs, carrying him through the underground command center as he struggles in vain. He's never seen on earth again.

Kenny Lee isn't very far away from Clem right now. He's in the bushes underneath the Harbor Bridge. He was shot in the back of the head in an apparent robbery, but the cops won't find his body until Tuesday.

Clem heads out the back door of the coffee shop to go to his apartment, but he stops midway. What he sees are two cop cars parked in front of his building. On any other day, Clem would have paid them no mind. But today, it's triply bad. There are other cars too. There are the black SUVs with smoked glass windows, generic white vans, and cars for detectives. The FBI and CIA are here, and they're expecting Mr. Reader. Clem reverses direction. It's time to go down another street somewhere.

SOMEWHERE BELOW BAJA, HUNDREDS OF METERS BELOW THE SURFACE

Attu is in the control room monitoring the magnetic interferometer. The green light goes up to the surface now and then to see his pets, but the rest of the time his day job is here. The interferometer is a vital component of an intergalactic dark energy generating network. The problem is that if the station stops broadcasting, the solar system suddenly ceases to exist. It's hell to replace the damn things, and the powers that be figured that since the earthlings still possessed one, it would be easier if they procured the thing from Fort Huachuca.

Installation went off without a hitch. The older models are easy to install. But Attu's discovered that it's a clear case of getting what you pay for. His co-worker Sajak is an orange light, and he's observing Attu as he fiddles with the dials in the control room. Concentrating on a bank of lights, Attu adjusts up and down. Two green lights turn to yellow. When Attu makes adjustments, the lights turn back to green. But the green lights last for only five to ten seconds before they revert to being yellow. And then they start flashing red.

"Pardon my French, but this magnetic interferometer blows chunks. Things are all right now, but they really can't be fixed. I'm afraid it's going to get worse, and you know what that means. We'll all be in trouble."

CLEM & SAROYAN

WORLD SECURITY COUNCIL MEETING, SITUATION ROOM

The problem is, they think they're in a secure location. They think that no one can eavesdrop on one of the most security conscious spots on the planet.

The situation room is the elegant bunker buried deep under the Blue House. It's traditionally reserved for the President's most secret briefings. It feels small and cramped, even if it has only a few people in it. Perhaps it's the low ceiling. Or maybe it's the knowledge of the lines and networks that can shovel information in from any part of the planet, or the sensors that record every action.

This afternoon's session of the World Security Council is a curious lot. It includes Secretary of Defense Corozon, the Secretary of Energy, the head of the World Monetary Reserve Fund, and the Secretary of Lands. The private sector is represented by Tutuwabi Mugabi, CEO and Chairman of the Board of Consolidated Hydrogen. President Hok is looking forward to this agenda item with dread. He'd rather eat a bar of soap than be sitting here. Mr. Mugabi is in charge here, and everyone else is a finger puppet. President Hok's assigned roll is to be the combination pushover/chump/rubber stamp. The Secretary of Lands is beginning the charade by outlining the world distribution of platinum reserves, noting that the South African mines are essentially exhausted.

"Booga booga," Hok thinks. It's an old joke, but it fits. A huge tribe of bloodthirsty savages has captured two explorers. The hapless duo are tied to large stakes as a thousand painted warriors dance around them, brandishing their spears. The big chief raises his arms and brings things to a halt. He approaches his captives, waving a decorated skull.

Going up to the first explorer, he asks the question, "Death or booga booga?"

The first explorer thinks out loud. "Death is not a good option. I don't know what booga booga is, but it can't be any worse than death. Give me booga booga."

BOOGA BOOGA!" The chief shouts to the crowd, and the crowd replies:

"BOOGABOOGABOOGABOOGABOOGABOOGABOOGA!" The hapless explorer is untied from his post and systematically gang raped by twenty of the chief's lieutenants. The second explorer is terrified! He tries to avert his eyes from the sexual tortures being inflicted on his companion. Finally the chief comes up to him, posing the same question:

"Death or booga booga?"

The second explorer steels himself. He straightens himself as best as he can, and he says, "I want no part of booga booga. Give me death."

The chief turns to the army of warriors and yells, "DEATH -- BY BOOGA BOOGA!"

The Secretary of Energy has just finished his presentation, and the Chairman of the World Monetary Reserve Fund is getting ready to explain the economic impacts the proposal would have on planetary prosperity. After that, Mr. Mugabi will get up to make his modest, entirely reasonable proposition, and Secretary of Defense Corozon will be there to say, "Why sure. We have one. No problem." The whole thing is about as free form as a TV wrestling tag team match, and it has the same purpose. And that is, to get President Hok to sign off on the whole shebang. Be a good guy, Mr. President. Roll over, and take one for the team.

Even the most bought and paid for pundits would call Mr. Mugabi's proposal controversial. Because platinum is necessary for converting biomass to hydrogen, and because it's in short supply, the hydrogen interests have decided that the best thing to do is to use an old H-bomb to extract platinum ore from the ice fields of the Magaden Peninsula. No one has ever called President Hok squeamish, but Hok is squeamish about authorizing the first use of a nuclear weapon in over 300 years. Just because mankind nearly committed hari kari messing around with the little playthings, just because children from the age of two onwards are told about the stupidity of the Holocaust, just because the very idea of testing an A-bomb is as popular as a swastika at a B'nai Brith meeting, why President Hok should be squeamish about signing off on this venture, no one can know. And although he is not much of a moralist, Hok is personally sickened by the fact that this proposal is an unhappy combination of corporate greed and the Defense Department's fascination of seeing if its toy will actually work.

Mr. Mugabi is wrapping up his presentation referring to a bunch of geologists' reports. All that remains is the statement from the Secretary of Defense saying that the Army has recovered some ancient atomic weapons, and the material is available to make them operational. It should be a done deal. But President Hok is ready. After the bureaucratic kabuki dance is over, the other members of the Public Private Partnership fold their hands, looking at the World Leader expectantly. President Hok says matter of factly, "I think we need to table this discussion. There are other ways of meeting the coming hydrogen crisis. They might cost a bit more, or take a little more time. But I think it's entirely feasible to extract platinum the good old-fashioned way. I just don't think the government's use of nuclear weapons is a viable option. I have to say no."

There is much hemming and hawing. Many eyeglasses are adjusted. Cabinet members give polite and respectful disagreements and arguments. This is their way of saying, "Fuck you, Charlie!" and still Hok does not budge. Speeches and rhetorical flourishes continue from the public sector boys. Mr. Mugabi pretends to be charming, hinting that President Hok is only kidding. The hydrogen magnate doesn't understand why the President's position could possibly be anything except for the only right way, which is to H-bomb Siberia. There are some attempts among the Cabinet members at intellectually stimulating ideas, consistent with the only right way as put forth by Mr. Mugabi, and yet it is all for naught. Hok is pretty much the stone face. His longest speech is to say, "Remember what I said before."

The meeting eventually winds down like some kiddy toy with a weak spring. Hok looks at his watch and says, "Thank you for your input, gentlemen." The high ranking government officials file out like a pack of admonished schoolboys sent to the principal's office.

Mr. Mugabi gives Hok an extremely evil eye, even though he looks slightly ridiculous in his leopard skin pill box hat, Ashanti robe and lion's tail flyswatter. Before he exits, he turns to Hok and he says, "You haven't heard the last word from ME on this issue, Mr. President."

Hok smiles cordially, but he feels the psychic arrow lodge in his aorta. He knows that the hydrogen trust is not to be trifled with. Mugabi and his band of plutocratic thieves are a ball of cranky puff adders, and the last thing he wants is to be bitten. But at the same time, there is principle -- morality, doing what is right, and doing right by doing good. And it doesn't do anybody any good to go around in an election campaign on the platform that you want to play with an antiquated old nuke just for fun, even if it is for the benefit of renewable energy. Now only the Secretary of Defense is in the room with him. "The butler did it," Hok thinks.

Corozon looks like he is going to go out the door too, but he turns. "May I sit down with you for just a minute, Mr. President? I've got something I'd like to share with you."

Hok thinks to himself, "Death or booga booga."

The Story of the Century

Corozon gets close to the president, a little too close. His chair is touching Hok's. His knee is touching Hok's knees. The president is mildly uncomfortable. Corozon has this slimy, oleaginous air of a funeral director who's just pawned off a deluxe bronze casket on some indigent widow. More thoughts enter Hok's head. "As slick as greased pig shit." His mouth is a slightly skewed line with tight cheeks that say in so many nonverbal ways. "I am so screwed."

Corozon begins by saying, "Mr. President, I admire your courage today. It takes guts to stand up to all of your advisors as well as the hydrogen industry for the sake of principle. There are not many people who would stand up for their beliefs the way you did, even if it meant risking world prosperity for what I know are your deeply held religious beliefs -- and I respect that."

Hok's about ready to utter his polite version of go fuck yourself, but Corozon beats him to the punch. He puts his hand on Hok's forearm while he fiddles with a manila folder. Hok is really uncomfortable, but he's trapped. Corozon doesn't miss a beat. Before the president can get one word out of his mouth, Corozon goes into his speech. He's like a spieler for one of those miracle knives. It slices. It dices. It julienne cuts. It's obvious that he's memorized the whole damn thing beforehand, being able to probably recite what he's saying in his sleep.

Hok thinks, "God, this guy has brass balls."

"Mr. President, I had hoped that it would never come to this, but I'm only the messenger. And you can still contain the damage. " He slides some large photographs in front of the president. "A copy of these came into my hands just today. Now I am sure -- with your cooperation -- we can just leave matters sit where they are. But if you don't change your position, I can't guarantee that these photos won't get into the hands of the wrong people -- the press or Marjorie."

Corozon might as well have driven an ice pick into Hok's skull. In front of the president are some "R" and "X" rated photos of one short, gone to fat, middle aged, Korean World Leader with his mouth hanging open in a ridiculous O as he is riding on top of the fabulous Yvette. Hok could probably tough out the world press' salacious inquiries -- but Marjorie! How many years of living hell is he willing to endure for this one stinky, little political issue? Hok knows when he is beaten. Point, game, set, match, checkmate.

And yet there is that cartoon of the frog strangling the crane, even as he's being swallowed up with the motto of "Never give up." Even in defeat, Hok has a few rabbits that he can pull out of the hat. He begins by saying, "Okay, you win. But let's negotiate." For a loser, he does pretty well. He gets stipulations that the government will not pay one thin dime for the project. This is going to be the world's first privately funded nuke test. The government will provide the weapons, parts, etc. as needed, but there is to be 100% reimbursement. Corozon is so anxious not to overplay his hand that he goes along with everything, including provisions that the private sector is responsible for all liability, and that any information on the test is to remain secret until after the election. The private sector is also going to be responsible for all information and public feedback. The government was in another city at the time this testing stuff happens.

FAR, FAR AWAY

The World Security Council is always supersecret, but today everything has been monitored in real time by the Earth Watch Subcommittee on the 34th floor of a government office building in the capital city of the fourth planet from Alpha Centauri. Ordinarily, this is a lowly collection of midlevel bureaucrats, but the equipment

The Story of the Century

failure has gotten the attention of higher authorities. In the conference room are a variety of beings. There is Z.X. Hawxe, a venerable gray who is the chairman of the committee. Nafta is a green shapeshifter. Saurus is an orange ball, and a mid level, middle aged careerist to boot. Tenotitchtlan, the Jaguar God has flown in from the Central Office, to ride herd on everyone. The committee members are following the H-bomb agenda item.

When Hok starts the meeting, Tenotitchtlan says, "I don't like the looks of this." When they get to the part where Corozon blackmails the president, all hell breaks loose. The green shapeshifter and the orange ball are resisting the urge to zoom around the ceiling. They're having a hard time controlling themselves, hovering, just vibrating and shimmying with anger.

"Excuse me, but what is it with these bastard chimpanzees?" says Saurus. "Didn't they learn anything from their die off?"

Nafta finally comes to rest in one place. His impulse has been to fly around the room in a rage, but somehow he's contained himself. "It's not only that, but the location of their test is in close proximity to the dark energy generator. If their test were a success, it would bring down the entire network, and you know what that means!"

The gray slices his finger across his throat. "There goes Earth. There goes the quadrant in one giant gamma ray burst!"

"Something MUST be done against this criminal test! Speaking for my hive, if these Earthlings are not prevented from their mindless experiment, my people will be happy to sterilize the Earth personally if the Alliance doesn't take IMMEDIATE action against this moronic species!" Saurus is so worked up that he's vibrating and changing to a burning white color.

Tenotitchtlan takes note of this. Unlike the others, he's a *macher*, a being of influence. He reports to the Lords of Pure Energy directly.

He has always balanced his feelings and his words, emphasizing diplomacy. By his nature he's a moderate, and yet this development has left him sharing the same feelings as his fellow committee members. He addresses his cohorts.

"Ladies and gentlemen, I share your feelings and concerns entirely. I am certainly going to pass this information on to the Lords. And I can guarantee that action on this will be decisive. Meeting adjourned."

SIXTH STREET, EL PUERTO

With the heat combing through all of his earthly possessions, Clem decides that it's time to hit the road, Jack! The fuzz has his description, and he's an easy guy to spot. He's near the Rainbow Thrift Store, and he has an idea. "Time to blend in with the scenery, Dude."

You should know something about Rainbow Thrift and El Puerto. Since it sits at the bottom of the Palos Verdes hill, this thrift store is the recipient of some of the finest junk in the world. The swells in their mansions need to refurbish their wardrobes on an annual basis, and the bums of El Puerto are the beneficiaries. Because of this Rainbow Thrift is the haberdasher to the homeless and the purveyor of sartorial splendiferisnous to eccentric street people. This is why you see winos decked out in three piece suits and four in hand ties. And some of the bag ladies have year-old fashions from Tokyo.

Clem is at the front door, and he knows that while the cops will be looking for a disheveled honkie reporter, they won't notice ordinary street fauna. It's early, but Mimi has opened the store. Once or twice upon a time, when Clem was married, Salma would do some volunteer work at the Rainbow Thrift Store. Clem would drop in after work to take her to dinner at the Caribou Café. There were a few times when he'd even help Mimi move some of the boxes of donations. What if

The Story of the Century

Mimi knows the cops are on his tail? But a strong defense is a strong offense. Clem takes a few deep breaths to calm down, and he walks in the store. Three seconds after he's inside, a police cruiser turns the corner, sweeping the streets for one Clem Reader.

"Hi, Mimi."

"Hello, young man. What can I do for you?" This is good. Maybe Mimi is getting old and forgetful. She doesn't seem to recognize him.

"I'm interested in some clothing. Where's your changing room?" Mimi absentmindedly points to the curtain hanging in the corner. Clem rummages around, and he finds exactly what he's looking for. There's a pair of black and white checkered pants, and a blue wool shirt with arms so long that they cover part of his geeky white hands. There's a broad brimmed garden hat that actually fits him, hanging down low and putting part of his head into deep shade. There's even an Army surplus backpack for stowing stuff in. Clem tries everything on. He looks at himself in the cracked full-length mirror held together with duct tape. From the standpoint of the fashion police, he has just committed a capital crime. From the standpoint of Clem versus the cops, he's just hit a home run.

"How much for all of this?"

Mimi looks him up and down. "$5."

"It's a deal." Clem has just gone a long way towards maintaining his freedom. Problems still remain though. There are personal hygiene issues for example, and there's that dead giveaway blond hair on his head. A hypermart is down the street a couple of blocks away, if he can get in there without being detected. Clem pulls the straw hat down over his head, and he ventures outside.

The Health Aid seems ten times further away than it actually is. Clem can appreciate how a blue crab feels after molting its skin, skittering across a bright sandy bottom in predator country. Perhaps because he's a rogue and a fool, his luck is with him. No one notices him on the street except for the security guard at the store, who eyes him as a potential shoplifter. Clem gets what he needs -- a toothbrush, toothpaste, dental floss, soap, shampoo, a wash cloth, towel, candy bars, bottles of drinking water, toilet paper, and most importantly -- sun glasses and hair dye. Another $39.34 is now gone. He's down to $103 and some small change. What to do? He knows he's hungry. There's a cheap Chinese place nearby, the Golden Dragon. It's a little early for lunch, but they might be open. Clem hotfoots across the four lanes of San Pedro Boulevard in the crosswalk of course. Cops don't take kindly to jaywalkers. He gets there, but he finds the doors are closed. There's a 24-hour tacqueria, but Clem knows that it's a cop hangout.

He needs someplace to eat, a place to monopolize the bathroom for a half an hour to color his hair and shave. Above all, he needs a friendly place that never asks too many questions. "The best defense is a strong offense." Clem says out loud to himself. He remembers that he's going to have to navigate through cop-infested waters. Instinctively, Clem takes the long way around, navigating through quiet, working class neighborhoods with small houses on cramped, tiny lots surrounded by waist high cyclone fencing. Eventually, he's back on the commercial drag near home. He turns into the alley, going down past the dumpsters, broken beer bottles, and used condoms until he gets to the metal door in need of a new coat of red paint. He tugs on the latch, and the door opens into a dark, fetid hallway. He's inside Shanghai Lil's.

He's in luck today. The Navy guy in the peacoat is off his shift right now, and the place is empty except for two hardcore alkys and Joe the bartender. Clem slaps a $10 bill down on the bar and says, "I'm ordering a plate of chop suey, but I need to use your bathroom for a half hour. Gotta freshen up. Is that okay, Joe?"

Joe looks at him, but he doesn't recognize Clem. "How do you know my name?"

"You're famous as a good guy. Is $10 enough for me to clean myself up in the john?"

"Is that all you're going to do? I don't want no funny stuff."

"Scouts honor. I've got a razor blade and some soap. Is that okay?"

"Sure Jack. It'll take time to get the chef activated. You're the first order of solid food today."

"Thanks. Thanks a lot" Clem takes his backpack into the tiny, smelly closet-sized space with old paint covering decades of barf and graffiti. Currently the bathroom is kelly green and yellow. The mirror looks as if it's covered with industrial grime. After an hour and a half, Clem emerges with a shaved face and a clean body. More importantly, he now has jet-black hair and eyebrows.

"Is my chop suey ready?"

"It got cold, and we put it back."

"Could you heat it up for me?" Another $5 bill appears from Clem's wallet.

"Can do," the bartender says, "Hey, you look different. What did you do in there?"

"Just cleaned up. Why do you want to know? Are you a cop? My money covers my rent, doesn't it, pal?"

"Okay, I'll get the chop suey." When Joe comes back with the grub, Clem hardly breathes as he inhales the food. It's hard to imagine how good mediocre food tastes when you're starving. Clem orders a second helping, and another $10 is gone, suddenly realizing that the burn rate on his money is going to make him flame out soon. After becoming a member of the clean plate club and thanking Joe, he walks back out into the alley, heading away from 7th Street. It's time to do some serious thinking. $68 will get you one more meal and a really bad hotel for one night only. Clem is getting close to the edge. He wanders around, trying to think his way out of the box he's in. He needs to buy some time. Who can he call on? He needs to formulate a plan. Slowly, in desperation, the answer comes -- Salma, his ex-wife. "Salma. What's the name of her gallery? The Iroquois? That's it." Within minutes, he's hunched over a pay phone. A face comes on the video screen, an attractive face with artsy bohemian earrings and makeup; a face with pencilled in eyebrows and braided black hair. Salma Aguirre Reader is on the line.

"Iroquois Galley."

"Salma! It's me, Clem!"

Salma looks quizzical. She frowns, and then she gets this sardonic look on her face. "Clem, -- darling! I didn't recognize you. You look so, -- how can I say it, -- different! We've been hearing all about your great adventures with the police. I'm expecting an FBI agent to drop by at my door at any moment!" Maybe she's joking. Maybe she isn't. It still makes Clem flinch.

"Did the FBI really contact you?"

"No, Love, but I've been wondering what you've been getting into."

"It's a long story, Salma. But to make a long story short, could I stay at your place for just tonight?"

"You've got to be kidding!!"

"Salma, I wouldn't ask you if I weren't in a really bad way. I promise one night and no more. I'll be happy to sleep on the couch."

"Are you crazy? You know that Christophe is living with me now, and you're a criminal! I could go to jail!"

"Salma, -- pretty please?" This always works.

"Oh, GOD! All right. You win, but only for one night only! I mean it! If you're hanging around when I get home tomorrow, I'll call the cops on you myself!"

The Story of the Century

"Salma, you're a peach."

"Now look here, Mister. I've got a gallery opening that's going to last at least until 9:00 tonight, so I won't be home until ten."

"Ten's okay by me, Salma. You're still at the same place, right? I promise -- only one night. I owe you big time. I promise I'll make it up to you. I'll ring twice when I get there."

"Look, Clem, I'm going crazy with the stuff I have to do. I've gotta go."

"Thanks, Salma." The picture phone goes blank. Although it seems like years since he woke up, it's barely one o'clock, and there's plenty of time to kill before he goes to Salma's apartment. What do you do when you're homeless and the most wanted man in the world? Clem starts looking around dumpsters until he has a collection of clean pieces of cardboard that he can carry. To the casual observer, he's just another bum on his way to the recycling center, but he knows where the cops go and don't go. As a reporter, he's been on police patrols in El Puerto. He knows about the homeless camps that the cops hardly watch, and the ones they hassle.

He's heading a couple of kilometers north, going up the great hill until he gets to the Eternal Rest Cemetery. The large wrought iron gates are open, and he trudges along the white gravel road. He turns off at the older part, dragging his cardboard behind him. Finally he finds a crypt. It's for Salvardor Dario and his wife Maria. He died five years ago, and she died last year. Clem looks around. There are nine or ten homeless people who have the same idea in a fifty meter radius, but it's more crowded because it's the day shift. Clem plops the brown sheets down on the tomb. He puts his backpack down as a pillow, and he gets out his white shirt to cover his eyes. The cops don't go here. They're superstitious, and the Dario family won't mind. Clem is doing them a favor by guarding the fort for them. The sun is high in the sky, and it's getting warm. He won't need a blanket. Clem lays down to sleep the dead, dreamlessness of an afternoon nap.

NORTH SANTA MONICA

The sun set three hours ago. Clem has visited Salma two or three times before, but never as a wanted man. He's walked forever, looking into store windows when he sees the cop cars. Although North Santa Monica isn't the swankiest neighborhood, it still takes less kindly to street people than El Puerto. He could have been picked up three or four times, but he's been a lucky dog tonight. Clem is standing in front of Salma's apartment building now He rings her doorbell twice and is pleasantly surprised to find that someone is buzzing him up. He takes the elevator to the third floor, and Salma's waiting for him. The dragnet is in motion, but the FBI hasn't gotten around to leaving a calling card at Salma's door yet. That won't happen for a few days.

"Aren't you the one? You certainly don't look like the Clemmie I know."

"Well, I lost my job at the *Times* yesterday I get drunk, wake up at the bus stop near the old homestead, and then I see police and detectives combing through the gallery space. After coffee at Sacred Grounds, I go over to Rainbow Thrift so I can be a homeless person. Not what I would call a good day. So here I am."

"How in the world did you ever get into such a fix? Here, put your backpack down." She points to a corner of the blue sofa that they both used to own.

Clem plops down on the couch. "It's really strange. I was just doing my job. I got some leads into a potentially very big story, and people start feeding me government documents. That's where my problem started. A girl who sent me some of them from some hotshot

The Story of the Century

professor at Cal Tech wound up dead the other night. I go to work and Pablo Lopez cans my ass, just like that! I've been raped pretty good." Clem's face changes from impassive remember to more pleading. "Uh, changing the subject a little bit, I'm awfully hungry. Do you have anything to eat? Have you eaten anything?"

"Just wine and cheese things from the opening. Business was pretty good tonight. Better than I expected. Christophe knows how to beat the bushes in order to make the sales. What if I order some Chinese?"

"Is it okay if you get pizza? I ate Chinese for lunch."

"Okay, pizza it is. I'll get a large with everything." Salma is in the galley-sized kitchen looking for the phone number to order. While she's on the phone, Clem is trying to sort things out. Not only does he have to contend with the incredibly bollixed situation he finds himself in, but he has to figure out what the near term future is going to be. Salma sits down in front of him on a small upholstered chair. "I still don't understand how you managed to get into so much trouble."

"Frankly, I don't know either. I can see that I got carried away following this story." He's thinking out loud. "I mean, I was investigating some big time secrets the government is sitting on, stuff like pieces of flying saucer equipment. But I don't have any proof of anything now. I know one of my sources was murdered. Fact of the matter is, I don't have any idea what they've got in store for me if I'm captured. I mean, it really scares me."

Salma listens intently. She's always been a good listener. "So you were trafficking in government secrets on a news assignment that blew up. And now the government and the FBI and the CIA and everybody are out looking for you." She shifts a little bit in her chair.

"But what do you want from me, Clem? Surely you can appreciate the predicament I'm in. I certainly can't keep you hanging around here forever. I'm sticking my neck out for you just by having you sit on my couch. Hiding a fugitive, -- isn't that what they call it? So what do you want?" She looks at him intensely, with her questioning doe brown eyes.

"Salma, I can't thank you enough. Just letting me stay here on your couch tonight is more than enough. I needed some time just to get my bearings to figure out what I'm going to do. As near as I can figure out, my immediate future is going to be flophouses or worse. But beyond that, I don't --." Just then the buzzer rings from the front door downstairs. They both jump out of their seats. Clem immediately thinks the coppers are there with an arrest warrant. Tentatively, Salma pushes the intercom.

"Pizza delivery for Salma Aguirre." Clem's heart rate slows to 160 beats per minute.

"I'll be right down." She grabs her wallet. "Clem, I'll be right back. Turn on the hologram if that makes you feel better. And get some plates for the pizza." Clem goes to the kitchen to get plates for the pizza. He resists the ugly urge to look at his boyish face on World News Tonight. While Salma is downstairs, Clem thinks about what he really needs to do. He doesn't relish bunking in a homeless shelter, but given his circumstances, his options swing from slim to none. She's back with the pizza, setting it down on the coffee table. Salma eats one piece in the same amount of time it takes for Clem to wolf down seven. He admires the artwork on the wall while Salma talks.

"Christophe is out partying tonight with some of his guy pals. He's really quite the party animal, but what he does helps to bring in the customers. I don't know what I'd do without him."

"Hmdmptfh." Clem says. His mouth is full. He doesn't want to comment anyway.

"So Clem, you have to tell me about what else has been happening in your life, -- besides getting in trouble with the law, of course."

Clem ignores these little zingers that only an ex-wife can throw. Foolishly perhaps, he engages in an exercise of self-disclosure. "Before this shit, I had the whole world going for me. I'm in love! Yes, I'm in love, and you won't believe who I'm in love with, and who loves me. Do you promise not to tell?"

"I promise."

Clem tells a white lie. "I mean, it really is a secret, and it's another big deal. But it's another worry because I haven't been able to contact her. That's a real bother to me. You've got to keep this secret because you're the first person I've told. So people around the office were talking, but I never told them anything."

"So who is it?"

"Can I keep you to the secret?"

"You know I can."

"It's Saroyan Pashogi."

Salma's eyes get very wide. "Saroyan Pashogi? You're kidding me, aren't you? You must be joking!"

"No, I'm serious. Saroyan Pashogi."

"Oh my God! So you're the one!"

This strikes Clem as more than just a little bit odd. The old philosophical question, 'What do you mean by that?' rears its ugly head. In God's green universe, what chain of causality made her say this phrase, 'So you're the one!'?

"What do you mean by that?" Clem doesn't think he's going to like the answer to this. He knows better than anyone that Salma is supportive and cutting, in only the way that ex-wives can be. There's her yin, and there's her yang.

"One of Christophe's best friends, Guy is the hairdresser to Saroyan Pashogi. He talks all the time about Saroyan having a secret boyfriend. I think it was even an issue in the tabloids, but they never found out who it was. I never paid it much attention. But you?! Are you her secret boyfriend? You're not making this up, are you? Is this a game?"

"No, I'm serious. She's serious too. We just both fell into it, and it's wonderful. But I'm worried. I tried calling her this morning -- all her numbers -- and I didn't get anything. I don't know what's screwed up, but I don't like it." He hopes he can use her phone.

Salma turns serious, no longer bemused. She's turned hesitant and questioning. Clem has read her body signals enough to know that a sledgehammer is coming, and he's right. He even notices her do that little inhale with a pause before she speaks.

"Clem, I don't know how to say this, but you are out of the loop, aren't you?"

"Let's just say I have pressing legal problems lately. What are you going to hit me with?"

Salma moves in close to Clem so she can look him straight in the eye. "Well -- Guy, you know -- Christophe's friend Guy called this morning from Mexico, -- from the *Zorro* set. They shut production down this morning indefinitely. He came back this afternoon. That's who Christophe is out with right now." The sledgehammer hangs high before it falls.

"What does that have to do with Saroyan?"

Salma holds his hands between hers. "I'm sorry, Clem. This isn't in the news because Guy says it's totally hush hush. But orderlies from a sanitarium and a doctor kidnapped her. They said she was having a nervous breakdown, but Guy said she looked just fine when he was working on her hair this morning. I'm sorry to be the one to tell you this."

The wind sucks out of Clem's lungs. He stares out the window in total shock. Then he curls into a ball, clutching his knees while he buries his head. He tries to stifle his sobbing, but he convulses instead.

He can't be quiet. There are the sounds of sobbing, gasping for more air, and then more sobbing. By now Salma has her arms around him, holding him like a baby. After some minutes, Clem comes up for air with his face red and snot running down his nose. Salma is there with a handkerchief.

"I – I – I -- didn't want this to happen." Then Clem sobs more before he continues. "She doesn't know anything." He is trying to get under control. "Oh, Salma, you're so kind. I got her into this mess. How could this happen?" He covers his eyes again, and tears run down his cheeks

"Here, blow your nose. Look, can you get up for a minute to sit in the chair?" She leads him like he's some kind of two-year-old. Then she busies herself, going to her closet for sheets, blankets, and pillows for the sofa.

'I am such a loser. I am so stupid. God, I should just kill myself. Maybe I should get drunk."

"Come on now. You know that that isn't going to solve anything." She stands over him, massaging his shoulders and saying, "There, there." As she tries to make him feel better, some thoughts come to her.

"You know, Clem it's getting late, and I think you need to think about getting some sleep.--"

Clem interrupts. "I'll never get to sleep the way I feel."

"I know. The first thing you need to do is to take a shower. You need one. While you're doing that, I'm going to run an errand. Is that okay with you?"

"I guess so. What if your roommate gets back?"

"I'm not expecting him for another couple of hours. Why don't you go to the bathroom and get cleaned up, okay? Everything is all ready and waiting for you." With the air of a condemned man, Clem gets up, and before he's out of the shower, Salma is back. Clem is spent, moving like a robot on low battery power. He's surprised to see how dirty he is, and how badly he needs the shower. He's in Christophe's bathrobe. He slumps on the couch while Salma looks in the medicine cabinet. She goes to the kitchen, and returns to the living room as the good nurse-mother combination.

"Look, I've got a sleeping pill and some warm milk. It's prescription, and it can knock out an elephant. Take it with this." She's holding the milk in a coffee cup.

"Thanks."

"Now, I have a couple of other things." She pulls out a cosmetics tube of cream that she holds in front of his face while he is drinking the milk. "This is a tube of More-Tan. Your complexion is too fair, and it needs to go on your face, ears, neck, and hands. Do you want me to put it on, or you can do it in the morning when you go."

Clem finishes with the milk and pill. "Could you put it on for me?" he whimpers.

Salma squeezes out some of the ointment and starts to massage his face. "That feels good, doesn't it? I got a couple of hundred dollars extra." Salma can anticipate what Clem is going to say. "I'm going to leave it on the table over there. You're going to need something to tide you over, you know. Right now, your prospects need improving, so the money will buy you time. It's a gift."

"You're too kind to me. I don't deserve any of this"

"Just because we're not married any more doesn't mean that I don't care about you." With that she gives him a motherly kiss on his greasy forehead.

"You'll wake up tomorrow, and you'll have a much better idea of what you're going to do."

"I hope so." Clem is reliving every possible thing that got him into this fix. His eyes are getting heavy as he falls into that bottomless pit of drug-induced sleep. He gives up on obsessing about his life, and he relives the time he took his first airplane trip from Guaymas to New Los Angeles. Somewhere around the border, over Mexicali, the seat belt sign goes on, and a subtle change takes place. Ever so gently, Clem can feel the plane as it begins to slow, entering its approach pattern. He feels himself weighing just ever so much less as the plane descends over the Mojave Desert. It's at night, and there is only that sinking and rising feeling as the plane descends. Everything is black.

Clem wakes up thinking about his weird dreams. The light is just turning from dark to gray, and no one else is awake. He goes to the sliding glass door that opens onto the tiny balcony. North Santa Monica is quiet except for the whine of a garbage truck. Off in the distance there's the slice of ocean compressed between two buildings. He goes to the kitchen and tells the robot to fix him a double espresso black, three scrambled eggs, a large bowl of cinnamon oatmeal with honey and raisins, along with a glass of grapefruit juice. Reluctantly, he decides the thing to do is to go to the bathroom, but this means that he'll have to pass by Salma's bedroom. He can see that her door is open. As he goes down the hall, he can't help but notice that Salma is asleep, being cuddled by Christophe. He can hear the sound of gentle snoring.

After the bathroom, he returns to the sofa where he puts on his cleanest dirty clothes. On impulse, he turns on the kitchen hologram with the sound low. It doesn't look like he's on the news today. He finishes his breakfast, but it's time to get going. By now the first rays of the sun are shining through the kitchen window. Clem returns to the living room, focusing on his backpack as he stuffs things inside. He looks at the $20 bills Salma has folded on the coffee table, and reluctantly he puts them in his pocket. At the other end of the living room is a small desk that has some stationary from the Iroquois Gallery. He writes:

Dear Salma:

You are kinder and more together than I will ever be. You don't know how much you've helped me to get on with my life, now and in many other times and places. Thanks for the money. I consider it a loan payable with interest.

Clem thinks some more before writing. He hears a slight shifting noise from Salma's bedroom. They're not awake, but they might be getting closer. He finishes up his note.

I really needed to see you, and you gave me strength. You've given me time. Thanks old friend. XOX, Clem

He wants to call Saroyan, but when and how? He puts his arms through the backpack before he completes his disguise. There is this vision that floats through his head. Once long ago, men went to the moon for the first time. Clem thinks about the ancient, grainy footage of Neil Armstrong stepping out of the lunar module. Clem thinks about what that astronaut felt like before opening the hatch door. He puts his hand on the doorknob. As he begins his life as a homeless person, he might as well be on the moon.

TEN BLOCKS SOUTH OF DOWNTOWN

Being a homie on the Mission District is never fun, as Clem has quickly discovered. Sandwiched in between the railroad yards and the corroded metal fence that demarcates the Forbidden Zone, the Mission District is a miserable collection of buildings mostly made out of crumbling concrete block, all of which have tin roofs that look like they're suffering from some kind of shit-stained disease. Hidden in the back alleys are warrens of shacks made of cardboard and skeletons of automobiles and shards of plastic sheeting. The unpaved streets are tan adobe, and they only have two conditions. One is the garbage-

The Story of the Century

infested dusty state. The other is the up to your knees mudsucking state. Sometimes the two coexist simultaneously in the same small area. Here and there a stray pig ruts around, moving between the urinating men and the way over the hill hookers.

Clem has come here to get some fake ID, but he doesn't have any idea of where to look. Without papers, there's no chance of work, but how do you go up to a stranger and say, "Hi, I'm one of the world's most wanted men. Do you know where I can get some phony identity papers?" What little social contact on the streets so far has been downright scary, and Clem has begun to classify the denizens by their mental state. There is the 'I'm crazier than a bedbug. Can I ramble on to you for two or three hours telling you how Jesus and the CIA have implanted these transistor radios in parts of my head?' state. Then there is the ever popular, 'Hey Bud, you wanna come in the alley with me (to see my friends that want to play with you)? I've got some good shit,' state. The last scary garden variety is, 'You look pretty nice to me. Do you want to see my cock?' Whenever possible, Clem looks for the people with the state he's in: 'I'm a real person, but I've been fucked over so bad, I can't believe it.' Thankfully, today this is the most common variety.

Being on the streets boils life down to fundamentals. When am I going to eat? Where am I going to sleep? Where is something to drink? How little money do I have left? Everything else that people busy themselves with, their possessions, family, friends, dreams -- is fungible. Survival is the key; and Clem has focused on the search for shelter. The missions are easy to find. They're the only painted buildings around, standing out among the tire and gypo auto repair shops, stolen goods tiendas, pawnshops, bail bondsmen, blood banks, and liquor and cigarette vendors.

Clem tries the Catholic missions. Since Rome went its atomized radioactive way, Catholic sects have proliferated into a spectrum of faiths; and Clem has bounced around like a pinball. Kilometers have gone under his feet, and he's found that there's no room at the inns. St. Peters is the sixth he's hit on, and it's getting late in the afternoon, time for the gatekeepers to think about closing up for the night. Clem is getting anxious. He's at the whitewashed stucco walls and the big Spanish door with its wrought iron and dark wood. He goes inside and finds a large space, a lobby for bed sitting rooms. In the alcove is a female priest sitting at a desk, who looks up at Clem with a gentle smile.

"Hello young man. My name is Sister Dorthea. Can I help you?"

"Uhm Sister, I'm in need of a place to stay, and I've been to six or seven Catholic missions without any luck. They're all full. Can you help me?"

"Things have been pretty crowded lately. Even though I don't have room I'll help you out. I'll tell you what. Let me ring my husband, and he can take you to the dining area. I'm going to phone around, and I guarantee you that you'll have some place to stay, even if it's not Catholic." She fiddles on her desk. "Honey, can you come out here? I've got a young man who's hungry, and I'm calling around to get him shelter."

About ten seconds later, an elf of a man comes bounding out from behind swinging doors. He is dressed in clerical garb. "Hello there. I'm Brother Andrew. Come with me." Clem follows the Filipino leprechaun down a short hall, taking a right turn to swinging doors that reveal a gymnasium sized space with a concrete floor, picnic tables, and a food lane. Covering a far wall is a bad copy of *The Last Supper*.

"You're very lucky. Ordinarily we wouldn't have set up for dinner so soon, but there were circumstances." There are about thirty men in the room, and Clem is hit with the pungent mix of institutional food smells. Clem picks up a tray and starts cruising through the food line. There's not a lot of high cuisine. He can choose creamed spinach or creamed corn. There are pieces of elderly fried chicken, synthetic mashed potatoes, five cent dinner rolls, and smatterings of bulgogi and kimchee. For dessert there are globules of rubbery yellow jello.

Clem and his food tray are looking for company, a specific type of company. He's looking for a person that he would not want to approach on the streets, someone from one of those states of mind. He spots a giant of a man with many tattoos. He has a diseased face and a wild growth of beard and hair, slobbering over his chicken piece because he only has half a mouthful of teeth. This wildman fits the bill perfectly.

Clem goes over, and he sits on the opposite side of the picnic table. He eats in silence for a minute before he speaks, "Pardon me, I've got a question to ask."

The fried chicken eater puts his drumstick down and snarls, "What do you want?" accusingly.

"It's only a hypothetical question." Perhaps this is a bad start. Maybe the man doesn't know what the word hypothetical means, but Clem continues anyway. "Say I know a guy who's lost his ID and his papers, and he has some legal problems, with the law, you know." The chicken eater relaxes a little, picking up the drumstick to gnaw at it like a dog, but he is watching and paying attention to Clem.

"Where would a guy like that go to get some new papers? Do you know?"

The chicken eater is polite enough to put the drumstick down, but he doesn't bother to stop chewing when he begins to talk. "Yeah, you go to one of the RPM Copy Shops around town. I think the closest one is at Bolivar and Sepulveda. It's about eight blocks from here. Ask for the premium service on ID papers, but it ain't cheap."

Clem puts his eyes down on his plate to concentrate on his food. But the chicken eater is feeling friendlier, and the ice has been broken. "My name's Raphael." It turns out Raphael used to be one of those 'you wanna come in the alley' types, but now he's more of a 'jesus loony tooners.' He goes on and on about being saved and salvation. Clem does his non-verbal reporter attending skills, and he pretends to listen. After a while, he realizes that the sun is getting low, and his shelter issue is still unresolved.

Sorry, gotta go." Clem beats a retreat back to Sister Dorthea as fast as he can.

"Did you find anything, Sister?"

The diminutive lady with the gold wire frames looks up and smiles. "Yes, a matter a fact, there is the Divine Light Mission three blocks west from here. Go outside and take Calle Munoz right. You'll run right into it."

"I have another question. How would I get to the intersection of Bolivar and Sepulveda?"

Sister Dorthea thinks for a minute, looking at a map that she pulls from her desk. "Calle Munoz runs into Sepulveda. Go north, towards the mountains for three blocks and you'll get to Munoz. Sepulveda is five blocks up the street."

"So, the Divine Light Mission is right along the way, right?"

"Right,"

"Well, thank you very much, Sister. I wish I could stay. If I don't like where I'm staying and I want to stay here, how can I do that?"

"Our situation changes every day. You should try to show up before 3:00 if possible. That's when registration is. You look like a nice man. There could be an opening in a couple of days. Give us your name, and we'll put you on our list."

"Think fast," Clem says under his breath. "Carlos, Carlos Castellon."

"Thank you Carlos." She writes it down. "God be with you."

On his way to the Divine Light Mission, Clem passes by some folks in **those** states and some tramps whose skins appear to be covered with diesel oil in order to hold the road dust better. A prostitute passes him by, and gives him a sultry look for someone with no teeth. Standing in front of Divine Light, Clem can see that while St. Peters represents the top end of flophouses, Divine Light says, "Why bother?" The front door has the ambiance of a Soviet border crossing, and the door buzzer is dangling by its wires. A security camera and a TV are shielded behind grimy bulletproof plexiglas. Once upon a time, this place was a movie theater, and it looks like there's a double feature that appears to be 'J-sus -aves' and 'Repen S-n-r.' A purple neon cross is lit, dangling at a perilous angle over the street, threatening to crush unwary passers by any second. It doesn't help that its wiring is on the fritz, jittering on and off wildly. Clem grasps the buzzer, and the face of a big, sweaty carny barker of a man appears on the TV screen. The tinny speaker yells, "Praise Jesus! What can I do for you son?"

"Uh, -- St. Peters called from up the street. Sister Dorthea said you have a space available for the night."

"Are you washed in the Blood of the Lamb?"

This must be some kind of code. "Uh,-- yes."

"Well, come on inside." The buzzer rings, and Clem pushes on the gulag gate, and now he's inside something like a tiger cage. Another TV camera is looking at him, and there is a pause before the other door opens. On the other side is what appears to be a small filthy office with very large portraits of Jesus on the walls. The hundred fifty kilo carny barker motions Clem to sit down on the swaybacked folding chair in front of a gray metal desk. He raises his hands to the flyspecked ceiling and says, "Thank you Jesus for giving us another lost soul." Clem is not exactly too sure to whom the man is talking. He stops looking at the ceiling, and looks at Clem with this man in the moon grin.

"What's your name, son?"

"Carlos, -- Carlos Castellon"

"My name's Roy, --- Reverend Roy Stringfellow. You can call me Reverend Roy. So how long do you plan to stay with us?" as if this were the Motel 6.

"I don't know. All I need is shelter for the night. I'm kind of living from day to day now."

"Just fill out some paperwork, Carlos. Here." Obviously there are high admissions standards to get a bed in this joint. There is a statement that he has to sign affirming that he is not a Jew or Muslim or other nonbeliever, along with a set of rules that includes 'no drinking,' 'no card playing or any other form of wagering,' 'no loud music,' 'no fornicating or self-abuse,' and 'no sleeping or disrespectful behavior during prayer services.' The list goes on. Clem sighs and signs. Reverend Roy looks at it and smiles. "That looks satisfactory. Follow me." They go up a dingy set of stairs to a dormitory of bunk beds and threadbare Army blankets. A short row of incredibly filthy wash basins, a horse trough pissoir and three feces-smeared open toilet stalls are at the far end of the dormitory. They walk midway down the rows of bunk beds, and they stop. The smell is overpowering.

"This one's yours, number 37." Reverend Stringfellow points to an upper bunk. "Your locker is over there. It's number 37. You signed that you know the rules, and you'll have to do ten hours of worship and Bible study a week in addition to doing twenty hours a week of missionary work. You're in God's Army, you know."

"Bible study begins tomorrow. Tonight's orientation starts at 7:30. You can get dinner now if you want to."

"That's okay. I had something to eat. Since orientation isn't going to start for a few hours, is it all right if I go out for an errand?"

The good reverend turns chilly. "I'm sorry, you can't. You can go without supper, but you have to do Bible study. You're a first-nighter, and we have to get you trained right." Clem sighs. The Divine Light

The Story of the Century

Mission is less a way station for the homeless than a sanctuary for a cult and a religious prison. Stringfellow hands Clem a Bible. "Sit over there on that bench, and start reading the Good Book. This is a test to see how worthy you are."

"Slim to none," Clem mumbles to himself. He opens the book of Genesis on the first page, and he starts reading. He discovers that Adam's family was a randy bunch. Both Cain and Abel slept with Mom. He gets into reading more. By the time he's in chapter 32, he's reading about Jacob wrestling with the angel. It appears they were touching pee-pees. Genesis 32:32 reads:

Therefore the children of Israel, eat not the sinew which shrank, which is upon the hollow of the the thigh unto this day: because he touched the hollow of Jacob's thigh in the sinew that shrank.

Clem is pondering all this wild and wooly behavior when one of the mission's trustees comes up and taps him on the shoulder. "Brother, the service is starting. Go downstairs, stash yer gear, and get seated." The newest prisoner of the Divine Light Mission slinks into the back row. He sits next to a skeletal man hunched over in his seat, who has tattoos all over his body and an ominous sounding tubercular cough. Reverend Stringfellow is standing behind a pulpit. He's changed into a clerical collar and robe, but he still looks like a greeter at Wal-Mart. Clem has perfect timing. Twenty more seconds, and he would have been tardy. The house lights dim and the spotlight shines on Reverend Roy.

"Brothers and sisters, Jesus is a fisher of men…" He launches into what seems like an interminable length of holy roller bushwa that allows Clem to have a chance to daydream about having sex with Saroyan in her bedroom, but he's diverted by the supergraphics on a big screen behind the Rev. "We have a special treat tonight, brothers and sisters. I have a special transmission straight from the Central Office in

Asuncion, Paraguay. Julie, hit the hologram!" The entire front of the room is suddenly filled with giant crosses flying out over the audience, and the dingy auditorium is filled with the sounds of a heavenly choir, singing from nowhere.

"Liiiiiiiiive!!! From the Crystal Cathedral! Give me your poor, oppressed and heavy in spirit! It's the man with the plan who knows Jesus is the reason! It's time for the REVEREND VATO LOCO DUDE!!!" More flying crosses whoosh by, disappearing into infinity. The words 'DIVINE LIGHT TIME' start flashing enough to give a screaming headache; and the view shifts to a helicopter, rushing across a flat urban landscape towards what appears to be a tight cluster of giant quartz crystals as the geological oddity reveals itself to be a supermodern, gazillion dollar church. Then there's a cut to the inside, showing that this house of worship has sufficient space for a small dirigible. Three story tall neon letters adorn the inside, suspended in space. On one side there's HEAVEN. On the other side there's HELL, and there's an indoor jungle at the back of the church.

The camera is somewhere over the pulpit. It rests for the briefest moment on the jungle at a distance before it zooms violently towards the five-meter tall solid glass doors that define the entryway to the interior. They must weigh a ton each, and they swing open by themselves. There is a deafening roar, preceding the appearance of triple chrome, straight-piped, turbocharged chopper with a solid gold crucifix where its headlight should be. If this were the 20th Century, a Hell's Angel would gladly sell his old lady into a white slave ring for the pleasure of this sweet hog.

Riding this gearhead's wet dream is a burly brown man with a red bandanna and a long flowing pony tail flapping in the motorcycle wind. He sports a Fu Manchu moustache and gold aviator sunglasses. The fringed black leather motorcycle vest appears to be covered with emeralds, diamonds, rubies, and sapphires that make a picture of a radioactive Jesus on the cross. The camera angle changes, and a close up reveals the jacket from the rear. The jeweled embroidery reads "Rev. Vato Loco Dude' and 'Jesus Saves' in the finest gangbanger typography.

By now, the holy hog and the raghead reverend are getting to the end of their hellfire run through church. The bike screeches to a stop, swerving sideways just before the steps to the nave. Dismounting and putting the kickstand down, the Reverend Dude bounds up the stairs to stand behind the pulpit, looking more like a wrestling hero than a man of the cloth. He throws gang signs to the church crowd while a speedmetal hymn plays at full blast.

"WHO'S YOUR DADDY?"

"JESUS!" the crowd shouts.

"WHO LOVES YOU, BABY?"

"JESUS!"

"Brothers and sisters, I can feel the heeeeeeeling power of luuuuuv tooonight!" The Reverend Dude has begun the service. As he continues with his opening remarks, the camera crews begin to zero in on members of the congregation. It's obvious that as rich as the Church of the Divine Light is, it's a magnet for the world's gomers and serious losers. There are the elephantine black ladies wearing polka dot dresses that are four sizes too small. There are the high school dropouts, sexually repressed teenage boys with overly tight collars and incurable skin diseases. Overly anxious welfare mothers with rotten teeth make their Mongoloid children wave at the camera.

"Hey, world, we're coming at you!" Reverend Dude is getting emotional. Clem thinks about the audience that wants to watch, not the prisoners trapped in this moldering auditorium. The Church of the Divine Light must be speaking to the trailer park resident in the tornado zone, the one who has been waiting for the big lottery ticket for the last seventeen years. There must be bitter old spinsters who never married because they loved Jesus too much, the lonely ones of questionable hygiene, and the religious crank addicts living in denial in their meth labs. This is the flock that the Reverend Vato Loco Dude must be speaking to. Most of the world's population would rather be seen coming out of a whorehouse by all their relatives than be seen at a Divine Light service.

Clem begins to lose attention, drifting mostly into longing for Saroyan, then alternating in sexual reverie. Floating over the auditorium, the Dude goes through the standard shtick. The choir sings. Their souls are made for Jesus. The Reverend goes into the congregation, giving blessings on the gomers who are pressed forward by the attendants. Between hosannas and obscure Bible verses, there is the sermonette, followed by yet more laying on of hands in the Parade of Miracles, with supplications to heal irritable bowel syndrome. The choir sings one more time. Nobody knows the trouble I've seen, and then it's time for the collection.

"Like, Jesus loves and lives in all of us, Man. No matter what kind of person you are -- sick, broke, drunk, or full of dope. He is the way, Man. I mean like right now and in the here after, understand? God so loved the world he gave his only begotten son, and I don't mean you, honey child."

The ushers and attendants begin to move up the aisles in order to vacuum clean the flock of their small bills. They run the tape, showing the Divine Light Missions around the world, spending precious time hovering over a drooling old bum, emaciated with matted hair as he tries to pretend he doesn't notice the cameraman hovering over him as he sucks on his thin mission soup. The hologram flashes in epileptic fits:

"MAKE YOUR LOVE DONATIONS! CALL 1-800-IMFORJESUS TO MAKE YOUR PLEDGE NOW!"

Eventually the charismatic reverend winds up for the big finale. God loves you, even if you're a sinner. Trust in Jesus, and make your sins go away. Bible quote. Bible quote. It could all go on in an endless tape loop with minor variations, and in fact it does.

Actually, the Reverend Vato Loco Dude isn't preaching now. He's standing in the counting room in the cathedral basement, talking to his accountant. The coin sorters are jingling, and the bill sorters are dividing the paper money into wrapped stacks of ones, fives, tens, and twenties. The Rev's mobile phone rings and he holds his hand up, silencing his cash flow advisor.

"It's Senator Srinigar!" Reverend Dude exclaims as he begins to listen. The leader of the opposition party tells the Reverend about Waldo Kitkeatlers, a TV variety show host, whom the senator believes could defeat President Hok in the upcoming election. Dude's eyes narrow as he concentrates. "Why yes, I think he'd make an excellent candidate!"

SECOND FLOOR, DIVINE LIGHT MISSION
2:45 P.M.

Because he was a good little Christian and did his four hours of Bible study, Clem gets some work release. This gives him enough time to buy his illegal identity papers, getting him back in time for a dismal Jesus lunch. Right now there's a short break between the lectures on missionary work and Bible study, and he's sitting on bunk #37 staring at a piece of plastic with a picture of some kind of proto-Clem with black hair and a dark complexion. He is moving his lips, trying to memorize some arcane bits of information about his new, false self that may keep him alive.

"My name is Robert Manley. I was born in Spanish Town, Jamaica on July 24, 231. My mother's name is Ethel Claymore. My father's name is Jeremiah. My mother's parents were Edward Claymore and Janet House. My father's parents were Ezekiel Manley and Margarita Cansino. My Social Security number is 011 562 151 601."

There are other things taking up brain space. Number one is that he despises the Divine Light Mission. Another is his overwhelming desire to call Saroyan, but this is problematic for a number of reasons. First there's the continuing manhunt for him. He knows now that the moment her number's entered, phone robots will begin burrowing through the wires until they've got his precise location targeted. Escape routes from the phone will be critical, and Clem won't have much time to make Saroyan certain that it's really him. Finally, movie stars don't usually take calls from bums in the slums.

During the morning Bible study, Clem spends hours trying to figure these things out, and he's got something resembling a plan. The first step is to write a letter to Saroyan by way of Pepe Lopez, addressed to Saroyan's fan club. He's already inked most of it during the morning scripture studies, leading Reverend Stringfellow to believe that bunk #37 is devout and truly worthy of spiritual redemption. Later he'll drop it in a mailbox, and even to the prying eyes of the Feds, the letter will look like some goober slobbering over Star. No attention will be paid to this message, except Saroyan.

CONFIDENTIAL TO PEPE LOPEZ
FOR SAROYAN'S EYES ONLY

I'm writing to you from the underground. Federal agents and local cops are on my butt big time, in case you didn't know. I tried to call you, but the telephones are bugged six ways from Sunday. The big story blew up worse than I could have possibly imagined. I got fired because it touched on areas "Vital to World Security," and it's lucky the cops weren't at the paper to arrest or disappear me.

I've got to be honest. I'm scared. At least one of my sources met a mysterious death, and I don't know what happened to the other one. If I'm caught, the best thing that could happen to me is an indeterminate stretch of time in some federal prison. The alternative is I could be dead.

I heard about the problems you're having. I can't imagine how horrible it all must be. I feel as if somehow I'm responsible for your situation. I want you to know that no matter what happens; my love for you is stronger and more powerful than it's ever been. We will triumph together. One way or another, I'll be back in your arms again, and we'll get out of where we are now.

Because the telephone is so dangerous, we can email each other as long as we use internet cafes or someone else's computers. Set up an email account under somebody else's name, and call it birdoparadise8 (because that's what you are!) My handle will be chimbila190 (because I'm batty about you). STARGATE.COM is where we should register.

Clem or whatever his name is looks around. It's about time for the flock to be herded into group bathroom scrubbing before getting into an intense three hour discussion on the meaning of John 3:16. Clem/Robert decides he's had enough of this place. He goes to the locker where his knapsack is, and he heads towards the rear exit. He's going to try his luck on the streets, and he'll finish Saroyan's letter later.

And it's a good thing too. As Clem is getting ready to go out the back door, a police detective is visiting Reverend Stringfellow in his office. He's showing Reverend Roy a picture of a blond, clean cut Clem Reader, as well as several images of possible disguises. The fat holy man has to admit that picture #3 looks vaguely familiar. He motions to the detective to follow him upstairs. Number 37 is worth looking into.

Karl Eysenbach

NEAR THE CENTRAL STATION

Clem has wandered west of the Mission District, pausing to sit at a park bench to finish writing to Saroyan. Feeling a little guilty, he writes a similar letter to Aunt Victoria and Uncle Carlos; then he heads towards Memorial Station, New LA's passenger rail hub. He realizes how dangerous his next action is going to be, and he gets into his hyperaware mode. Walking through the great hall with its Spanish architecture, he notices the security guards. Eventually he settles on a public phone located near an exit. There's a wide view of the parking lot and Sepulveda Avendia, and there are five or six bus lines running along this street. He picks up the phone and says, "directory assistance."

"Hello Operator. First I need to get directory assistance for Matzatlan, Mexico for Clyde Castellon, and then I'd like to make a collect call to him. Can I do that? Good.

Yes, could you tell him it's from his cousin, Clem." He hears a new click on the line.

He can hear the operator. "Hello, this is the North American operator. I'm calling Clyde Castellon. I have a collect call from Clem. Will you take the call?" There is a long pause at the other end. He can hear some animated talking in the background at the other end of the line.

 An annoyed, very cold voice finally says, "Put him on," and the operator says, "Go ahead."

There is some history you need to know. When he was young, Clem used to dread visits from his cousin, as he was a horrible bully. There's no love lost between these two even now, and that's what Clem's counting on. "Uh, Hello,---- Clem?" There is a pregnant pause. "Is that really you? Why are you calling ME?"

"Hey, Clyde. You sound really great!" Clem is lying through his teeth.

"Uyh,-- you've been in the news lately, haven't you?"

"I guess, but that's not what I'm calling about. I've been having problems in getting touch with Aunt Victoria and Uncle Carlos. Have you talked to them lately?"

"Uyh,------" The pregnant pauses go on forever. Clyde works in the phone company, and sometimes it seems he has his own wiretap system set up in the central exchange. His words are parceled as if someone spliced together a response. In this case, paranoia is probably just being realism. When Clem said 'Aunt Victoria' there's another click on the line. "No." The word finally leaves Clyde's mouth. "The last time I heard----- they were all right." There is that strange twist in Clyde's voice.

"That makes me feel better. I'm on my way down the coast to Tijuana. Could you do me a favor? I was hoping that maybe you'd call them up to tell them I'm coming."

The pregnant pause goes for another geological era. "Yes." And then there is another pause. By this time, the phone robots are going crazy, and the cops have figured out that Clem is in a one square kilometer area. No doubt Clyde is doing his best to cooperate with the authorities in his own way. Enough damage has been done.

"Well, Clyde, it's been great talking to you. Thanks for taking the call. I gotta go." With that, he slams down the phone. Some buses have gathered outside, and Clem starts running to catch one, any one. Soon Memorial Station will be swarming with local and federal dicks of all persuasions.

After he gets on, he discovers that the bus is headed towards the Ferry Building, and the neighborhood gets more and more familiar. Clem is still thinking about how to call Saroyan when the bus passes by Sochi's. It might be a big imposition, and it might get Sochi in trouble; but it might be worth a try. He buzzes to get off at the next stop, and he walks back. It's the middle of the afternoon, and it's set up time at the restaurant. Clem turns the corner and walks down the alley towards the back entrance, and he bangs on the rear door.

"Sochi? It's me, Clem Reader."

Sochi comes out, and he's scowling. "Are you begging? What do you want?" He barks.

Clem takes off his hat and glasses. "Sochi, it's me, Clem Reader. Can we talk for just a minute?"

Sochi's demeanor doesn't change. He just stands there with his hands folded across his chest, scowling. "So it IS you. So what do you want Mr. Big Time Newspaper Reporter in Big Trouble? You don't even look like him!"

Clem is standing with hat in hand. "Sochi, I know I look funny and stupid, and I'm probably a mess, too. Yeah, I'm in big trouble, and I'm going to ask you for a big favor. It won't last more than three minutes, I promise, and you can time me. Then I'll get the hell out of here, and you'll never see me ever again if that's what you want. But gosh, Sochi, you're my friend. I just need one tiny favor from you, -- a phone call. Can you give it to me?"

The samurai warrior of the sushi is not pleased. He just stands there, looking at Clem and shaking his head, while Clem's standing there, looking like a puppy and holding his hat in his hand so hopefully. Sochi is pissed, and Clem has caught him after his fish gutting, and he's in the middle of supervising the dishwashing.

"I'd like to call Saroyan on your phone. Can you do just this much for me?"

"Are you crazy? With the cops lookin' for you all over the place?" Clem gets down on one knee. He's being cute, but he knows he's on his last shot. "For Saroyan's sake and my sake. She's your friend too, and I think she's in trouble."

The Story of the Century

Sochi folds. He knows the truth of what Clem speaks. He can't stand it any longer. Rolling his eyes a little, he motions. "OK, Kid, get the hell in here. Do you know where the phone is?" "Sure." Clem pats Sochi on the back as he goes inside. "Thanks. You're a pal." In the kitchen, he dials the number, and it rings. There's only one click. That's a good sign. A female voice answers on the other end of the line. But he's disappointed when he finds out that it's Saroyan's answering machine.

"Hello world, it's me Saroyan. I'm doing something else right now, so leave a message, and I'll get back to you." There's a pause and a beep.

Clem thinks, "It beats a poke in the eye with a sharp stick." He says, "Saroyan, it's me Clem. I've been worried sick about you. I'm glad I got your answering machine at least. I've been blocked from getting any calls to you, and I've tried lots of times."

Clem sucks his breath in, and he continues. "Look, Saroyan, this is a horrible time to talk, so I'll be brief. Somebody in your organization is going to give you something from me. I need you to look at it, okay? It explains some of the things that are going on with me. I just want to say I miss you, and I love you more than you can ever possibly imagine. Okay, I gotta run. Cops are on my tail."

He turns to Sochi. "How long did I take?

"One minute I guess."

"Good. That's all I need. Look, I better get going even though I'd love to hit you up for some food. I'm starving. But I've got a question. Do you know where I might be able to get a job in a restaurant if I've got okay papers?"

"I'm not going to give you any food. You got enough off of me with the phone call. But you're sure as hell not going to get a job here."

"I didn't ask for that. I know. But I want some advice as to where I should go."

Sochi jerks his finger; "Maybe you can try down PCH towards Malibu. They've got a lot of restaurants there."

"Gosh Sochi, you're a pal! I owe you big time for the phone call. You don't ever have to do a favor for me ever again!" Clem puts his arms around the chef. He pulls away a little bit, and he looks at him.

"You are the best. You're a real pal! I love you, Sochi." He gives Sochi another bear hug. Sochi looks up at Clem.

"Get the hell out of here."

KILOMETER 12.3, PACIFIC COAST HIGHWAY 5:30 A.M.

It's not quite dawn, and Clem is walking along the Pacific Coast Highway in the gutter. He feels like he's struck out. It was all very well and good to nearly get his ass in a sling by using the telephone, but what did he accomplish? He left a message, but he might as well have been a telemarketer. He's certainly not going to try to do that stupid pet trick in the near future. He's doubly screwed, and he knows it. It's way too late to go back to the Mission District, and maybe St. Pete would let him in. But there sure as heck aren't a lot of homeless shelters around here. So what is he going to do? Sleep in the bushes? That's strictly Critterville! Yuck a gob!

Clem fantasizes. Maybe it will be like one of those romance novels where the rich dowager takes pity on the wandering vagabond and makes him her love slave, turning him into the Malibu pool boy. Not hardly likely, Bub! There must be some homeless people hidden in the underbrush around here, but then you're taking chances with the unwanted homeless states. And of course, there's the money factor. There is none. If he had a fire, he'd roast and eat one of his shoes. Clem is getting damn hungry, not to mention thirsty. Maybe he can sneak into

The Story of the Century

one of those bathrooms on the beach, taking his chances with the cops and his phony ID. So Clem doesn't have a clue here. Question: How much does it take one loser to be shit out of luck? Answer: Not much.

Clem is funked out, confused, lost in thought circles that go round and round, and his mouth feels like used sandpaper. The highway is totally deserted. Once in a while a luxury convertible drives by at excessive speed, coating Clem with yet more road dust. The only walking thing he's seen was a raccoon. Clem would immediately settle for discovering the next hobo jungle. This is risky of course, in so many ways. But what in the hell is he going to do? How is he going to get out of this mess?

But miracles happen. Way off in the distance, there's a figure approaching. Clem has no idea who it is, and yet it has a familiar gait. Clem has seen that walk someplace before, not in New Los Angeles. Where was it? Mexico? Maybe. What part of Mexico? He racks his brain. Ejido San Mateo? Did he see that walk in Ejido San Mateo? The figure is getting closer. He's too far away to recognize, but he looks Mexican. There's an outline of a person, and the outline looks familiar, but from somewhere out in the distant past. Who is it? The figure is getting closer. Clem can see the figure getting larger with more detail as he gets closer.

"Jose? Sumi? Chaparro? Jorge?" Clem thinks to himself.

"Jorge?" Clem says this out loud softly.

"Jorge?" The figure is approaching. He does look familiar.

"Jorge? Are you Jorge Estrada?" The guy is looking at Clem really weird now. He's tensing up. This could be trouble.

"Are you Jorge Estrada from the Ejido San Mateo in Baja?" The figure stops, glares, and puts one hand in his pocket menacingly. He's maddogging Clem. If looks could kill.

"Who the fuck are you, *chingado*?" he says with a sneer before he spits on the ground. There's an ominous edge to the body language of this familiar stranger. Clem could be a John Doe with a toe tag in the morgue tomorrow, but he doesn't care. He doesn't care. This guy might recognize him and help him. Clem's going to let it all hang out.

"Jorge, you're a fisherman. You used to be married to Jennifer. I'm Clem Reader. Look, I'm wanted by the law big time, and I'm throwing myself at your mercy. Is there any place that you know where I can stay?"

"You say I'm Jorge Estrada, right?"

"Right"

"And you're Clem Reader."

"Right," At this point the Jorge takes a red handled folding knife out of his pocket.

"Well Señor Reader, why don't I gut you like a fish?"

Here is Clem standing by the highway, God's fool if there ever was one. He doesn't know that Jorge is on the world's most wanted list as a terrorist. It does enter Clem's dim bulb of a mind that he doesn't look like the Clem Reader that Jorge used to know, but Mr. Chucklehead decides to tell his life story, regardless of whether Jorge recognizes him or not.

"Look Jorge. I'm sure it's you. I know that I don't look like the Clem you knew in the village, see? But I had to disguise myself because I'm the most wanted man in the world now. All the cops are after me, and the FBI and the CIA too. They know I had something to do with some secret government documents I got on my job as a reporter, you know, with the *New Los Angeles Times*? Anyway, a bunch of people wound up dead I think because of the information they gave me. Since I'm a blond guy, I had to dye my hair and darken my skin so the fuzz wouldn't recognize me." I could go on narrating what Clem had to say, but it's all blah blah blah.

Little does Clem know, but he's actually making Jorge secretly happy. First, Jorge has had a hard day's work, and he's not really into killing people

The Story of the Century

unless he absolutely has to. Second, it gradually enters Jorge's mind that this guy might actually be Clem Reader. Third, it amuses him to think that someone he knows -- someone -- supposedly a man of respect and substance, might actually be in as deep a pool of legal shit as he is.

"… and so that's why I'm here walking here on the highway."

Jorge puts his knife in his pocket. He steps forward towards Clem, and gives him a big *embrazo*. *"Compadre!"* he says with the hug. "So you're wanted big time by the Federales?"

"Yeah," he says somewhat reluctantly. "I suppose you saw me on hologram."

There's one more test. "You say you're from the Ejido San Mateo. How do they make a living?" Jorge is still fingering his pocketknife. He can still dress a hog if he needs to.

"That's easy, there's fishing, tourism. My Uncle Carlos has a hacienda. He's in the road building business, and he sells some citrus on the side."

That's all that Jorge wants to hear. "So you are Clem Reader! It must have been years! You don't look like a reporter, or whatever you are, and I can tell you need a bath."

Clem is positively sheepish now. "I guess I said that I'm homeless. I woke up from a bender, and I found an army of cops going through my studio. I decided that it'd be better to be a homeless person than to go to jail or be disappeared. Problem is, I don't have any place to park my head tonight, and I'm getting awfully hungry and thirsty."

Here Jorge has a chance to be a big man, turning the social tables from the ejido. "I'll tell you what. This is your lucky day. I just got off my shift at work, and I'm headed home. I got paid today, and I know where we can get a beer or two. After that, we can head to my house in Pacoima. I'm living in a bungalow with a lady friend, and you're invited for dinner. I know you can stay with us sleeping in the living room."

Clem is extremely grateful. "Do you really mean it? That would be swell! Thanks, Jorge!" It's his turn to give Jorge a hug. Then he realizes how flat busted broke he is, and he gets another sheepish look on his face.

"You know, I don't have a thin dime to my name right now."

Jorge smiles," Don't worry. This is all on me. Just follow me." They stop at an all night Shop & Rob, picking up a six pack, and they lollygag around behind the store drinking their fill, talking old times. Clem is elaborating on his blah blah blah.

"This whole thing started with that massacre of Marines at Santa Ynez." This freezes Jorge cold. He turns into a statue while he's having acid flashbacks of killing people at the Ybarra Loncheria.

"Did I say something wrong?"

"Yes and no." Jorge/Insecticida turns to Clem. "You've told me all about your story. It's time I told you some of mine." But Jorge is beginning to fish for words because he's never told anything to anyone, not even his girl friend Maria."

"You know about the ALF?"

"Sure, they were involved in that killing, weren't they?"

"I don't want to talk too much, but there was a lot more stuff going on with the ALF than anyone could ever know. I saw what some of those guys did."

Clem's eyes get big. "Wow! I had no idea. Did you really know some of those guys? Were they really as bloodthirsty as the government was talking about?"

Jorge clams up. "Just say, I knew people who knew people. I wasn't in the center. I just saw stuff." It's emotional shutting down time for Jorge now. "I don't want to talk about it."

The hunger and cerveza must be going to Clem's brain. "Wow! What a coincidence! There must have been ALF people around San

Mateo. It must be that artesian water. You and me, we come from an ejido of superbad hombres!" Jorge rolls his eyes. This is not funny.

"Let's talk about something else, like what happened to Netto."

"The last time I heard, he got religion." This is an appropriate topic. They trade names back and forth as they start heading towards the subway station. When they get there, the security guard gives Clem the evil eye, but Jorge is a regular. He waxes effusive.

"Relax, Man, this is my homie, man! He's hanging with me. I'm taking him to dinner. He's on my pass." They're being observed by the men and robots of the security cameras, but no close attention is paid. All anyone sees are two old pals, a working stiff and a weird homeless guy. These are not people on the #3 and #7 positions in the World's Most Wanted list. The train comes from the valley. There's time out for the conductor, and eventually the train line goes all the way to Pacoima, the other end of the line. After an hour they get off, and they wait for the bus. Then they walk. The sun is up now. All the while, they're talking about the old times.

Finally they're standing in front of a ratty looking bungalow that's badly in need of paint. Tufts of brown grass struggle to stay alive in the adobe soil, and there's a refrigerator with a door off lying down in the front yard, at the end of a street that used to be paved. The two caballeros go up the two cracked concrete steps. *"Mi casa es su casa,"* says Jorge as he opens the corroded aluminum screen door. Inside isn't much better, but an attempt has been made to keep things clean.

Maria is sitting on the floor in front of the sofa with a broken spring. She's eating deep fried pork rinds and watching a *telenovela* on the hologram. The moment she hears voices at the door, she turns the tube off and gets up off the floor. She is mildly attractive and slightly overweight, the way that Mexican ladies are of that age. She tries not to be deeply pissed as Jorge does the introduction.

"Maria, you're gonna hate me, but I found Clem here on the way home. And he's from my *ejido*. So, if it's all right if he spends some time here, isn't it?"

Maria would rather that the stranger be invisible and not be here in the first place, but what's a gal to do? "It's not much, but we call it home. I have a pot of beans and rice on, so there's no problem about having enough to eat."

Clem is just about a monomaniac now on the subject of food, and he's still dirty and thirsty as all get out. "Could I have a giant glass of water? Whatever you've got cooking, it smells like food for the gods to me."

Maria smiles. "Thank you. The glasses are in the kitchen cabinet by the sink. The bathroom is over there. And feel free to take a shower."

By the time Clem has freshened up, a cloth has been placed over the flimsy plastic table, and dinner is ready, even though it's early morning. Now Clem finds out more about Maria as he wolfs down the chow. To make a long story short, it's a good thing that Jorge found Maria. They talk about life on the streets, and how important it is to have a job, any job. It turns out that Maria is a food prep worker at the same restaurant that Jorge works at, and between themselves, they have enough for beer at the end of the week.

After dinner, Maria cleans up and Jorge brings out a bong for smoking. They trade hits, and this loosens Clem up enough to start complaining about the impossibilities of finding a job. "You know, I spent all my money on getting this phony ID card. (I'm Robert Manley, you know. I was born in Spanish Town, Jamaica." He goes off on his litany. "And I don't have a clue about what I'm going to do for a job."

Truly, Clem is living now in the land of Christmas miracles. By luck, Jorge has one more chance to play El Grande Señor. "Funny you should ask. One of the pearl divers where I work just quit today. I guess since you've got your papers, you can work with me. I can put in a good word for you. The bosses, they trust me." Of course there are the usual qualifications, but I will cut to the chase and tell you that in three days time Clem will start work as a dishwasher in the bowels of the Tour de L'Argent.

Clem and Jorge continue to trade bong hits, and their topics of conversation expand, as things tend to do in such circumstances. They talk about whether robots have feelings, and whether they're really just slaves. They talk about how the powers that be want everything in the world frozen in amber so they can control things better, but society doesn't work that way. They talk about Central Africa, where the people live in REAL poverty, not like the good poverty here.

Clem says, "Earth is like a noisy neighbor, and we don't realize that somebody has already called the cops."

Jorge agrees, and the ex-Subcommandante loosens up enough to tell Clem about his relation with Attu, how Attu has always been there for him until recently, and how it was that Attu arranged for everything -- even helping him to get him the dishwasher's job to where he is right now, in this shabby living room in Pacoima. Clem thinks that this is the best story he's heard in decades, but what does he know? He's stoned.

"Why doesn't your flying saucer pal come and visit you here?"

"In Pacoima? No, Man. He doesn't like cities. He says the pollution gets to him, and besides, he's a wide-open spaces kind of guy. But you're right. I sure do miss him -- wish I could see him right now."

Think of Jiminy Cricket. When you wish upon a star, Jorge is more right than he knows. Attu has been tied down in the control room under the mountains of Baja. The magnetic interferometer from Fort Huachuca's been nothing except a major pain in the ass. Its wobble has progressed all the way up past the subatomic level. At this rate, the whole thing has only 100 earth days before the whole thing goes shebang, and there goes the solar system along with the rest of the neighborhood. So there are more important things than loafing around and visiting old friends, but this doesn't mean that Attu can't see what's going on in Jorge's life.

Although he's trapped in the control room, his alien TV keeps a live running commentary on the Clem & Jorge Show.

"The Earth is a noisy neighbor, eh? I'll have to remember that." When Jorge talks about how the little green light never comes to visit, he can't help but get choked up.

"I'll come and get you Buddy. Don't worry, I'll save you. I'll get you out of here before this whole thing blows up!"

HAPPY VALLEY REHABILITATION CENTER

She's wearing nothing but a hospital gown, pacing back and forth in the padded cell. It's taken quite a while for her to come to her senses, and it hasn't been easy, what with all of the weird drugs that they've been pumping into her system. There she was, sitting in her trailer, getting ready for the morning shoot. Her character, Doña Maria, was going to be in the cantina when *Zorro* was going to break in to battle six of the evil lieutenant's soldiers. She was looking in the mirror practicing her reaction shots when there was a knock on the door. Standing outside was Doc Aguilar, the set physician, and he looked awfully worried. There were some ugly fuckers in dark glasses and white coats standing behind him.

"Miss Pashogi, these men are here, and they have some papers for you to look at."

"Laundry or ice cream delivery?' The fuckers didn't smile. She took the paper from Aguilar, and she began to read it. She got as far as the headline, 'Notice of Psychiatric Commitment' followed by a few sentences of legalistic gumbledegook. There wasn't even enough time

The Story of the Century

to ask, "What does this mean?" when the goons began to manhandle her. You better believe that she fought like a bloody banshee, and she screamed at the top of her lungs. Then she felt a sharp pain in her arm as someone administered a hypodermic needle. She remembers wriggling and screaming for help as she was dragged through the movie set, barely remembering being strapped into the ambulance.

She woke up briefly, or at least she thinks she woke up briefly, but maybe it was part of the dream too. She was strapped to a bed in a cabin in a jet plane, but it was mostly empty. There was a doctor and a nurse, and another nurse with a hypodermic needle. Behind them were two creepy looking guys in gray suits that looked like they worked for the government or something. One of the creeps said, "Give her the sodium pentathol." Then there was the missing time again. The next thing she remembers is feeling like homemade shit in some kind of hospital, this hospital. The nurse is taking her vital signs.

"Blood pressure's still a little low, but that's a side effect of the medication. Her temp's normal."

She's in this awful hospital gown. She has no idea of what happened to her clothing or telephone or jewelry. She feels violated. What kinds of paws were all over her body going through her things and putting her in this rag? A doctor comes in. He seems like a nice black man as he shakes her hand. "My name is Doctor Chabarki. Welcome to the Happy Valley Rehabilitation Center Miss Pashogi." Before he has a chance to finish, Saroyan is saying:

"What am I doing her? What is this all about?" These are #1 and #2 of a million other questions she has.

"You certainly have the right to feel worried and confused Miss Pashogi, but consider this a brief vacation. You're here for therapy. You've been working too hard, and you've been diagnosed as a substance abuser. Marijuana and cocaine, isn't it?"

Saroyan is getting angrier and angrier, and almost as if on cue, Dr. Jagan is there. Dr. Chabarki may be a good cop, but Jagan is the bad cop from central casting. While Chabarki is a reasonable, pleasant looking man in a slightly overweight, middle aged kind of way; Dr. Jagan has a perpetual expression as if he's just tasted some sour milk. His complexion is bad and gray, and he has the darkest circles under his eyes. His intentions are not the best.

The first thing he does to establish rapport is to loudly declaim, "Aggressive behavior, eh? An injection of Respiridal, and a big one." He snaps his fingers, and the orderlies pounce on her again, struggling with her, until they throw her in the padded cell.

Saroyan remembers being naked because she tore her hospital gown off, and those goony guards were spying on her. Then they gave her another shot, and other than for test tube static in her brain, the only coherent thought she came up with was, "Gee, this is bad shit." You'd think it was bad shit too, if they force-fed you some cousin of PCP. On top of mental flatlining, she's got the hiccups and water retention. Other than for sitting on the toilet or being spied upon by the staff, there's way too much time to think about her situation; that is, between the times the drugs wear off. The only way to fight this crazymaking place is by doing exercises as long as she can to the point of exhaustion. Saroyan doesn't know what to think about her situation. She's angry. She's scared. She's bored.

But the number one motivating factor for Saroyan is TO-FIGURE-HOW-TO-GET-THE-HELL-OUT-OF-HERE. Even though they've tried to make the most beautiful woman in the world look like a hag, they really haven't succeeded. There have been a parade of different eyes parading past the peephole, and 80% of it's prurient. She's decided that extreme actions are needed if she's going to blow this popcorn stand, but there are pieces missing to the plan.

The PA announces that it's time for group therapy; and it's showtime as an orderly opens her cell, escorting her to the group grope already in progress. "What are you feeling now, Estella?" Nurse Banton is asking, but there's no answer. Nurse Banton is just a clockpuncher, but what can you expect when you've been in an insane asylum for fifteen years; being paid to be as proper, attentive, and as caring as can be, when you're supposed to lovingly elicit some kind of response from a basket case of a woman with a drooling mouth?

"Will you share your feelings with us, Estella?" Nurse Banton asks one more time, but Saroyan can see that Nurse Banton has made yet another check mark on the clipboard on her lap. She's asked Estella one or two times already, and Nurse Banton at least acts perpetually optimistic that she can get a response out of the catatonic woman with the vacant eyes. God only knows what Estella's original problem was, but it's obvious that her problem now is the severe overmedication that she's been given. Estella has less personality than a defective robot, and yet Nurse Banton continues.

"Concentrate, Estella. Look at me. Make yourself speak, and tell me how you're feeling. Are you all right Estella?"

Estella's lips begin to quiver. She jerks a bit and shifts her great weight on the rickety folding chair. Her right leg gives a small involuntary kick, and she begins to stammer. "I----I----I." She pauses and inhales twice. A drop of spittle from her protruding tongue drops to the floor. "I----- feel--------sick."

"Oh, Estella, thank you ever so much for sharing that with us. That was wonderful! Everybody, give Estella a round of applause!" She looks at her captive audience of lost females. Most obey, but only half-heartedly.

"I know that took a tremendous amount of effort, and I'm sorry that you're not feeling well. But we're all here to get better, and I think you made a very important statement. I'm so glad you could share that with the group." She turns a page on her clipboard, making some notes before she focuses on the next victim in group therapy.

Saroyan looks around the therapy room, painted in institutional tan with cheap thin wall to wall carpeting. Two floral prints on the wall do little to diminish the oppressiveness of the place. Besides Saroyan and Estella, there's Yoko, a rather frightened looking older woman who plays with her fingers entirely too much, and Juanita, -- a pierced, tattooed, punked out teenage girl with thick bandages on her wrists. And then there's Anna.

Anna is different from the others. Unlike the other innmates she's wearing street clothes; even though they look like they came from some cheap hypermart. Not only does she look incredibly more normal than anyone else; her hair is combed and styled. She has some make up on, and she's wearing a bracelet. She's a Happy Valley statement of what many good institutional psychiatric brownie points can do for you. She acts normal too, but Anna poisoned three lovers in a row for their insurance. She's the perfect psychopath.

Nurse Banton has turned her attention to Anna. They're carrying on quite a conversation with each other, and Saroyan is smart enough to look at them with a deep pretending to be 'I'm so interested in what you're saying' expression and body language while she thinks under the influence of her bad drug .

"Everything is so flat. I wish I could concentrate. What am I going to do with that stupid question? Somebody in the studios must have done this to me. Who was it? Probably one of Ravi's associates. Maybe it was Jose Feliciano. How am I going to get revenge? Wait until contract negotiations! What's going on with Clem? I miss him so much. He's kissing me there and there and there, mmmmm -- all the right places. I hope he's all right. That was a weird story he was working on. Who were those strange men lurking around the movie set? This is going to play hell with my career. We're going to have to spin some publicity on this one. God! We're losing money on the production costs. I don't think they can shoot around me, but they can try. Oh, I wish I had a baby! Why couldn't I be a normal person, and just settle down and live in a little house with Clem and one or two children? I must look hideous. It's been a century since I've had my hair done and a massage. It's hard to stay focused. Why can't I remember times. Whoops! There goes another hiccup! Look at those love handles! I feel so fat!"

She can see Nurse Banton turning the gun in her direction, and she feels like she's trying to hop on board a moving freight car in her train of thoughts. "Saroyan, what are the feelings that you are having right now?"

What she wants to say is, "I want to get out of this little hellhole as fast as my legs can carry me!" but that's not an appropriate answer. Saroyan looks serious and wistful at the same time. She has marvelous eye contact. "I was just thinking about my boy friend, and how much I miss him."

"That's nice Saroyan. What's his name?"

Saroyan thinks, "Are you a cop? Just saying his name could be dangerous!" but she lifts her chin a bit as she says, "Gary." The conversation goes on about what Gary is like, what she's done with him, and why she likes him. At least that much is real in Saroyan's conversation.

Nurse Banton looks sympathetic as her pen makes checks on the clipboard. "That was very appropriate. Thank you for sharing so much so well with us, Saroyan. Perhaps as a reward, if you get enough positive points, you could eventually use the telephone."

The telephone! This sure crystallizes Saroyan's thinking! How can she get access to the phone here PDQ? She can't afford to wait for the brownie points to pile up like chunks of ice falling off of some glacier.

Karl Eysenbach

Maybe the drugs are beginning to wear off, but maybe they're building up. She's beginning to focus on the great Here and Now. It makes no difference what kind of intrigue it was that got her in here. It doesn't even matter if it was some CIA plot. *Zorro* is big bucks no matter which way you slice it, and the one thing that the suits hate more than anything else is losing money! All she has to do is to start the legal machinery, and a Panzer division of legal storm troopers will descend on this snake pit, shoving their writs of habeas right up some shrink's corpus.

It's closing time at the group therapy bar, and Nurse Banton gets everyone's attention, except for Estella. "I'm very proud of the sharing experience we've had here today, and I'm happy to announce that everyone here has earned the right to watch an hour's worth of hologram in the lounge tonight.-- I" Nurse Banton emphasizes the word 'I." I will choose the program, but I anticipate that we will be able to spend time in the lounge after dinner. Now Ladies, if you'll follow me to the recreation room."

There is the shuffling of feet and chairs as the inmates line up like good little goslings behind Mother Goose. Saroyan hates the regimentation and everything else about this bean farm, but she's beginning to think that she can be a free woman in less than a day's time. As the motley crew shuffles down the hall in their slippers, Saroyan looks at an office door. She knows now how it can be done.

The dinner certainly isn't much to write home about. If you decided to check yourself into Happy Valley, you'd have to pay over $5000 a day one way or the other, and you'd get to eat the same thing that everyone else gets tonight; creamed synthetic beef on dry toast, plastic mashed potatoes, and your choice of either overboiled spinach or tough old green peas. Dessert is stale peppermint candy, and the drinks are best used in a car radiator. Certainly no expense is spared in procurement by the hospital nutritionist.

The Story of the Century

The goslings have been herded into the rec room early, and have been encouraged to socialize with each other. The interior is like the therapy room, except that it's bigger and has some boxy Naugahyde lounge chairs in some pukey color. Along one wall is a ping pong table and a Velcro dartboard, but they're never used. The end tables have dog chewed copies of five-year-old magazines on how to be a better suburban mom and flower arranging.

Saroyan is leafing through the magazines, realizing that she's never been much interested in either one when she's interrupted. Yoko, one of the ladies from the therapy group tentatively sits down next to Saroyan, looking all over before she begins talking.

"You're new here, aren't you? I apologize for being so forward. You're Saroyan, aren't you? The talk around here is that you're kind of special."

Saroyan isn't very interested in mixing camellias with Spanish moss. Yoko looks like she's been around the block more than a few times, and she might provide some background information. And besides, what's so bad about a couple of chicks dishing the dirt?

"Sure. I don't have any problem. Why do they say I'm special?"

"They say you're a movie star. You're rich and famous."

"That may be the case, but as for me, I just want out of here yesterday."

"I wish I could get out. Once upon a time I thought I had everything. I was young and rich and beautiful and in love with my husband. He was president of Mitsubishi -- a *chaebolista*, and he worked himself to death. He died of a heart attack. Tomiichi was so young. That's when it all began to happen." It is here that Yoko stops and scans the room one more time, as if she is afraid that an ax murderer is stalking her. She lowers her voice to a whisper and draws closer to Saroyan.

"Dr. Jagan, -- Dr. Jagan is my brother in law. What a shit! He married Tomiichi's sister, and he spent all his time brown nosing my husband. It was almost as if he had it planned." She looks around one more time.

Tomiichi appointed Chedi –," she says this name so bitterly that it can only be Dr. Jagan. "Chedi was, and is, executor of the estate. Tomiichi said there were too many trusts and foundations. It was all too complicated for me." Here she clenches her fists as if she's going to pummel Dr. Jagan if he comes into the room.

"So Chedi is the executor. And lo and behold, all sorts of things begin to happen. The first thing is that my inheritance disappears. 'Bad investments,' Chedi says. 'Bad luck.' "

"Didn't you talk to people in your family? Didn't you have any children or relatives?"

"No, except for Tomiichi's sister, and you know -- she had to be into it up to her head with Chedi. I never liked Miko." She looks over her shoulder one more time. "But you better believe I fought him. I had lawyers and accountants, but they could never prove anything. That just made the money go faster, and Chedi begins to get hostile to me. It was then that he began to accuse me of being paranoid. Mentally ill, you know. One time he got angry at me, and he said, 'I'll make book on you!' Yes, that's what he said, he said, 'I'll make book on you.'" Then Yoko glances backwards one more time again.

"So one day, I was minding my own business, and these men came with papers and a hypodermic needle and a strait jacket."

"I don't know if I want to hear about it much more." Suddenly Saroyan is feeling very cold, and there's a pain in her stomach.

Yoko looks attentive. "Is that the way it happened to you?" Saroyan can only nod.

"Poor baby, you're right. We should change the subject." Yoko looks around. Her eyes shift back and forth. Turning to Saroyan she says softly:

"I said before you were special, but there's another reason. You're government." Saroyan lifts one eyebrow high at this statement. There is the "I'm trapped, wedged into this bus seat with this raving lunatic and I have to humor her." feeling. There's shock, confusion, surprise, paranoia, and the general impression that things aren't exactly what they seem. She puts her hand to her forehead, suppressing temporarily the spinning in her head, and yet she's absolutely riveted by what Yoko is saying.

"Governments are not ordinary crazy people. Governments have been railroaded. I call them governments because that's who puts people like you here. They decide that you know too much, and they get papers to say that you're crazy. This usually shuts them up. I've heard that military people who discover unpleasant things wind up in the naval hospitals. If you're committed to a naval hospital, you just disappear. You're never heard from again."

A touch of skepticism enters Saroyan's brain. She says, "That sounds like an interesting story, but what kind of proof do you have about these so-called governments?"

Yoko smiles weakly. "You should see the men's section. It's loaded with engineers from Lodestar. There are at least four or five of them. You're the only female who's a government."

Saroyan does what she can to move gracefully away from Yoko. "That was a wonderful story. Thank you for telling me all this. Pardon me now, but I have to go to the bathroom." What is really inside of Saroyan's head is, "Too much information, way too much information." Saroyan is halfway across the room seeking sanctuary when she's waved to a stop by Nurse Banton, who's standing there with the hologram remote control in her hand.

"Ladieees! May I have your attention please? I hope that we have been socializing appropriately, and I promised you, and now it's time for the Presidential Debate. Please be quiet and sit down everybody!" With that she presses a button. President Hok is on one side of the room at a podium, and Waldo is at the other end. Everyone knows the popular hologram variety show host and UPPP standard bearer. One of these men will change her relationship with Clem.

THE NEXT MORNING, 11:45 A.M.

Saroyan has been granted an hour of freedom for her build-up of behavioral brownie points. The first thing she does is to see Anna the serial killer. Anna might not be the best loved inmate, but at least she has some essential cosmetics. And she's willing to let Saroyan use them. During lunchtime, Saroyan takes step number two. She approaches Nurse Banton. She's interested in her treatment regimen, and she has a lot of questions. Saroyan knows that Nurse Banton will kick her upstairs.

"You know, Saroyan. I can't really answer some of these questions right now."

"Well, do you think that Dr. Chabarki could?"

Nurse Banton thinks for a minute. "Yes, Saroyan. That's a good idea. I'll talk to him about that."

Saroyan wants to jump, but she has to act cool. "Well," she says casually, "What if I could see him this afternoon. What time does he usually have free?"

Nurse Banton is distracted. "Two o'clock usually. I'll let him know you're coming."

After lunch, Saroyan returns to see Anna. Shortly before two, an orderly comes to Saroyan's cell to escort her to Dr. Chabarki's office. The halls of the insane asylum are empty. Most of the inmates and staff are outside playing volleyball, but Saroyan hasn't gotten enough plus points to do this yet. Dr. Chabarki is doing some paperwork when there is a knock at the door. The first thing that he notices when the orderly opens the door is the walk. It's a demure and somewhat tentative as the walk of a patient should be, but it's also alluring and fetching. It doesn't register consciously, but unconsciously.

Dr. Chabarki does register the second thing, which is Saroyan's hospital gown. It's actually shapely. Some parts of her gown are downright tight, and they're tight in *those* places. Dr. Chabarki is slightly uncomfortable now. His underwear is tight, and she's standing there in front of him in all her movie glory. "May I sit down, Doctor? I have some questions I'd like to talk to you about with my treatment modalities." Saroyan has just spoken to him in a breathless little girl voice.

"Have a seat, Ms. Pashogi." Dr. Chabarki finds that he's more clumsy than usual. He drops a pencil. He's looking for Saroyan's case management file, and he can't seem to find it. She's just sitting there, watching the good doctor expectantly, waiting and watching. She's encouraging the doctor to look back at her, deeply into her eyes, which seem more beautiful than anything he can remember.

"You are mine, all mine. Let me reel you in." Saroyan thinks to herself.

"What, what can I do for you Miss Pashogi? Did I say that before already? I'm sorry."

"Oh Doctor," Saroyan breathes seductively before proceeding, "You don't have anything to be sorry about. I was wondering about how my positive and negative points are scored, the particulars you know. I'm interested in details. I'm working for just one good behavior goal, you know. Perhaps you'd be interested in finding out what that is." Dr. Chabarki begins giving some very technical, very boring psycholingo about treatment modalities, and he's suffering now from sensory overload. There's the slight aroma of cologne that has only just now consciously registered. He hadn't noticed that before, and this makes him rattle on more.

It's time for Saroyan to interrupt. Almost imperceptibly, she licks her lips. She is now looking at him so seductively that Darth Vadar would turn into a puppy dog. "Oh, Doctor." There's that eye contact again and that subtle shift of head and body. "Do you know what I really need? I really need to use the telephone for half an hour, just a half an hour. That isn't asking much, is it? I'd do **anything** for it" She shifts her legs slightly, just ever so slightly. Dr. Chabarki sees that her hospital gown is beginning to ride uptwards her crotch.

"Miss Pashogi. I'm afraid you haven't earned enough points yet." But Saroyan can tell his no means yes.

She thinks to herself, "Buddy, if I were a guy right now, I'd whip your ass. But since I'm a girl, I'm going to pretend that you're the only stud I could ever love." What she says is, "Doctor." She bats her eyes, just a bit. "I'd do -- anything, just anything to get phone privileges today." She's moved herself out of her chair, going around his desk, getting closer to him. She kneels in front of him in order to be at eye level.

"This is really corny. I never had to work this hard when I was a starlet." This is Saroyan's thought balloon. She's looking at Dr. Chabarki, and he's looking at her, full time now. He has that look of the fish that is willing to be reeled in. His defenses have are terminally crumbling. With the skill of a pro, she loosens his belt and unzips his pants.

"Would you like to kiss me? You can kiss me anywhere you want." This is all it takes for Dr. Chabarki to start pawing at her, groping clumsily but eagerly. Saroyan is taking control now. "Ooooh Tiger, you can just stay in your chair. Just move a little bit -- right -- there." She guides him forward to where she wants him. As she unloosens his tie and starts to unbutton his shirt, she can feel Dr. Chabarki's hands as they begin to move under her hospital gown, discovering some interesting places on her skin.

Saroyan has taken his shoes off, unbuckled his belt, and is in the process of taking his pants and underwear off too. She stands up to remove her hospital gown (no underwear, no surprise there), giving Dr. Chabarki just enough time to take the rest of his clothing off. She thinks for half a second as to whether she should go down on him, but she decides that it's not necessary. "Tiger, stay there -- just -- like -- that." She moves his legs ever so slightly under her own. "There, that feels good, doesn't it? Just what the doctor ordered."

Dr. Chabarki isn't bad to look at, but there are lots of better guys in the world than him. He's just another graying, middle aged guy who used to be somewhat muscular, but now he's gone to fat. He's very busy now, and he's engrossed in his work, moving back and forth towards the main chance. But Saroyan is far more detached. Her mind is far, far away. One of her thoughts is to try to recall the phone numbers for her agent and that friendly legal eagle at the studio.

It could still be the effects of the medication, but her mind is in two places. Saroyan moves back and forth. It feels mildly pleasurable. She likes it this way, but her physical, sexual self is existing in a different dimension, a different universe, while her rational self thinks about how to dispose of Dr. Chabarki for that precious half hour. She thinks about the last time she was with Clem. She thinks about being kidnapped from Loreto all over again. She fakes a moan of incredible pleasure. "To hell with it, don't call the studio, just call Pepe." She can feel him inside. He's big, and big is a good thing. Let Pepe handle the details. She feels wet inside, and the doctor gasps as he comes. "Good. We can get down to business." She rides him for thirty seconds more before she slides off.

"Oooooh." She says. This is a half-and-half mixture of reality and acting.

The doctor is having mixed emotions. "I'm a Christian, you know. I shouldn't have done this."

Saroyan looks at the picture of his wife and kids on the desk. She gives him a long peck on the cheek before she whispers in his ear, "God will forgive you." She pulls away and looks at him. "Doctor, you were fabulous, but you need to get dressed. There must be some place you can go to freshen up? I need to be alone for a bit. Would you mind if you showed me how to use your telephone? I need an outside line."

"Just dial nine and the number." The doctor begins to gather his things together, and Saroyan sits in his chair, still naked. The doctor pulls up his trousers and buttons his shirt while Saroyan looks at him. She's moving her legs back and forth just watching the doctor get dressed while she gives this hungry, seductive stare.

"There'll be more of this, the longer you stay out. Don't hurry back, at least not for half an hour," Saroyan says while the doctor backs up against his door, geting dressed. It looks like he's spent the night in a clothes dryer. But he's happy, very happy.

"Come here for a minute." Saroyan has covered herself with her gown. The doctor is now the patient, obeying Godess. "You need your hair in better shape." She diagnoses as she runs a hand through his hair. Then she hands him his tie to make him look more presentable. Almost as an afterthought, she adds, "Why don't you go to the lab or the library? You've got research to do." As he slinks out the door, the only thing Saroyan has to say is, "ta ta." Saroyan pounces on the phone like a wolf.

"Hello, Pepe? You won't believe were I am! I'm at the Happy Valley Rehabilitation Center and it's a hellhole! What a dump! Some bozo railroaded me here." She doesn't even care that she's still buck naked, and that Pepe can see her from his end of the line. But then, it's not the first time that this has happened.

The Story of the Century

Pepe is always suave and diplomatic, but on hearing what Saroyan has to say, he's upset and concerned. "Oh Saroyan, you can't believe how relieved I am to hear from you. We're all worried sick about where you disappeared to. Thank God you called. No one had any news. I don't know how such a thing could have happened. You say you're in a psychiatric hospital as a patient? How horrible!"

Saroyan is in overdrive now. "Let's get to the point. First call up all our legal chits with the studio, and get me the hell out of here. I want every Bollywood lawyer ready to declare total war on Happy Valley and its quacks in charge. This fiasco is costing *Zorro* plenty in production costs. Tell everybody their cash is on the line in grave danger, total loss, and they've got to get me out if there's going to be any recovery on what's been sunk into the picture. I want out of here yesterday."

She hardly pauses for breath. "You've got a lot of work to do. This is serious damage control, and you're going to have to figure out how to crank up the publicity machine full blast. You know what to do."

IT'S THE CHEESIEST! -- WHICH ONE OF THESE PLAYS MUSIC? -- NO EXERCISE AND TAKE OFF THE KILOS! -- BAD CREDIT IS NO PROBLEM WITH MONSTERCARD--- BEDROOM BARGAINS ARE YOURS -- **LATE BREAKING NEWS:** SAROYAN PASHOGI TO BE RELEASED FROM HAPPY VALLEY REHABILITATION CENTER: WHAT DOES THIS MEAN FOR HER CAREER?

Happy Valley has seen its share of commotion before. You should have seen what Mr. Amin did when he tore up the joint, but Happy Valley has never seen anything quite like Saroyan getting out of stir, escorted by her entourage while her fans crowd around. The morning begins with Dr. Jagan enjoying his coffee. Nurse Banton comes in, announcing that several attorneys are waiting outside. This is unusual enough, but the legals are being followed by camera crews. This can't be good news. Taking a moment to compose himself, he goes out to greet these invaders. A process server hands him the writs, and the lawyers start explaining what it all means. Dr. Jagan can haggle all he wants, but the fact of the matter is, all of Saroyan's paperwork is more than in order.

It's an ironclad mandate for Happy Valley to immediately set its most famous charge free, signed not by one judge, but a panel in Singapore, with concurrent final determinations of no cause for commitment from the Federal Psychiatric Review Board. This is the equivalent of taking out a .357 magnum and holding it to his forehead. Saroyans' lawyers made sure there were a host of financial and accreditation penalties attached for any failure to comply. Dr. Jagan begins to sweat profusely, asking for clarification that the high-priced legal talent is only too happy to explain to him. He mops his brow, gets this sick smiley face expression (Smile for the cameras!), and agrees that everything appears to be perfectly in order. Dr. Jagan has Dr. Chabarki paged to handle the rest of the arrangements. Once Dr. Chabarki is front and center, Dr. Jagan slinks back to his office so that he can pulverize his desk, pulling over his bookcases and filing cabinets.

Every media outlet flashes the news by every which way except tin cans and string. Like iron filings to a magnet, every lookie-loo in a 300 kilometer radius flocks to Happy Valley just to say they were there. Police from 27 jurisdictions go on overtime to handle traffic and ground control. The white media vans descend, circling like a troop of marauding Indians on a wagon train; and the reporters cover the reactions of the people in the crowd to the incredibly significant, incredibly riveting and incredibly moving news that yet another Bollywood star is checking out of rehab.

The Story of the Century

Pepe has decided that the best way for Saroyan to avoid the crush is to leave by helicopter. Dr. Chabarki spends the entire morning and half of the afternoon dealing with the press on where they can film and not film (patient confidentiality, you know), security arrangements, crowd control, and the landing area for the copter. Once the networks pick up on the airborne angle, the skies become more polluted with the Saroyan air force. Right now, six helicopters are circling. At a higher altitude the small private planes circle for the stringers and the tabloids. Thousands get sore necks gawking at the spectacle.

Even Dr. Chabarki begins to lose it with the logistics of Saroyan's need to look glamorous when she makes her public appearance. Ordinarily, Dr. Jagan would have a visit with a soon to be released charge, giving a sermonette of psychobabble followed by some treacly panegyric that all boils down to "After all, it was for your own good." Unfortunately he's sleeping off a heavy dose of tranquilizers now, leaving Dr. Chabarki to deal with Pepe Lopez, the dressers, hairdressers, hangers on, and the circus outside. This inmate has taken over the asylum! Saroyan and her entourage commandeer not only the therapy room but the rec room, leaving no space for the other inmates to congregate inside except for the cafeteria. The rehab center might as well be one giant star wagon today.

There has been much back and forth about what is appropriate for her coming out party, and she has been poufed, stylized, and accessorized. Pepe gives the signal, and Saroyan starts heading toward the door to face the publicity lions. On the way out, she flips the bird at the doctors' offices as her high heels click. Pepe is at her side, and her legal talent, hair dresser, make up, wardrobe, masseuse, and press people follow a respectful five paces away so as to not interfere with the paparazzi. The press has already been fed CD-ROMs and videos of the trailer for *Zorro*, with Pepe to handle the interviews.

Saroyan pauses just inside the main door in the hospital lobby. "How do I look?"

Pepe says, "Just fabulous." The doors open, and there's the roar of the crowd and the aircraft, the noise and movement of bodies against the police barricades. The crowd is an incoherent beast. It could be the Academy Awards, except that it's daytime. The official line is that Saroyan was hospitalized due to drugs and overwork, but that's a lie. The legal boys have tracked the bona fides of the two doctors who signed the commitment papers, and they have no previous connection to Saroyan. But they do have plenty of connections to obscure government agencies. The attorneys have decided that discretion is the better part of valor; and that it's better to tell a damaging lie, rather than trying to shine flashlights into peepholes where right thinking people don't go.

Saroyan is wearing large dark glasses to hide her fragility. One thing that goes wrong before she's free this morning is Yoko. Saroyan wanted to talk to her, but she saw Yoko being led down the hall by two orderlies. She was informed that Yoko was being taken for electroshock therapy. How much of what Yoko is true, and how much is it the delusions of a crazy woman? No one will ever know. Her fragility increases after she's taken her first five steps out of the door. She finally has access to her cell phone, and the screen highlights a curious voicemail message. She clicks it on to listen as the cameras and crowd focus on her. She's transfixed, horrified by what she hears.

"Saroyan, it's me Clem. I've been worried sick about you. I'm glad I got your answering machine at least. I've been blocked from getting any calls to you, and I've tried lots of times."

She hears Clem suck his breath in, and he continues. "Look, Saroyan, this is a horrible time to talk, so I'll be brief. Somebody in your organization is going to give you something from me. I need you

The Story of the Century

to look at it, okay? It explains some of the things that are going on with me. I just want to say I miss you, and I love you more than you can ever possibly imagine. Okay, I gotta run. Cops are on my tail."

Saroyan hears these sinister clicks before she turns the machine off. The entourage walks over to the area just outside the hospital entrance that has some nice foliage in the background for the cameras. Pepe is standing by her side, and they sit down behind the folding table with so many microphones and so many black snakes going to so many sound engineers. The commotion dies down when Saroyan starts her statement. She has her little cards in front of her, and she takes her dark glasses off. She takes a breath, puts on a happy face, and goes into her routine.

"Having a stay in a mental hospital is not something I would do as a publicity stunt. It's a simple case of working so hard on my picture that I got into a dangerous state of exhaustion. Working hard on something you really, really love like *Zorro* can be dangerous if you put too much energy into it. This has never happened to me before, and it won't happen again. We all make mistakes, and hopefully we can learn from them. Don't try to stay awake for five days to try to rush something though."

Now she ad libs. "If I rest up for a few days and relax at home, I'll be ready to finish the picture. I can't wait to show it to you." At this point, Saroyan squeezes Pepe's hand, signaling that she's absolutely had it. It's time for him to take charge. He reaches for the main microphone.

"Miss Pashogi has had a tremendous ordeal, and she's not prepared to take any questions at this time. I will be happy to." At this point, Pepe is drowned out by the media mongooses, who yell their questions anyway in machine gun order.

"How are you feeling now?"

"What drugs were you on?"

What was it like on the inside?"

"Who's your secret boy friend?"

"What was the real reason you were hospitalized?"

Pepe finally gets control to say that his office will be happy to handle any written requests, but that the most important thing is for Saroyan to rest. They walk to the helicopter where the rest of the entourage is already. The wolves tag along, surrounding them -- only being kept at a distance by security. Saroyan waves at the crowd straining at the hospital fence, but her heart's not in it. Manager and Star get into the helicopter, and Saroyan is helped into her jump seat, with someone buckling her in.

"How was I?" Saroyan asks Pepe, and four people immediately say,

"Fabulous!" and they almost mean it. The phone call and Yoko have shaken Saroyan up badly. Everything seems surreal, and Saroyan is beginning to feel a serious disconnect, not only from her associates, but from herself. Pepe begins to talk schedule, and Saroyan cuts him off. It's taking all her effort just to be sane right now. Saroyan almost feels as if someone else is speaking inside her body. The real Saroyan is screaming inside doubled up with pain. The external Saroyan is mild and reasonable.

She hears herself say, "Pepe, everybody. I appreciate the fact that you're here for me right now. I really mean that. You don't have any idea how much I've missed seeing every one of you. It means so much to me, but I just want to go home. And I don't want to talk to anybody. I just need time to be by myself so that I can do things right for me."

Her mind spins with flashbacks of psychiatric torture, and she's showing that haunted, teary look when she remembers one more thing. "If Clem sends me something, anything, will you deliver it to me, Pepe?" Pepe nods, and Saroyan buries her head in her hands. The rest of the helicopter ride might as well have been a noisy tomb as everyone else gets to listen to Saroyan yell and wail. When the copter lands, assistants help her into the limousine. It's just her and Pepe.

Jeeves is at the door, and the house is quiet and dark. Pepe asks, "Is there anything I can do for you?" It takes all of Saroyan's strength just to shake her head no. She's already beginning to schedule her nervous breakdown. "Well, call me immediately if you need anything, anything at all." Turning to Jeeves, Pepe says, "Please make sure that she doesn't get into any trouble. I don't want her to get hurt." The robot understands.

For the next two days, she won't sleep at all, even though she spends 90% of her time in bed with her head under the covers. This is followed by twenty-four hours of sleep. She'll try masturbating repeatedly, but she won't be able to feel anything. As bad as her psychiatric kidnapping was, Saroyan is in for the worst month of her entire life.

SINGAPORE & BEYOND

The Story of the Century

SOMEWHERE DEEP BELOW BAJA

Attu and Sajak are sitting in the control room monitoring the early warning system, and things are not right. Attu's jobs are to monitor the equipment and recommend fixes, and Sajak is a technical geek and the dude that does the heavy lifting. I wish that I could give you a better description of the control room. You know there are a whole gob of knobs, dials, and lights, but the problem is, we're only human. There are things we know, and things we don't know. But how do you describe a veeblefetzer? We are also dimensionally handicapped. Sure, you know length, breadth, width, height, thickness; and you have some understanding about time. But what kind of drugs am I going to take to describe to you what something in the tenth dimension looks like?

So we're seriously handicapped, but what we see looks a lot like your average super hi-tech control room in your ordinary science fiction flick. But pay attention to the fact that although most indicators are green, there are three red lights and about a dozen yellow ones.

This is a problem. Attu and Sajak told the Lords of Pure Energy that the old magnetic interferometer was way past its prime. The bosses decided that the old earth model would be just jim-dandy, but what do the big cheeses know anyway? Nobody counted on the fact that the monkeys on this rock would be playing patty cake with it for a couple hundred years. And you know what happens when you get old parts put into your car, and they aren't even rebuilds. Mexican engineering will only take you so far, baby!

Sajak and Attu have done all that's inhumanly possible to keep the magnetic interferometer going, as it's the most critical piece of equipment in the whole station. If it goes, the whole station goes. If the station goes, the earth goes, and the blowup takes out a small portion of the Milky Way galaxy along with it. Our space boys have been doing

Karl Eysenbach

what they can to keep the old MI running, but it's been a bitch with triple overtime! Knobs have been adjusted to max and min, and then they put them on a new range. They've used more than one set of shims. Our boys have done far more than their share of tightening, loosening, adjusting, shunting, buffering, wiring, and rewiring the thing. They've increased the maintenance, and they've hand(?) built components that have been jury rigged on. But those damn monkeys have sure screwed up the works!

And still the problems continue. The magnetic interferometer is warm to the touch, and that's not a good sign. Of course, there are still a few million degrees to go before the whole thing blows. And there are the vibrations. It's almost to the point where a human being might be able to feel some kind of back and forth motion if he or she had the right machines. Attu and Sajak are mechanical geniuses in an interdimensional hierarchy of superintelligent beings. They've written and rewritten the manual on the care and feeding of the magnetic interferometer, and they're not about ready to throw in the towel. But there is such a thing as prudence.

Attu turns to Sajak and says, "There's only one thing to do, pal. We've got to call Kryll." They don't want to do this. In time and space, there are beings who know, and beings who don't know, and then there's middle management. O.H. Kryll is a gray; but if this were the Army, Kryll would be a lifer. Imagine a short, blubbery, bantamweight rooster with an old school crew cut, a slightly dingy white short sleeve shirt, a cheap polyester tie, a clipboard in one hand and a cigarette in the other. No, this is not what O.H. Kryll looks like. But the gray alien fits the mindset to a tee. The only thing you know for sure, when you call a Kryll, you'll automatically start the fabulous run around.

"What's the problem, gentlemen?" O.H. Kryll is there.

The Story of the Century

Attu speaks, and his green light flashes as he speaks. "Boss, we're at our wit's end! We've tried everything six ways from Sunday, and the earth equipment is just plain lousy."

Kryll radiates skepticism. The last thing he wants to do is to start some more damn paperwork. He's up to his armpits as it is already. "Are you sure?!"

If Attu could shrug, he would. "Boss, would I lie to you? This old thing is nearly toast. If we do everything we can, there's three, four earth months before the whole shebang goes blooey; and they can do the memorial services for us on the other side of Orion."

"Are you REALLY sure?!"

"Look at the control room readouts, for chrissakes!"

There is this thing that middle management always does that drives the hired help wild. Kryll goes over to tweak some dials. The yellows go to red, and more greens turn yellow. Eventually Kryll bungles the knobs back to where they belonged in the first place, and things return to abnormal. "Guess you're right. I'll start the process. You got the requisition forms filled out and the start of the purchase order?"

"Right here, boss." Sajak hands him the goods that were finished three days ago.

Kryll puts the papers on his clipboard reluctantly. "Guess I'll have to expedite. Gee, I hate doing that!"

"We don't have much choice!" Attu and Sajak would like to scream this, but they know which side their bread is buttered on. Attu's no dummy, though. He's in an organization of superintelligent life forms, and lowly mechanics have more juice than their earthling brothers. Some things are possible that would not be the case on earth. Attu inquires, "Boss, is it all right if I'm in direct contact with the Lords of Pure Energy?"

O.H. Kryll pauses and scratches his head. "Can't hurt. Go ahead and do it!"

Karl Eysenbach

IN THE 12TH DIMENSION

Attu talked with the Lords of Pure Energy (the LOPES). In the hierarchy of things, if your run of the mill flying saucer boy is 10,000 times more advanced than you are, then the LOPES are to the average space alien what the Trilateral Commission is to your local plumber. The LOPES are usually busy with their tinker toys, experimenting with different kinds of electron spins and varying mixes of neutrinos and leptons. When they make new universes and new dimensions, the rules that apply for us, don't apply there. Once in a while something wonderful happens, like Earth.

All of this earth stuff is annoying them, even though it's only taking up .000001% of their brain space. But the squeaky wheel, and what's going on down here is diverting their attention away from the next Big Bang.

"Dark energy station number seven, what's its name?"
"Earth."
"Earth?"
"Right."
"And what star is that around?"
"Sol, in the Milky Way galaxy. They call it the sun."
"Right."
"And the machine?"
"The magnetic interferometer."
"Do we have back-up anywhere?"
"Just operational ones at stations one through six."
"Not enough."
"Right."
"Shit. I hate those things. Damn, they're hard to replace."
"Everything is custom, and the suppliers!"

The Story of the Century

"Far, far away."

"I know."

"I was having fun doing adjustments on Euler's Constant."

"And I'm still working on something to replace DNA. There's got to be something better."

"I'm trying to put more and heavier lanthanides in the mix for the next universe"

"We know you, Mr. Anti-Gravity."

"Same to you, Mr. Life Processes."

"What are the odds?"

"50-50"

"Shit. Then we better expedite."

"Right."

"If it doesn't get there in time, we'll have to stitch up the rip in the space-time fabric."

"I hate that, and it'll leave a bad smell."

"Hey, but that's what insurance is for."

"And you know about their proposal for a nuke test near the transmitting tower in Siberia."

"That too? Holy Mackerel, didn't those clowns try to get rid of Gaia once before?!" You'd think they'd learn."

"They don't know."

"Remember the Magaden peninsula."

"Right."

"We could still get the bug spray out."

"Is that place worth saving or not?"

"It's questionable."

"You know the Prime Directive."

"Right."

"Right."

301

"So we see what the damn suppliers do, and cross our fingers?"

"Right."

"We got this transmission from Attu -- the mechanic at #7."

"What did he say?"

"Not much, besides getting everybody off if #7 is going to blow, and his tour of duty is about up."

"Provide one emergency packet, and let him take his stuff with him when he leaves. Standard operating procedures."

"Anything else?"

TOUR DE L'ARGENT, 1:48 A.M.

Clem is on the graveyard shift, and he's bone tired. He's on part of the swing shift too, and he's never worked so hard in all of his life. He spends more time in the bowels of the Tour de l'Argent than anyplace. The working conditions are as close to slavery as the law will allow. Clem might as well be on one of the better spots in hell, and to some extent he is. Every day's the same. The only two days of the week that he knows for sure are Monday and Tuesday. Monday is his one day off when the Tour is closed, and Tuesday is when he goes back to work. Otherwise, he's engaged in this crazy-making job six days of the week from late lunch until dawn. And all of this is for less than minimum wage.

He crawls back to his hot sheet, two-bedroom bungalow in the Valley, the one that he shares with ten other men, all illegals. He gets his five hours of sleep in the morning (if he can), taking the place of some guy who's a gardener; and then he's rousted out of bed at noon by some janitor working a trash machine. Showering? Shaving? Clean Sheets? Rarely. And don't even go near the toilet, it's too scary! His unconscious part of life is called 'sleeping at home,' trying to ignore the banging around of the small crowd that's either snoring or looking

The Story of the Century

for someplace to pee. The commutes are the best parts of the day. The trains are clean, and Clem can get some precious sleep without being disturbed. Crawl to the station at one end of the line, and sleep until the train gets to the other end.

The conscious part of his day is something else. Late lunch in the kitchen is like entering some overheated pandemonium on the edge of the Bottomless Pit. There's ten minutes to eat. Then he has thirty seconds to strap on his apron before he straps on his job. There's a pile of greasy, encrusted pots and pans that goes halfway to the ceiling. Everyone in the kitchen might as well be running for his or her lives. To get to his workstation, Clem has to dodge waiters and cooks who hurl insults at him while they scream at each other. Everybody is doing the work of three people during lunch rush.

At four o'clock, work stops. Lunch is over for the swells, and this means the workers have a time to chow down. The scullery employees go down to the basement to the employees' lunchroom, a filth-encrusted closet that's a good habitat for vermin. The first thing that Clem does is to swill down a liter or two of liquid, any liquid that's available; coffee, water, or wine. If it's wet, it replaces his sweat. Lunch is short, made up of hand me down food. And then it's time to go upstairs to serve the waiters in their closet of a lunchroom, a pantry space just swinging doors away from the grand dining room.

There's an eternal pecking order in fine restaurants. The manager is the kahuna. Clem has heard that he has a real office where he eats and fornicates with God only knows what. His food is prepared with better ingredients and more care than even the customers get. The maitre d' is the overseer, who's snotty to all the waiters and most of the customers. He gets kickbacks from the liquor distributors. Then there's the head cook, who's always big and fat. He can plunge his hands into boiling water to pluck out a lobster, and he has apprentices serve him dinner during the slack periods, critique-ing them severely. Waiters are not allowed to have moustaches, and they enforce this on the pearl divers. The male cooks have moustaches to show their contempt of the waiters.

None of the highrollers has any idea what goes on behind the scenes. The slightest mistake at rush hour gets you a severe tongue-lashing, and sometimes fights break out. But usually, there's just the heat-seeking insult. After work or between rush periods, all is forgiven, and the management plies everyone with bottles of leftover wine. The rationale is that if wine isn't freely given, the employees will steal it anyway.

Clem has learned job necessities like picking up customer's food off of the floor, cleaning it up, and putting it on the plate for service. At rush hour, there's no time to do it any other way. Then there are the miscellaneous chores like spreading sawdust, cleaning the floor, carrying out the garbage, hefting boxes and crates of food, and taking things from the kitchen to the cooler (like going from India to Greenland). And there's pest control.

But most of the time, Clem is touching the potato skins of the stars. For endless hours he's spraying jets of boiling water onto a conveyor belt of used silverware, dirty dishes, and baked greasy pots before they go into the maw of the Lodestar/Acme Model A1000 institutional dishwashing robot. The room sized stainless steel cube kills germs in six ways, leaving even your toughest cleaning jobs spic and span. Clem remembers what they told him at school. Get an education, or else all you'll ever do is work in a restaurant if you're lucky. Journalism school sure did him a lot of good. His first day at work was mind boggling, but after that, it became zombielike. Clem can't possibly imagine doing this year after year, until he dies. And yet, there are plenty of people do exactly that.

But Clem thinks that he's lucky. He's glad he's got a job instead of being homeless, collecting cans and bottles. It's the best way of staying

The Story of the Century

out of trouble. He's not in prison or disappeared. He even drops into internet cafés to leave messages for Saroyan, but so far he hasn't got any answers. The one advantage to the job is that it's so boring. Boring is not as bad as you might think because Clem's a dreamer. For example right now he's dreaming about having sex with Saroyan 26 different ways; missionary, 69, doggy style, tantric, in costumes, with emollients. I could go on.

2323 ALVARADO DRIVE

Oddly enough, at this very moment Saroyan is having the exact same dream. She's in her bedroom thinkng about the two of them, standing naked together in front of her full-length bathroom mirror. It's funny how things work that way. She's getting over her nervous breakdown, and she's feeling better; although she's still damaged goods. One moment she's fine. The next moment, she's sent to a hideous depression by seeing a butterfly. Her journal is a pastiche of bad writing and mood swings, writing fit only for blackmail. One thing that is therapeutic is a needlepoint canvas and colored yarns that Pepe dropped off. Saroyan spends hours stitching the picture and forgetting about her problems.

Food containers litter her bedroom, and the bed's been unmade for weeks. Her dresser is wet where a cola can spilled. The only thing being taken care of is Junior, who somehow still manages to get fed and his litter box emptied on a regular basis. She is sitting on her bed wearing a soccer jersey, and nothing else. She finds the remote, and she's watching WNN and its ongoing coverage of the election. President Hok is touring Africa to obtain greater regional cooperation between states.

She pays more attention when Waldo's coverage comes on. Waldo's organizing a cavalcade of stars in support of his candidacy. They're at a press conference, and they're going to do some Bollywood fund raiser. It's funny. There's hardly an "A" list on the roster, except for Gary Chindowarry. In fact, their average age appears to be about 80. Saroyan focuses on Gary for a moment. On a better, more normal Saroyan day in an alternative universe -- she'd be in Loreto right now wrapping up filming with Gary on the *Zorro* set; Gary Chindowarry of the Gary Chindowarry line of action figures for boys, along with his video games, series of *Gary Chindowarry, Spy* books, and his bazillions of royalties; but the only thought that enters her head is, "I guess he's got to do something with his time. He's not working on the set. That's for sure."

Now she fixates on how much money she's losing by staying in her bedroom. She worries about what is happening to the set in Loreto. She worries about what is happening in the studio executive suites. She worries that maybe Pepe won't be able to defend her interests this time. She worries about the publicity from her stay in the bean farm. She obsesses on how she hasn't even been able to email Clem, and how much she loves and misses him. She thinks about what a bozo she is, and she begins to cry hysterically. Again.

DEEP UNDERGROUND AND FAR AWAY, SOUTH

Meanwhile in the Baja control room, Attu is getting the alien equivalent of a migraine headache. Another indicator has just gone from green to yellow, and five more have turned from yellow to red. An audible alarm chime is going on and on, softly but persistently in the background. He can turn it off, but it starts up five minutes later. And so on towards infinity. He relays this image of the control room and panel lights to the LOPEs, just because he is pissed.

"What do I have to do to get some attention around here?" He thinks to himself.

TOUR DE L'ARGENT, 6:23 P.M.

Clem is in the middle of one of the Tour's daily feeding frenzies. He's wheeling a cart that has a huge collection of pots and pans that he's just cleaned. In the middle of the boredom and insanity, a strange thought has just entered his head for no reason. At the very face of it, it's totally ridiculous; and yet it is there with a certainty. It will happen. "Someday, I'll save the world!" Clem smiles to himself at both the idiocy of it and the necessity that it must be true. Unfortunately, he is going to intersect with Pierre, the waiter, whose real name is Jesus. Pierre/Jesus is rushing towards the dining room with a full tray of food, and there is a huge collision, with waiter and tray slipping. High priced meals turn into instant slop, and dishes break. Many colorful oaths are given against idiot Clem (AKA Robert Manley).

"God Damn you! You sonofabitch! Can't you look where you're going? Pick up that food! Get some sawdust to throw on the floor! I ought to cold cock you one right now! Howdareyoudosucha **thing** to **my** customers! You ought to be fired! Wipe that crap up off of the floor! No! Not with that! Use that! You are the most ignorant donkey I have ever seen in the world! Get rid of those broken dishes! Over there! Wipe it on your apron, you moron! Throw those potatoes away! Get out of the way!"

The damage is righted in a short period of time; but a few hours later Pierre complains to the manager about Clem, saying that he should get fired. He almost does just that, but he finds that staffing is short-handed today. And it's a good thing. If he had fired Clem, the world would end.

Karl Eysenbach

IN THE PARKING LOT OF A HUGE FACTORY

On a planet circling our North Star, a factory service crew is boarding a ship with the newly upgraded model of a magnetic interferometer.

2323 ALVARADO, 6:23 P.M.

If you have to choose between a nervous breakdown and a root canal, go to the dentist. Saroyan is in her bed crying hysterically, and she feels the need to go to the bathroom. There she is with unkempt ratty hair, mascara streaming down her cheeks, and the snot running out her nose, looking at herself in the mirror. At the sight of all of this, the most beautiful woman in the world begins to laugh hysterically.

She reaches for some lipstick, and she begins to draw on the mirror. As carefully as she can, she traces the outline of her head, messy hair and all. It surprises her when she's finished, and she steps away. The screen goddess with the perfect bone structure, whose face is at this very moment being projected in a 3-D image thirty meters tall, is in fact the owner of a mirror image no larger than a peach. This fact has never occurred to her at all. There is an epiphany, the moment her financial backers have all been waiting for. She realizes the absurdity of being thirty meters tall, the size of a peach, and Saroyan at the same time. She says to herself, "You're crazy. But are you really crazy? Do you want to go back to Happy Valley and spend the rest of your life there? Do you really want to do that?"

She thinks about how fucked up she looks. She thinks about the conspiracy. She thinks about how she became a star. She thinks about what a snakepit Bollywood is. She talks out loud again. "Paranoia is when you think you have more enemies that you actually have, except when you're in Bollywood. There you think you have fewer enemies than there are. But do I really want to give up on *Zorro*? Just walk away and never see it again? But is that what I really want?"

She looks at life. She looks at her identity. She ponders the universe. "What do I really want? What do I really need?" She asks herself that question over and over, and then there is that name, Clem. "Out of all the men I've ever, Clem's the best, so kind, so funny, even though he's a klutz. And he's a natural man, not one of those Bollywood dudes in love with themselves too much."

She thinks about the conspiracy again, but she tells herself. "Don't go there. But what about Clem? Is it right that he has to live like some kind of hunted dog? Can you see yourself married to a homeless person? We're going to have to talk about doing something."

She remembers that although drama queens are by their very nature good at histrionics and self-indulgent whining, such behavior needs to be put into a bottle to be used as a weapon against other people, and not against oneself. Going back to her bedroom, she finds the journal she's been writing, and she leafs through it briefly. Then she goes out to the brick barbeque pit by the pool, gets out some charcoal lighter and a match, and she burns it.

TWO WEEKS LATER

Saroyan has gotten on a computer and pulled up the email messages from Clem. She's sent back a big long message of what she went through, and they've started text messaging. Most importantly, she's set up a date to meet him so that they can have a talk. Right now, she's in an editing studio, going over the stuff that's already been shot and taking copious notes. She's been in conference with Pepe, Gary Chindowarry, and the suits, and shooting is going to begin tomorrow on some crowd and background scenes.

She's putting in eighteen and twenty hour days, and she's never been so artistic or creative in her life. There is this drive of not only making up for lost time, but a drive that an artist gets very few times in her life, when she knows that what's she's doing is revolutionary; not political or a paradigm change, but revolutionary in the sense that it will insure her immortality. Fifty years from now, revival houses will still be playing *Zorro*, getting big crowds.

> C:Darling, I've sent you so many messages. I've been so worried about you. I can't believe that we're actually instant messaging.
> S:I've been worrying about you. I was super competent when I was in Happy Valley, and when I got home I just fell apart. I analyzed everything in my life all the way back to my first memory, but that wasn't very productive. You are one thing that's worthwhile. But the other thing is work. That's why I'm in Loreto. *Zorro* is very important to me for a whole bunch of reasons. But I'm very worried about you. If you stay in that horrible job, it could affect our relationship. We have to talk about your future.
> C:I hear what you're saying. All of this is very hard for me to talk about.
> S.Guys don't display things like emotions.
> C.I don't like this life I'm in at all, but if the government got me, I don't know what would happen to me if I surrender. I heard about Salinas getting assassinated at that farmers' meeting.
> S.Yes, it was horrible. I had a relapse when I heard about that.
> C. But I'm still trying to figure a way out of this stupid situation that I'm in. I sure know that I'd like to see you.

S. I want to see you too. I think I know a way out, but you'll have to decide.

C. I want to tell you something really funny that came to me the other day. I don't know whether it's funny ha-ha or funny weird. Maybe it's both. Here I am a lowly pearl diver, and yet I feel like I'm doing something important. I can't say that I've enjoyed the experience, but it's made a better person out of me.

S: You said something weird happened darling. What was it?

C: Call it male intuition. I'm almost embarrassed to say this, but I feel like I could save the world.

S: Darling, I've got to get back to the set. We've got to talk face to face. I'm going to do publicity dinner at the Tour the Monday after next. I'll see you there in the evening, and I'll post a more exact time. But it's very important that we have a serious talk. I love you much xoxoxoxo.

412 KILOMETERS ABOVE THE CENTRAL BAJA

It's very quiet over the Sea of Cortez right now. That's because it's 3:43 AM Ejido San Mateo time. Night fishermen went to bed early, and rancheros are asleep in bed with their families. Every 40km or so, there's a gypsy trucker being a ping-pong ball between Tijuana and Cabo. The sky is the lushest black velvet, with the finest, eternal light show; thousands and yes, millions of stars. Some are nearby, but there are plenty of nebulae, star clusters, galaxies, and even quasars set into the black half dome above you. But tonight's even more spectacular. The Lords of Pure Energy are in the neighborhood doing things on the QT. That's why they've scheduled a meteor shower as a diversion. Every one or two seconds there's a blade of light slashing through the velvet, giving off sparks as it goes. Look! One just whizzed by the planet Mars. That's something you don't see every day!

You may think that the LOPEs are just showing off, being gaudy, but there's method to their madness. It just so happens that there's a reconnaissance satellite making its run over the Pacific on its way to the North Pole. This modified ripoff of the Hubbell Space Telescope is on the scene like some two-bit divorce gumshoe, just saying "Howdy" while it cruises in its polar orbit looking for UFOs. Unfortunately, the big spy eye in the sky has a date tonight. A small piece of grit the size of a grain of sand is aimed squarely at the camera eye, with an estimated speed at impact of 87,000 km/hr. There's a wave of cursing coming out of an underground control room that's heard in all sorts of places. The LOPEs are happy campers.

A week ago a mother ship materialized out of another dimension to hover in that sweet spot of gravity between Jupiter and Saturn. The black rectangular box was roughly the size of Rhode Island. It hovered here for the shortest period before it vanished, allowing a small convoy to exit from its hanger bays. On board are intergalactic big time spenders, anthropologists, travel agents, and collectors that want unique stuff that can't be found anywhere else; stuff like tobacco and Soupy Sales videos. Did you know that there's one alien who actually has all those socks you lost in the dryer?

It's 3:43 AM, and the convoy is entering the right orbit. Lights appear over Ejido San Mateo that have not been seen in over a million years. All at once, it's a psychedelic bouquet in the sky. In the center is a black triangle with dozens of silver observation ports on its sides. Surrounding it are dots of green, orange, white and red lights, hovering like bees. These are your security dudes and media coverage for the folks back home.

The Story of the Century

The whole flying circus hovers over a small mountain that just so happens to be shaped like a 20th Century over the horizon radar station. The triangle is the center of attraction; and the other ships are like a troupe of ballet dancers following Dame Margot around as it sashays back and forth, moving this way and that ever so slightly before they all becomes locked in some atmospheric concrete. The light show freezes, and the red lights go out. From the triangle's belly, four solid columns of blue light shoot down, carrying beings and stuff that floats down. Faraway cops on the graveyard shift in Loreto and Los Mochis report seeing something that looks like some kind of weird-ass ball lightning. The big triangle has done its thing. The tractor beams go off, and the red lights come on again. In two seconds the UFOs shrink from covering the whole sky to pinpoints of lights before winking out entirely.

A couple hundred of meters below the surface things are just starting to move in what everybody hopes is the right direction. Attu, Sajak, and O.H. Kryll welcome the pilgrims, some industrial strength robots and Wanda. Wanda is a tall statuesque Viking with blonde hair and blue eyes who's dressed in a tight silver lamé jump suit. As the official greeter, Kryll blusters on and on. After all, he's the big dick in charge, but he has sense enough to let Attu do the talking about the technical stuff when they start walking around the place. Since everyone is the product of technically advanced civilizations, there's much multitasking going on. They talk sports. They talk about filling out the required paperwork, who's going to win the race for President of the Earth, soccer, and the condition of the equipment

It's getting to be crunch time. There's been too much bubble gum and baling wire already. Wanda, Kryll, and the industrial robots have uncrated the parts and tools, and they're ready to go. So far things are going smoothly. Kryll is hovering in the background, providing documentation while Sajak assists on shuttling the parts and tools.

There is a rod of transparent aluminum about two meters long and a quarter meter thick, and it takes three robots to manipulate it into the position that it's supposed to be in. They hold it there, and they hold it there. They're still waiting. Attu rotates around for light while Wanda bends down to inspect it. She frowns.

"There's something wrong." She runs her hand over the metal.

TOUR DE L'ARGENT KITCHEN, AUGUST 14TH, 3:39 P.M.

Clem and Jorge are on the same shift today. They're sitting in the hot and humid, grease-encrusted lunchroom. It's been a slow day at the Tour, and there's some rare slack time going on. Clem is describing the latest events of what's been happening to him and Saroyan. "I've been emailing Saroyan, you know, and I get this uneasy feeling."

Jorge raises one eyebrow. "Why is that?"

"Well, I'm kind of caught between a rock and a hard place. On the one hand, I have this stupid feeling that I'm going to accomplish some great thing in the near future. And I think that this has kind of spooked Saroyan as far as our relationship goes. And on top of that, I think Saroyan doesn't like the idea of a Bollywood movie star maintaining any kind of relationship with just a bus boy. But her plans for me don't look very appetizing either given what I think is in store for me."

Jorge is just listening. "How so?"

"Well, she talks about the high-priced legal and publicity talent she can bring to bear on my case, you know, of being a fugitive." Jorge starts to pay some serious attention now. He turns and faces Clem, folding his hands and being very intense. Fugitive is a word that he understands.

Clem continues. "We'll get the publicity machine up and the lawyers up. Fine and dandy, but I don't see how I can get out of the rap that the government has set up against me. I mean, even if I have all the high-priced legal talent in the world, I think that the World Prosecutor is still going to have a serious hard-on about my case." Clem is winding up and beginning his rant.

"I mean, what *are* Saroyan and her team going to do for me? Sure, I can get my picture plastered all over every hologram and magazine, and the talk show boys can have a field day with their call-ins expressing my guilt or innocence. But how am I going to get out of the fact that the powers that be have been hunting me like a dog for months, vowing to the world that they will bring Clem Reader, #1 Criminal to the justice that he deserves?"

"What are they going to do? Have Save Clem Reader rallies? Maybe they can have celebrity concerts all over the world to raise money for my legal bills, but the bottom line is, I don't see how I'm going to escape doing some time in prison, given the way the powers that be are positioned against me. And if Saroyan doesn't relish having an affair with a bus boy, how is she going to feel about having a long term relationship with a felon, even if by some miracle, the high priced talent can get my time down to something like a reasonable six month sentence?"

Jorge looks at him while he lights a cigarette. Clem can see that he's not pleased. He's not pleased at all. He looks at Clem, and then he exhales. "I understand what you have said, Amigo, but remember -- we both work here." Then he walks away.

What Jorge doesn't say is what he's thinking. "So, you want to turn yourself into the authorities, eh? That will bring the pigs to the Tour de l'Argent, won't it? And what about me? You think you committed a crime, but you didn't do shit! What about me? Do you think my little world will stay the same when Federales start pawing through the trash in the kitchen? Do you think, for just one minute, that they might find ME? No! You can only think of yourself! If you turn yourself in, maybe

I should just kill you like a dog. No one would pay any attention if they found a bus boy with his throat slit lying in the ditch along PCH, would they? Maybe tonight, Amigo, maybe tonight."

AT THE BAJA BASE

"I can see that it doesn't fit. It's just too big." Attu has calculated the discrepancy to within a millionth of an angstrom, but that's immaterial. It's not close enough for government work. What are we going to do about this? That's the most important thing."

Wanda is thinking multiconceptually on her feet right now. If something goes wrong, do the math; and do it quick. "Either the manufacturer got the specifications wrong, or there was some distortion due to hyperspace. And of course, the engineers could be just plain fubars. It's not common for either the manufacturers or transportation to screw things up like this, but something happened."

Kryll has been overhearing what the real workers have been saying, and he feels that he has to put his two cents in. After all, it is middle management's right to be an asshole on a periodic basis, and Kryll plays his part so well. "It seems to me that the chuckleheads in the central office should be paying more attention to things instead of playing tiddlywinks or whatever they're doing with all of their discretionary time." He puts his arms akimbo and gives his most sour expression. But this exclamation is not good enough for him. It's necessary to continue.

"This is the worst fuck-up I've ever seen in my forty millenia as a supervisor! Somebody better figure out what the hell to do about this situation pretty damn quick or you, me, and this entire quadrant is going to go critical!"

"As if it weren't obvious enough to everybody." This is the thought that everyone else has, even the robots. Since everybody is a mind reader, Kryll gets the message. But he doesn't care. He has the sensibilities of a wart hog.

Wanda is being as controlled and competent as she can be, "Computer, can you give an estimation of estimated mean time to failure if all ameliorative steps are taken to compensate?"

"In Earth time, estimated mean time to failure is 7 days, 11 hours, 38.2 minutes plus or minus 0.4 days."

DOWNHILL ON TOPANGA CANYON ROAD

Saroyan has been an absolute miracle. Whatever troubles she went through after that trumped-up stay at Happy Valley, she's more than made up for it. The shooting on *Zorro* went remarkably ahead of schedule. Every scene was done on one take only, and every scene was done brilliantly. Saroyan didn't know much about editing beforehand, but she picked up on it immediately with no problem. And she became an instant editing genius. Despite the Happy Valley delay, *Zorro* has come in ahead of time and under budget. Truly, it's a movie that defied all the odds that were stacked against it.

The buzz on the movie is phenomenal. The sneak preview audiences laugh. They cry. They hold their breaths in fear, leaving the theatre with the images and characters embedded in their brains for weeks. To a person, every reviewer gives *Zorro* his or her highest rating. The movie isn't even regularly showing anywhere yet, but the talk on the streets is that it will sweep all the awards. Phrases are being bandied about like 'Movie of the Decade' or 'Movie of the Century.' The trade rags are going gaga and even the highbrow, intellectual publications are talking on about how Saroyan has transitioned from an ingenue sex kitten into a woman of the ages.

Of course, she's overjoyed. There's that sense of accomplishment and that feeling of having hit a home run when everything was stacked against her, but she's also keeping things in perspective. "My next picture will probably, absolutely stink." She thinks this sitting in a limousine as it snakes down Topanga Canyon towards that publicity dinner at the Tour. As a Bollywood war veteran, she's trying to keep a level head and not believe the hype.

But there are other things on her mind as well. "I've got to come to some sort of closure with Clem about his situation. We'll see what happens when we get to the restaurant." Here she's very confused and insecure. There's this different side of her brain at work. On the other hand, she's emotionally attached to Clem in a way unlike any other bonding she's ever had with a man. She deeply loves him, and she frets and stews about the life he's living now. On the other hand, she just wants to kick his ass. "Get over it, Dishwater Boy! Be a man and not a mouse!" This thought runs through her head over and over. Although she doesn't show it, she's a little nervous as the great black car winds its way down to the water's edge before turning onto the Pacific Coast Highway.

Her thoughts change as the car takes another curve. She starts to toy with the flawless five carat blue diamond hanging around her neck, practicing responses to the questions the reporters will ask in her mind. "What made you want to make *Zorro*? How did you conceive your role? What was it like being a first time producer? Is it true that you also had your share of editing and directing, is that right?" She runs through her responses bit by bit, making her answers just that much smoother, wittier, and more fabulous. Of course, she'll have to go over what she's been working on with her publicity committee in the next few days. She makes a note to herself to review the tour schedule one more time, being sure to set aside enough down time for rest, exercise, and sightseeing.

She suddenly realizes that she hasn't been paying enough attention to her date this evening. Her sophisticated and handsome costar,

The Story of the Century

Gary Chindowarry has been sitting beside her, dressed in his tuxedo on their just pretend romantic date. "Oh Gary, darling I'm sorry I've been ignoring you. My mind has been so elsewhere. I've been thinking about the interview schedule and the answers to the questions. What have you been thinking of?"

Gary turns from looking out the window, giving her a catty look "My boy friend." He pauses as he lights a cigarette, being careful to open the window just a crack. "Suppose some people think this publicity stuff if glamorous, but to me it's practically drudgery. I know, everything is written into the contract beforehand, but I can hardly wait to get back to my villa outside of Zamboanga."

It's time to use diplomacy, and go for something completely different. "Darling, would you do me a favor and open that bottle of champagne? It's Wolverton Estates." Saroyan reaches into the cabinet behind the driver, pulling out the bottle and two glasses.

"Darling, I thought you'd never ask," he says. Saroyan holds the glasses as her co-star does the ritual with the bottle. He opens it without a pop. There's only the slightest hiss of escaping gas, and he pours a glass to sample for himself.

"The Australians finally figured out how to do it right. This is a good vintage, but not as good as the previous year." Then it's time to fill Saroyan's glass. He goes into an extended wine monologue, talking about acidity and the undertaste of currents and peaches and figs. Saroyan smiles as she listens. Significant communication is no longer necessary for a while.

A small army of paparazzi are waiting for her. Cordoned off farther away, are more people -- a couple dozen of her fans. She's hardly out of the car when she's in front of a bank of microphones saying, "Thanks everybody for coming. I'm just overwhelmed by the support you've already given *Zorro*. Gary, is there something you'd like to say?" She smiles as she cradles her arm with Gary's as he talks about his role in the movie.

A thought crosses her mind. "Beauty is so overrated. I've used it to my ends well, but it's put me on such a high, high ladder. It's about time for me to assume a new phase in my life. I wonder about Clem." Then it's time to respond to all the questions that the reporters throw at her. She can hear her stomach growl. She thanks everybody, and the highly stylish couple enters the restaurant arm in arm. The maitre d' effusively greets them, and the whole restaurant greets them with applause.

Saroyan whispers to her co-star. "Appearances, appearances. How many reporters assume that I'm sleeping with you now?"

Gary looks at her and whispers back. "Ah, Tinseltown! Every one of them is going to imply a love angle, and thirty percent will come right out and put it in their story."

Saroyan looks at him, "It's good for business. This can't hurt our residuals from the box office receipts." Inside, Booth #1 is waiting for them. There are the candles. There is the linen. There is the security. Everything is just the same as it was before, except with a different love angle. Well, okay, maybe Saroyan is having something different to eat -- perhaps some baby lamb chops in wine and mint sauce with fresh miniature vegetables and garlic potato au gratin. And maybe she likes her co-star better than Rhadavan. But the real deal is the dishwasher back in the kitchen.

Saroyan finishes her meal quickly, and she reaches for Gary's arm, touching it gently. "Dear, I want to go to the kitchen to complement the chef. Would you mind terribly if I left you alone for fifteen minutes? And would you mind terribly if you went outside afterwards to talk to the reporters again?" With that Star gets out of her seat, heading towards the double swinging doors.

The Story of the Century

Everyone in the kitchen is surprised to see the most beautiful woman in the world enter into this overheated chaos, and the screaming stops for less than a second as the entire crew freezes in their tracks. But the pandemonium starts up again when someone smells the turbot beginning to burn. The head chef delegates his chores to underlings, and he wipes his hand as a he comes forward to greet this most famous intruder.

Saroyan thanks him for the fabulous dinners that he's prepared for her over the years, and his eyes get wide when she says that she wants to see that Robert Manley dishwasher person. Nonplussed, he takes her hand, and they navigate the slippery minefield of the kitchen floor until they get where Clem has been working up a powerful sweat.

"Clem!" Saroyan is surprised by Clem's appearance. Clem's still Clem, but he looks harder and leaner. Since he knew that she was coming, he actually doesn't smell too bad, having taken a shower today, and he's freshly shaved. There's a new edge to him, and he's sporting short hair where his blond roots are beginning to show.

"Actually, that's Robert." The chef says.

"Robert!" Saroyan runs towards the pearl diver, and to everyone surprise plants a big long one right on his face, being careful not to let his dirty togs contaminate her evening dress. Clem/Robert solves this problem by taking his apron off and retrieving a fresh clean apron that he puts on over Saroyan's gown. Once this is accomplished, they go back to more serious kissing. This is too much for everyone in the room (especially Jorge, who steams away in a huff.) Saroyan eventually looks at the crowd that's gathered around the two lovers embracing.

"Could you leave us alone for a few minutes? I haven't seen him in so long." Turning to Clem she says, "We need to talk."

Karl Eysenbach

T MINUS 66 HOURS TO TOTAL FAILURE

Wanda is beginning to sweat a little bit, "The only thing we can do right now is to not fool with the new piece, and put the old part back in. It's not the option I'd like, but it's the only one I can think of until I talk with the engineers."

This makes Attu get emotional, something that his species does not ordinarily wallow in much. He's getting to be beside himself as he's broadcasting all of his feelings everywhere as he begins to whirl around the room. Attu is even beginning to affect Kryll, who's beginning to ramp up on his conniption fit.

"Put the old part back until we examine the alternatives. Is that what I heard you say?"

"Yes, that's correct." Wanda gives a little expression of 'What else can I do?" as she says this.

"Well, the only problem with that is, that that part ain't worth shit. Look at this piece of junk!" He goes over to the old aluminum column. Its surface is too shiny, and it has millions of spider web cracks that go from top to bottom in its core.

But Wanda is the boss among bosses. She's thinking faster than the speed of light; and she's diplomatic, even though she'd love to throttle everyone."I know. It's not something that I would ordinarily recommend, but I've got to talk to the engineers to find out what they have to say about this and what their recommendations are."

Who's responsible for this mistake, and what we can do to get out of this jam?"

Wanda takes the bull by the horns. "Look, let's call the engineers right now."

To make a long story short, the engineers admit that they made the mistake, and they're working on ways to safely install the

The Story of the Century

interferometer. The bad news is, that being engineers, they want to consider the 20,000 alternative ways in which the project can be most safely, cheaply, and effectively done. Everyone in the Baja base knows that this is not the answer. Kryll crys, "For God's sake, just send a rod that meets the specs!" For once, Wanda backs him up.

"Look, get me one part to spec, and I want it on overnight delivery!" She can see the engineers blink.

"That'll cost a pretty penny. Overnight delivery."

"I don't care if you take it out of my salary. Just get it to us overnight, okay?"

There is a pause at the other end. "Okay."

When she does this, the Lords of Pure Energy decide to make a conference call to see why the project is suddenly over budget. Attu stops packing up to go home, and everyone else pays attention to the big cheeses.

Wanda speaks, "My Lords, I've talked with the engineers, and they've admitted they made a mistake. They assure me that all the answers will be coming by tomorrow".

One of the LOPEs says, "What are we paying these people for?" The LOPEs are not pleased. Wanda knows that when you're the hired help, it's not generally a good idea to call the bosses on their head games when they're having a bad day.

"I had to order a new part on overnight delivery. I know that costs money"

"Money? Did you say money? Don't get me started!" The LOPEs begin a long rant about running the arrow of time backwards, but in physics that's a little like driving on the wrong side of the freeway. The one thing that's consoling Wanda is that the engineers are being forced to listen to this tirade too. She senses that it's time for a little feminine sensitivity.

"Boss," Wanda puts her hands on her hips and assumes her most forthright expression of concern. "Can I ask you a personal question? You seem a little cranky."

There is an audible sigh from nowhere. "You're right. Things have been eating us." With that everyone at the Baja base is no longer where they are, wherever they are. Now they're hovering over the Siberian ice fields. Far off in the distance are the icy fingers of the North Pacific Ocean. Below in a small glacial depression is what looks like a boy's sandbox. Everyone zooms down, and they can see, that it's a construction site. There are prefab construction sheds. There are loads of heavy construction and drilling equipment, work lights, and maybe a couple billion dollars of government contractor stuff on top of a lot of frozen mud underneath the snow on the ground. A Sno-Cat with its tank treads slowly chugs in from over the hill. The diesel motor stops, and men in parkas get out, holding their collars tight as they struggle through the wind to get to one of the sheds.

"Look at that mess! Those fools! Hairless chimpanzees, every one of them, and they don't have a clue of what they're doing! Do you have any idea of what they're doing?"

Sajak says,"Offhand it looks like a primitive nuclear test."

"Precisely," comes the very annoyed voice of one of the LOPEs. "These worse than morons really don't have a clue. Listen."

The scene shifts, and Wanda, Attu, the engineers, Sajak, Kryll, the robots, and the Lords are all standing inside the construction shed that's the office of the big boss man. He's in a white shirt, tie, and hardhat while his underlings are clustered around like abominable snowmen. They're gathered around a set of plans lying on a government gray table. The whole scene freezes.

"Look at Test Well Number Two." They zoom overhead and see the schematic plans for the drilling. One of the robots points outside, and they can see the rig all spotlit up. It's dark, and it's snowing outside.

"Now look where the pond scum is going." The whole view goes 3-D geological. They burrow several hundred meters below the ground. Looking through the rock, they can see a large dull metallic cube about the size of a semi truck only ten meters away from the bore hole.

Wanda's eyes get wider and wider, and a look of horror appears on her face. "That's -- that's the main antenna! You mean they're drilling on top of the main antenna? I can't believe that they are doing this! What are the odds of something like this happening? How long have you known about this?" She can hear the engineers in the background murmuring their concurrence. "Is there anything you can do about it? I'd think you could." Everyone is agreeing all at once.

The LOPEs reply, "As to the odds, don't ask. They've been doing it too damn long. There's ALL sorts of things we CAN do, but we're still considering our options. I can tell you this. This little double bogey between Base #7 and this nuke test are making us think about sterilizing the whole joint. Maybe we should just turn the keys over to some more worthy species than the trailer trash inhabiting this place now. Our patience with *homo sapiens* here is running thin. Quick Henry, the Flit -- if you know what I mean?"

Wanda is playing dumb. "The planet? The whole planet?"

There is a sigh. The LOPEs are not quite as cranky as they were before. "Maybe We're just losing our temper. After all, this drilling project is not even in the ground yet, and it will be months before it begins to be a critical issue. And the repairs in Baja take first priority. I guess the thing is, it's just another brick in the wall. They tried to blow themselves all away not too long ago. We do what we can to help them, and then they go off and try to do something stupid like this."

Attu takes it upon himself to change the subject. "If we can get back to base, that would be a really good idea," and suddenly everyone is in the control room again. He starts busying himself with more jerryrigging while Wanda works on the final touches of the automating.

"The good news is, the automated systems on line already. Preliminary testing shows that they're working fine."

One of the engineers says, "Good. If everything was operational the whole thing could be done by remote control."

"Obviously that's going to make active staffing redundant when it's in place. What are the plans if automating proceeds successfully as planned?"

Attu speaks. "I've been thinking -- besides the stuff around the base, I'd like to take back some souvenirs and specimens. Does anybody have any problem with that?"

"Why that would be a good thing."

Attu's mom is on the party line now. She says, "Sonny, anything you bring back home is fine with us."

From somewhere, a voice tells Attu, "We're ready to beam you up. For your carry ons, do you want live specimens?"

"Yeah. I'm also thinking of some fruits and minerals."

But the wobble factor in the magnetic interferometer is getting worse. One out of every ten indicators is red, and there's a forest of yellows. The pings, klaxons, and verbal warnings have become a kind of symphony for Chinese water torture, and Attu is just practicing triage. Wanda has gotten the blessings of the engineers, and the parts and equipment are in place for the industrial robots. The interferometer is making its own side effects for the planet. On the surface, more havoc is breaking loose as the laws of probability break down. Lately the money supply has begun to have a major case of the whim-whams. One day it's hyperinflation. The next day, interest rates dive through the floor. Winning lottery numbers end with nothing but fives or zeroes. It was 90° at the North and South Magnetic Poles today. President

Hok has made an official statement to reassure people about all of this, and he sounds pretty lame. But against the laws of probability, his popularity rises as a result of his speech.

Attu is absorbing this, but it's all background Muzak to him now. He's got his kit packed. A lot of things have already been teleported up to the mother ship parked behind Jupiter. Wanda's the whole show now, and he isn't even a bit player any more. He is officially non-essential personnel. Now the only thing necessary is to go upstairs to collect some stuff. Then, he's out of here, Man! Hello, Mom.

TOUR DE L'ARGENT, 10:35 P.M.
58 HOURS, 56 MINUTES TO TOTAL FAILURE

Clem leads Saroyan by the hand to the deserted break room. Once they get there, the first item on the agenda is more serious kissing along with plenty of second base and third base. "Oh Darling, I've missed you so much." Clem has just enough time to say this, coming up for air before they go into another extended lip lock and body hug.

Saroyan is temporarily swept away, but she comes to her sense and pulls back. "Oh Clem or Robert or whatever your name is, I've missed you so much. Email isn't the same as being here with you now. You don't know how much I've missed you, but we've got to discuss some things." She looks around. She can see a cockroach scurrying over the rolls of bread in the corner. "If we were in a better place, we could sit down and have a long talk or make love. But we don't have much time, so this is gonna have to do." Saroyan sighs, looking mostly at Clem's face as she continues to hold both of his hands.

"Clem, I don't know how to say this, but you've got to get off the dime. I mean what kind of life are you living anyway? Did you grow up really wanting to be some kind of dishwashing fugitive?"

Clem's angry, but he doesn't show it. In the past, she's criticized him for not listening well enough and for being slow on the uptake, but he realizes that this is just about the most critical time in the relationship. He does the best possible thing he can do after remaining silent and stewing about it all. He lowers his head, bites his lower lip, shuffles his feet, and says, "No."

"So why don't you take some steps to get out of your problem?"

What Clem would like to do is to pound his fist angrily on the table shouting, "Goddamn it! Don't you know what I'm up against? Don't you know that two people died trying to give me information on some damn government conspiracy, and God knows how many other people bit the biscuit in the process? If I get out of this so-called problem as you describe it, what guarantee is there that I won't disappear? At the very least, I see myself doing probably years in some godforsaken penitentiary thousands of kilometers away from you. Is that what you want?!" Wisely he suppresses this. He's smart enough to realize that Saroyan cares deeply about him, deep enough to be here in some cramped little vermin-infested room. And there's that glimmer of a thought that maybe she has some kind of angle that he hasn't thought of.

"Concentrate on your feelings." The voice inside him speaks.

"Well?" Saroyan is there looking at him, waiting for an answer. Clem looks up taking her face in. He swallows, and then he speaks.

"I'm afraid. I know that people have died trying to give me information, and I'm still one of the most wanted people in the entire world. Prison and death or disappearance are not my friends, and either is a real possibility."

Saroyan softens up, relaxing and drawing closer to her lover. She puts her arms around him, gives him a kiss on the cheek and says, "Oh Clem, I know how afraid you are, but it's time to get proactive."

The Story of the Century

"What do you mean by that?"

"I think it's possible to negotiate with the government." Clem backs away when Saroyan says this, and his anger is beginning to show."

"What do you mean by that? What kind of negotiating power do I have against them? The moment I turn myself in, the district attorney and the rest of the government will hold a press conference about me, putting just the kind of spin they want to railroad me and send me to prison for a million years. Or else they won't say anything at all, and I'll just evaporate!"

Saroyan reaches out and touches Clem's face again. She strokes his hair. "Darling, Have you ever heard of Bollywood lawyers? They're as mean as snakes. How do you think that I managed to get out of that horrible hospital? Why don't you let Pepe and my legal team handle this? It worked for me, and it can work for you."

Clem pulls her closer to him. His eyes get wider. He looks at her with a mixture of love and surprise and tenderness. "Gosh, you'd really do that? I never though of that! That'd be swell!! He kisses her and he kisses her again. He's beginning to lose track of time. One thing can lead to another.

"Do you --." Saroyan interrupts Clem. She pulls away from him slightly, putting her finger to his lips.

"Darling, I mean it. I'll talk to Pepe and activate the lawyers from the studio too." She's facing him -- backing away, holding hands. She glances at her watch.

"Darling, it's time for me to go. There are a herd of hungry reporters at the front door just cooling their heels, and I've got to go feed them. Is there anything else you can think of before I go?"

Clem immediately responds by giving her a long, passionate embrace, and then it's his turn to draw away from her. "Since your legal team is going to rescue me, is there any way I can get out of this?"

With that, he sweeps his hand to the lunchroom. "I'm tired of being a dishwasher. Maybe you could hide a fugitive from the law."

They kiss again, and Saroyan smiles. "Okay, killer. You win. What time does your shift end?"

"4:00 AM."

"Okay, I'll get a car to come and pick you up then."

"Saroyan."

"Yes."

"Just one last kiss to last me to the end of the shift?"

"Okay."

One more time they go for the lip lock attempting yet another relativity experiment. Checking in at thirty three point three seconds, it's a short eternity, and just a moment to the two lovers. To the reporters and Gary cooling their heels outside, it's another length of time entirely. They think of asking their nastiest questions, but they decide to give the gal a break. Saroyan has already turned on her heels when Clem calls out. "I love you Saroyan. See you tomorrow morning." Before she has a chance to respond, Clem has one more short speech. "I know it sounds stupid and funny, but I still think I was put in here for a reason, and not just for what I reported on or being a wanted man. I really do believe that I'm here to do something really important."

In the past, Saroyan's response has been something like, "Sure, sure." It's the same kind of remark you give to an eight-year-old when they suggest dining at Chucky Cheese.

"We'll see," or maybe "Maybe we can do it in a few hours." But it strikes a chord in her that wasn't there before. She turns and thinks and looks at Clem.

"You might be right. I love you so much. See you tomorrow." Clem suddenly finds himself back on his job. He trudges upstairs, putting on his grease-stained apron to hump butt on more pots and pans. He accidentally touches Jorge, and Jorge turns around with a spin to glare at him. He's snarling, and it looks like he wants to clock Clem on the spot. "Where the fuck you been, you fuckin' asshole Bro? I've been hauling my *chingaste* ass in two places at once while you're making ficky fik with some candy-ass movie star!" Clem is taken aback. Jorge looks like he's really angry, and he doesn't quite know what to think of it. Jore's thinking about where he can hone his knife to dispose of Clem later tonight.

ON LINE

"Thanks for the celebrity pet interview, Myra. Hate to interrupt, but there's a late breaking news development. Just let your peepers wander over this footage! It seems that a convention of flying saucers has parked over the Baja peninsula in Mexico. Our teams are on the way for full coverage, but this home video shows a real light show. Well Barbara, there certainly appears to be enough little green men over Mexico. Don't you think?'

On screen, a huge selection of pie plates, floating cigars, globes, silver amoebas, triangles, and Christmas lights of various colors hover over a Baja landscape. Oh those hologram newscasters! They certainly get their chuckles out of the footage they've purchased.

"Flying saucers over Baja? What does it mean? Is this the end of the world? We'll find out after this commercial break."

Unfortunately, the troops from Cassiopeia, Polaris, Alpha Centauri, the Pleiades, and the sixteen points of the galaxy have gathered for the same reason that the Romans went to the Coliseum, or the hicks from the sticks go to the NASCAR rallies. There is always the pleasure that living things get when they can watch the whole world go to hell with some brave warriors (and innocent bystanders) get their meat chewed up real good in the grinder, while the looky loos capture the event for one of their funniest home videos. After saying, "Aw shucks, wasn't that a horrible thing?" they drive away with the kids. Now everybody will have something to talk about. The LOPES are letting it all hang out.

NEAR THE TOUR DE L'ARGENT ON THE PACIFIC COAST HIGHWAY, 2:58 A.M., AUGUST 15TH
54 HOURS, 19 MINUTES TO TOTAL FAILURE

The streets of Malibu are deserted. Coastal fog has moved in, and it's cold and spooky looking outside. A stray police car cruises down the boulevard before it turns, and then the whole town might as well be empty. That is except for the lone figure that emerges from the shadows, walking along the Pacific Coast Highway. If there was anyone around to see this, they would think it profoundly strange. The cops would flash their lights, get out of the car and ask for ID, but this isn't going to happen. This thing is smarter than cops.

It could be a kid, because it's not that big at all. It's not dressed provocatively. Anything but. But, but, it's profoundly strange. It's getting close to being an autumn morning, and the fog is cold. It's in from the ocean. It's October, but you've never seen a Halloween costume like this one. It looks like a beekeeper, but how many cosmic beekeepers have you ever seen? The jacket and pants look more like a spacesuit than a flimsy canvas coverall. There's a broad-brimmed hat with a heavy wraparound veil. There are tennis shoes and white socks, but they might as well be duct taped onto the uniform. It's all hermetically sealed. Everything's white except for the veil. But it's not a clean white, more like a white that has been exposed to moon dust.

It's a gray white, a dirty filthy white, a white that looks like it's been dirtied into not being any kind of color at all.

And that's from a distance. If you were brave enough, if you were foolish enough, if you were to get closer, you'd even be more amazed. Peering under the beekeeper's veil you'd see a deathly, whitish masklike face, withered and drawn. Even more frightening, you'd see those bug-eyed wraparound sunglasses hugging the face. Is this some zombie hipster hopped up on dope, afraid that anyone would see his pinhole eyes?

The zombie/cosmic beekeeper keeps walking, eventually getting to the rear parking area of a certain world famous restaurant. There he finds a xeriscape with carefully planted oleanders and cactus. Turning -- he/she/it moves towards the back where the dumpsters are, going up the concrete stairs to pound on the metal door. Pound! Pound! Pound! There is no hurry, and there is a pause and then pound-pound-pound again. Eventually the door opens.

"What's this all about?" Clem asks himself this question, but he's talking out loud, trying to remain cool while he masks his fear. The thing standing in front of him might not be human, and it doesn't look like a robot. He feels the hair rise on the back of his neck. A moment ago, he was just tired and annoyed. He didn't mind closing the joint with Jorge, and no one bothers him. But it's late. He's been working overtime, and he wants to see Saroyan after a hot shower and a shave. At any other time, he'd be thinking about taking a shower with Saroyan, but the thing in front of him has made him profoundly dreadful and cautious. His mind is racing, who knows where? Clem doesn't know whether he's dumbfounded or paralyzed.

"Is Jorge there?" Clem hears the cosmic beekeeper in his brain, but there's no sound. And it's not like it's even speaking to him. It's more like the voice just appears directly inside his skull, bypassing his ears entirely. Clem can chalk it up to 3:00 AM and closing time, but there is this strange and disorienting feeling. Is it the fog, or is the landscape actually shivering slightly?

"What the hell is this?" This is Clem's thought.

"Don't be so rude. Where's Jorge?" Again, it's this voice inside his head.

"Uh, -- over there." He thinks to himself. Before he can point his finger, the beekeeper heads into the kitchen that way.

"Hey Jorge! There's someone to see you!" Clem yells. He thinks, "What the hell is this?!" Turning around, Clem can see that he should probably play catch-up ball to the little guy. Running ahead of the thing, Clem says, "Follow me, and be careful. The floor's slippery and wet. Walk like a duck." The odd couple sort of shuffles over to where Jorge is wrestling with a wet mop. There is strange, and there is quantum strange, and there is stranger still. It's plain that Jorge is as confused as Clem is about this strange visitor.

"Jorge! It's me, Attu!" At this point, the earthlings just freeze solid. They might as well be dishwashing statues. Clem is standing beside the beekeeper, standing diagonally from Jorge as the beekeeper pulls the veil away from his face to the top of his hat. The beekeeper's hand reaches for the hideous face, and pulls it away from his body like some cheap Halloween mask, revealing cosmic deep space with galaxies in the distance and a glowing emerald shining, suspended from nothing. The white-suited devil or whatever it is casually rolls up the death mask into something resembling a badly misshapen cylinder before it's placed in a front canvas jacket pocket like some decorative handkerchief. Inside the beekeeper's bonnet is the glowing emerald, floating in infinity. The humans' faces and bodies are bathed in emerald green light. Clem suppresses the impulse to shit in his pants. He's scared beyond all belief, and yet…. Every impulse in his body is screaming at him to run away from this horrible, horrible thing -- the kind of thing that reminds him how tiny he is, how stupid he is, how insignificant he is, until he's reminded that there are beings who shrug off glimpses of eternity in the same way he does when he looks at a tiny fact. And he's sharing that space, and he feels afraid, but he still watches because he can't help it.

Attu transmits his thought waves. "Jorge, it's me. How are you doing?"

Clem is still terrified, but Jorge is nonchalant. "Not so bad I guess. Things are steady. I work here. I've got a girl friend. I can't complain." He even gives the beekeeper an *embrazo*. It's old school home reunion for Subcommandante Insecticida and the green light, just two long lost friends. Clem thinks that he's privileged to be witnessing something that has never been reported in the history of mankind, at least not on the five o'clock news.

"I've come to see you for a reason. It looks like the powers that be -- my bosses, have decided to destroy the earth, and I've come to see if you'd like to come with me."

Jorge is puzzled. He scratches his head. "I don't know. You mean that someone up there is going to destroy the earth? Why are they going to do that?"

The green light flickers a few milliseconds. "Some of the earthlings have been messing around with our equipment. One piece is in the Russian ice fields. The other is the magnetic interferometer that you delivered to us."

Like the proverbial man about to be hanged. Clem's mind is concentrated suddenly with horrible precision. The old reporter's instincts come forward. You know those obnoxious newshounds. They don't care a fig about who they embarrass or who they interrupt. Some people just have no idea of that adage about being seen and not heard. The first order of business is to interrupt with some questions.

"You say that the earth is going to be destroyed. Is that correct?"

For some reason this actually gets the full attention of Attu, who is now ignoring his friend.

"Yes, that's correct."

Who are your bosses?"

"They're called the Lords of Pure Energy, although you would probably call them God."

"When are they going to destroy the earth?"

"On your time, in approximately fifty four hours, and forty six point two minutes."

"You said that earthlings had messed with some equipment."

"Yes, there was a magnetic interferometer that Jorge (Subcommandante Insecticida) delivered to us in Mexico."

"As part of the Atzlan Liberation Front, is that correct?"

"Yes."

Clem's mind is racing faster than it's ever gone before. And by some miracle, he's asking all the right questions.

"You said something about Russian ice fields. What do you mean by that?"

"That's a good question. Actually, our base in Baja is the radio station, and the Magaden peninsula in what you call Siberia is the signal's transmission unit. You might call it an antenna. The World government has allowed for a nuclear test in this area that endangers our antenna. For this reason, sterilization of human life is scheduled."

Here is where Clem just about loses it. "What?! Are you serious?! I can't believe what I'm hearing. You've got some things lying around, and some people are messing with them. So the only way you can deal with this is to destroy the whole planet? Is that what's coming down? It seems like a pretty indiscriminate thing to do. Can't your God guys be more selective for Christ's sake?"

Now for a short discourse on the nature of mankind in particular and life forms in general. We all know about human beings -- the good things and the bad things. You don't have to be a student of history to know how despicable and yet godlike we all can be. We assume that the UFO guys are better than us, smarter than us, with more civilization and superior values. But think about *homo sapiens*. Aren't smart people often stupid? And don't even the densest bricks among us sometimes demonstrate flashes of pure genius? The truth is, even the Lords of Pure Energy sometimes have the IQs of flatworms. Attu has just realized that the LOPEs have been suffering from a significant logic gap, and it's time for emergency measures.

This actually gives Attu some pause. The green light flickers some more. "That's a very good question, but I'm just reporting on what's happening. I can only tell you that the Big Boys, -- my bosses, are inclined to sterilize the earth particularly because of the proposed atomic weapon test in the Magaden peninsula."

"You say because of the proposed weapons test in the Magaden peninsula."

"That is correct."

"Then why don't your bosses just punish the people who are responsible for messing with your equipment instead of taking it out on innocent human beings?"

It's the green light in the beekeeper suit's turn to freeze now. It's reboot time. Control-Alt-Delete. The green light flickers on and off. The deep space behind the floating green light changes color to dark blue and white for a second before it becomes black again.

The green light flickers before speaking. "You said, 'Why don't your bosses just punish the people who are responsible for messing with our equipment?" That's what you said Clem, wasn't it?" There is some urgency in Attu's voice.

"That's right." A frown crosses Clem's face, giving that look of having a third eye on his forehead. He's just not sure where all of this is going.

"That's what I thought you said, Clem. I just wanted to be sure. Pardon me for one moment." Attu starts patting himself, searching through various pockets until he finds what he's looking for. He reaches into the place where you keep your wallet, and he pulls out a shiny piece of gold foil covering what looks like a large piece of bubble gum. Unwrapping the foil, the beekeeper's fingers reveal an oblong piece of putty with short fine wires sticking out of it. The beekeeper mashes the gum between his fingers, and he puts it on top of the beekeeping bonnet.

"Create file copy. Transmit to Lords of Pure Energy. Priority One Alpha." There is another pause and color change while Attu blinks some more.

While Attu is busy, Clem turns to Jorge. "Do you have any idea of what's going on?"

Jorge shrugs. "I don't know. I've never seen anything like this before, and I know this guy."

Now Attu has come back on line. "You did a good thing, Clem. The Lords of Pure Energy considered what you've said. Life is precious, even when it's stupid and destructive. Your world will not be destroyed, but it's still in great danger. This whole place could still be vaporized if the installation in Baja goes wrong. But there's a good chance that nothing will happen. We have equipment that's being repaired. When that happens, hopefully everything will return to normal. Thank you for your idea."

Now it's time for Attu to get back to where he once belonged. He speaks to Jorge. "Jorge, the reason why I came to see you tonight is to ask you if you want to be assimilated by the blue light. I've been declared non-essential personnel, outsourced if you will, and I'm leaving Earth. Do you want to come along with me? Do you want to see Puto again and maybe a few other friends? What do you think?"

Clem would like to ask a few million questions for this most exclusive interview in recorded human history, this scoop of all scoops, but he's shut out of the game now. It's just Jorge and Attu. Jorge puts his hand to his chin, and he tells Clem in no uncertain terms to his face, "Shut up. I'm thinking." It takes about ten seconds. Turning to Attu he says, "Oh, what the hell? Why not? What do I have to lose?" Jorge faces Clem. He takes some keys out of his pocket and tosses them a Clem.

"I'm out of here, Man. You're in charge now. You get to close up the joint all by yourself. Maybe I'll see you around some day. You don't know it Man, but you're one damn lucky dude."

Clem looks at the keys, and he looks at Jorge, who is already hanging up his apron. "What do I tell your girl friend, and what do I tell the boss?"

"Tell the boss, I quit. Just see that Maria gets my last paycheck." Now he gets more sardonic. "I'm sorry about Maria. I wouldn't want to leave her, but it's something I have to do. I hope she understands. Give her a kiss for me." He's on his way out the back door. Clem rushes up beside him and Attu.

"Jorge?" Clem looks him in the eye.

"Thanks, thanks for everything you've done for me. A lot of people are going to miss you." With that, Clem gives Jorge an extended hug.

"It's better that I do this than what I was going to do. Goodbye, Clem. Maybe some day you can tell the story in San Mateo." It's one more hug, and they close the door behind them. Clem's alone in the restaurant now. There's not much more to do to shut down the kitchen, perhaps only fifteen minutes more work. The buckets need emptying and putting away. The mops need wringing and to be put in their drying place. Tomorrow, there's going to be a mini-personnel crisis when it's found that not one but two dishwashers have called it quits. Clem looks around for paper so that he can write a note telling the restaurant management that they're going to have to do some pretty quick hiring.

But there's one more chore that didn't exist before. Clem reaches down, picking up the gold foil wrapper that Attu has dropped. He looks at it. It seems surprisingly strong for such a flimsy thing. He flicks his finger at it, and it's like he hit a concrete wall. This is all very curious. Clem scratches his head, and he looks at the little piece of space junk in his hands. Later, he'll do some experiments, starting on the way home. These are experiments that will give him his freedom and his total happiness.

DISTRICT ATTORNEY'S OFFICE, NEW LOS ANGELES
AUGUST 15TH, 10:57 A.M.
47HOURS, 18 MINUTES TO TOTAL FAILURE

District Attorney Gil Rivierte is sitting in his office, and he's concentrating. He's trying to get it off by examining the files of the kiddy porn cases. The intercom buzzes, and he immediately shuts down his hologram files. Damn, it was so close! He'll have to wait until later.

"What is it?"

"Mr. Rivierte, there are two people here claiming to represent Clem Reader."

"Really? Oh, all right. Send them in in just a minute."

Rivierte zips up his fly before he adjusts his position behind the desk, and you can bet he won't get up to greet his guests. In walk Pepe

The Story of the Century

and Olive Montgomery, a Eurasian cutie in severe bangs and a power suit. She happens to be short, pierced and the legal firepower. And yes, she is shaped like a brick shithouse. Rivierte looks down at his crotch before he motions them to sit down.

One thing you have to say about Pepe is that he's smooth. "Oh, Mr. Rivierte! I can't tell you how much I admire your work against child pornography. Too many people don't know the courageous fight you're making!" He shakes the DA's hand in one motion as he continues talking. "Allow me to introduce myself. I'm Pepe Lopez representing Clem Reader, and this is Miss Olive Montgomery. She's senior attorney with Tata Studios, you know."

Olive steps right up to the plate. "Pleased to me you Mr. Rivierte. We're here to discuss the case of World versus Reader."

Mr. Rivierte, the Western America World District Attorney, doesn't know what the hell is going on. Reader's still a fugitive, and the case is cold. What are they doing here? It's Pepe's turn to take over. "Mr. Rivierte, we're here to cut a deal on this case. I have a proposition that I'd like to run by you."

It's the mule's turn to be hit on the head with a brick. Gil gives a little start. These dudes are playing tennis, and they're obviously seeded at Wimbledon. Gil's a player too, and he coolly fires a lob shot that lands right between Pepe and Olive. He leans back in his chair, and he puts his hands behind his head. "Why should I? Do you know where Clem Reader is right now?"

Pepe doesn't blink. "No, no. Not right now." He doesn't know that Saroyan's car picked him up from the Tour and took him to her house where Clem is by the pool, looking at a script. Saroyan is out shopping.

Gil's acting tough. He takes his time, keeping the fugitive's reps waiting while he slowly lights a cigarette and drags on it. "Frankly Mr.

Lopez, I'm disappointed in you. Mr. Reader should be here with you right now. You know that. I don't even see any reason why we should be talking until Mr. Reader is here so that he can be in custody."

It's Olive's turn to go to bat. "Let me butt in here. I am legal counsel here both to Mr. Lopez and Mr. Reader in this matter. If you have any questions, you should be addressing them to me."

"Aha! I'm up 30-love already. What do you have?" This is what Gilberto thinks. What he says is, "Okay, Ms. Attorney, -- what's your name again? Why shouldn't I try to throw both of you in the klink for harboring a Class A felony fugitive?" Olive is pretty cool, too. She's dying for a cigarette. She would practically give out state secrets for a cigarette now. But she doesn't show it. She's all business. She looks at the poor thing with the horrible five-cent toupee sitting in front of her in his cheap-ass suit at his cheap-ass desk.

"A little lob over the net, perhaps." She thinks to herself.

What she says is, "Mr. District Attorney, you're well aware of the highly classified aspects of this case, I presume." Oh oh! Olive AKA the Evil Mrs. Tooth is showing some topspin on the ball.

Rivierte is still stone faced, but he knows he's got a weak backhand. "Why – uh, certainly. I'm aware that Mr. Reader is charged with multiple violations of the World Code on a whole host of world security issues. We're very aware of his theft of government documents, and his intent to disseminate them to compromise world security in any number of sensitive areas." He's bullshitting, and Olive knows it. She moves in for the kill.

"Perhaps I didn't express myself clearly. Do you know the specific pieces of information that Mr. Reader allegedly stole or intended to use for criminal purposes?"

Rivierte gulps and shrinks. "Why -- uh, no. Not actually. The documents in question are highly classified, and they're being held *in camera* by the CIA as far as I know. But I've been allowed a declassified summary and depositions from the CIA."

Olive smiles. "Then you can appreciate that my client has substantial new classified information to present that has a direct bearing on this case."

"On what grounds can you say that? It's my understanding that world security forces successfully recovered all evidence that Mr. Reader was pursuing, and besides that, the charges preclude him from disseminating any information he might have."

Olive continues to grind Gil slowly into powder. "You're right as far as you go, but I can assure you that Mr. Reader has new evidence on the matter that he was pursuing, and that no one else has ever seen this information before. We can understand your reluctance to make any deals with us, but we need to have a little discovery process with the proper authorities. Once the people who need to know see what Mr. Reader has, I believe that then and only then can a determination be made regarding the charges facing him. I would go so far as to say that the ultimate disposition of World V. Reader can only be made at the highest level, far outside the jurisdiction of your office I'm afraid." Olive smiles sweetly.

Gil still has to jerk things around. After all, this is what lawyers are paid to do. "What do you mean by that? Maybe you have a magic lamp you can rub a genie out of, or maybe you can arrange for a flying saucer to land in the plaza out there." He points out the window.

Olive can't stand it any more. She lights a cigarette for payback time and to keep the DA cooling his heels. "Not exactly, but close. Look, here's what we want. First, I'd like you to get in touch with your world security contacts -- at the highest levels, so that we can arrange a meeting at the police shooting range."

Gil is incredulous. "The shooting range? Downstairs? You want the CIA and FBI to meet you at the shooting range downstairs?"

"You heard me. How soon can you make it happen? We want to do a demonstration."

Gil is getting sarcastic. "Oh, you've got an atomic death ray that some space alien gave you, right?"

Olive smiles sweetly. "Not exactly. When can we go to the shooting range?"

"Now I've heard everything! This is the craziest thing I ever heard of."

It's time for Olive to get serious. She sends a smoking shot into the backcourt where Gil can't possibly reach. "Look Mr. Rivierte. If you don't want to humor us, you can just let us out, and you won't have to hear from us or Clem Reader again. We'll take our deal upstairs to Singapore and Kuala Lumpur."

Gil's behind one set already, and it looks like he's on the verge of losing another one. He sighs, "All right. You win, but this better be good. This is crazy. You want me to contact local World Security interests in this case for a meeting at the shooting range downstairs. Is that right?"

"Right."

"What time do you want it for?"

Pepe looks at his watch. "Why not after lunch? It would be good to get a bite to eat."

Gil knows when he's been screwed. "Okay, so this afternoon. How do I let you know?"

Olive gives her card to the hapless DA. "Just instant message us when you have the time arranged."

Pepe has, by just his body language, signaled that the meeting is over, allowing Gil to unlock the door. "It's a pleasure meeting with you and doing business with you, Mr. Rivierte."

IN THE COURTHOUSE BASEMENT
1:30 PM
44 HOURS, 45 MINUTES TO TOTAL FAILURE

At the shooting range, Gil is still hoping that he can be a player in all of this, but he's not sure. This is making him insecure with the spooks. He keeps nattering on about legal points and precedents. FBI Special Agent in Charge Mendoza looks like the old Marine sergeant that he is, and he's accompanied by some Wild West CIA guy who says his name is John Smith. Everybody is getting bored with Riverte's legal exposition.

"... The variety of criminal and world security issues in World V. Reader mean that we're only here to review evidence pertaining to the criminal charges, isn't that correct Ms. Montgomery?"

CIA Agent Smith (a grizzled old Mexican sheriff type with a white moustache and a bulletproof vest) says, "Let's get on with it. I want to see what they have."

Olive is in charge. She whispers in the ear of the wizened spook before she speaks. Agent Smith nods his head in agreement as Olive talks. "Given the sensitive nature of what we want to show, does Mr. Rivierte have the security clearances to see what I'm going to demonstrate?"

The FBI and CIA dudes look at Rivierte for the briefest glance before Smith says, "I doubt it." Turning to the District Attorney, the FBI agent says, "Gil, why don't you go back to the office. We can report back to you on what we've found. If this is anything like she says it is, you're not supposed to be here."

The District Attorney does not like what he's hearing. At least in his mind, he's a Very Important Person, and worthy of all access to this case, no matter what the world security establishment has to say about things.

He sneers to Mendoza, "So I'm just a paper pusher, an errand boy, eh? Well listen to me! I am the District Attorney for the Western District of America and I am the lead prosecutor of this case! I am the man who is going to recommend that Clem Reader gets a minimum of ten years in prison and a $100,000 fine for the crimes that YOU say he's committed! And here we are. I arrange for this little téte a téte with you and the criminal's legal help, and all I get is, 'Thank you very much. Get the hell out of here?' Well, let me tell you something! I'll carry your damn water for you, but I'm just the prosecutor -- not a REAL man like you!" He stops and gives his parting shot just before he leaves.

"Mendoza, why don't you go screw yourself?!" The door closes with a bang.

Pepe looks at the door before he speaks. "I wouldn't have had any problems with Mr. Rivierte seeing this demonstration, but I'm not a legal or security expert. But Mr. Mendoza and Mr. Smith, I'm sure you're wondering why we're really here. This is the reason." With that he takes out of his vest pocket a small strip of gold foil.

"Mr. Reader has most of this material in a safe place that only he knows about. He is willing to turn the rest of this over to the government for safekeeping in exchange for immunity from prosecution." Pepe passes it around for the security dudes to feel.

The CIA guy is skeptical. "Looks like a piece of a gum wrapper to me."

Pepe has the stage. "Precisely, but I can guarantee you that this is actually a piece of alien technology. What we need to do is to attach this foil to the clamps that holds a target. Then we need to have a sharpshooter hit the strip of foil."

Now Mendoza is in charge. "Let's see what we can do. He calls out, "Bring this target forward. I need to install a new one." Ten seconds later, he's mounted the pitiful looking strip on the target mount. Then he turns to Pepe. "What kind of ammo do you say this thing can stop?"

Pepe smiles,"Any kind you want. Why don't you start with your handgun if you want?"

"Move the target back four meters," Olive says. The CIA guy takes out his pistol, checks the chamber, and double hands the gun in his firing posture. Turning to Pepe, he says, "You're sure about this are you?"

"Absolutely."

"Here goes."

The firing range is filled with the sound of an incredibly loud explosion that echoes off of the concrete block walls. There is the smoke and recoil, and there is what everybody sees. Not only does the flimsy little strip not even give a millimeter of a budge when the bullet hits it, but inspection proves that the strip actually split the bullet in half.

Pepe says, "Not only has the foil stopped the bullets totally, but if you felt the strip right now, you'd find it cool to the touch. This strip is 100% successful in absorbing any kind of energy you want to impart to it."

Special Agent Mendoza puts his hands on his hips. He's already thinking about what kind of firepower he can bring in for tests. "Uhm, Mr. Lopez and Ms. Montgomery, would you object if we maintain custody of this foil strip?"

Olive assents. "No problem at all, as long as you remember that my client wants immunity from prosecution in exchange. And please review and sign this paperwork first."

John Smith now nods his head just enough. "We'll have to do legal review."

Mendoza says, "Impressed me. Let's look at the paperwork."

Karl Eysenbach

NEW LOS ANGELES
PRESIDENTIAL SUITE, TANG'S HOTEL
AUGUST 16TH, 1:26 P.M.
22 HOURS, 47 MINUTES TO TOTAL FAILURE

It's beautiful from up here. You can get the sweep of the line where the ocean meets the shore. The sky is filled with puffy clouds, and the digs are swell. Where else would you stash your fugitive boytoy while you're away on your publicity tour? Although Clem has a scheduled court appearance, by some freaky-deaky technicality, he's still a wanted man who should be properly rotting in jail. So one Robert Manley is a bird in a truly gilded cage. Room service has come and gone, and there's not much to do except to look out at the skyline, which includes the *Times* Building. He gets tired looking at Pablo Lopez's office. Clem's bored, and he turns on the big screen hologram to GBS. They're usually more amusing, even if their coverage is the butcher's thumb on the scale of journalism. The news is on, and there's Daniel Maria R. going on and on in his usual way.

"The Presidential campaign has taken a nasty turn. Some commentators have said that this negativity is to be expected, considering that the election has moved into the final stage of internet voting. Both sides have been slinging more mud than an Oregon tractor derby in the middle of winter. Just look at these two ads." Yadda yadda yadda. Then it's back to R.

"If you stack all the polls on top of each other, President Hok looks like he can win the election. He's ahead by five points, but that's inside the margin of error, which has been pretty huge lately, so hold onto your hats, you Waldo supporters. Let's cut now to the First Presbyterian Church in Singapore. Gupta Dalivan is outside to report on opposition candidate Waldo Kitkeatlers leading the congregation with the Apostles' Creed. The votes are being counted as we speak. Come in, Gupta."

Clem turns off the hologram. The election is beginning to come out of his ears. There is fear. There is loathing. There are liars, damned liars, and there are politicians. He lights a pipe of the good stuff, and his mind begins to wander. Come to think of it, the whole world has been weird and cranky lately. For some reason, everything is more radioactive all at once. The traffic has been insane. It's either smooth sailing all the way one day, or road rage supreme. On every street corner it seems there's some mad holy man, or holy mad man crying about the end of the world. And there have been just too many weird things happening outside of the laws of probability. He counts himself in this category.

He picks up the *Times* on the coffee table. Central Africa is bleeding all over the front page in 100-point type. The stock market is up or down a thousand points an hour. The money supply has gone wild or disappeared, depending on what day it is. The magnetic poles have both suddenly developed massive volcanoes. Of course Clem's stoned now, and his mind is as sharp as a golden retriever's. Maybe he can call Saroyan.

SHIT HAPPENS

So far, everything in the Baja control room has been installed smoothly. The operating system is completely automated, and it's already up and running. The last order of business is to transfer the operations of the old interferometer to the new one that beamed down with Wanda. They're side by side, and the robots are connecting conduit and wiring together between the two. The place might as well be some disco with the red lights flashing all over the place. Klaxons are howling, and annoying things like '2 hours, 37 minutes 45 seconds to criticality' keep booming. Wanda's looking at the robots, "Ready?" The robots nod their heads, and Wanda gives the signal to tighten things up. There's a boom, and a giant blue spark fills the control room.

A housewife in Recife, Brazil is the first person to notice something extra screwy. Every morning for the last 17 years, she's been in the habit of toasting an English muffin or a slice of wheatberry. There have been times when she's been careless, but she knew that it was due to her own negligence. But not today. The first piece of toast that she tries to make just lies there in the toaster. The toaster is on. The power is on. Everything looks operational, but it's dead. The toast is as cold as it had been when she took it from the refrigerator. She checks the plug, puts the bread back in the toaster, and suddenly it gives off the fiercest heat, clutching the hapless slice of bread in a death grip as it incinerates it, nearly causing her kitchen cabinet to singe. When she pulls the plug, the surly toaster expels the charred remains with such force that it breaks a china plate.

She indignantly phones the local TV consumer activist, and within hours, the substandard performance of consumer products is the number one topic of worldwide discussion; that is, except for those radios, televisions, and holograms that did not explode while they were reporting on this news. Electric razors, blenders, microwaves, power drills, drill presses, dental equipment, and streetlights are all behaving badly.

"It was just a loose connection. No problem. It's okay now."

"So far, so good! Let's see how Part Two fits." Wanda can hardly hear herself telepath with all the racket going on. The robot is shaking like some low-budget cartoon character holding onto Part One. The vibrations are that bad.

"We're trying. We're trying to put it together." The robot delivers this message as he moves back and forth two times a second. "It's frozen!" Part Two has gone in smoothly, but Part Three is not a good fit.

"What's the matter?" Wanda looks down anxiously. Time is running out.

"It doesn't want to go in!"

"Oh, God!" Wanda's mind is racing. "What are the alternatives? Oh well, you know the saying. Don't force it. Use a bigger hammer. Get that sledgehammer over here and pound away."

The assistant robot complies, dragging the hammer over as quickly as possible. He raises it above his head and aims.

THWANG! -- THWANG! The sledgehammer reverberates.

At the World Elections Division, electronic voting is in its final day. The crew here is having their own set of problems. The control room is monitoring the voting traffic, and things are not running smoothly. The votes come in fits and starts, jamming lines and making for 'think fast' diversions on the traffic patterns to prevent total overload.

"There's a spike coming from out of Oceania -- Easter Island? I've never seen a traffic load coming out of a place like that, not even on the financial statements!"

'Jeezus H. K-riest! Everybody votes all at once five times over!"

"It's cascading -- Equador -- Amazonia -- Recife. It's arcing across the Atlantic!"

"Bypass! -- Bypass!"

"Sahara and Subsahara are jammed. The Sahel countries are too!"

"Secondary failure! Looks like tertiary is --"

At this moment the internet control room goes temporarily black. In three seconds, the emergency generators have kicked on, and the lights begin to flicker on again. Thrumthrumthrumthrumthrum. This is the sound of the emergency generator as it kicks on, echoing through the control room as the technicians attempt to check their equipment. Every monitoring screen is either flashing or sending fatal error messages. The control room chief is getting status reports, and he doesn't like what he hears.

"Fire control report."

"Smoke alarm activated in storage retrieval area. Suppression is in progress."

"Storage retrieval? -- Storage retrieval? -- Do you read me? Over." There's nothing but silence.

"Can you get me a video feed to the storage retrieval unit?" The big screen on the wall eventually flickers on with the view from a security camera. It shows a picture of workers and robots going up and down the banks of internet servers and computers, blasting fire extinguishers at black boxes that are still sparking.

"Art, somebody run down there and return so that I can get some feedback. Environmental is okay, isn't it? Things are being ventilated, right? Computer: Advise whether total evacuation is in order."

"Minor smoke and equipment damage. Evacuation is not necessary." It's time to turn to what's happening in Electionland.

"Asia desk, status report."

"We're having trouble retrieving even basic default mode. Status of elections returns is uncertain at this point."

"Africa -- what is your situation?"

"Not good. It looks like most of our equipment is fried."

"South America."

"Nothing but fatal error messages stacked on top of each other."

"Icefields."

"North American server looks okay. The Eurasian server is not responding right now."

"Oceania and Antarctica"

The Story of the Century

"We've got some data, but it looks awfully corrupted." The chief has only one thing to say besides the 'Oh Shit' that he keeps thinking to himself. He reaches for the intercom that will take his voice to every part of the elections facility.

"This is an emergency lockdown. Secure all doors. This is not a test."

"THWANG! -- THWANG! It fits!" Wanda breathes a sigh of relief. Suddenly, there are no more alarms or red and yellow lights. Everything is suddenly green and quiet. She says, "Can we get some confirmation on how the system components are doing?" The data and command robots assimilate billions of inputs and pieces of information, and they come up with the response in ten seconds.

"All systems are operating within normal parameters. Fine-tuning is needed, and will take an estimated four hours, forty-seven minutes to calibrate. All systems are go and fully functional." Maybe this neck of the galactic woods will survive for a while.

For the first time in who knows how long, Wanda feels the air let out of her, and she feels ten kilograms lighter. She hasn't fully absorbed how demanding all this has been until now, and she's quite pleased with herself. She's already getting kudos from the LOPEs and God knows whom else. She announces to the robots, "It's cleanup time. Let's recheck the automated systems so we can get out of here and go home."

Baja get one more visual treat. One by one, the congregation of flying saucers zooms up into nothingness. A black triangle hovers for a few hours, waiting between mountain ranges in an uninhabited valley before it moves back to the intercept site. Finally, it shoots down a blue tractor beam, and a cutie with a load of tools and some robots comes floating up. The holdout ship shoots toward Jupiter too.

Karl Eysenbach

ONLINE

Oh that the election for president had gone so smoothly! Hologram viewers get so sick of the whole thing they wish that election coverage was replaced with TV wrestling. While the votes from the polling places give President Hok a 55% majority, the internet voting produces an astounding 99.999% majority for Waldo Kitkeatlers. Dozens of rational senators are replaced by a variety of gurus, imams, swamis, diaperdomes, yahoos, and holyrollers of the UPPP. It's an absolute electoral rout. The only people who are happy are the legal lounge lizards, who have discovered a new source of billable hours for the foreseeable future.

The screaming, the yelling, the street protests, and the punditry go on until an independent investigatory commission is appointed, coming out with a report in fine print the size of a large phone book. The commission on the election labors mightily for many months, producing an encyclopedic rehashing of the entire process, complete (except for the deletions and redactions necessary for world security.)

It finds rats' nests in campaign financing, unexplained mysteries, systemic breakdowns, and faulty management. There are curious and questionable campaign practices, incredible biases and slantings of the truth in the mass media, as well as assorted hanky-panky by low level field operatives. The entire process is examined with a fine toothed comb, and the commission's report is not afraid to criticize shortcomings when it sees them, proposing a host of small but sweeping legislative and administrative procedures that would be easy to adopt if everybody would just put their shoulder to the wheel.

Despite the exhaustive listing of voting irregularities, (and just plain weirdness), the report's final conclusion states that the constitutional framework still exists (strong and robust), and that despite whatever

The Story of the Century

problems the election had, it fell well within the parameters of what was in fact just another ordinary transition to power.

The pundits say, "Thank God, the system worked one more time."

NEW LEGAL CHALLENGES TO ELECTION RESULTS

MEDIA GATHERS FOR PRELIMINARY HEARING OF FUGITIVE REPORTER

WHAT IS CLEM READER REALLY LIKE? WHAT DO LEGAL EXPERTS THINK ABOUT THE CASE? THIS IS WHAT OUR FOUR PANELISTS HAVE TO SAY

The line of policemen restrains the unruly horde of reporters as they compete with each other in the yelling contest to question the celebrity fugitive.

"Clem, what was it like being on the run?"

"Why did you decide to surrender now?"

"Do you think you can beat the rap?"

"How has Saroyan Pashogi helped you in your case?"

The reporters might as well be players jostling each other in a soccer scrum. Sex always trumps politics, and Saroyan's involvement in this case is hardly a secret. For after all, how's a poor boy going to get good results from the judicial system if he can't get the full Bollywood treatment?

Clem has had time to get his wardrobe makeover, hair styling, and media coaching for his court appearance. That's half of the game, but it helps to have Olive Montgomery, who's Ms. Outside, with her sex appeal and pithy sound bites. Then there's Mr. Inside. He's a slightly elderly, distinguished man with wavy gray hair -- just your average Joe in a $4000 suit. Lashkar Jhangvi is trial attorney #2, a former presidential chief legal advisor and general counsel to the CIA. He also cut his teeth many years ago, being the only attorney in a celebrity murder case where it was a lead pipe cinch that the guy was guilty. That jury voted to acquit.

Of course, this doesn't count Pepe and the rest of Clem's handlers. But all you see today is the defendant moving his way through the media mob with Ms. Outside and Mr. Inside blocking for him. He's just gotten out of the black town car with them, and they head up the steps to the giant marble columns framing the giant bronze doors. Clem has even been coached on the way to walk through his fellow reporters, in that dignified way, looking straight ahead as everyone heads for the courtroom.

At the microphones outside the courthouse, Olive and Lashkar stand just long enough for her to say, "This is a preliminary hearing, and we are going to listen to what the prosecution has to say. But we have a lot of information and issues as to why Clem Reader is innocent of these charges. Beyond that, we can't take any questions. I'll be happy to tell you what I can after the hearing." With that, they get to the elevators. The doors close and suddenly there's quiet.

Olive turns to Clem and says, "They won't broadcast a single word. All they want was the visual of you and your attorneys."

Clem says, "Yeah, I can figure that one out. I can remember doing that on the other side."

The only thing that Mr. Jhangvi has to say is, "Showtime." The elevator has arrived at the courtroom's floor, and they walk down the hallway that dwarfs humans to another set of bronze doors. On one side, there's a long line of people cordoned off with a series of velvet ropes. At the courtroom, the officer opens the door and ushers them inside where they find a packed house. People have been waiting for hours to be admitted, and they've had to endure a variety of petty cases and metal detectors. Some unlucky souls have only been able to see the workings of ordinary justice, not celebrity justice.

Inside the courtroom, it's a neon oven. People are sitting like cigarettes in a pack, but the press and sketch artists have comfy seats. Judge Montaña's space is a square redwood box, spare in its decoration except for the giant insignia of the World Court. The early crowd has been entertained by a case of petty criminal intent. A luckless nineteen year old schmuck is given the choice of either doing time for messing with mailboxes, or being sentenced to the Marines. Guess what the outcome is? The judge recesses -- taking his fifteen-minute bathroom break, and the bailiffs sweep out everyone except for Team Clem and the reporters. There's an island of quiet until they shepherd in the new crowd from the hallway.

"All rise. The Right Honorable Guillermo Montaña is approaching the bench." There is the shuffling of three hundred people getting out of their seats.

"You may be seated."

The bailiff reads, "Now on the docket, preliminary hearing number 23-235, in the matter of World versus Clement Reader." The thin old wizened man with a pockmarked face and thick glasses might be considered silly looking if he weren't towering over everyone from his judge's bench.

The judge clears his throat, giving a small cough before he speaks in this elfin, squeaky voice. "As this is a preliminary hearing, we will accept a plea from the defendant. But the major purpose of this hearing is to only establish a determination of whether there are sufficient facts for the establishment of findings allowing for a trial pursuant to the World Code, Section Four, Subsection Seven. How do you plead Mr. Reader?"

Clem stands solemnly and says, "Not guilty, your honor," and then he sits down. The judge turns to the district attorney and asks, "Do you have any opening statements of fact pertaining to this case Mr. Rivierte?"

"Thank you, judge." Gil Rivierte, with all his importance, stands up; beginning his litany of the horribleness of the crimes of stealing vital government documents with willful intent to subvert world security. He natters and meanders on.

"One Clem Reader knowingly encouraged the theft of such documents on April 23rd of this year with malicious intent to publish said documents he knowingly held, all of which had a restricted classification that Mr. Reader was not authorized to possess." Like a trained seal, he details legal chapter and verse of when the secret documents were stolen, when they were passed to Clem, and when the warrant was issued for his arrest, and the basis of the law, and why the defendant should have the book thrown at him.

It's Olive's turn. Standing to face the judge, she deftly reviews the conspiracy charges acknowledging that Mr. Reader had a series of meetings with Ken Ho Yunghai Lee, but she notes that Reader had no knowledge that the documents posed a threat to world security, and that he was not responsible for their theft. She also stipulates that at the time, he was acting for the *Times* as part of his job.

"The government has a collection of documents that it has retrieved from the *Times* newsroom. The facts are that Mr. Reader was working on a news assignment from his editor. It was his job. He met with Mr. Lee as part of his investigation into the story. These were provided -- volunteered to him by Mr. Lee, and Mr. Reader was not even aware that these documents posed a threat to world security. On top of this, the government has retrieved 100% of the documents supplied to Mr. Reader."

Olive continues. "A key legal question is whether or not Mr. Reader broke the law in doing his job. He never told Mr. Lee to break the law or any of his other sources. He was an innocent victim, caught up in a web of conspiracy and intrigue."

The Story of the Century

Judge Montaña takes control. Adjusting his spectacles, he peers down at Gil Rivierte. "Mr. Prosecutor, do you have anything to say?"

The DA sees his chance to be a drama queen. He begins to strut back and forth in front of the bench, making dramatic gestures as he speaks. "Mr. Reader and his defense crew can claim him to be an innocent ingenue, but ignorance of the law is no excuse." He waves a sheaf of documents.

"This preliminary hearing will show a trail of felony that leads from the initial theft of sensitive information that leads step by step directly to the desk of one Clem Reader!"

"If I could say something your honor." A distinguished voice comes from the defense table.

The judge bows his head in deference ever so slightly before he speaks. "Mr. Jhangvi, do you have something to say?"

"Yes, your honor." The elegant patrician rises. "I don't want to take up too much of your time, your honor. After all, this is only a preliminary hearing. I just have a few questions." Solicitor Jhangvi appears to be the kindliest and most urbane gentleman. There's a Santa Claus twinkle in his eyes. Almost imperceptibly, he pulls himself up to his full height, and he faces Rivierte.

"Mr. District Attorney – do you have a complete list of the documents that Mr. Reader received from Mr. Lee or anyone else in this matter?"

The only thought that goes through Rivierte's mind is that picture of little Billy with his legs spread apart. Everyone else only sees the DA looking like some stupid cow. There is silence, long silence.

The judge cocks an eyebrow, and he leans over the bench. "That seems like a good question to me. Answer the question, Mr. Rivierte."

The mighty DA suddenly turns. "No, your honor. While I have a partial list of the documents in question, there are many documents identified by numbered code only with no reference to subject matter, and other documents have been redacted entirely. I have no knowledge of what is underneath the black lines on this list. I would say that we have a good idea of the total number of documents stolen. We think we are close to knowing the count, but no, I do not have access to any of the documents that Mr. Reader had in his possession."

Jhangvi raises a finger. "I have a few more questions, your honor. Does anyone in this case have any idea of the contents of these so-called documents, or are they in fact will-o-the-wisps? -- Imaginary things of no substance? And if no one in this court has any idea of what Mr. Reader did or did not actually have in his possession, how can this court make a determination that Mr. Reader in fact committed a crime?" Is there a case here? I'd like the District Attorney to answer this."

The judge is getting secretly amused, taking pleasure out of seeing someone publicly humiliate Gil Rivierte in a big time way. Judge Montaña has always thought that the DA was a major bottom-feeder. But judges are paid large salaries to look as solemn as all get out, even when they're busting a gut inside. Putting on an extra stern face, Judge Montaña peers down his glasses at Hapless Gil. "Well Mr. Rivierte? That is a fair question?"

Gil's poker hand is awful weak, and he's giving tells. Yet the District Attorney is going to continue to keep fighting. "Your honor, I would not have continued to press charges as long and as diligently as I have without the assurances from other branches of the government that a grave threat to world security had taken place here by Mr. Reader's reckless acts."

Solicitor Jhangvi and Judge Montaña are beginning to play a tag team match with the DA. Raising little more than a pinky finger, Lakshar gets the attention of the bench to ask another question of Rivierte.

The Story of the Century

"Mr. District Attorney, can you show me the legal brief from the CIA or wherever detailing why and how Mr. Reader's actions constitute a threat to world security?"

Gil knows that it's time to fold when you're not holding any cards. In a voice so low that the judge has to cup his ears to listen, Rivierte says, "Your honor. I would like to present these documents to the court as evidence, but the powers that be showed me heavily censored charges one time only for my visual inspection, and they maintained possession of crucial documents known only to them. The CIA's legal documentation is classified, and they have not communicated with me. Whatever basis for prosecution is in their hands only."

It's point, set, game, match time for Mr. Jhangvi. "Then, how can there be a basis for a trial if the government doesn't even take the time to allow for an **in camera** inspection of the evidence by any attorney in this case, or even the presiding judge?" Saroyan is sitting at home listening to this on the internet, and she gives out a whoop, jumping up and down while she can hear the courtroom audience quietly murmuring its assent.

Judge Montaña bangs his gavel once. "Order in the court. That's a very good point, Mr. Jhangvi. I have had no contact with the security services on this case, and Mr. Rivierte has a very bad list of documents that he claims list those stolen, but it's clear to me that insufficient evidence exists at this point to proceed any further."

Clem is feeling pretty good now; but Judge Montaña's about ready to pull a legal rabbit out of his hat. He folds his hands before he speaks. Lakshar Jhangvi sees this, knowing that it spells bad news. The tiniest smile appears on the judge's face. "I'm going to make a ruling that the government has thirty days to make its case fully, providing me with an in camera inspection of all stolen documents, and that a full trial on all charges is scheduled for December 16th, starting at 9:00 AM." He bangs his gavel.

Olive Montgomery can't control herself. She jumps to her feet, yelling, "Your honor, -- your honor -- I object!" There is a serious hubbub from the courtroom audience. The judge bangs his gavel twice.

"Order in the court. -- Order in the court." Admonishing the Olive, he says, "Ms. Montgomery -- watchy watchy! To answer your objections, bail will be set at $1,000,000. This court is recessed."

JUST BEFORE DAWN, DECEMBER 16TH, -- TWO HARBORS, CATALINA ISLAND

She spreads her legs more, wrapping them around his. He looks away from her face as he slides down towards her breast, to suckle gently and insistently as his hips move more and more totally under their own control. Saroyan moans, breathing in and out in short bursts. She moves to her own rhythm too, faster and faster. There is her warm flood, and he returns back to her lips, moving their tongues together. Finally there is his sweet release. They lie there, together for a while, exchanging kisses. She has no birth control with her, and neither does he.

"Ummmm -- Tiger," she coos. "Do you have time to go round again?"

Clem looks at her. "You cute and sweet thing. Not now. How about some coffee?" He gets out of bed in the cramped boxlike space that is the bedroom. He puts on his bathrobe, and he goes to the galley of the sailboat. He holds the terrycloth close to his chest as he tries to keep the chill out as he busies with breakfast.

They had gone down to the docks, unobserved the afternoon before to the 11 meter sloop *Casablanca* with only the two of them aboard. Pepe was told that they were going to be alone for up to a month, and that no one would be contacting them. "We'll call you on a periodic basis. Don't call us. The phone will be switched off." This is what Saroyan said.

It's a good thing that Clem isn't a fugitive from justice. His court appearance was cancelled because the case has been declared moot. One of President Hok's last official acts was to give Clem a full pardon from any of the charges against him. The mainstream journalists have had their field day, hawking their wares aplenty by plastering Clem and Saroyan's face all over. But the news cycle goes on. Clem's airtime is shrinking from two minutes to thirty seconds to ten seconds before it will disappear from the respectable media radar altogether. This isn't the case with the paparazzi, who continue to grind the couple through the publicity mill with enthusiasm. This is one of the reasons why they've decided to make a run for it in the *Casablanca*.

Clem's life and times are still examined with an electron microscope. Every detail of his life history, including what his grandfather did, has been news fodder. Great attention has been paid to his interest in doing something about the homeless, and every detail of the presidential pardon is analyzed with a fine tooth comb. Well, almost every detail. There are a few things that the boys in the press just don't get around to covering. There's the little fact that Clem has signed onto a lifetime consulting contract for a dollar a year with the CIA, complete with non-disclosure agreement on penalty of death.

This doesn't mean much to the two shipmates right now, though. Clem's busy with breakfast. Coffee is ready, and he's chopping onions, peppers, and baked potatoes for a vegetarian frittata. While he's cooking, Saroyan has time to pull on a sweater and jeans. She gets around to sitting down at the foldout table in the galley, and he gives her a cup of coffee, just the way she likes it.

"Your coffee, Ma'am."

"For a novice, you're a pretty good sailor."

"It's fun. I've always wanted to know more about real boats. Ferries and water taxis on the way to work and pangas for squid fishing -- that's my experience. You know, if we're ever down in San Mateo, you should go squid fishing with Netto. It's a gas."

She tastes what Clem has fixed for breakfast. "Not bad. This tastes great. This frittata is excellent."

"Just one of my many talents. I saw how the chef did it at La Tour." He sits down across from her and starts digging into his breakfast with gusto. Clem is still thinking about his first major sailing lesson with Saroyan.

"The weather was pretty good last night. There wasn't much traffic, and the moon was out. How much trouble do you think we'll have if there are rough seas?"

Saroyan sips her coffee. "This boat is as steady as a rock, and it can practically sail itself. I've got the best intelligent systems on board that money can buy. There shouldn't be anything to stop us from just being tourists as we sail down the coast. We're not going to get too far offshore. We'll have to pay some attention to the traffic between here and Ensenada, but after that, we'll pretty much have the whole ocean to ourselves."

They continue talking ship. Saroyan becomes a teacher again, reviewing with Clem some of the fundamentals of sailing. It's obvious that Clem has an aptitude, as he remembers every query that Saroyan can throw at him, both about equipment and situations. After a while it's time for a different course of conversation. Clem touches Saroyan's hand across the table.

"We make a pretty good crew. You're the best captain I've ever had."

Saroyan brightens. "Say, I've got an idea. Why don't we take the rubber dinghy to the beach? I'll bet the sunrise is going to be spectacular." She puts down her cup off coffee and looks at Clem.

"That sounds good to me. I've been looking forward to messing around on the island again. It's been years since I've been around."

The Story of the Century

They go topside, and Clem climbs into the raft carefully. He steadies himself with one hand while he helps Saroyan into the dinghy. Saroyan casts off as Clem sets the oars. In less than two minutes he pulls up to the beach, jumping out and getting his bare feet and jeans wet in the cold water. He wades ashore; pulling the boat with Saroyan in it until it's almost halfway up on the sand. Saroyan steps out, handing him his shoes.

The dawn is truly spectacular. The sky is aflame with yellow and gold in the mackerel sky. The sloop is the only boat in Two Harbors today. The park buildings are dark, and the concession stands are closed for the winter. Clem stands up after getting his loafers on. He gets close to Saroyan. He needs the body heat. "It's cold. We need to stay close together to stay warm." The two lovers kiss and kiss again. They kiss some more. He feels her butt. Saroyan breaks free from the clinches and holds his hands.

"Let's climb up the hill to get a better view. Last one to the top is a rotten egg." This isn't fair to Clem. Saroyan is a much better runner. She sprints off the beach towards the isthmus, while Clem huffs and chuffs behind her. Finally he follows her up a hundred meters to a boulder in a meadow where the famous buffalo roam. Saroyan has been waiting for more than thirty seconds, while Clem comes trailing up the hill, sweating and slightly out of breath.

"Just you wait. I'll get into shape again, and I'll beat you, I swear." He grabs hold of her, and they start to wrestle around in the grass like two puppies. After about thirty seconds of wrestling, he manages to get on top of her, pinning her down gently. He stops tussling to look at her. She looks up at the sky and says, "It's a beautiful day, isn't it?"

Clem looks at her -- deeply in her eyes. "I haven't noticed." Their lips meet open-mouthed, and their tongues start to play with each other, doing their tongue dance. One thing leads to another, and they begin to take off their clothes. The sunrise passes into early morning, and they don't pay any attention at all.

EPILOGUE

A number of strange and unfortunate deaths occurred after the flying saucers left. First, Secretary of Defense Rigoberto Corozon committed suicide in a naval hospital after a brief period of depression. The psychiatric reports (hushed up), said that Corozon was under the delusion that beings from outer space were telling him what to do. His last act on earth was to jump out a window, thinking that he was going to be beamed up by a space ship.

Oddly enough on the same day, Professor Wong Fat was delivering an academic lecture in China when he began to falter, sweat, and fall behind the podium he was speaking at. When people rushed up to assist, they found that he had died of spontaneous human combustion. The bad news is that this is the first fully recorded incident of a death like this in human history. The good news is that the evidence provides several large, multiyear government grants to study this phenomenon, providing many graduate students with minimum wages for many years.

Tutuwabe Mugabe, corrupt plutocrat of the hydrogen barons, met a more ordinary death. His private plane merely disappeared over the ocean, joining Amelia Earhart. For all we know, he may be one of Attu's less viable specimens

THE MAGADEN PENINSULA

It was amazing how well things went. Things were humming along, and the whole operation was running as efficiently as a Swiss chronometer. But things changed around the time of the election. There was a lot of weirdness then, and things were never the same ever again.

The first thing that went wrong was the main drill hole collapsed from an earthquake. People got a little rattled, and nothing seemed to be wrong at the time. When they tried to drill again, they encountered a huge amount of quicksand, and when they tried to seal the hole with grout, they found that they had been sent substandard concrete. Nothing held together anymore.

This delayed the game, and the geologists re-evaluated the site. They determined that maybe it was better to move a couple of hundred meters south, but the whole project began to be plagued with mechanical failures. Gears broke. Equipment froze and just turned into expensive stones. Computers crashed, and there would be weeks of downtime when people were paid big money for watching their porno holograms.

The government and the hydrogen companies began to burn the midnight oil trying to figure out what was going on, and more material and manpower was devoted to the project. Instead of speeding things up, this actually slowed things down even more. Coordination problems began to occur, and fistfights broke out on the test site between the government observers and the contractors. Everybody had to admit that this antique atomic weaponry was more complicated than they had originally thought, and more time was wasted examining and reexamining the weapons system.

All of this was duly reported to both Singapore and Sao Paolo, and the Public Private Partnership wasted its valuable time examining the factors that were slowing progress. The hydrogen companies funneled more cash into the program, and they screamed bloody murder at what was going on! The boys in the Defense Department were getting unhappy too, as their money was being diverted from their pet projects.

Karl Eysenbach

Things managed to be kept out of public view for a long time, but this only worked for a while. One problem was the financial drain that the test was having on the hydrogen companies, and irate shareholders began to pick up on the accounting notes in the glossy annual reports, raising holy hell at the annual meetings. The public pension funds were particularly obnoxious and persistent in bringing attention to this in the press. But still everyone was clever enough to hide the government involvement in all of this. Singapore claimed to know nothing. The new CEOs of the hydrogen companies were a little bit more flexible than their predecessors, and they started up alternative and more expensive methods of platinum extraction. The problem was that implementation of these more conventional methods was several years down the road, and the profitability of the companies began to be affected in a major way. Hydrogenia SA and the others were now paying for two platinum extraction projects at the same time, and their share prices began to suffer.

One of the things that was done was to increase the level of government financial participation through black programs and the issuance of more government debt for false purposes. Back channel funding was approved by the President, but the bomb specialists just stood by while the roughnecks drilled a hole to watch it collapse again and again and again. Back to the porno again. The meters were running. After several more years, and fifteen billion of dollars in cost overruns, everybody actually got a successful hole drilled, and the bomb was securely placed where it belonged. They pretested the warhead systems and telemetry, and everything appeared to be working. The detonation date was set at T-minus three days. Everyone responsible for the project from all over the world flew in to observe the test.

Finally all systems indicated go, and the obstacles had been overcome. Five, four, three, two, one, ignition. Nothing happened. That's when the problem began. Override systems were activated to put the bomb into sleep mode, and it was decided to pull the atomic weapon up out of the hole to see what had gone wrong. All the instrument readings indicated that it should have been a successful detonation.

This went off without a hitch, and they brought the Mark VII warhead back to the surface. Its software program appeared to be improperly programmed, and the techies started to work to correct this glitch. For no damn good reason, the explosives malfunctioned and detonated while workers were removing the shaped charges for inspection.

While there was no thermonuclear explosion, there was a huge area that became contaminated with plutonium. Everyone at the test site was killed. News of this disaster was flashed around the world, and it set off a series of political and economic firestorms.

President Waldo Kitkeatlers was eventually forced to step down when his own party gave him a congressional vote of no confidence. The senators and the press screamed about false promises and betrayals, and the Vice President stepped in before he suffered a fatal heart attack three weeks later.

As to the hydrogen companies, a series of class action lawsuits were filed by trial lawyers on behalf of insurance companies, workers compensation victims and environmentalists that eventually led to several major bankruptcies and reorganizations, including Hydrogenia and Consolidated. The nuclear test project was abandoned, and a new Forbidden Zone was created.

Eventually the hydrogen companies' alternative methods proved far more successful than anyone realized. Thank God for strip mining!